JORDYN ELLERY

Retribution

That's the thing about karma, it always comes back with a vengeance.

ELLERY
PUBLISHING

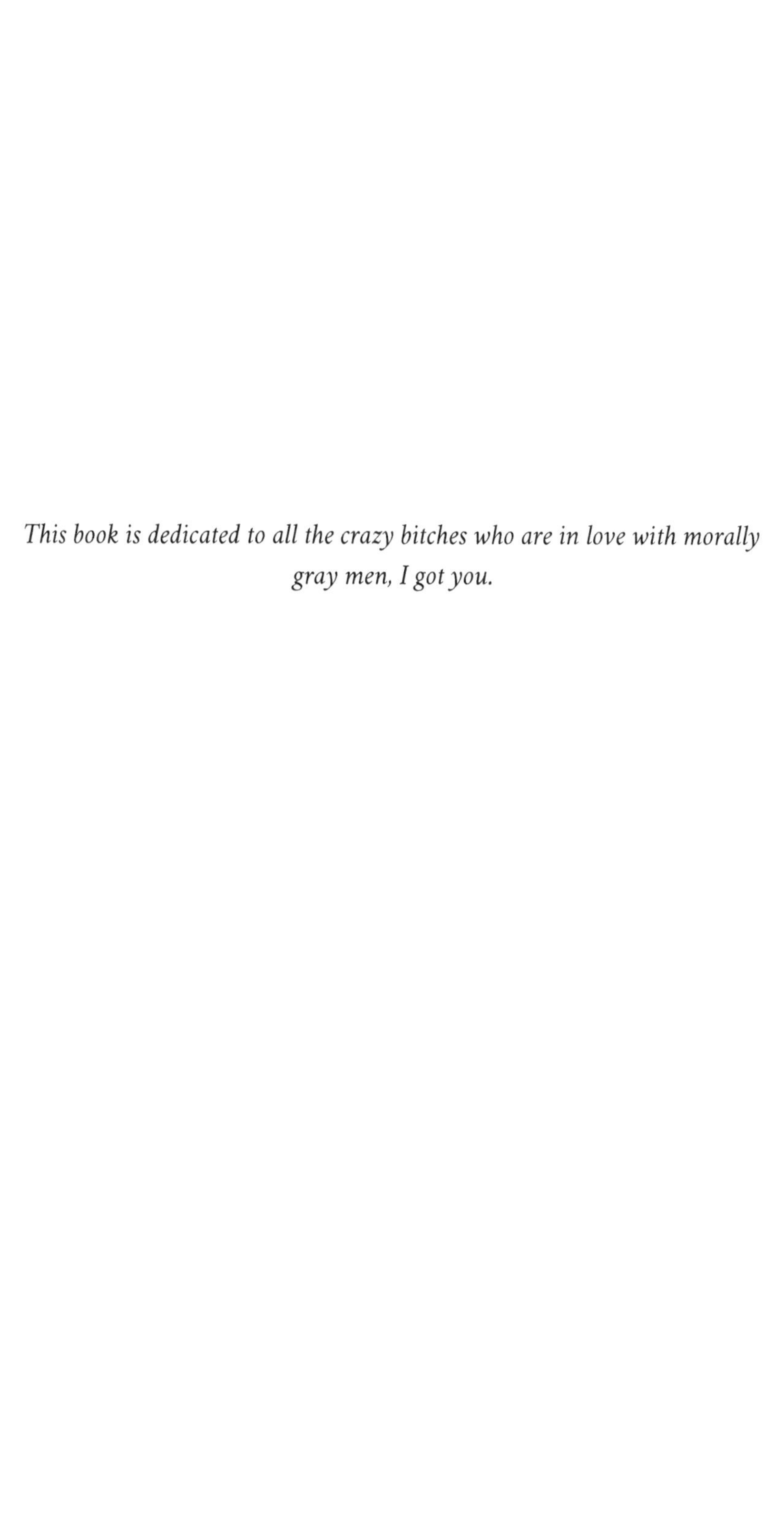

This book is dedicated to all the crazy bitches who are in love with morally gray men, I got you.

Contents

Acknowledgement

Thank you to each and every person who has supported me along this journey.

My first thank you is to my parents (all four of them) for believing in me and allowing me to become obsessed with reading and writing from such a young age! (I'm sure it cost you guys a fortune haha).

The next thank you is to my fiance, Dan. Without you, I wouldn't have had the courage to delve into writing my book in the first place, you gave me the extra push that I needed to believe in myself.

Of course, my two darling daughters, Luna and Rome, who are far too crazy most of the time but I'm so thankful to have you both. I hope that one day, I can share the same passions with you both.

Wow, my next thank you is to my twin flame, Courtney. Almost two decades of friendship, some questionable One Direction fan-fiction and an addiction to Wattpad, we've come a long way. Without our endless face time calls and your 'quotes and notes', (many bottles of wine), I couldn't have done it without you!

I want to thank each and every one of my beta and ARC readers, who gave me an insight into ways I could improve my book, things you loved and things you hated, it was all an amazing credit to me. I can't thank you enough for the amazing encouragement along the way!

A huge huge thank you to the most amazing woman in the form of an English teacher, Laura Travis. You gave me the most incredible experience and introduction into the literary world, I'll never forget your insane Hunger Games costume! (I also still have your copy of 'The Time Traveler's Wife' that I promised I'd return many years ago, oops. I promise, it's still very much looked after.)

To every person who has followed me on social media, shared my posts, and to all of my future readers, thank you so much. You're all bloody beautiful.

I hope you fall in love with Indie & Reed as I did whilst writing this book, prepare to fall into the world of the Billy Boys!

Thank you.
Jordyn Ellery x

Prologue

Reed

Nothing can truly prepare you for the unexpected moments in your life. I mean, I had to see it to believe it. It's unexpected for a reason. You can't prepare yourself for something that was never meant to happen; something that shouldn't have happened.

I've never fully understood the concept of grief until I had to experience it through the eyes of my 9-year-old.

It's been 64 days since her death.

44 days since her funeral.

32 days since I discovered the truth.

14 days since my world came crashing down around me.

3 days since I picked up the scattered remnants of my heart.

2 hours since I had the phone call that would alter the course of my life forever.

Chapter 1

Reed

I stare at the documents I've just opened in the mail. None of this makes any sense. I bring my hand to my jaw and rub through my stubble, stressed. Taking a sip of my coffee and leaning back in my office chair, I take a glance at the busy traffic in the city below. I wonder how many of those people have been divorced. The divorce rates in America sit at around 50%.

Am I about to become part of that statistic?

I'm pulled away from my thoughts with a knock on my office door. I glance up and look through the glass door to see Maddy, my assistant.

I beckon her to enter, and she opens the door with a huge grin on her face. I'm not exactly in the mood for any of her usual jokes this morning, so I keep my lips pressed in a tight line. Her grin drops when she notices my obvious sour demeanor.

"Reed, how on earth are you not celebrating?"

I huff and shake my head, eyeing up the papers in front of me. I have no idea what I would have to celebrate. Congratulations, Reed. Your wife, the mother of your child, has served you with divorce papers. Just, perfect.

I stay silent, waiting for the follow up conversation.

Maddy sits at the chair in front of me with a concerned expression across her face.

"Are you not happy? I thought this was exactly what we wanted?"

Now this girl sounds like she's gone absolutely nuts. There is no way we're on the same page here.

"Maddy, can you please enlighten me on what it is you're actually talking about?"

Placing my elbows on my desk, I lean forward, propping my head upon my folded hands.

"Named partner? It was emailed out this morning, I thought –"

Shit. I wiggle my mouse and head straight to my email. My mind was so distracted the moment I'd opened my divorce papers this morning, I didn't even care to refresh my emails.

The Future of Atlas & Burhan

There it is. I read the email's subject with bated breath.

Following the recent retirement of Mr. Richard Burhan, one of the most reputable lawyers in the Atlanta district, we have been on the hunt for our next named partner. After conducting extensive interviews with some of our best and most successful lawyers, we would like to congratulate and welcome our next named partner...

Mr. Reed Breckenridge

We would like to thank each and every one of you who applied for the position. Your hard work has not gone unnoticed. A meeting will be conducted further in the week to discuss the new direction of this law firm.

Sincerely,
Mr. Jonathan Atlas
Atlas & Breckenridge

I re-read the email three more times to allow the news to sink in. I did it. I'm named partner.

Maddy is watching me quietly, trying to read my reaction. Breaking out into the biggest grin I can manage, I jump up from my chair. She jumps up too, squealing and lunges forward to wrap her arms around my neck. I swing her around as we both celebrate in unison. After all, she gets a promotion out of this also.

"I can't believe you've done it, Reed; I am so proud of you!"

I plop her down, straightening out my tie and gather my wits again. I did it.

I've gotten everything I've ever wanted.

Maddy pulls me into a conversation about some of the new protocols we were going to have to run through, booking in an official meeting with the rest of the firm to discuss new management. It's then that I pull up my phone to ask Allie to meet me for lunch, to discuss the bad news and boast about the good news.

* * *

The first part of our lunch runs smoothly, as you would expect from a husband and wife. It's far too platonic for our usual encounters so, I begin to call the shots.

"Divorce papers, huh?" I chew on some pasta and take a sip of my water, not bothering to pay attention to her reaction to my forwardness.

I can see her placing down her cutlery in my peripheral vision and I could almost roll my eyes at her dramatics. She was always one for the 'movie-style' scenes.

"We both knew that it would come to this eventually, Reed. We had no other choice with you being so busy at work and I don't want Willow getting mixed up in our family affairs." She stares intently at me, her green eyes piercing and battling with my blue ones.

I nod my head agreeing.

"I just didn't expect it so soon, you know? What's the rush?" I say accusingly.

"There is no rush, it's just something I'm certain of, something that is long enough in itself that I didn't want to drag out for any longer–"

I couldn't help but cut her off. "Were you aware that I've been named partner?"

She looks out of the restaurant window and contemplates for a moment before returning her attention to me.

"Of course," she offers a tight smile and leans forward with her elbows propped up on the table, "It couldn't have fallen at a more perfect time."

I shake my head and tsk, a scowl evident on my face. She always was a conniving little bitch.

"Ah, I presume you have a plan. Take me for half of everything I have, yes?" I smirk and gaze back at her with fire in my eyes.

The thought of her trying her best to clean me out ignites an anger within me that burns, the flames thrashing and begging to surface.

"When do I ever not have a plan, Reed?" She smiles at me sweetly and refills her wine glass, the red liquid thick and tempting.

Something about her calmness makes me nervous, like she has

another trick up her sleeve. Like, she knows a way to make sure I end up with the lesser half of everything.

"I'm just warning you; I am one of Atlanta's best lawyers, Allie. You are not just going to battle in court against me, honey. You are going to lose in such a way you'll wish you'd never even come across me." I relax in my seat, glad that she seems anxious.

"Reed, darling. I don't think you know how to be a father if your life depended on it. The courts will see you for the heartless human that you are and Willow will belong to me."

"You say 'belong' like she is an object" I snarl, the tension between us beginning to hold me in its grasp, tugging at the darkest parts of me.

She lets out a laugh, dotting her lips with a napkin at the same time, "Object or not Reed, she is my daughter and I know that your busy work schedule will be a huge issue for your case. The job you treasure so much will be your biggest hindrance."

My lips part as I try to re-evaluate this situation. My brain is currently thinking of all of the ways that I can sow her mouth shut so as not to hear her speak anymore.

"And we both know what you'll choose between them, your job or your daughter, Reed? The ball is in your court." She reaches down to pick up her bag and as she stands up, her crimson colored body-con wraps to her, leaving little to the imagination.

"You don't mind paying for the bill, do you? I suppose that's all you've ever been good for." She spits at me, strutting obnoxiously past me and out of the restaurant.

Releasing the knife, I didn't realize I had gripped so tightly inside of my hand, a wave of relief immediately washes over me at the lack of her presence.

I chew on the inner side of my cheek, pondering over how I can make this situation disappear, how this can all be stopped. Losing Willow or my job is despicable, to even compare the two as if they are the same.

Can you imagine if I had done this to her? If I had made a mother choose between her job and her child, the world would be in absolute uproar, and I'd be burned at the stake.

It is completely unfair the lack of support and favor for fathers, who tend to be the providers for the family, leaving them at a complete disadvantage in the eyes of the law.

Yes, maybe I can't attend every father-daughter day. Maybe I can't attend all her parent evenings, but does that make me less of a parent than those who do? I'm at risk of losing custody of my child just because I have a career. But, there's no way that's happening.

Not if I have anything to do with it.

Chapter 2

Indie

It's a Saturday, why am I being awoken from my precious beauty sleep?

I begin to stretch out my arms and legs, kicking the blankets from my body, as I reach for my phone, vibrating on my night stand.

3 missed calls and 2 text messages.

I swipe across the screen to uncover who it is that desperately needs me this early in the morning.

(Lola): *Please tell me you have not forgotten about today! You said you'd be here!*

(Gracie): *Lola is freaking out, pls call her xx*

I draw my eyebrows together, confused about the urgency. I dial Lola's number and it only needs to ring twice before she picks up.

"Indie Thorne, you are one huge pain in my ass."

I whine as I'm stretching once again, waiting for Lola to fill me in on the reasoning behind her stressful outburst.

"I'm freaking out, I have waited 8 months for this appointment everyone is here but you –"

My hearing shuts off as my brain becomes crowded with the internal cussing at myself. Sitting upright in the bed, I swing my legs over the side.

"Lola, I'll be there in 20 minutes," and I cut the phone call off.

If I decided to take a look at the world around me for a second, then maybe I wouldn't be so ignorant. Just maybe.

There are pros and cons to being the eldest sister, getting the final say so, getting the fresh clothes and getting to be the one to break all of the rules. Cons? Well yeah, the responsibility.

I climb out of bed and rush to the bathroom to make myself appear less zombie looking.

Why didn't I remember? I have been so preoccupied lately with the upcoming show for my ballet girls that I didn't even remember my own sister's wedding dress appointment. She's been dreaming of choosing her wedding dress from this designer since she was thirteen years old, and here I am, almost ruining her day.

I turn on the faucet and splash some water onto my face and dry it with a hand towel. I take a glance at myself in the mirror, the dark circles around my eyes are prominent. I need to work on getting my eight hours of sleep each night, but it's hard whilst running your own business independently.

Rushing around to give some life to my dull complexion, I think about if I'd have just got up earlier, I might have been able to make myself look a bit more presentable.

Throwing on my three-day worn jeans and a bra, I grab my phone and exit the bedroom into the living room, in search of my jumper. Scott turns around at the sound of the door closing.

"Hey baby."

Holding my index finger up, to tell him I need a minute, I find my jumper hanging over the side of the sofa and slip it on over my head.

"It's Lola's wedding dress appointment, I can't believe I forgot!" I glance up at Scott leaning over the kitchen island, wearing just pajama pants, and holding a plate of waffles.

He lets out a nervous laugh and strides towards me, without the waffles. He wraps me in between his arms, my head naturally falls into his chest as he squeezes me.

"I hope you're not going to be this disorganized for our wedding events."

I shake my head and pull away from his embrace.

"Nothing would get in the way of the most important day of our lives," I smile sheepishly, squeezing his hand as a comfort.

Scott worries that I have too much going on, biting off more than I can chew. He isn't wrong, I'm a bit of a people-pleaser and struggle to say no.

"Take these waffles to go, I won't be here when you get back as I'm meeting with a client at noon."

Sighing, I reach up to kiss him.

Lately, we only see each other in passing. Our lives are so busy, we hardly get to spend any quality time together anymore. Things between us haven't been the same since I began the ballet school, which took off with full force. It's one of the many perks of already being an internationally recognized ballerina.

"I love you, Scotty."

Scott looks down at me and presses his lips against mine.

"You too," he says, returning to the couch to watch whatever program he's into these days.

I roll my eyes at his ignorance and the fact he didn't bother to actually box up the waffles for me. I suppose I'll go without breakfast.

Inserting my keys into my purse, I look down at the photo frame in the hallway as I'm slipping on my shoes. It's the photo that was taken just after he proposed to me nine months ago in New York. It was one of the only few trips we'd been on before we both made the decision to begin our businesses.

I've never been in such a nerve-wrecking moment, not knowing if we would be able to financially cope. I'd personally say it's been a success, but Scotty would probably disagree. His side of the decision hasn't been as smooth sailing as mine, but that's what makes us a team.

* * *

Backing up onto Lola's driveway, I honk my horn to alert them of my presence. Lola fires out of her front door towards my car, pulling open the passenger door.

"I don't want to hear your ravishing apologies, Indie. You can take me out for lunch later, just get me to this goddamn appointment."

I smirk, knowing I always manage to get off lightly with Lola. Gracie and Erica climb into the back of the car, giggling at Lola's antics.

"Where's mom?" I ask Lola.

"She's already in Kingston, no doubt waiting to absorb the free champagne." She rolls her eyes.

* * *

We've been here for two hours, and so far, it's been terrible. Lola has tried on possibly twenty-five dresses, none of which have been a contender.

If this is what wedding dress shopping is like, I might skip it and just order one online. How on earth can one person be *this* pedantic?

"Indie, help out your *darling* mother and grab me another bottle of champagne." Her eyes are flitting between me and the complimentary selection.

I look towards Lola, then to Gracie, giving them a side eye.

Lola shakes her head slightly mouthing 'no' through the reflection of the mirror. Standing up, Gracie grabs Mom by the elbow.

"How about we go for a walk, mom?" Gracie says, steering mom away from the temptation.

Lola's head drops to her hands and I immediately rush to her side.

"We've got this all under control, don't worry. This is *your* day," I whisper into Lola's ear as I caress her forearm.

She gives me an apologetic smile and wipes a tear that had managed to escape. I knew it was a mistake inviting our mom to such a monumental event. As per Lola's request, she's here in all of her glory, addictions and all.

I haven't remained in contact with Celia (Mom) since I moved out, we never really had a great relationship.

She disapproved of my love for ballet, didn't understand the importance of it being more than a hobby.

The day I told her I wanted to pursue ballet as a full-time career, she laughed and asked me if I would also be moving to England to marry a prince.

You see, my mother and father have both been strict surrounding education whilst we grew up. It wasn't that I wasn't academically gifted, I achieved a 4.0 GPA. But, when I informed them of my decision to apply to the School of American Ballet as opposed to Harvard, they pulled my funding.

It wasn't something I'd comprehended before making my decision.

I never expected them to welcome the idea with open arms, but I thought they would come around to it.

They never did.

Daddy passed away three years ago, leaving mother half of his estate, and splitting the rest among Lola and Gracie. I suppose I didn't apprehend being cut out of the will either.

Lola discusses with the designer, Evelina, what her plans are for her dream wedding gown. She takes notes and begins drawing on a digital sketchpad, Gracie and mom still absent. Erica takes full advantage of the mini vegan cupcakes and snaps pictures for the wedding memory book. Erica is Lola's best friend, and luckily a brilliant photographer.

I look up to the sound of Lola clapping and cheering. I gasp when she says, "That's the one, it's perfect!" she squeals, jumping up and down.

I head over to Lola and smother her in a giant hug, looking at the sketchpad with her perfect design on it.

Evelina disappears as another assistant escorts Lola back to the changing rooms to change her out of the other wedding dress she was wearing. I sit on the plush cream couch, admiring the luxurious decor as Gracie walks back in, mom stumbling in tow.

"She's going to have to catch a ride with us, we have room." Gracie states with a lack of enthusiasm.

We all know that the longer that me and mom are in the same proximity, the meaner she gets. I've been lucky to escape today with only a few sarcastic questions about my life choices. The last thing any of us need is a fight between us, today is about Lola.

I roll my eyes and start to gather up the wedding planner papers and pop them all back into the folder. This girl wasn't kidding when she said she's had everything planned out since she was thirteen-years-old.

Sometimes, I can become a little envious of my sisters, knowing that they are able to plan these fantasies and live out their dreams, where I can't. Wanting to follow my dream, meant sacrificing the rest of my dreams.

I'm sure most people wonder why I didn't just cave, drop the idea of having a career in ballet and have it simply, as a hobby. But it could never work that way, ballet is like another language to me. No, it is like my *first* language.

I was first introduced to ballet at the age of four. Mom wanted to have each of us grow up to be placid and well-composed, it was also a status boost. All the wealthy families in Buckhead had their children attending every extra-curricular activity to add to our resumes.

They knew that when the time was right, their children would be competing for a place in an Ivy League. Nothing and no one would get in the way of their future heirs and heiresses from securing a place in Harvard or Yale.

Most other kids weren't like me, though. I lost sight of Harvard early as I began to excel in ballet. I mean I'm good, insanely good. Which was exactly how I managed to secure my scholarship for the School of American Ballet.

I competed for years after finishing school, partaking in numerous shows of *Swan Lake*, *The Nutcracker* and *Romeo and Juliet*. I won awards and became fully established with an online presence big enough for me to step away from the spotlight and open my school.

Lola finishes signing all the paperwork as mom steps forward, swiping her credit card to pay for the expenses. Ignoring the envious and bitter energy she draws from me, I focus my attention elsewhere.

* * *

After taking my sisters home, I head straight to the dance studio, grabbing the mail on my way inside. Turning on the lights in the studio, I enter my office, throwing my bags onto the couch and tearing into the mail. Bills, bills and more bills.

I huff and lay down on the sofa, kicking my bags onto the floor. Closing my eyes for a moment, I think of the huge show next weekend, the qualifying gig for the Atlanta Youth Ballet competition. The youngest of my class of sixteen ballerinas, is only five years old. I'm hoping to expand the business at some point, to teach different age ranges and give me more spare time.

"Indie?" A female voice calls. I jump up from the sofa and pop my head out of the office.

Willow walks across the floor and Allie follows close behind her.

"Allie, Willow! How are you girls?" Hugging them both, I notice a frown upon Allie's face.

"About the competition this weekend… Willow's father is taking her, I'm out of town," She says as she begins to set down the gym bags she'd been carrying.

"Oh, it's such a shame that you're not going to see Willow qualify!" Pouting, I turn towards the office as Willow skips off to the locker room.

Allie hesitates for a moment, staring longingly into the distance.

"Everything okay, Al?" I whisper, trying not to alert Willow.

She groans and pulls her bag into her suit jacket.

"Is it obvious?" She mumbles.

Placing a comforting hand on her back, I flick my chin towards my office.

Allowing Allie to sit first, I sit to the left of her.

We've been quite good friends since Willow has attended my classes. It's common practice when she shows up to every dance class. She is everything I would have wanted from my own mother growing up.

After a few moments of comfortable silence, Allie sighs, "I'm getting divorced."

I still, trying my best to conjure up a sympathetic response.

"Oh, I'm so sorry, Allie."

Thanks to my parents, I've never had to experience what divorce is like, despite a divorce being well overdue. It was just circumstantial that before it got to that point, my father expired.

Allie slumps against me as I pull her into my arms, rubbing my thumb along her arm. Sometimes, sympathy can be displayed best when it is unspoken.

"It's the right decision but I know it's going to tear Willow apart. I can't help but feel guilty and selfish, we have nothing between us anymore. He is never away from work; I feel like I don't even have a husband." Her voice breaks at the end, drawing my chest tight.

"You know what's best for your family. If it's any consolation, you're an amazing mom to her, she's old enough to understand. I think you'd be surprised how mature she is, how strong she is."

She smiles coyly at my comments and sits upright.

"Thank you, I feel like I really needed that right now. It's nice to have someone be on my side for once, and, you're right. My girl is tough, she could conquer the world with her courage." She's nodding as she speaks, her eyes slightly glossy.

"If you ever need anything, don't hesitate to ask." I pat her knee, standing up as she follows me out of the office.

"You'll make a great mother one day, Indie." Her voice is quiet.

Blushing at the thought of when my time will come, I head into the changing rooms to prepare for my class.

Despite my absence at home, Scott disappears throughout the day, working, supposedly, even though he brings little to our income at the minute. We're surviving off of my income alone. I just have to keep thinking of the better times that we've had, the times when we were so in love the world didn't matter anymore.

10 Years Ago

I struggle to pull on my heels after drinking for the last 5 hours. This 'welcome back' party has very nearly caused me to ruin my reputation along with my new dress. The effect of my intoxication becomes apparent as my need to head home heightens.

Pulling myself up from the couch, I step over a bunch of drunken, passed out teenagers. None of us are legally old enough to consume alcohol, but I suppose that's the perks of being friends with a bunch of 21-year-olds.

Britney is nowhere to be found so I head out of the apartment and stumble into the hallway.

Spinning my head left and right, I try to remember which way it is to the elevators. I squeeze my eyes shut a few times to try and straighten out my focus. Each way looks the same, so I head right. Surely right is the right way, right?

I stroll along the hallway, for what feels like hours, until I finally come to the elevator lobby. Thank God, I didn't take a left.

My head pounds from the harsh lighting while I wait for the elevator to climb to this floor. Pulling out my phone, I squint, trying to make out the numbers on the front screen. It's 3 AM.

I groan and slump down the wall, closing my eyes to avoid the intense headache brewing.

I feel myself being shaken by someone.

I just want to sleep and my head hurts.

I brush their hand from my shoulder and turn away. Instantly, my eyes spring open as a wave of nausea strikes through me.

I keel over and empty my stomach contents onto the carpeted flooring, wiping my mouth afterwards.

Slumping back against the wall, someone moves my hair out of my face and pushes it behind my shoulders. As soon as his fingers graze my skin, goosebumps spread across my body and the hair stands up on the back of my neck.

Instinctively, I angle my body towards them, catching a glimpse of the person sitting beside me. His eyes are a mesmerizing chestnut brown, matching his swooped fluffy hair. Admiring his fair complexion, my gaze drops to his plump and pink lips.

Oh, his lips.

I'm staring.

"Let's get you cleaned up," his deep voice echoes through my head and pushes through my headache. I nod slowly as he stands up, taking my hands in his.

I shiver as my body ignites with goosebumps as I stare at the connection between our hands.

Who is this beautiful specimen of a man?

I pull myself up, trying to hold my balance as the alcohol still pulses through my system. Wrapping one arm around my waist, he steadies me, allowing me to lean slightly on him. We turn away from the elevators and down the corridor that I have a vague memory of.

We reach a door, and he fumbles in his pocket, pulling out some keys and unlocking it. He flips on a light switch, introducing me to a small apartment, a kitchenette and living room visible. The next thing I remember is the warm comfort of a blanket and a soft pillow beneath my head.

And I sleep.

I roll over to pull the blanket closer to me and open one eye to check the time. Where is my alarm clock?

Sitting up and looking around the room, I come to the realization that this is not my apartment.

Oh fuck.

What happened last night?

I instantly enter panic mode and hop out of the bed, knocking over a glass of water on the nightstand. Turning to the commotion, I see two tablets now dissolving in the puddle of water on the surface and an empty glass on the floor. A beam of light floods the bedroom, as the door behind me opens.

"Is everything okay?"

A very attractive-looking man appears in the doorway, a concerned look etched across his face. My mouth gapes open as I glance from the unkempt bed to his disheveled look.

"Um..." The confusion is clear through my tone.

"Don't worry, nothing happened, I swear. I'm not that kind of guy." He declares quickly.

I glance at him again, nothing about him is concerning. Internally, I'm just glad I haven't gotten myself into a mess that I can't get out of.

"Well, I'm thankful that you're 'not that kind of guy,'" I chuckle.

He smiles. Mm, I'm melting.

His smile is worthy of 100 photographers waiting to capture their muse.

Shifting awkwardly on my feet, not really sure how to act, I bow my head.

After all, who is this man?

Why am I in his bedroom?

I remember leaving the party... trying to find the elevator to leave...

Britney?

Shit.

Where is she?

I glance towards the mystery man, standing in the only exit of his bedroom, eyeing me right back.

If he didn't take advantage of me, why am I in his bed?

"I found you asleep at the elevator lobby. You were incredibly intoxicated, I couldn't live with myself putting you in a cab and just hoping you make it home safe." Almost as if he was answering my inner conscious.

Where have they been hiding this guy?

I smile at his confession, glad I'd fallen into the hands of this man and not some crazy psychopath.

"Well for that I thank you, but I do have to leave." He agrees and steps out of the entrance of the doorway, gesturing his arm to the rest of his apartment.

Despite my lack of experience with guys, I can't imagine many of them would be so kind.

I make my way towards the bedroom door as a wave of fresh peppermint floods my senses.

Oh boy, he smells good.

Peering up at him as he stands just outside of the doorway, I gaze into the most heavenly brown eyes I'd seen.

"Thank you for not being a dick," I reach up and peck the corner of his mouth, the stubble stinging me during my encounter.

Instantly, his cheeks turn a shade of crimson, revealing his bashfulness.

Smirking, I walk towards his apartment door. I notice the planning board upon the wall, littered with lectures and timetables. Grabbing the pen held on by blue-tac, I scrawl my phone number across the whiteboard partition. Adding a love heart next to it, I pop the pen back where it belonged. I make a swift exit towards the front door when he calls out,"Wait, what's your name?"

"Indie." I grin, leaving the apartment with a newfound confidence. I have a small feeling this is not the last I'll be seeing of him.

Chapter 3

Reed

I return home to greet Bridget, the new nanny for Willow. I place my briefcase by the door, adjusting my suit to appear presentable, being at work for twelve hours comes with a cost.

Bridget is washing the dirty plates in the kitchen, her blonde hair tied up on the top of her head.

"How's she been?"

"She's been brilliant, aside from throwing a hissy fit over missing… Ballet?" She responds, not bothering to turn to look at me.

I run my hands across my face.

"Oh, I'm sorry. She attends ballet classes a few times a week, I'm just not used to managing her schedule," I grimace.

She offers a curt nod whilst she finishes drying a plate, proceeding to put it in the designated cupboard.

"I'll be sure to ask Mrs. Breckenridge for a print out of her schedule.

I'd be more than happy to take her, I'm not opposed to ballet myself." She rubs her hands on her jeans, tapping away at her phone.

"Yeah, I'll be sure to get you a copy," my face pulls into a tight smile, a shiver running along my spine.

"I'm all finished up now, Mr. Breckenridge. I'll be seeing you tomorrow!" She begins to throw on her green parka.

"Call me Reed, there's no need for last name basis here."

"Well, Reed. Good night." Bridget waves as she walks through the hallway, leaving the house. As soon as she closes the door behind her, the silence becomes daunting.

Inhaling deeply, I let myself falter. This week has been stressful, not only with my new job ventures, but with the news of this impending divorce and the long road ahead.

I hope Willow isn't angry at me for her missing out on dance practice. In all fairness, it was Allie who had decided to take a business trip earlier in the week and disrupted their usual schedule, hence the need for a nanny now.

Sitting at the kitchen island, I scroll through the business news. Yet another law firm has lost clients due to sexual harassment case against one of their employees. I raise an eyebrow but deep down it all works best for me in business favor.

Taking leftover takeout from the refrigerator, I give it a sniff before popping it into the microwave.

I've been staying in the spare room for months now, not even because of our relationship struggles but because of the clashing of our working hours. We kept disrupting each others sleep that it just became easier to sleep separately, until it became favored.

If I'm being truthful, I do miss her. I hate allowing myself to feel these moments, remembering what we once were before life decided to test our limits, push and pull us in completely different directions.

We weren't always so bitter, so eager to displease one another, wanting to hurt each other in every which way.

It's like we began a battle of who can do the worst damage, who can break each other first. So far, it seems she is winning with her new plan of destroying my life by taking my daughter away from me, as if she is something that can be traded and spent.

Surprisingly, I have expected it would come to this. It's one of the last cards she can pull, she's tried everything else and if I'm honest so have I.

I'm broken from my thoughts by the ping of the microwave, the hunger I had diminished from the thoughts of Allie.

Leaving the food in the microwave, I choose to lounge on the couch, using the remote to flip on the TV. The evening news fills the screen, something that can take my mind off of my own troubles. Paying attention for a measly few minutes, I drift off into a slumber.

"…a horrific accident with several casualties on route one-four-one, emergency services have been tirelessly trying to attend to the victims. However, we can confirm there are three deceased victims. The other two victims have been airlifted to Piedmont Hospital, updates to follow."

Inching my eyes open, they focus in on air footage of a horrific accident between a trucker and two vehicles.

I rub my eyes and sit up. I squint at the sixty-inch TV sitting in front of me and my eyes grow wide. The camera zooms in on a stray registration plate on the highway.

I blink.

"The scenes are too graphic to display, but we can confirm three deceased victims and two seriously injured victims airlifted Piedmont Hospital, we warn other drivers to avoid route one-four-one at this moment in time."

This must be a coincidence.

Standing up, suddenly nauseous, I grab my phone and instantly dial Allie's number.

Straight to voicemail.

I try again.

Voicemail.

Pacing around the living room, I dial the usual driver for Allie.

Voicemail.

This is really happening.

It can't be.

Two victims at Piedmont Hospital, three deceased.

Finding the number to the hospital, I call them.

"Hello, hi, yes, I'm checking if my wife has been admitted, Allie Breckenridge, blonde hair, slim–"

"Hi Sir, please slow down."

My chest heaves with anxiety. I need to know, is she one of the surviving or one of the deceased.

"Sir?"

"Yes, yes. My wife. Allie Breckenridge. I believe she was involved in a traffic collision, route one-four-one"

I hear typing in the background. A pause.

…

"Sir, can I ask your relationship to Miss Allie?"

My frustration bursts its seams, "She's my wife!" I scream, agitated with the clearly incompetent receptionist.

"Sir, I need to ask you to remain calm during this–"

The next moment, everything becomes a blur. I fall to the ground, crushed by the words that were being spoken to me.

Peeling off my suit jacket, the phone drops to the floor beneath me. My head sinks into my hands as her words play over in my head.

"…we have her in surgery at the moment, she's a fighter…"

There is no way.

Picking up the phone and placing it back to my ear, I brace myself.

"I'm so sorry, Sir. We are trying everything we can. We will call you with any updates." Fuck that, I need to see this for myself.

I end the phone call and dial Allie's sister, Britney. As much as we despise each other, it is the least of my worries right now.

It rings out, going to voicemail.

Standing up and pulling on my hair, I scream, loathing with anger, "Fuck!"

Hearing the door creak open, I freeze.

My darling daughter enters the living room, confusion written across her sweet face.

"Daddy?" Her voice is lined with sleep.

Crouching down, I wrap her into the tightest embrace and kiss her head as the smell of her strawberry-scented shampoo comforts me.

"Willow baby, everything is going to be okay. Daddy's here, I've got you," I assure her as I continue to kiss her luscious brown locks of hair.

She latches to me like a koala bear, exactly how she used to when she was so much smaller.

"Daddy's got you, princess," I whisper into her neck as her arms tighten around mine.

I stand, carrying her with me to her bedroom, my eyes grimacing with tears from the love I feel towards her. My little girl deserves the world. I would do anything for her.

My phone rings out downstairs as I place Willow into her bed, making sure she is content before rushing back to the living room. I grab my phone, on what I predict is the last ring, and swipe right.

"Britney."

"What do you want?" She groans, not pleased with my contact attempt.

"It's Allie,"

Her tone shifts entirely.

"What about Allie?" The arrogance in her voice is overbearing.

"She's been in an accident, she's in the hospital. I need you to be here for Willow, so I can be there for her."

Her breath hitches, "What I don't under–"

"There is no time for questions, Britney. You need to get over here, now." My voice is cold and unnerving.

I hear shuffling in the background, "Yeah absolutely, of course. I'll be there as fast as I can."

Ending the phone call, I take in the sudden temperature drop. The lack of warmth in the air adds to the building chill in my bones.

***

Britney arrives within record time, no belongings, just herself.

"Thank you." I whisk past her, not looking for any sort of conversation.

Putting my car into ignition, I screech out of the driveway. Every red light I surpass, doesn't register within my eyesight. All I can see is Allie. A broken shell of a woman that is suffering inhumanely, because of matters that are beyond her control.

Leaving the car outside of the emergency department, barely remembering to shut the door, I sprint inside of the foreboding building, my heart pounding.

Stumbling upon the reception desk, I'm greeted by a woman in her sixties, not sensing my matter of urgency.

"Allie Breckenridge, where is she?" I breathe.

"Date of birth, Sir?" She murmurs, the lack of interest in my words has me spiraling. I gawk at her, not because of her ignorance, but because I don't remember. Surely, this is because I'm in shock?

"April… 5th, 1993." I say.

The tapping of the keyboard thrums to the beat of my heart.

"Sorry there is no one–"

"April 3rd 1993. Run it again."

Her face screws slightly, judging me for my lack of knowledge.

"Yes, we have an Allie Breckenridge. She's currently up in the neurology department, if you head up the elevator–"

"I know where it is." I snap, bolting off into the hospital, my heart beating out of my chest.

It clouds my ability to hear as if it were a typhoon jet, soaring the skies.

I jam the button of the elevator continuously until I'm comforted by the 'ding' of it arriving. I walk inside, persistently pressing floor six until the doors finally close.

The elevator stopped at every level on the way up, dragging out the incessant need to find out what's going on.

It occurs to me that most visitors in a hospital are here for someone they love. Whether they are in a tragic accident, suffer from a horrific disease, or despicable circumstances. We are all in the same boat. Each one of us, potentially seeing someone we love for the last time.

My stomach drops as the doors open to reveal the sign reading 'Floor 6 – Neurology'.

Rushing to the neurology department reception, I repeat the same information as I did downstairs. They inform me Allie has been in surgery for four hours already, she has suffered significant head trauma. Then, spouts the usual, '*When we have any new information, we will let you know*'.

I sit in the waiting area for what feels like years, but in reality, is only three hours.

"Mr. Breckenridge?" A woman in scrubs interrupts my train of thought.

I stand up, making my presence known.

"Mrs Breckenridge is out of surgery and she has been transferred up to the ICU, the surgery went as well as we could have hoped. However, she will be closely monitored following the surgery. The doctors in the ICU can provide you with a lot more information regarding her condition."

Thanking her, I begin to make my way to the intensive care unit.

My eyes rest upon her, the reality of the situation now sinking in. I haven't slept properly in weeks, the reason of it all is lying right in front of me.

Here she is. The most vulnerable state she's ever been in, her shield, shattered and her guard completely down. She has ceased fire.

The visualization of the situation only makes it worse; it cements the consequences of it. Her luscious blonde locks are now partially missing as a wide bandage wraps around her head with numerous tubes and drips connecting to her body. The body I loved so much, the beautiful body that birthed our only child, now damaged and broken.

I take hold of her hand, as cold as ice, as cold as her heart. Her face that was once a light tan, now a washed gray. Her lips once plump and pink, now a tight blue. Her forehead is littered with cuts, her nose swollen, and deeper wounds sit across her jaw and chin.

Poor Allie.

I pull the chair up to the bed and hold her hand tightly, I'm never going to leave her side, until death do us part.

Chapter 4

Indie

Awakening at the crack of dawn, I creep out of the house before I could wake Scott, not bothering him with my usual goodbye kiss. Especially not after his distance last night. If anything, I'm avoiding him because he decided to roll in, in the early hours of this morning and disturb me, reeking of alcohol.

It's disgusting and disrespectful.

I haul all of my bags into my car trunk, before accelerating towards Buckland Hall.

The sun has barely begun to rise, but I have to make sure I'm prepped and raring to go as the girls are due to arrive in a few hours.

I'm of course eager.

This is one of the most exciting times of my career, finally getting to see the hard work pay off and get the recognition we deserve.

Pulling up to the beautiful gates, I drive along the pebble stone driveway, the hall pillars echoing the entire front of the ancient building.

Once inside, I set up all of my equipment, makeup, hair, and spare costumes. I want to ensure nothing is going to get in the way of our inevitable winnings. Every single one of my talented dancers has been carefully selected, according to their skill level.

Most dance moms bring their own makeup and hair employees, but you never know when there could be a slip up. I've experienced far too many of my own to be ignorant to it.

***

By the time the show ends, I feel like I can finally breathe.

The star of the show is of course Willow Breckenridge. Every other girl is amazing but there is just something special about that Willow.

I've never felt such excitement, finding out we've won the prize funding for our ballet school.

Scott's of course, not in the audience, despite my invitation. His lack of presence doesn't deter me though, I don't need him to witness every moment of my success.

Willow gets to take home the 'Star Quality' award, which I already knew she'd get, I have every faith in her talent and ability. I'm glad the judges can see her how incredible she is.

It's disappointing for Allie not to be able to experience this moment, knowing it's something she takes pride in.

Instead, her father is in the audience as Willow proudly pointed out. It's difficult to make him out in the crowd but I'm just glad he finally decided to show his face for the sake of his daughter. I'm all too familiar with having a lack of parental support in situations like this.

I crouch down as Willow hugs me so tight, her arms crush against my rib-cage.

"Congratulations, little miss! I knew you could do it!" Cheering, as I hug her back equally.

I was astounded by her performance; she was most definitely the star of the show. Trust me, I don't like to make favorites. But as a dance teacher, you can tell the difference between a skill and a talent, Willow's got both.

The crowd begins to clear out so I start gathering up my equipment backstage.

A knock sounds at my dressing room door, my heart jumping at the thought of Scott making the effort.

With his face in my mind, I swing the door open with ease.

I'm taken aback by the man that stands before me. I peer into the most stunning blue eyes I've ever seen, piercing into my soul enough to take my breath away.

His hair, a dark shade of brown, appears disheveled despite his prompt appearance.

"Hi, are you Indie?" His deep tone sings.

Still analyzing his appearance, I find myself encapsulated. Entranced. And honestly, I'm not one to look. Scott is incredibly attractive but, I can appreciate beauty when I see it.

"Yes, she is me. I am her," my voice squeaks out, finally.

He stares at me, no words following. We both continue to fight for dominance, a gaze so intense it causes my chest to tighten. Unable to stop myself, I scan him from head to toe, feeling him doing the exact same in return.

I've not felt this level of intrigue since I had met Scott.

Shifting uncomfortably, the silence between us begins to overpower my thrumming heart.

His ocean blue eyes focus on me until he blinks, realizing I've responded.

"Hi, yes. I'm Willow's father." *The mysterious father.*

"Nice to meet you..." My voice trails off, not knowing what his name is.

"Sorry, Reed Breckenridge." He gestures for a handshake before we're interrupted by Scott.

"BABY!" he shouts. Reed steps back from the doorway, startled. Scott protrudes through and wraps his arms around my waist. He begins to kiss me over and over again on the lips.

"Well done baby, I am so proud of you, you would not believe!" He pulls me into a tight embrace. Counteracting his grip, I pull back due to his ridiculous need for affection in front of an audience.

"Are you not going to introduce me?" He stands up straighter.

Scott turns towards the door, staring down the attractive well-kept man. He places his hand out as a greeting and Reed complies, shaking his hand.

"Your girlfriend is an extraordinary woman," Reed compliments.

Scott turns to me with a lazy smile and then nods in agreement.

"My *fiancé*, is most definitely extraordinary," he replies, clearly trying to assert dominance.

He turns back to wink at me. I almost gag at his public display of affection, the unnatural and forced actions are purely for his own benefit.

"Well it was lovely to meet you, Indie." He smiles at me and I swear I'm melting under his gaze.

His voice so deliciously husky, my name sounds perfect coming from his lips. He turns away, disappearing into the darkness of the hallway.

Scott kicks the door closed and grabs me by the waist, proceeding to kiss me along my jawline.

"God, baby you just fascinate me," he pants.

"Scott, I have so much to do, can this wait please?"

It's been three weeks since the last time we were intimate, his ignorance persists as he continues to try and push me up against the dresser.

"Scotty, come on, just stop," I say whilst shoving my hands against his chest as I turn my head away from him. His head pulls back, the look of betrayal is written all over his face.

"You're so fucking uptight all the time! Can you not just relax for a moment?" he stresses, his body still pressed up against mine. I can feel how much he wants me but my head isn't in the right place at the moment.

"Can we just, wait till later?" I sigh. He retreats and his shoulders drop.

"Okay, whatever," he runs his hands through his hair, pondering as if he is debating saying something, but decides against it.

"I'll just see you at home."

He shakes his head as he follows the same route Reed did, leaving me alone.

I collapse into the dresser chair, placing my face in my hands.

When did things get so difficult?

I inhale through my nose and let out a long breath, trying to alleviate the tension in my shoulders but, there is something I can't shake. The excitement and the buzz that I felt from speaking to Reed for a matter of seconds, like I'd been reborn, awakened and blessed, all at once.

***

Since I've got home, Scott is seemingly distant.

As the exhaustion begins to overwhelm me, I kick my shoes off, throwing myself onto the couch and turning on the TV.

Scott groans in the kitchen, capturing my attention. Turning, I watch him mess around with the laundry machine, twisting the dial and repeatedly pressing buttons.

"Is everything okay?" Directing my voice towards the kitchen.

"Yeah, I just can't get this damn thing to work," he grits, jamming the buttons aggressively.

Rolling my eyes, I get up and walk over to the kitchen.

"Twist the dial to the correct setting, add the detergent and press the 'on' button," I explain, as if he is a toddler and breaking it down as simply as possible.

"Thanks babe."

He proceeds to do as I instructed and the machine comes to life, the water dripping out and soaking the clothes.

It's then my gaze draws on the clothes, the outfit that he was wearing today, only those in the washer.

Things are beginning to change, things already have changed, I can feel it.

Trying to not let my mind run wild, I eat a banana on the sofa, focusing on the news.

"...Four people were unfortunately deceased following a horrific traffic collision between a trucker and two pedestrian vehicles last night..."

Grimacing, I change the channel over, not wanting to hear any more negativity than what's already going on in my own head. An episode of *Friends* will have to do.

The tiredness becomes too much, so I get up from the couch, turning off the lights in the living room and heading to the bedroom.

The bathroom door remains closed and the steam pours from the gap at the bottom, indicating Scott's in the shower. I suppose I'll entertain myself with my skincare routine whilst he finishes up.

Part way through moisturizing, my ears prick at the sound of the phone vibrating to my left, on the dresser top. Picking it up, I notice it's Scott's.

My registered face ID instantly opens the phone to a conversation. I cover my mouth before I'm able to make a sound.

*(**Faye**): Thanks for the meeting, we definitely need to do it again.*

*(**Scott**): Absolutely, Faye you were great. We need to do this again.*

*(**Scott**): St. Regis Room 238.*

*(**Faye**): Looking forward to our next 'meeting'.*

*(**Scott**): Same place next week? I'll text you the time on the day*

*(**Faye**): Of course baby, anytime ;)*

The last four texts were sent today, beginning almost immediately after he left my dressing room. The sweat begins to bead on my upper lip, the anxiety from reading a private conversation and the content of said conversation, has my pulse racing.

This must be a mistake.

But it can't be.

Reading over the texts, for what felt like three-hundred times, the shower cuts off.

Panicking, I swipe the message to read as unread, throwing the phone back onto the dresser.

Diving onto the bed, I pull the covers around me and turn on my side.

Scott enters the bedroom in a towel, tied around his waist. He looks at me and smiles before making his way to the closet to get changed.

I let out a breath I didn't realize I was holding. My face is burns with trepidation as I stare at dresser top, at the phone that's holding so many secrets.

This has to be a misunderstanding,

This is Scott, *my* Scotty.

Maybe, I'm just reading it wrong?

Closing my eyes, I lay with my back flat into the pillows of our bed, hearing Scott come back into the bedroom. He turns the lights out, taking his sweet time to get into the bed. I feel it dip when he does.

The mobile phone light shines through my eyelids and does so for the hour after he assumed I was asleep.

I'm not wrong.

Chapter 5

Reed

I t isn't until the following day that I hear anything specific from a health professional.

"...Allie is currently in a medically induced coma..."

"...It's what we advise to be best for her, based on the intense surgery on her brain and the injuries she sustained..."

"...It is the best way for her to recover, but we cannot guarantee any level of recovery. The injuries Allie suffered during her accident were very serious and, in most cases, fatal. So far, she has proved she is a fighter..."

The words I'd heard from the doctors in the past half hour were more than I can comprehend.

The air in my lungs is not enough to keep me oxygenated. Each breath I take feels sharp and unfulfilling.

Britney came to visit this morning whilst Bridget took over the care of Willow.

I know that she has her dance competition today, to which I made a promise to attend.

I keep the details about Allie to a minimum, when I speak to Bridget. I don't want Willow to find out anything until I've spoken to her myself.

She's an extremely intelligent nine-year-old and sometimes, too much for her own good. I've been trying my best to act perfectly normal around her but, last night she had seen me break.

Normally, I can contain my emotions and control my reactions. That was flipped on its head when I had to prepare myself for life changing news.

***

Entering the busy hall, I take a seat amongst the chattering crowd.

A stage sits central, spotlights cast over it in different directions.

After scanning the audience to see if I recognize anyone, I pull up the brochure I was handed at the entrance. Flicking through the pages, I land on a photograph of Willow.

She is positioned with her right leg stretched outright, her arms in a beautiful arch. Her face is very different to the usual happy and smiley girl I was used to. It was much more taut, focused, and serious.

It makes her appear so much older and mature; she looks exactly like Allie. Her brown hair is pulled back into a tight and neat bun, the opposite to her usual wild and curly locks.

I really have missed out on this huge aspect of her life. Not for any longer.

The situation with Allie seems to have put a lot of things into perspective, like what really matters to me. It's time for me to put my daughter first.

I look across the rest of the page that's labeled with '*Thorne Ballet Studios*', in cursive writing.

A group photo of the entire class is the largest image on the page. Searching each face looking for Willow, I notice her as she's stood in between the arms of a woman.

The woman stands out from the rest of the group as she is dressed differently, in a black leotard rather than the opposing pink.

Her eyes pierce through the photo and stare right back at me. I hadn't realized I was completely staring until I'm interrupted by the panel of judges, announcing their greeting and the awards that are up for grabs tonight.

I quickly fold the brochure and pop it into my suit pocket, returning my attention to the stage.

* * *

Here it is, the final performance of the night.

The stage draws dark, and a line of black shadows scurry across the way.

A harmonious violin fills the room and the lights return. Willow is presented in the middle and slowly begins to arch her back and her arms move with such elegance. Her feet move quickly, but with ease.

I barely even notice any of the other dancers throughout the full performance, my gaze entirely upon my daughter.

She looks so beautiful, I really feel like I've begun to understand why Willow is so passionate about ballet, the grace and luxurious skill-set that comes with it.

The performance comes to an end and the room erupts into applause. I beam with absolute pride, knowing how much this means to her. Her smile shines out as she takes a bow in front of the judge.

There's my girl.

The rest of the dancers from other schools come onto the stage, preparing for the results.

My gaze is pulled towards the woman I had seen on the brochure. Her slender figure is obvious in her tight-fitting ruby dress, it clings hungrily to her breasts and hips, complimenting her in every way.

The girls from the performance crowd around her and she laughs, a stunning smile spreading across her face. Within a split second, the spotlights are no longer as bright as they once were.

"This decision was incredibly difficult for us as each and every one of you performed to your full potential…"

I bite my lip with anticipation.

"But of course, the decision we have made represents the true talent of their performance. We would like to announce that the winners of the annual *Atlanta Youth Ballet Competition* are…"

"*Thorne Ballet Studios!*"

I jump up from my seat and cheer the girls, as do the rest of the crowd. Seeing Willow light up with such happiness brings a tear to my eye.

The woman from the brochure steps forward and accepts the microphone from a staff member. Her smile is mesmerizing, causing her dimples to pop. I feel like I can't take my eyes away from her, she radiates a warm energy that makes me feel at home.

"Thank you so much to every one of the judges for this opportunity. Our team have worked tirelessly, and I couldn't be prouder of them, they put on a beautiful performance!" She turns back to the class, each of them cheering whilst the whole room applauds.

"Thank you, Miss Thorne. Well done everyone for participating, we can't thank you enough for your hard work and effort. Without further or do, we would like to announce the awards for the individuals who stood out to us the most within their performances…"

They announce three solo awards. Willow looks nervous and slightly wounded that she hasn't won any of the awards, yet.

"The final award we have to announce, is our most prestigious award we can offer at youth level, the '*Star Quality*' solo award."

My heart thumps.

"Willow Breckenridge!"

I whistle and ferociously clap my hands, grinning so hard my cheeks hurt. She looks afraid to step into the spotlight to accept the award so Miss Thorne grasps hold of her hand, walking out with her.

"Thank you so much everybody, especially you, Indie!"

Indie. The beautiful face has a beautiful name.

There it is. The dimple pops out. They are like an aesthetically pleasing game of hide and seek, and boy did I want to play.

As the show ends, I make my way backstage, on the hunt for Willow. I find her completely giddy and showing off her new award.

I kneel, sweeping her up into my arms swinging her around, her tiny body being encased in mine.

"Daddy! Did you see me? Have you seen my award? We won, Daddy!" she rambles, proud.

I erupt into laughter, nodding my head at her eccentric energy.

Setting her down, I kiss her on the cheek, "You were fantastic, Lo."

After a while of talking, I ask Bridget to take her out for a well-deserved milkshake and I'll meet up with them shortly after.

There is just someone who I want to thank, for making my girl so happy.

As the dressing rooms begin to clear out, my eyes rest upon the sign that reads '*Thorne Ballet Studios*'.

Doing a quick once-over in the mirror nearest to me, I button up my blazer jacket. I clear my throat and knocked twice.

Almost straight away, the door is thrown wide open and what stands before me is nothing like I have ever seen.

Those green eyes are even more enticing in person, they pierce straight through me as if she can read every thought that was going on in my head.

I move my eyes down her face to her lips, painted seductively in a deep shade of red.

I clear my throat again in an attempt to take away the sudden dryness.

"Hi, are you Indie?" I barely manage to choke out.

"Yes, she is me, I am her." she giggles.

God. That laugh, and oh, there they are again. Those dimples.

Reed.

What are you thinking?

Allie is in hospital, barely alive. And here you are, flirting like a lovesick schoolboy.

This mad level of attraction is clearly because of the lack of female company over the past few months. Even before the divorce, the intimacy within our marriage has been long forgotten.

I'm drawn out of my subconscious by a sudden awkwardness between us.

"Hi, yes, I'm Willow's father." I quickly try to recover.

"Nice to meet you..." She blushes.

"Reed Breckenridge," I reach out for a handshake, hoping to diffuse the building heat I am feeling from inside.

Taken aback by a loud presence from behind me, I watch as he surpasses me ignorantly, proceeding to kiss Indie multiple times.

Attention returns to me as Indie introduces me to the man, who is around three inches shorter than me, that rudely interrupted us. I use my usual formal introduction and shake hands with him.

"Your girlfriend is an extraordinary woman." I smile.

"My fiancé is most definitely extraordinary." *Fiancé.*

I thank Indie and remove myself from the situation before I give myself any other ideas. The last thing I need is to torture myself, wanting what I can't have, yet.

I exit the building and slide into the driver side of my black Mercedes.

Now, is time to celebrate Willow's achievements, before I must break the terrible news to her.

Chapter 6

Indie

It's been a rough week. I've tried to keep preoccupied, trying to distract myself from the messages I discovered three nights ago. I've avoided Scott as best as I can, leaving early and going to sleep early.

I can't look at him.

The messages are engraved on my memory, making my stomach twist with knots as my heart aches.

I don't cry. I've been through too much in my life to allow myself to give in to what I'm feeling.

Pulling myself off the couch, I walk into the kitchen to get myself a glass of water to sooth my dry mouth. Gulping down the full glass, I set it on the counter-top.

I press my hands against the solid marble as I stare off into the distance, confused as to how things have even gotten like this.

Scott is out, a 'client meeting'.

Blinking a few times, I realize my gaze has settled upon the Mac computer. It's almost as if a light bulb had gone off in my head.

Should I?

Surely, I'm only going to cause myself more pain.

I groan and squeeze the counter-top hard before pushing myself off, heading towards the desk in the dining space. I sit in the cold chair, giving myself a few minutes to think before I do something I may regret.

Fuck it.

Typing in the password we commonly share, the computer unlocks.

I'm met with the bland looking home screen as I now lose all sense of composure. My hand shakes on the mouse, the sickness feeling rising in the back of my throat. I act like I have the confidence to be snooping, I most definitely do not.

Where do I even start with things like this?

After trying to rationalize, I realize I'm not the person to be doing this.

So, I call the only person who should be doing this.

Britney.

No more than twenty minutes later, she's at my door.

"Where is he? That cheating scumbag has so much to answer for!" She growls, storming into the apartment with her blonde hair tied into a neat bun, gym bag over her shoulder.

I was skeptical to call her, considering what she's going through right now with her sister, Allie.

I couldn't believe the news when she told me, my heart ached for their entire family. Especially little Willow, she danced her heart and soul at the weekend and went home to find out her mom had been in a terrible car accident. I'd felt selfish, knowing I've been so concerned with my own worries, that now seem incomparable.

But, Britney insisted that she needed something to take her mind away from it all.

After all, we have been best friends since kindergarten.

"Gosh, you look a wreck, darling." She grabs my face in between her small hands as I pout.

I look up at Britney, so pristine.

You would never be able to tell this girl was going through anything, she was the epitome of being 'put together'. I lean into her and rest my head against her stomach. She pats my head like a dog as I heave a deep sigh. This was about as comforting as she gets, but I'll take it.

"Now, let's do this!" She peels me off her and grabs a dining chair, scooting it up beside me.

I move out of the way of the computer screen and allow her full control. My leg bounces up and down with anxiety as the sounds of the mouse clicking haunts my ears. I zone out completely, wrapped in the thoughts of happier times.

"God, Scott. Just wave your arm a bit more obviously, that's the fourth cab that we've missed!"

"Listen, little lady, I'm trying, okay? See, I told you I wasn't cut out for city life," he retaliates. I huff and push him aside. I wave my arm frantically towards a passing by cab that pulls to the side in front of us.

I turn back with a smirk to see Scott shaking his head at me.

"Look, you're gorgeous, that's clearly an advantage!" he jokes. I roll my eyes as we jump in the cab.

The snow outside makes it incredibly difficult to navigate our way around the city, road signs are coated, and the pathways don't feel safe enough to walk on.

Back in Atlanta, it's rare we have snow, and when we do, it's minimal.

It's partially why I wanted to visit New York in the winter season, and I wanted to see the Rockefeller tree.

We get as close as we can to the Empire State Building. Scott slips the driver a few extra dollars as a tip. I exit the cab, the wind whistling around us hard.

I pull my coat around me tighter, as I feel my breath become harsh in the cold air, misting in front of me.

I look up at the building in front of us, it's barely visible above the height of a traffic light.

I press my lips in a tight line.

Maybe winter isn't the best time to be a tourist in New York.

Scott grabs my gloved hand, pulling me towards the entrance of the Empire State Building.

After a short elevator ride to the floor one-hundred-and-two, we make our way outside to see the view.

It's crowded still, despite the weather. It's also even more ridiculously cold, and I thought downstairs was bad.

I peer out through the barrier, but all I'm met with, is white clouds.

I don't think I can mask my disappointment well as Scott turns to me,"Not what you expected, honey?"

I look back at him with a sheepish smile,"It's great," trying to sound grateful.

Of course, I am, it's just hard when I feel like we'd planned this trip so well and it being one of our few chances to escape for a getaway.

Scott reaches up to tuck my loose hair behind my ears, my beanie not containing them very well against the strong winds.

"Don't worry, darling, we will come back one summer. I promise." He pushes his warm lips against mine.

I close my eyes with satisfaction at the comfort it provides me. The taste of mint spread throughout my senses. It's like all of a sudden, it didn't matter that the view isn't great. What's important is that we did it, we've managed to go on my dream vacation.

We've worked so hard to save up, sacrificing quality time together and becoming extremely stressed in the process. It's all worth it to be here with him, right now.

He pulls away and grins at me, before looking startled at something behind me.

I quickly twist to face what he is staring at. I scan the view and each tourist.

What on earth was he looking at?

Confused, I return to face Scott.

Scott?

My gaze drops down to see the most nerve-stricken, but sweet, face staring up at me.

Shifting my eyes to the glimmer in the small green velvet box, I gasp. My hand rises to cover my mouth in shock.

"Indie Margot Thorne," he begins. I can't believe this is happening. In my favorite city, with my most favorite person.

"I never knew what love felt like until the moment you scribbled your name on my planning board. The way you make me feel is like I am invincible, like I can take on the world. Since you've walked, or stumbled, into my life, I've been dreaming of this moment. The moment I can make you mine forever. I love you so incredibly much and my hand is freezing off so please Indie, will you marry me?" He looks up at me with pleading eyes.

I nod so quickly, I can barely see.

I whip off my gloves and let him slide the ring over my finger. His poor hands are shaking from the cold, but at this moment in time, I can't feel it. My entire body burns with thrill and excitement; nothing could ruin this moment.

It was only then, I heard the cheers and claps of the crowd that had witnessed the proposal. Scott takes me into his arms and spins me around, kissing all over my rosy cheeks. This smile, his smile. He has just made me the happiest girl in the world.

I'm pulled away from the beloved memory.

"Girl, are you crying?" Britney makes a pet lip and reaches over to wipe the stray tear that's escaped.

I sniffle and shake my head, making sure I'm not going to let my guard down any further than I'd already let it. I try to distract from the tears and point at the screen.

"Wait, what's that?"

An alert pings up on the notifications tab. The email sender listed as 'monroef@aandb.com'

Subject: Regis

A small part of the email is visible from the notifications tab:

'Mr Scott Lowrey, in regards to our recent meetups, I would like to offer you ...'

Both me and Britney dare not to move a muscle. We are both frozen, staring at the small pop up that could ruin my entire life.

"You read it," I say, as I bow my head.

Picking at my fingernails, I hear the clicks of the mouse. Britney takes in a sharp breath.

My heart sinks.

I feel dizzy, I feel sick.

I need some air.

I retract from my seat and exit the apartment swiftly. I hear Britney try to scramble up and the faint call of my name, but I'm too fast.

I feel everything closing in on me as I make my way down the emergency exit stairs. I can't wait for the elevator. I take the stairs two at a time, hoping my jelly-like legs wouldn't give out on me.

This is all too much.

I leave the staircase and enter the apartment lobby, ignoring Jimmy, the doorman who I usually greet. The second I feel the gust of wind from the outside, it's like my lungs have taken their first breath.

Keeling over, I lean my hand against the brick wall, trying to normalize my breathing. I can't tell if it's the pace I've ran down the stairs or if it's the inability to breathe from what I fear the most.

I slump down the wall, pulling my knees up to my chest and burying my head in between.

After a few minutes, the door to the apartment building bursts open, a familiar scent sitting down beside me. The second she puts her arm around me and pulls me into her, I break.

I cry.

I don't need to know logistics, I know. I feel my heart tearing apart, I feel every part of my body being ripped to shreds.

If this is what love feels like, I don't want it.

No one should ever have to experience pain like this. I never ever wanted to feel this, how could he do this to me?

I can't think rationally, I want to burn every memory I have with him.

In rage, I yank the engagement ring from my finger and throw it out into the street. Britney doesn't speak because she knows I don't need to know any more than I already do. Her reaction is confirmation enough, as well as the incriminating text messages.

"Sh, baby it's okay," she rubs my arm comfortingly.

I stare at the ring, that once had so much meaning, so much happiness contained within it; that now lay in the gutter. Looking at it makes me infuriated, distraught, disappointed.

I look up at the sky. The clouds begin to cover over the sun, darkening the outside world. It's quite symbolic really.

It's strange, feeling connected to something that isn't actually alive, something that represents exactly what I'm feeling internally.

We sit for a few more minutes before Britney ushers me to go back up to the apartment. Passers-by begin to stare, no doubt at my very apparent sorrow.

I struggle to find my balance, whilst she guides me back indoors.

One thing I can promise myself is that, from now on, it's going to be me on my own.

Chapter 7

Reed

"...We are so incredibly sorry for your loss Mr. Breckenridge, if there is anything we can–"

I end the phone call.

Staring at the art on the wall of my new office, the silence threatens to swallow me whole.

I don't breathe or blink.

I sit, and I think.

I think about everything. The moment I met her, our first date, first kiss, first time, Willow, our wedding.

My eyes drift to a picture on my desk. My heart pulls and the tears start to arise. I grab the picture and launch it towards the wall, the overwhelming sensation of guilt overpowers me.

"Argh!" I cry out.

All I can see is her face.

The face that once lit up every part of me, now haunts me.

I lash out and throw things.

This feeling needs to stop, the feeling that I've fucked up big-time, something needs to get it to stop. Being in public, only makes it worse.

My body is pushed to the floor as I'm pinned down, but I can't see by who.

I don't even bother to resist.

"Everyone, out now!" A male voice bellows.

After what feels like hours, the tension in my body begins to subside. I look up to see a face that only makes my pain and guilt boil into anger.

"Harrison." I grit through my teeth.

Here he is in all his glory, eating up the satisfaction of seeing me like this.

"Reed," he responds, climbing off me.

He offers a hand to help me up, which I gladly decline. I hop up independently, looking around at my once pristine office.

Papers and glass lie everywhere, artwork hangs off the walls.

I place my fist in my mouth and bite down, hard. Seeing it all only makes this all seem, so much more real.

"Reed, look I–"

"No, no. Not now. Not ever. Leave." I point to the door.

That's when I notice the audience. As soon as I look over, they try to make themselves appear busy.

I didn't get to where I am from being gullible.

Scrambling together my papers and my laptop, I slide them into my briefcase whilst his eyes burn into the back of me.

He makes no attempt to leave.

"Harrison, if you don't leave this building immediately, I'll string you out by your neck myself."

I instantly stop packing my stuff and turn towards the stubborn bastard. He makes eye contact with me, his face melting before me.

"It's Allie, isn't it?"

Even just her name made me spiral. I grab my desk to steady myself. I can't do this. This is too much. I need to leave.

"I'm so sorry, Reed. Please just–"

The sound of his voice boils me to my core. Gripping the scruff of his collar, I throw him against the wall behind him.

I snarl into his ear, "Stay the fuck away from me, and my family," his eyes grow wide with fear as he stares back at me.

Releasing his shirt, I close my briefcase, not even caring to look back at my brother before me.

I need to escape; I don't need a reminder of any other fucked up situations in my life. Taking my briefcase, I leave through my office doors, employee eyes burning a hole into the back of my head.

I walk through the door to our– my home, leaving my shoes and bag in the corridor.

I feel numb.

Willow is spending the night at a friend's house, she has dance practice in the morning and one of the other moms offered to take her.

Nothing can prepare you for this moment. Even the thought of her name makes me want to climb inside my head and rip it out of my brain.

Charging straight towards the cabinet that holds the alcohol, most of it remains untouched, I pull the door open.

I stare at the numerous bottles of liquor, positioned perfectly.

Taking in a sharp breath, I read over the different brands, the options.

Reed, don't do it.

Everything else is a mess right now, you need to be strong for Lo.

Squeezing my eyes tightly shut, I find my grip on the first bottle my hand met with.

Removing the cap, I prop it onto the counter-top, sitting on the stool in front of it.

I lower myself to its level like I'm having a staring contest, but we both already know who's going to win.

Count to ten, Reed.

Do, as you practiced.

One...

Two...

Three...

Four...

Five...

Six...

Before I could reach seven, Allie's face flashes across my mind.

Strong, burning liquid gushes down my throat. I gulp and gulp. Allie's face flashes with disappointment and I don't stop.

Gulp.

Gulp.

Gulp.

Everything begins to subside, the pain, the guilt, *her.*

Allie.

I keep drinking.

My phone begins to vibrate. Pulling it up, I see a number of missed calls and text messages from people offering their condolences.

I shut it off.

I can't be here right now, in this house, surrounded by... *her.*

Throwing on my coat over my partially unbuttoned shirt I put my wallet into my pocket, heading out of the house. I leave my car keys and phone at home.

***

There's a chill in the air as I walk down the block to the nearest bar. The buzz of customers sounds through the opening as I push through the door.

It's not too late yet, so there is still spaces for me to sit.

I pick a space at the bar, ordering a whiskey on the rocks, telling the guy to keep them coming.

He looks at me for a second before giving me a slight nod.

I knock them back in one. Each shot chipping away, burning what little feeling I have left inside of me.

In the bar, people are generally in groups, chatting away, laughing, without a care in the world.

My mouth turns sour.

Alcohol is an interesting concept. It is used in several ways; to celebrate, to socialize, to wind down. Or the one I'm most familiar with, to numb pain.

I don't have a good way of dealing with my feelings. Hence, a therapist from the tender age of 12.

I began consuming alcohol around the time when my mother died; she committed suicide, leaving me, my brother Harrison, and my sister Charlotte to be brought up by my Aunt Lucy.

My father?

We parted ways a long time ago.

After he and my mother divorced, he barely kept in contact with us. He sent us gifts on birthdays and Christmas, financially supporting my mother. The bitter truth was, he left her for another woman.

As far as I'm aware, my mother couldn't deal with the strain of being heartbroken and raising three children, alone.

What my father did to her was unforgivable, and I've always resented him for it. Harrison and Charlotte, however, didn't see it that way.

Once they reached the age of 18, they tried to build a relationship with our father, something I was never be able to do, something I will never do.

Both, Harrison and Charlotte, work for my father's law firm as prestigious lawyers, under his thumb.

I drink another glass of whiskey.

The nerve of Harrison is eating away at me.

Being in one of the rawest moments of my entire life, reveling in the loss of my wife, he had to be there.

Looking down at my empty glass, that has not yet been refilled, I scowl. Searching for the bartender, I beckon him over and point at my glass.

He shakes his head.

"Look, buddy. I think you've had enough for one night."

I furrow my brows.

This. This is *my* choice.

I turn my confusion into a smile as the rage I've tried to dim, fuels the rising temperature of my blood.

The bartender seems to relax and turn away. Hm.

"Not to worry, I was finished anyway," I smirk as I take the whiskey glass, dropping it to the floor.

Instantly, the bar quiets. Their eyes on me, watching for my next move.

The bartender backs away, holding up his hands.

"We don't want any trouble." He tries to reason with me.

"Well, I wanted another drink!" I yell, standing up from my stool and slamming my hands down on the bar as a wave of intoxication begins to consume me.

"If you don't calm down, I'm gonna have to call the cops, dude."

Stealing an onlooker's glass from their table, I flick my head back and drink whatever concoction it was.

"If you won't get me a drink, I'll get one myself," I slur, reaching down to take another mysterious glass.

The commotion heightens as the bartender grabs the phone.

The world looks at me with absolute disgust, as if I'm just some sleazy alcoholic.

Nobody knows what I am going through, the shit I've got on my plate. And here they are… sitting, judging, pitying.

A perfect representation of the world as it is, bitter and unforgiving.

I kick back another drink from a random table as a presence looms over me. A guy, who is a good few inches taller than me, covered in tattoos, bares his teeth at me.

"You think you intimidate me?" I snarl, the fury inside of me only increases.

I'm sick of people thinking they have a say so on my life.

He begins to square up to me just as I puff out my chest, anger pulsing through my veins.

I need this, I need some way to get rid of this torturous feeling that reminds me so much of the innocent 12 year old, who lost the most important person in his world.

"You should be intimidated, pretty boy." He smirks.

I see out of my peripheral someone darting towards us as the guy in front of me raises his fist.

Go on, do it.

Hit me.

I need this.

I need to feel the physical pain, I can't take suffering with any of this mentally anymore, I need to be punished.

As I brace myself for impact, a high-pitched voice shrieks, "STOP! He's with me!"

My eyes flicker open, casting upon the last person I expected to see

tonight.
  Indie Thorne.

Chapter 8

Indie

Since I found out the vile truth about Scott, I've been staying at Nina's place.

She insisted on having me stay after Britney told her all about the tragedy, that is my life.

Britney has far too much going on with Allie, I don't want to burden her with looking after me.

The first few nights are horrendous. I can't sleep.

I spend every waking moment thinking about Scott, thinking about his hands all over another woman. Her getting to experience what was once mine.

The absolute disgust that turns my stomach, whenever his face enters my mind, has me wondering where we went wrong.

I have arranged my entire life to include him, my past, present and future. Now, all of that has been flipped upside down, inside out and left to rot.

There are so many things in life that you can predetermine, prepare for, and manage to work through.

This right now feels like an abyss of darkness, pain and sadness surrounding the memories I have, the memories that I will now, never have.

I've been wondering over the past few days if there is anything I could have done to change the outcome, if I could have paid more attention, been more affectionate, been more present.

None of which seems to comfort me.

Getting to grips with doing everything that I had planned for the both of us, on my own, is going to be a lengthy process.

It feels as if my brain is in constant overdrive, thinking far too logistically and not having much to distract me.

Tonight, isn't going to be the same.

I need to stop thinking about the hypothetical, I need to blow off some much needed steam. Anything at this rate is better than sitting here, wallowing in self-pity.

I towel dry my hair, looking at the same three outfits I've been wearing all week. Washing in between, of course.

Sighing at the bland selection, I text Nina, asking if I can raid her wardrobe for something to wear. Once she offers me her permission, I search through the different outfits, looking for something that would make me appear presentable, endearing.

A gorgeous black dress captures my attention, strappy and short. Rather promiscuous for my usual choice of attire but, Britney's advice?

The best way to get over someone, is to get under someone else.

I've spent the days crying, being hurt and sad. I'm tired of feeling the same emotions over and over. At this point, I am desperate.

It doesn't matter that I'm not feeling up to it, I'm taking back the slightest bit of normality that I can have right now.

Pulling the dress from the hanger, I study it in the mirror, holding it against my body. Fortunately, Nina has the same 5'3 frame as me, meaning her clothes will mostly fit me.

Helping myself to her wine collection for the first time this week, after declining the countless times prior, I select a pretty bottle of white Grenache.

The last thing I need is to look like I was coming straight from a funeral so I add a bucket load of concealer, in an attempt to cover up my purple circles.

The next thirty minutes are spent indulging in wine and trying to mask the damage that is now hidden beneath.

Eyeing up the black dress, hung in the corner of the room, my mind drifts into one of its spirals.

How did things go from being so normal and simplistic? I'm about to go out and drown my sorrows in alcohol and someone other than Scott.

The breakup went as well as you'd expect an unfaithful breakup to go. His excuses consisted of; you work too much, we never see each other, he was desperate, it didn't mean anything. Typical responses from a man who is clearly intimidated by an independent, successful woman.

Of course, things weren't as simple as just leaving and never having to see or speak to him again. Technically, I'm a partial owner of his company, the majority of the investment came from me. so I warned him he would be hearing from my lawyers if he made any attempt to make my life any worse than he had already.

You'd think after everything we'd been through, it would have been that he is distraught in emotion that I was leaving him, he wouldn't care about trying to grip me within his claws. His concerns resided in the logistics, where am I going to live, how do we split our finances, the apartment. The last thing on his mind was the hurt he'd caused me.

It was almost like another kick to the gut, the final moment where my warm beating heart turned to solid ice, for good. No more feelings, no more love and relationships.

I'm truly becoming everything I never wanted to be, emotionless and helpless. But, I can't allow myself to become so vulnerable again, the indescribable amount of pain I'm suffering with has only proved, I am on my own.

You'd think, losing the relationship with my parents would have built me up enough to deal with this kind of trauma.

Nope. Still hurts like a bitch.

Sliding the black silk dress over my head, I pull it down to a comfortable position, admiring the way it compliments my figure. I slip on a pair of Nina's black strappy heels, lacing them up to mid-calf.

Glancing at myself in the mirror, my eyes focus on my hair, tied up in its usual neat bun. I shake my head as I yank the hair tie from my hair, letting my natural waves settle around my shoulders. Messing with it for a minute or two, I decide it's good enough.

As I wait for my Uber, I finish off the rest of the bottle of wine, feeling the buzz of the alcohol in my system

Not forgetting my clutch, I exit the Uber.

The numerous buildings light up the streets with their flashing neon signs. The city is stunning at night-time, it breathes life. It feels strange to not have someone by my side, guiding the way. Instead, every decision from now on is purely my own.

Lucky and independent me.

The cute bar across the street appeals to me the most, the blinking 'Rolling Stones' logo has caught my attention, small tables line up on the sidewalk outside.

Glancing left and right for clear traffic, I walk over to the other side of the road, pushing open the heavy glass door.

I check out the busy room, looking for a seat. A bustle of commotion draws me away from my search, maybe I've picked the wrong bar?

A guy, in an expensive looking suit, has his back to me whilst a larger guy towers over him. The conversation they are having looks extremely heated, I think its best if I get myself out of here, before this escalates.

As I begin to turn back towards the exit, the suited man turns and squares up to the bigger guy, revealing his full profile.

Oh god.

Reed Breckenridge?

The muscular guy begins to raise his arm up and before I can stop myself, my instinct claims hold of me, and the alcohol.

Darting forward, I cry out, "STOP! He's with me!"

Both men stop, turning towards me in annoyance that I had interrupted their battle.

Reed's eyes rake over my entire body, almost in disbelief.

"Indie, what are–"

"Come on hon, let's get you home."

He's blatantly intoxicated and not thinking clearly, judging by the strong smell of alcohol coming from his breath.

If he thought I'd leave him to get beaten up, he's wrong.

Allie would never forgive me for letting her, soon to be, ex-husband get into some kind of bar brawl whilst she's in the hospital.

He has Willow to prioritize.

Pulling him towards me, I place my arm around his waist and he doesn't resist.

I mutter some apologies to the staff and other customers on our way out of the bar, using all of my weight to keep Reed steady.

Once we make it a bit further down the street, definitely not gracefully, I plant us on a bench near to the sidewalk. He hasn't muttered a word since we've left but I can't tell if it's out of embarrassment or if he is purely just too drunk to notice what's going on.

The confusion overrides me, "What the hell happened in there?"

A mumble escapes his mouth, barely even trying to make it understandable for me. Slouching back, he covers his face with his hands, revealing a very expensive looking watch.

If I didn't think he was rich before, I certainly do now. That watch could probably pay my entire year of bills.

My gaze drifts from his watch to his hands that completely cover over his face and then some. Those long fingers that are currently entangled in his locks tempt me in ways I didn't think possible.

My eyes trail along each of the veins on his hands and up to the exposed skin of his wrist, continuing to his torso, a tight-fitted white button up sculpted to his obvious abs underneath.

Lingering on the belt at the bottom of his torso, I find myself biting my lip. I can't help but wonder what's hidden beneath, the buckle taunting me, knowing that it's protecting something that I want.

Coughing, I try to pick my mind up out of the gutter.

Clearly, the bottle of wine I had before leaving has ignited emotions within me that had been long forgotten, until now.

Reed startles, removing his hands from his face, eyes meeting with mine. My lips part as his glassy eyes wander all over my face.

My mind wonders, questioning why he's in such bad shape, drunk and almost getting into a fight with some random guy.

"Is everything okay with you?" I question.

"Right as rain," he beams with a perfect set of white teeth.

The smile he gives represents how I'm feeling internally, pained, and sad.

Trying to reassure him, I give him a small smile in return. I know that Allie is seriously injured from the accident, I don't know the full extent, but I've heard she is in some sort of coma.

It can't be easy, seeing someone you love to suffer, knowing there is nothing you can do about it.

His hand reaches up, stretching his finger out as he jabs it into my cheek.

My brows instantly furrow with confusion, and I gasp. What on earth is going through his mind right now?

He grins to himself, his eyes twinkling under the streetlights. Folding my arms across my chest I raise my left eyebrow, hinting I want to know what is *so* hilarious.

"I love that."

"Love what?" Has this guy had more than alcohol?

"Watch, do it again," he speaks confidently.

"Do what?" I try to think back to what made him poke me in the cheek. I give him a sympathetic smile. This time, he attacks me with two of his fingers, one on each cheek. What the fuck?

Standing up from the bench, I place my hands on my hips, "Are you okay, Reed? Do I need to get you a cab straight to the nearest loony hospital?" He smirks up at me, revealing the most mischievous look on his face.

"I'm perfectly fine, dimples." *Ah.*

"Very original, Reed. I need to get you home before you start harassing other random strangers for their facial features," shaking my head and offering him a hand to stand up.

"Actually, harassment is usually offensive or demeaning which is the exact opposite of what I did," he smirks at his arrogant nature.

Who even recalls definitions of words off the top of their head like that? Should I be alarmed that he knows exactly what harassment is?

"What exactly would you define it as then? Smart ass."

He ponders for a moment.

"Simple, a compliment." His arrogance swarms the air.

Rolling my eyes, I sit back down beside him, the smell of alcohol still floating around. I find myself becoming distracted once again, with my poor attempt of forgetting about it.

We sit in front of the restaurant that was once one of my most favored places. Through the window, it buzzes with life and happiness; couples and families enjoying a candlelit dinner without a care in the world. Mine and Scott's first official date had been here, paired with the time he asked me to be his girlfriend; some sort of meaningful gesture to our history. Scoffing at the memory, I prohibit the emotion that is bursting to pour out of me, shutting down the thought and locking it away with a key.

No more of this. No more dwelling on the past.

"I'm sorry I didn't mean to offend you."

Angling my body towards him, I give him a small smile.

"You didn't offend me, don't worry. I just haven't been much of myself lately, I'm sorry for being uptight."

"Could say the same for myself," he shifts, looking downwards and withdrawing from the conversation quickly, avoiding to spill anything else about how he's feeling.

For a few moments, we both just sit in silence.

I don't know whether to probe him for more information, or if that would be overstepping.

I certainly wouldn't want him poking questions around my personal life, we barely know each other. But then again, would that not be better? To be able to vent to someone you don't know so you get minimal judgment in return. Before I'm able to speak, I'm interrupted.

"How about we both blow off some steam? We can stay at a hotel, have a few drinks and relax?" he looks up at me, his blue eyes dancing in the reflection of the streetlights, or the glassy-eyed look from the alcohol.

I know better than to act on impulse and take him up on his offer, he's Allie's husband for Christ's sake. Shaking my head, I tuck a strand of hair behind my ear.

"Come *on*, it'll be fun, I promise," he winks at me. I let a shy laugh escape, looking around to try and stop myself from submitting to temptation.

"I can't I have–" I find myself about to say that I have a fiancé, which clearly, I very much don't anymore. After years of saying I have a partner, it's definitely going to take some getting used to, now that I'm single.

I meet his gaze, him looking at me with an arched brow.

Sucking in a deep breath, "Yeah, fine, sure." I pull my lips into a tight line and stand up, tugging my dress lower.

What's the worst that could happen?

Wearing a lazy grin, he stands up alongside me, but not as graceful as me.

He offers his arm, towering almost an entire foot above me.

Linking my arm through his, we begin to walk further down the street, away from the bar, the warmth of his touch sending signals to the rest of my body.

After engaging in small talk for the walk, avoiding bringing Allie into the conversation, we come up to the entrance of an extravagant building. One look at the huge signage makes my heart skip a beat.

'St. Regis Hotel'.

Planting my feet to a stand still, I pull away from Reed's arm, my obvious demeanor causing him to question me.

"Um, is everything okay?"

Everything from the past week resurfaces, flashing through my mind, the text messages, the email, the conversations.

Closing my eyes, I flare my nostrils as pure anger begins to pulse through my body. I clench my fists, I squeeze my eyes together tight, trying to shut out everyone and everything around me.

After a few seconds I feel the warmth return to my side, a large hand caresses my arm patiently, comfortingly. I like the way he makes me feel, the protective nature and the ease of being around him.

Slowly opening my eyes, I look at his, an ocean of concern.

"I- I'm fine" I assure him. His gaze doesn't leave mine, though.

"It's just some bad memories…" I trail off.

Shaking my head and raising my chin, I act as if it's proof that I've got rid of the thoughts that haunt my mind.

Reed plasters a comforting smile on his face, pulling me closer. I look up to him, slightly leaning back so I can keep my eyes on his due to our height difference.

His face looks as if it's been crafted carefully, with the perfect sharp and soft points, like an actual work of art. Despite his eyes looking tired, they are such a unique shade of blue that glows almost white as it gets closer to the pupil of his eye.

Sinking against him as his strong arms pull me in for a hug, he practically squeezes the air out of me.

Normally, I would resist but it's exactly what I need right now. The muscles of his chest rest against my cheek, the buttons of his shirt pressing into my skin. I stand there for a moment before I realize, this hug isn't just for me, the situation with Allie and the divorce they're going through can't be easy.

Maybe, we both just need a person right now. Maybe, we just need to forget about life and all its worries and need someone to distract us from this reality. Pulling back slightly, he loosens his grip fast, coughing to cover up his awkwardness.

Finding a newfound confidence in my revelation, I promised myself tonight would be about forgetting. Tonight, would be about change and finding myself again, what better way to start that off, than finding someone as equally damaged to pour my heart into.

Grabbing Reed's hand, I pull him towards the entrance of the hotel before he has a chance to speak, or before I have a chance to fall back into whatever hole I've managed to climb out of.

No looking back now.

Chapter 9

Reed

I slide my key card into the hotel room door slot, pushing it open, allowing Indie to enter first.

As I follow in after her, I walk past the full-length mirror barely recognizing who is looking back.

Hanging up my blazer jacket in the corridor, I watch as she starts to unstrap her heels, bending over as her dress becoming restrained against her backside.

In an attempt to avert my attention, I drink in the stock artwork on the walls whilst I wait for her to finish up so that I can get past her.

The last thing I want is to have to squeeze past her, crotch to ass. That part can wait until later.

Standing up, she saunters away, looking around at the different rooms that lead off. Giving her a moment to feel comfortable, I head towards the mini bar, grabbing a bottle of red wine and heading back towards the kitchen.

"Wine okay?" I call to her, as she proceeds to the living room.

"Wine is fine," she responds.

I grab a corkscrew and two of the large wine glasses from the cupboard, rinsing them as the fingerprints on them have me uneasy.

Strolling back over to the living space, I pop all three items onto the glass coffee table. She leans forward and grabs the bottle, bringing it straight to her lips.

She takes me by surprise as a laugh erupts my throat, "That bad, huh?"

Her eyes flick to mine as she scoffs a laugh into the wine bottle, trying not to spill anything in her mouth. I watch as her lips wrap around the top of the bottle once again, her lipstick slightly smudged. Something about the way she is doing that is so fucking seductive.

When she is finished, she licks her lips, her tongue lingering out of her mouth longer than necessary causing my mind to run to images of her on her knees, licking my entire length tauntingly.

Taking the bottle from her, I split the remainder of it into the two glasses I brought over, trying to calm my brain from the dirty thoughts I'm having. I hand her one of the glasses and take a large gulp from mine, letting the warmth of the liquid burn my throat on the way down.

I can feel her watching me, her beautiful green eyes wander all over my body. The sexual tension in the air is thick and tempting, we both know what our intentions were when I asked her to come here.

"So, Indie," I begin as she takes a sip of her wine, waiting for me to finish.

"How about we cheers, to forgetting about reality tonight," I raise my glass to hers, my grin bearing teeth.

She beams at me, clinking her glass with mine.

"Cheers to forgetting about reality."

The silence finds its way to us soon after that. How does one simply, forget about reality? It's easier said than done. Grabbing my phone, I hit shuffle play on my Spotify, the sounds of 'Fleetwood Mac' drift through the surround speakers.

"I love this song!" she squeals.

"Who doesn't?" I smirk.

She sways to the music, closing her eyes and singing along to a few of the lines. I watch her for a few moments before standing up to get us more alcohol from the mini bar, noticing the empty bottle of wine.

As I return, she's sits cross-legged on the couch, peering up at me, looking so damn cute as she flutters her eyelashes at me.

She reminds me of Allie in some ways, the similar eye color nestled into large round eyes as opposed to Allie's smaller, sleek eyes.

I want to forget badly about her, but I'm almost finding a new way to deal with this grief, this guilt. Even just thinking about her causes my stomach to twist and turn into knots, but I also can't tell if it's the shock or the excessive amount of alcohol in my system right now.

I can tell I'm drowning. I'm doing everything I can to shut myself out, but the woman I have in front of me offers me everything I would ever want. I regret everything that has ever happened between me and Allie, the falling apart of our marriage and the last few years. We became so distant, we were like two strangers stuck in some sort of agreement to bring up a child together rather than the passionate, loving couple we were, once before.

I would never ever regret Willow. In some ways, she solidified us together, bringing us a connection we would never have had.

Although, I think my mistakes wouldn't have been so apparent if we didn't have a child in the midst of it all. But Allie always put Willow first, more than I ever did. For that, I will forever respect her and make sure that Willow knows how much her mother loved her and wanted her to have everything she ever desired.

I definitely need to figure out where I go from here like how I try to fill the role that Allie created. It will be inevitably difficult to do, but it is something that must be done to make sure I'm worthy of the role.

The playlist shifts onto a few random suggestions, some questionable.

"How about we play a game?" She asks me.

Raising an eyebrow, I respond,"Hm, what kind of game?"

"Two truths and a lie?"

I ponder a moment, "We can, but I wanna spice it up, let's make it... interesting."

She looks at me puzzled, I need anything to draw me away from these haunting thoughts.

Forget about reality, tonight is about letting go and having fun.

"For every time the person guesses the wrong lie, you must remove an item of clothing," pulling a half smile and lounging back as I take another sip of wine.

Her eyes grow wide.

"But I literally only have one piece of clothing on?"

"Well, you best hope you have a lie detector then," I snicker into my wine glass whilst she huffs out a breath.

"Well, I get to go first then." She props her wine glass down on the table and sits forward, facing me straight on.

I beckon for her to go ahead.

"Okay, um... I have 2 sisters, I am single and my favorite alcoholic beverage is a gin and tonic,"

I laugh to myself, knowing that she is about to have to take off that very seductive dress of hers. I couldn't care less if she has a boyfriend, or *fiancé* as he so obnoxiously confessed. She's clearly here with me right now, looking as gorgeous as she does. I almost cheer internally.

"Easy, the lie is that you are single." I remember back to the day of Willow's dance competition, meeting her beloved. Not that I care anyway, reality is no longer going to cross my peripheral.

"Wrong, remove your shirt," she says confidently, drinking the last of the wine in her glass.

I frown as the confusion draws across my face.

"How can I be wrong? I do remember the over-confident *asshole*." She meets my eyes.

"Long story short, he's just like every other guy and also as you put it, an over-confident asshole, who cheated on me." The pain flashes across her eyes even from that brief statement.

My hand reaches out for hers instinctively and I notice a silver line of tears coating her eyes. She begins to laugh out loud, shaking her head and blinking away the tears that were about to spill.

Damn, when I met the guy, he was all over her, and I knew straight away he was way out of her league. And that guy cheated on… her?

The nostalgia brews.

I instantly begin to feel an anger I had buried deep down inside of me, reminding me of my disgusting excuse of a father that had done the same to my mother. Why do they always throw away a diamond for a piece of dirt?

If I've learned anything from my father's mistakes, it's that I know my respect for women, I know boundaries and the purpose of being a husband.

Well… I did.

"Just refill my drink will you… oh and remove the shirt." She winks.

I begin to unbutton my shirt, one by one, fumbling slightly, purposely.

"Here, let me help you." she leans across me and swings a leg over my lap.

I jolt at the sudden movement, her dress shifting up her thighs. I look up to her as she begins to take over the unbuttoning. Her eyebrows crease slightly as she concentrates, a small line appearing in between them and her lips part slightly as she leans further forward, casting shadows across my face.

I can feel the heat of her breath smother me, the scent of the wine filling my senses. I flutter my eyes closed as my hands find their way to her waist, holding her in place.

She pulls my shirt fully open as her eyes devour my body, taking in all of it. She rests her hands on my chest carefully and softly, sending a ripple of sensation straight to my groin. Her touch feels magnetic on my body, demanding a response from me.

"Your turn."

Snapping out of my trance, I focus my attention back to her sweet face.

"Right, yeah. So I'm allergic to shellfish, I have a foot fetish and I've only ever slept with one person my whole life."

She concentrates on me for a while, her hands remain on my chest. The pressure in my body to stop me from flipping her onto this couch and running my hands all over her body, is bordering on weak.

"I'm gonna say… the lie is that you've only ever slept with one person. I can one-hundred percent see you as the kind of guy to have a foot fetish." She giggles.

I burst out into a laugh, almost offended.

"Well, I'm not opposed to foot play, but I most definitely don't have a foot fetish," I say in my defense. Her laugh falters as she realizes, she didn't guess the lie correctly, finding it hard to mask my succeeding grin.

"Refill my drink, darling… oh, and remove the dress." I sit back and spread my arms out across the back of the couch, repeating her words from the last round.

We lock eyes as she bites her lip nervously, all whilst she remains straddled on me. Her hands slowly find their way to the bottom of her black silky dress, and I clench my fists in apprehension of what's to come.

She grips the thin fabric and ever so slowly tugs it upwards, revealing more of her skin on her thighs. Instinctively, I run my hands along her smooth legs, the feel of it is like she herself, is made of silk.

My eyes dart back up to hers, the vibrancy of her green eyes have now darkened, almost swallowing me up with lust. She continues pulling the fabric up higher, now just above her waist. I glance back down to see the black lace that caresses her most prized possession. *Fuck.*

Swallowing hard, my mouth all of a sudden dry. The material keeps moving upwards, exposing her smooth, toned stomach. I move my hands up the sides of her, causing her to shudder.

God, I am so fucking turned on right now.

As the dress reaches her underarms, her head disappears as she wrestles the material over her head. I cast my eyes down her entire front, taking in a harsh breath at the sight of her plump breasts, her nipples hardened and begging for mercy.

The sound of her dress hitting the floor brings me back to her face. She wears a smart look on her face at my obvious flushed appearance, the heat apparent on my cheeks.

"You are so goddamn beautiful," I breathe.

She brings her face closer to mine, the shifting of her body making me groan. The pants I am wearing are painfully restricting my growing package, any slight movement is making it so much harder.

"I have something to tell you," she whispers into my ear, sending chills throughout my body at the seductive tone. I mumble some sort of response.

"I've only ever slept with one person too," and she sits back up straight, her breasts bouncing from the sudden movement.

I can barely even string a sentence together right now as I lift a hand up to touch her chest before she bats my hand away.

"My turn again."

I don't know how much longer I can carry on; my building frustration is about three grinds away from exploding into an orgasm.

I just nod my head and squint my eyes at her.

"My favorite ice cream flavor is mint choc chip; I have a dog named Barney and I've only ever left the state to go to New York."

I want this game over and done with. I need her. Now.

"Lie is your favorite ice cream flavor, who likes mint choc chip?" I grimace in disgust.

"Remove your pants, Reed." She hops up from my lap and I can barely take my eyes off her.

Seeing her stood up in front of me lets me take in the entire curves of her hips and the way her stomach has toned lines from top to bottom. Struggling to undo my belt, I shuffle to kick off my trousers onto the floor. My boxers can barely contain my pained erection.

I watch as she looks at me from head to toe, my breath going ragged. I've never had a woman be this forward with me, this in control. And, I am fucking loving every second of it.

Indie flicks her hair to one side of her shoulder and drops to her knees in front of me. I part my legs wider to allow her closer, my cock is begging so hard to be touched, I can't take it anymore.

She runs her long fingers along my groin, my body shuddering at the insane amount of pleasure from that alone. I haven't had sex in months, and I feel as if I'm going to end up releasing all over her before she's even had chance to begin. I've never wanted someone so much.

She grips me through my boxers, and I let out a hiss at the touch I am so dearly craving. I look towards her face as she's licking her juicy lips, God, them lips. I want them all over me in every way possible.

"Do I make you nervous, Reed?" She taunts me.

"Fuck, yes."

"Do you want me to help you out with your little problem here?" She gestures to my cock.

"Fuck, yes please. Indie, God," I say as she tugs down the waist band of my boxers, allowing me to spring out. The release itself ricochets pleasure from my groin to my toes. She grips me.

"Indie, fuck yeah," I choke out.

My entire body is radiating, sweating with suspense. I watch as she very slowly licks from the bottom of my length all the way up to my tip, the sensation making me moan out loudly. The way her tongue curls around my tip causing my toes to curl likewise in order to hold back my orgasm.

She takes me in her mouth as she makes eye contact with me. I put my hands behind my head and grip onto my hair hard as she struggles to cope with my size. I can't break her gaze, her eyes welling with tears as she tries her best to take me in fully. Fuck, she is fucking divine.

I begin to feel the intense orgasm try and burst through my control, I am trying so hard to resist right now. It feels far too good to want her to stop.

She bobs her mouth up and down, licking around the tip and pushing it all the way back to her throat. I moan and groan with pleasure, not sure how much longer I can hold myself off. Every time it hits the back of her throat I cry out and fist her hair.

She puts me in her mouth one more time and pushes down, holding me in the back of her throat as she moans. The vibrations that pulsate through my body send another wave of pleasure and I can't cope anymore. Moaning loudly, my legs begin to shake as I feel myself explode into her throat and she swallows it submissively.

"Oh my fuck, Indie fuck," I pant, sweat beads forming on my

forehead from holding back for so long.

Something about her innocence, her seductive eyes and her delicious body have me higher in the clouds than I've ever been before. She is the angel, guiding me to the heavens above.

I relax my hand in her hair as she pulls up from me, climbing on top of me.

She peers down at me and I pull her closer, glancing at her swollen lips as I crash mine straight onto hers. I wrap my hand around the back of her neck as I chase her tongue with mine, electricity entering my veins once again.

Who the fuck is this woman?

We battle breathlessly and I tug on her lip with my teeth as I begin to caress her right breast. She stifles a moan as I brush across her hardened nipple and slightly rub myself against her wetness between her legs. I rub my other hand along her ass and squeeze it roughly, my body craving the touch and feel of her. Wrapping a finger around her, I tug the string of her thong, causing it to ping back against her skin.

"Mph," she mumbles against my lips. The kissing doesn't cease whilst I take both of my hands to tear the string. I'm impatient and hungry to feel inside her.

Throwing the skimpy piece away from us, I return one hand to her breast, this time entertaining her left, whilst the other finds its way between her legs.

"Oh, God, Reed," she moans when I slip a finger against her wetness.

I tear away from her mouth and take her left breast to my mouth and swirl my tongue around her nipple. She cries out with pleasure as I begin to slowly rub my finger over her clit, her beautiful writhing body can barely keep still as she hovers over me.

I flip her over onto her back and take to my knees on the floor, the loss of the warmth of her body, devastating me. Pushing her down,

I pop her legs over my shoulders and I come face to face with her pretty little pussy, begging for me.

The wetness of it glistens in the light from the lamp and I starve for her. I part her slightly with my tongue and her hands grip my hair, the beautiful moans of her, blessing my ears. I'm going to tongue fuck her so good that she doesn't remember anything but the feeling of me inside of her, that no other person can replace.

Slowly, I place long licks down her slit, agonizingly slow, as I take in her taste. The sweetness of it tantalizing my taste buds. The whirling of my tongue inside of her has her crying out.

"Reed, *oh*." My name sounds perfect coming from her lips. I devour her, licking, sucking and flicking my tongue across her.

I reach up and put one hand on her right breast, taking her nipple between my fingers and playing with them whilst I eat her. Her breaths start to become ragged and desperate, so I know she's close. This sweet pussy is about to become mine.

I raise my other hand and push one finger inside of her, it slips in without any resistance. I glance up to see her writhing, her eyes closed as I deliver her to the devil myself, my sacrifice.

"Yes, oh fuck, yes," and I feel her legs tense around my head as she begins to reach her peak.

I keep my rhythm the exact same as she struggles to contain herself, pumping my finger inside of her to match.

She starts unraveling before me as she climaxes, her euphoric moans like music to my ears; her beautiful juices fill my mouth and I lap it all up, still sucking and licking her whilst she finishes.

She catches her breath and peers down at me whilst I slowly drop her legs down. I smirk at her flushed complexion, her eyes hazy and disoriented.

"I'm not finished with you yet."

Her eyes glisten and gleam in the light and I take in her beauty once more.

Dropping to my knees I position myself, causing her to suck in a breath as I press my tip against her. I slowly push myself inside, my eyes fluttering closed as the intense pleasure ripples throughout my body, my knees barely able to keep me upright.

She cries out, holding onto my forearm. I fill her more, waiting for her to be able to accommodate my size. I lean over her further and she wraps her legs around me. Beginning to thrust slowly, I keep my focus entirely on her.

Her cheeks are blush pink, her mouth parted and gasping every time I move. I'm not quite sure if this is how hook-ups are supposed to feel but if it is, then this is fucking addicting.

Picking up the pace, I bury myself inside of her, watching as her breasts bounce with the movement. I lean down and kiss her neck, feeling every single inch of her. I grip her wrists with one hand, pulling her upwards towards me as I my other hand grab onto her hip, hoisting us both up.

I start to kiss her again, craving the need for her sweet mouth on mine. The same mouth that just absolutely annihilated me. I keep myself inside her as she writhes to try and get me to continue moving. I smile, tugging on her lip with my teeth again and carrying us towards the kitchen island.

Resting her on the surface, I break my kiss from her mouth, propelling down her neck, that smells sweetly of coconuts, until I reach her breasts again. I start to move against her again and she moans in agreement.

I lick her nipples and start to thrust faster into her. Indie wraps her arms around my neck and gives me easier access. I can't help but wish I was able to fuck her like this forever.

Starting to feel my orgasm building again, I want to resist but I only grow even hungrier for her. I grip onto her hips and start to pound her over and over. She falls backwards, her arms grabbing onto the island to keep herself upright. I lap up the view of her, so sweaty and disheveled, her nipples hard and sexy.

All I can hear is the slapping of our skin together as Indie tightens her legs around me whilst I fuck her into oblivion.

She cries out in ecstasy, dropping backwards unable to support herself anymore whilst she orgasms. Her tightening pussy tips me over the edge as I follow close behind her, my thrusts becoming sloppier whilst my legs shake.

I jerk out of her, allowing myself to expel into my hand.

"Oh, fuck," I moan and lean forward, resting myself against her stomach. Both of us are panting, hot messes. It takes us a few moments of us being in that position before we can both get enough energy to move.

I slowly pull my body upwards, offering her help with my spare hand, to get down from the counter.

She accepts, taking hold of my hand as I pull her into an embrace, pressing a kiss to her forehead.

"If you'd like a shower, there is one in the en suite."

She scowls at me, "Are you suggesting I need a shower?"

I stutter, "No, no I just meant–"

"Relax, I'm kidding!" She taps me on the shoulder and turns away, retreating to the master bathroom.

Picking up the wine to take to the bedroom, I walk in to find her struggling to work the shower.

"Need some help?"

She turns to me with confusion on her face.

"Why are all showers different? Shouldn't it be universal to make it easier for everyone?" She whines.

Laughing, I lean in front of her, switching the dials to the correct temperature.

"How's that?"

She tests the water with her hand, "Perfect." She smiles, climbing inside and resting under the stream of water.

I once again find myself admiring her as she closes her eyes, her cute dimples prominent as she runs her hands over her hair, allowing the water to soak it.

Despite her reminding me so much of Allie, my conscience telling me my attraction was her similarity to her, I hadn't even thought about her once.

Chapter 10

Indie

I wrap the plush towel tightly around myself and feel my body ache from the activities I've just participated in.

Reed is in the shower and I retreat to the luxurious bedroom. The large king bed is branded with the gold 'St. Regis' detailing, a collection of accent pillows littered in gold and white crisp bed sheets, that seem to be calling my name. I look around the room, not an item out of place. Everything looks pristine, as does the rest of the suite.

Hearing the shower shut off, I enter the living room to find my clothes. The shower helped me sober up a little, but my mind is still in disarray.

I recount the events that have taken place, how it happened and how I've ended up here now. I don't know where that side of me came from as I know I've never been so forward before.

I wasn't like that with Scott.

Usually, our sex life consisted of however he wanted it and if I ever tried to take control, he would find some way to regain it.

With Reed, it was different. I can't pinpoint how, but it just felt… *right.*

I don't have any experience with sleeping with other men other than Scott, and now Reed. Maybe Scott was just terrible in bed?

There is something else though, I felt something. It was when he kissed me, it gripped me and drew me in, leaving me hungry and wanting more, feeling empty when he wasn't kissing me. I can't quite explain it, it feels like there is some sort of bond between us. It feels warm, comforting, and loving.

I look towards the cream couch, seeing the pillows and underwear sprawled all over the floor, clothes draped over the side and an empty bottle of wine on the coffee table. I lean down to get my dress and find my thong that is now good for nothing. Well, I suppose you could say it was worth it.

Shuffling the dress over my now dry body, I pick up my purse from the other end of the couch, opening it to get my phone, requesting an Uber. It's early hours in the morning, and I'm returning to work tomorrow evening, I need my sleep.

Hearing the bedroom door close, I turn to see Reed standing by the entrance of the living room, leaning against the frame. His boxers cling to his hips, highlighting his godly body. I find myself blushing, not really sure how to act now that we've both given each other our most damning body parts.

"Going somewhere?" He looks up at me through his wet hair hanging over his eyes, the strands looking a darker shade of brown now.

Cringing internally, I smile sheepishly, holding up my phone.

"Uber is on its way." I shrug.

This must be the awkward walk of shame, the part that people dread after a hook-up. I keep my eyes to the ground and twist my hair around in my finger as I hear his feet padding closer on the carpet.

A finger rests under my chin and brings my face up to meet his. He leans down and his breath fans across my face, freshly minty. His ocean-like eyes bore into me as he brings his lips to meet mine, soft and subtle.

My eyes flutter closed at the sensation, the vibrations of pleasure spreading throughout my body.

He pulls away but keeps his face close to mine.

"I'd like to see you again," he whispers.

I pull away, reality settling back in. We really did manage to forget about reality tonight, and it was so incredible.

Now, I need to go back to my life and face my problems head-on.

My phone vibrates in my hand, signaling that my Uber has arrived.

Looking back up to Reed, I appreciate his beauty one final time.

"I had fun, but I need to leave. Thank you for taking my mind off of things for some time, I really needed it."

His jaw tightens at my words, and he looks like he wants to say something.

Before he gets chance, I put my phone in my purse and make a swift exit out of the room, practically running towards the elevators.

Drinking in my appearance in the elevator mirror, I realize I'm a far cry from the girl who left Nina's house, hours ago. My makeup has all been washed off in the shower, my hair is flat to my scalp and the dark circles under my eyes have decided to delight me with their presence. I flick my wet hair over my shoulder and shiver at the coldness it propels onto my skin, the smell of Reed has been washed from me and I can now return to normal life.

Exiting the elevator, I begin to walk through the lobby.

I can hear him before I can see him.

My feet falter, refusing to budge.

His gaze travels from my bare feet to my attire and then finally to my face. His brows furrow in confusion, my gaze goes to the red-headed girl standing next to him.

And then back to him.

"Indie..." he starts.

I begin shaking my head as the tears line my eyes, I'm unable to cope with having to witness it right in front of me. Scott and no doubt, Faye, or some other girl he was screwing behind my back.

Keeping my eyes to the floor, I continue on my way and out of the lobby doors, yanking open the door of the Uber and climbing in. I mutter a quick 'hello' before the driver takes me back to Nina's.

I lean my head against the window, the coldness somehow not affecting me. I keep replaying the image in my head over and over. Seeing it in real true form, hits the hardest. At least with messages you can kind of make your own mind up about it, read between the lines, ignore it if you want.

When the devil himself is looking right at you, it's pretty fucking hard to not stare back at him.

I close my eyes and allow a tear to escape, watching the buildings whiz by through my blurred vision. After the first tear, the rest of them unleash one after another like a dam that has just burst its walls.

My chest becomes tight, restricting my ability to breathe.

My brain buzzes at the tension in my head.

I can't breathe, I can't breathe.

"Can you let me out here please," I barely manage to choke out.

The driver nods and I dash out of the car just as the car stops moving.

Waiting until the Uber driver has disappeared before I fully try and allow myself to breathe, I bend over, trying to draw in a breath, my eyes burning. It feels like I'm so deeply trapped in my own mind; I'm drowning.

I set myself down on the grass by the side of the road and lay down, staring up into the midnight sky. I intake a sharp breath again, struggling as my gut wrenches in pain. I can't stop, why can't I just breathe?

Please.

I just start to scream. Well, more like a hoarse cry at this point. I get onto my knees and fist my hair and cry out.

"Why," I scream at nothing and no one.

I repeat it over and again until my chest aches from the screaming and letting go of all the pent-up anger and hurt that Scott has caused me. I drop my head back, the tears free-falling from my eyes to my cheeks and beyond.

I whisper up to the starlit sky, "Why?"

Laying back down, I am finally able to get some oxygen into my body, my brain suddenly quiet.

All that can be heard is the distant sound of crickets and my harsh breathing. My tears become dried, and I eventually muster up the courage to walk the rest of my way to Nina's, my strappy heels in one hand and purse in the other.

My body feels completely numb, empty, and broken.

I thought I was doing well, I thought that I was finally able to let go of the pain.

Turns out, I just got better at hiding it.

***

I unlock the door and wince as my feet ache from the barefoot twenty-minute walk I've just had to endure. I don't even bother changing into anything else before I dive into the bed sheets and fall into a deep slumber.

***

My eyes hurt, my head hurts and God, my chest hurts. I wince at the light that pours through the open curtains, of course I didn't even bother to close them last night.

Turning over, I pull the duvet over my head, the hangover well and truly kicking into gear. Sitting up and groaning at my tense body, I glance towards the alarm clock on the bedside table. Ugh, it's too late for breakfast now.

Finding my phone on the floor, I swipe up to call Britney.

She doesn't answer.

I send her a quick message for her to call me ASAP and throw the covers off from myself.

Sliding out of Nina's dress, making a mental note to make sure I return it to her, I slip into a pair of pajama shorts and a plain tee. I throw my tangled hair up into a quick bun on the top of my head and make my way downstairs to see Nina lounging in the living room.

She glances towards me, biting her nails.

"Morning, sunshine." I mock her.

Her usual happy self seems, not so happy.

"What?" I bark at her, not in the mood for any lecturing about the time I strolled in last night.

"Britney tried calling you last night, but obviously she knew you were busy. She called me instead." Okay? What's wrong with that?

I wait in silence for her to explain.

"She said that…" her voice trails off and the next part barely comes out as a whisper.

"Yesterday morning, her sister, Allie, died."

I freeze. My entire body tenses and my mind quietens. I blink a few times, trying to process what she's just said.

Opening my mouth to speak, I try but nothing comes out. I blink again.

"Is… Is she okay?" I barely manage to stutter.

My mind rushes back to last night, me and Reed. The bar. The state he was in when I found him.

Oh my god.

"Not really," Nina mumbles, casting her eyes to the window.

I don't even know what to think. What to say. How could this have happened? I thought she was getting better. I've just slept with a man who had lost his wife less than 24 hours before, if I had known… A haunting, sickening feeling overtakes my senses.

What the *hell* was I thinking?

"I should go see her." My is hangover being pushed to the back of my mind as I rush back to my room to grab the remainder of my stuff.

Quickly gathering all of my belongings, I throw them into my gym bag.

This makes my problems with Scott seem minuscule; Britney needs me right now, and I need to go home.

✳ ✳ ✳

Pulling up outside of Britney's apartment building, I shut off the engine, taking a minute. I rest my hands on the steering wheel and close my eyes, letting out a breath I didn't realize I'd been holding in. My head pulses at the pressure of what is coming, hangover or not.

I knock for the fourth time.

"Brit, it's me Indie," I shout again.

After a moment I finally hear signs of life.

The door unlocks and what I see standing before me is not the girl I know.

This girl is an image of grief and despair, a ghost.

Her usual tan skin is almost a sickly green, her well-kempt hair is in a messy ponytail, no makeup in sight. This is the disgusting truth of losing someone, the bitter horrible truth. Her eyes appear hollow, dark, and miserable.

I reach forward, pulling her into the tightest embrace as she falls apart in my arms, her sobs muffled by my chest.

I hold her, my eyes also welling with tears for the pain of their family, but also the immense guilt that's circulating through my body, knowing what I was doing and with whom, whilst their entire world has been tipped upside down. The anger stirring in me once again, at the complete ignorance of Reed.

I feel disgusted knowing that during the entire time together last night he didn't feel the need to share something as important as this. I sure as hell wouldn't have agreed to a grief fuck.

I walk us into her apartment, and I glance around the small kitchenette, the selection of flowers littered across the counter tops causes me to wince at the sight.

Sitting down onto her green leather couch, I hold Britney as she leans into me again, allowing myself to absorb the pained sobs that manage to escape her as I stare at the picture of Britney and Allie on the wall above.

Chapter 11

Reed

Buttoning up my suit, I pop on my cuff links and straighten my tie. I rearrange my hair in the mirror just before I walk out of the elevator into the bustling office. I keep a stone hard face as I make my way to my personal office, the noise in the room ceasing as I walk around the numerous desks, feeling every single pair of eyes on me.

Just keep walking, Reed. Let them stare.

I swallow hard and tense my jaw as the journey to my desk seems to stretch for even longer than normal.

I close the glass doors behind me and take a seat.

The disastrous events from yesterday have been cleared up and my office has been organized back to its usual state – minus a few picture frames.

I log onto my computer and load up my email, checking over what I need to complete today, diving headfirst into a criminal case of fraud and embezzlement for a marketing company.

I'm interrupted by a knock at my door, looking up to see the one and only, Jonathan Atlas, my partner. I give him a slight nod as he enters the room, looking at me with a skeptical face, his hair growing grayer by the day.

"What are you doing here, Reed?" He cocks an eyebrow, his cold brown eyes burning into me. Brilliant, straight down to business.

"What do you think? Working," I mutter, acting impatient.

"You've just lost your wife," he starts.

"Indeed." I look at the blank wall next to him.

"You need time to grieve, Reed. You need to be with your family right now." He tries to reason with me, his tone almost coming across as condescending.

"I've grieved, my family have each other. I need to focus on my clients right now." The silence in the room threatens to swallow me up.

I don't need people to constantly remind me that my wife has died. I've been through all this before with my mother, I know the process and I understand it, understand she's not coming back and there's nothing I can do to change it.

"Reed, we're just trying to–"

"I'm *fine*." I snap.

I grit my teeth, I'm sick of people deciding what's best for me. I'm a fully grown man with a hell of a lot of responsibility, I can't just drop everything and take time away to sit and dwell on something that cannot be changed.

Jonathan stands up and walks closer towards me and he pats my shoulder gently.

"I'm here if you need anything." He offers a tight smile and straightens his suit before walking out.

Huffing, I return my attention to the papers in front of me.

Maddy has bothered me the entire day, so much so that her constant presence irritates me to my core. I've been mollycoddled by each member of staff, the 'I'm sorry for your loss' permanently etched in my brain.

My phone buzzes with a text.

(Bridget): *Hi Reed, just a heads up that Allie's parents are here and want to chat with you about Willow.*

Groaning, I rub my hands through my overgrown stubble. This was not something I wanted to have to deal with yet. They've always been the overbearing type, sticking their noses into business that does not concern them.

I check my watch and decide to close for the night. I've dealt with six separate clients today and my brain is fried trying to make up for lost time.

Flicking off the lights to my office, I walk past the receptionist.

"Goodnight, Reed," she murmurs.

I barely look at the redhead as I pass her.

"Night, Faye."

* * *

I park on the driveway and look up at the house that holds far too many painful memories.

The gray colored sliding is in desperate need of paint, it's started peeling again. I glance towards the garage that still has the dented door from Allie's unfortunate misjudgment with how long our driveway was.

The shrubs that line the driveway have withered into dry brown eyesores, I told Allie she wouldn't be able to keep them alive, that girl most definitely didn't have the expertise for keeping plants alive. I chuckle at the memory of being at college with her. I'd bought her a small, potted cactus as a moving in present for her dorm and she somehow managed to kill that also, despite them being the easiest of plants to keep alive.

I walk up to the large porch to see the wooden porch swing, hanging on by just one rope, something I was meant to fix months ago.

The house appears in a worse way than it did even this morning.

Twisting the doorknob and pushing the door open, I'm greeted by a low chatter that hums from the living room. I instantly hear her footsteps.

"Daddy!" She squeals and runs towards me.

I swoop her up and spin her around, planting a kiss on her forehead.

"Hi, baby." I grin at her.

Lowering down onto my knees, I pull her in for the tightest embrace. Her hair is loose and smells of strawberry shampoo. I soak up every last bit of her scent as I feel her grip onto me as if she let go, I would disappear.

Carrying her through into the living room, her face remains tucked into my chest. Feeling my shirt become damp, I peer down at her to see she has tears rolling down her cheeks.

"Lo, baby. Don't worry, okay? Daddy's here, everything is going to be okay, I promise." She doesn't respond, but wraps her arms around me tighter.

I rub my hand across her back and sit down with her still attached to me, attracting the burning eyes of my in-laws.

"Where were you?" Allie's mother spits at me.

I meet her eyes, her entire face is screwed with anger and the raw sadness, apparent. I tuck Willow further into my side and lean back, finding the family portraits on the wall incredibly interesting.

"You are one despicable excuse of a husband, Reed, and even more so a father," she practically growls.

My body grows ridged, and I sit up straight. This woman has constantly had a say so in our marriage, in the way we parent, I don't need to hear any more of her biased opinions.

I remember when me and Allie first started dating in college, the control she tried to maintain over us only propelled us closer together. I'd never had a strong mother figure since mom died, but she made me resent the thought of ever wanting a mom. It drove Allie to be a better mom than hers ever was, she made sure she listened to Willow and let her have free rein of whatever it was life could offer her. No limitations.

"I find your opinion to be insulting." I scowl.

She scoffs at my words.

"Insulting?" Her voice raises a few pitches.

"What I find insulting, is the fact that you have decided to keep me and her father out of the loop, we had to find out through Britney that she'd even had the accident. What I find insulting, is the fact that not even twenty-four hours after she has left this earth, instead of stepping up and being a father to our granddaughter, you decided to put work first. Again." Her tone growing harsher as she continues.

"We always knew you would prohibit Allie from reaching her full potential, and now you're doing the same to Willow."

My heart thumps in my chest.

I work to provide for my family, I work to ensure that Willow never wants for nothing. I work so that I can create a stable environment, to pay for Willow's eventual college tuition, so she can be anything she has ever dreamed of. I want to give her every possibility in the world, so nothing can hold her back from being the person she wants to be. I will not accept someone thinking they know better than me about my reasoning.

"Rachel, Allie chose to step down from her career, not for me, but for Willow. I worked my damned ass off to make sure I could give them the life they wanted, the life they both deserved."

She shakes her head and looks towards her husband. Bridget enters the room with a tray of tea and notices the obvious tension in the air.

"Come on, Lo." She gestures a hand towards Willow, and she hops up out of my lap, not before giving me another heavy hug. Lo takes Bridget's hand, and they head towards the kitchen. Thank God, she doesn't have to listen to any more of this, she's been through enough.

I pour myself some tea and take a sip, the liquid singeing my tongue.

"Do you even care that she's gone?" Rachel whimpers.

Bill, Allie's father, pulls Rachel into his side and grabs the box of tissues from the coffee table, offering them to her.

"Of course I care that she's gone! Don't act like you know anything about our relationship."

"Watch your tone." Bill finally speaks.

I narrow my eyes towards him, his face stone cold and pale.

"I know enough to know that you neglected your wife when she needed you, you let our daughter suffer for the last few months of her life," she sobs.

I've had enough of this, I have never wanted their opinion and I sure as hell don't want it now. I place my teacup onto the coffee table and stand up from the couch, straightening my jacket.

"Thank you for your concerns, but I have priorities that relate to my daughter." I turn to exit the room.

Rachel reaches into her bag and throws a stack of papers onto the coffee table in the middle of the two pieces of furniture, her hand shaking.

I glance at the table and then back up to their faces. Both stare at the floor, giving away nothing.

"What's this?" I gesture to the table.

A long pause.

"We're filing for full custody of Willow"

* * *

I order them to leave after they spilled the news. They are no longer my in-laws; they are my competition. Like *hell*, they will get custody of Willow. My brain can't even comprehend the situation, how they even think they have the right to try and take her away from me.

They have lost Allie and they think by taking Willow, it will somehow subsidize their loss.

The initial hearing is in a few weeks that will determine where Willow will stay for the duration of the custody battle, I have little time to plan and arrange a funeral and gather enough evidence to prove that I am what is best for her.

What kind of evidence do I even need?

This is not my area of expertise, and I am not going down without a fight. I'm going to give it my everything to ensure my daughter stays with me, her father, I am who she needs.

I know what I need to do. I pull open my contact list, scrolling down until I see his name.

Harrison.

Chapter 12

Indie

Pushing my key into my apartment door, I twist it to open. I take hold of the gym bag from the floor and struggle to manage the heavy stack of letters I collected on my way into the building. The apartment is dark, and the coldness creates a chill across my bare arms, creating a layer of goosebumps.

I drop the bag and kick it under the bench in the entrance, flicking on the light switch.

The room fills with light, revealing the empty room at the end of the hallway. I slowly begin to walk, remembering the last time I was in here. I peer at the photo frame that sits on the sideboard, *New York*.

It grips me, the happy couple that stare back at me, no longer recognizable. His face causes my stomach to tighten and writhe, the face that once could brighten my day with the simplest of smiles.

I snatch the delicate frame and place it face down; I don't need a permanent reminder of the mockery that has been made of me.

My body aches, the tiredness settling into my bones from the last few hours of ballet. I'd missed the studio, missed the girls, missed the feeling of escape through my dancing.

It haunts me, knowing the reason why Willow wasn't there. I'm can't even begin to comprehend what that little girl must be going through. I really wish I could help her out in some sort of a way, to try and soften the huge gaping hole that she now must live with.

My mother was never any sort of example to me, she barely speaks to me anymore. But, at least I know she is still alive and breathing, despite our indifference.

I climb up onto the bar stool and face time Lola.

It's pretty late now, but I'm sure she'll still be up watching whatever trashy reality TV show she's into.

She picks up practically straight away, I swear that girl is glued to her phone.

"How's my favorite big sister?" she beams.

I roll my eyes. "I'm your only big sister Lola."

"Exactly." I shake my head at her, giggling.

Since I told her about what happened with Scott, she's been exceptionally chirpy on all of our phone calls. She's tried to avoid talking about her wedding, despite the date growing closer. I appreciate it but, I don't want her to feel the need to tiptoe on eggshells around me because my plans for the future haven't worked out.

I'm so glad that she has someone like Greg, someone who would move the world for her if it got in her way. She's a hothead when it comes to protecting the people she loves.

She's like a shooting star in a sky full of darkness, she manages to bring people around her up to her level and make sure that we're all okay.

Maybe she should have been the big sister?

"You look terrible. In the best way," she jokes.

I glance to the small square that reflects the worn out, tired version of me.

"Exceptionally worn out," I grimace, trying to laugh off the apparent trauma ongoing in my life.

I can't even begin to think of the mess I've got myself into.

First, the obvious. Scott and his little mistress.

The next? I close my eyes just even letting it cross my mind, what was I thinking? Reed and Willow and Allie. I have enough drama in my personal life to even think about getting in the mix of the loss of a mother and wife. I was meant to be Allie's friend, and before she has even been buried, I've jumped into bed – not quite but not the point, with her husband.

I groan, causing Lola furrows her brows in confusion.

"You do know I'm always here for you, don't you?" Her innocent face concentrates on me.

I don't deserve any sort of sympathy right now, I don't deserve the goodness of Lola's heart. I may as well run right back to Scott, I feel as bad as he should.

I've always taken pride in my loyalty, my dedication to people and here I am being the biggest hypocrite in the room.

Maybe I just need to keep to myself for a while? Britney's advice certainly hasn't worked in my favor, it's just landed me in an even bigger hurricane.

Instead of Lola worrying about whether her wedding cake will arrive in time, she's concerned about my well-being. This is certainly not meant to be her issue as my little sister, so I plaster the widest smile across my face.

"Of course, I know, how could I ever forget? Now, have you managed to get the wedding cake delivered on time?" A well-thought-out subject change.

The conversation carries on for a long time, rambling about the changes that have been put in place for the wedding as well as my input for the final seating arrangement. Thankfully, I don't have to endure any small talk with my mother.

I end the call with a few words of affirmation about how the day will turn out.

Drawing myself away from the rest of the apartment, I enter our – *my* bedroom. I focus on the bed and stand in the doorway as the unmade sheets glare back at me.

My chest rises and falls before I'm pulling them from the bed, tearing at them with frustration and regret. It's almost like they're taunting me, knowing something I didn't.

By the time I finish, the bed is stripped bare, pillows litter the floor and just a naked mattress lay on the bed frame.

My lungs feel flexible, like they have permitted me to finally relax.

Diving onto the bed, the nakedness welcomes me into a slumber I so desperately need. The familiar scents of my bedroom, blanket me with a warmth of protectiveness, allowing me to endure in the best night's sleep I've had in years.

Days go by in a blur. The constant grind of keeping myself indulged in the dance classes and figuring out my new independent life manages to keep me distracted from the rest of the world.

That is until, I'm hand-delivered a court summons regarding ownership and shares of Scott's accountancy business.

Talk about being sucker-punched in the gut.

It's also hugely embarrassing to be getting your morning coffee in your usual café and having some guy in a suit expose a huge aspect of what's going on in your life.

Let's just say my coffee tasted extra bitter that morning.

I've pondered too much about what to do with the papers I've reread probably a thousand times over.

I haven't told anyone that Scott is not only trying to claim rightful ownership of the business, but he's also trying to claim partial ownership of the dance academy.

I scoff, *the audacity.* He can try and fight a case regarding his business but coming after my dance academy that I formed with blood, sweat and tears, is another matter. And one I will not take lightly.

The dance academy is rightfully mine and it isn't something he is going to get his filthy, cheating paws on.

I practically drag myself into my apartment, exhaustion sweeping over me both mentally and physically.

I look at the calendar on the side of the refrigerator, the '18th', circled in pink love hearts and Lola's name written in a red glitter gel-pen.

Only three more weeks until she becomes a wife, three weeks until I watch my youngest sister surpass me in life, knowing I've been reset to square one.

I did think that my busy schedule and career-driven self would be perfectly capable of conquering life alone, but I can't deny the aching feeling in the back of my mind. The thought that I am twenty-eight years old and have no intentions of getting into anything long-term or serious for a while.

The worst part for women can be the ticking clock. The idea that we must find our life-long partner at a younger age so that we can bear children, something that I know I want very much for myself.

I want the chance to provide and become everything my mother never was. I want to be able to create a safe and loving family dynamic, a home.

This is never anything a male has to worry about, they can reproduce until the day they die if they want to, swap out the old for the new constantly.

Placing a mug under the coffee machine, I pop in an espresso pod and notice how much my brain is hurting, knowing how much I still have to do.

Looking around at the dark and cold room, the glistening lights of the outside world pour in through the windows. The world outside, living and breathing.

The machine beeps and I take the cup over to the desk in the living room, allowing the heat of the mug to warm my icy hands.

I am barely in the apartment long enough to adjust the heating, and to keep the bills down for my lone income.

Filtering through my emails for some time, I respond to queries and potential sponsors for the academy. The espresso has relieved some of the strain on my mind, allowing me to focus on some overdue tasks. My phone pings a notification next to me and it comes from an unrecognized number.

Who is texting me at this time of night?

(Unknown): *Hey, can we talk? It's Reed.*

Reed? What could he possibly want to talk about? Surely, he knows that I now know about Allie. I lock the phone and return to updating the studio website with fresh pictures of our awards, including the new availability.

I smile fondly, knowing the huge progress I've been making over the past few years, the competitions we've entered and won.

My phone vibrates again, erupting a groan from me.

(Unknown): *I know you probably don't ever want to speak to me again, but it's really important. It's about Willow.*

Willow? I find myself texting back before I can consider any awful situations.

(Indie): *What's happened with Willow? Is she okay?*

(Unknown): *She's fine, but something is going on. Something I would prefer to speak to you about in person. I need someone who knows her, like you do.*

His tone sounds serious. God knows how Willow is coping, how much she is hurting right now.

I can't imagine being so young and losing a mother, especially one that was so devoted and loving as Allie was.

I've tried to be there for Britney as much as I can, but the guilt became overbearing. I've decided to distance myself for a while, probably why I've been so invested in the dance academy at the minute.

Dancing has always been my escape, I've found myself there at all hours, even outside of class time. I've managed to excel my feelings and pour them out through the days I've been spending at the studio.

(Indie): *Well, I'm free tomorrow midday? We could meet at a public place, coffee?*

The last thing I want is to be in a private, enclosed environment with him again. Despite the inevitable grief and guilt I feel, my mind still can't ignore the way he makes me feel.

That night is not something that can ever occur again but, I find myself reliving it at times when I'm alone at night, the shame less than I'd like to admit.

He responds quickly.

(Unknown): *Of course, Coffee & Creamer at the boulevard, around 1pm?*

Interesting place of choice, I'd have considered him a more commercial *Starbucks* man myself.

(Indie): *See you then.*

Without pressing on the matter, I return to planning my finances but, the worry washes over me.

I can't help but wonder what could be going on with Willow, if she's become withdrawn from things, if she is not attending school. I know she hasn't been attending ballet practice, and that will be the very least of her worries at the moment.

The huge gaping hole that is now vacant, almost like shouting down into an empty space and your voice not receiving its echo. Walking among the sidewalk under the daylight sun, glancing around and not being able to find your shadow. I don't know how the world expects a child to deal with such events, despite having a shitty mother myself, I would never have wished her dead, at any age.

Closing the tabs, I turn off the computer, leaving my empty mug on the desk. I'll deal with that in the morning.

After changing into something more comfortable, I let my hair down and climb into bed. The one perk I've discovered from being single is that I can starfish all I want in the king-size bed, the sheets all to myself. I tuck a pillow under my head and stretch out, the coldness of the covers kissing my bare skin. Willow's face flashes through my mind a few times before I'm deep into a much-needed sleep.

Chapter 13

Reed

Harrison.

Harry.

Haz.

Whatever he goes by now, I've lost count of the numerous nick-names he's accumulated over the years. Harrison suits me just fine, its non-personal and professional, just how I like to keep our relationship.

As far as I'm aware, I stand a chance in court. But I'd stand a stronger one if I was not alone.

Turns out, my working schedule and the commitments I have mean that there are certain activities that Willow would have to draw back on, she would have to move schools that would allow for a more extensive after-school package. I have so many things I need to figure out before I can stand up in court and prove myself as being worthy enough for custody. I currently don't have a permanent place of residence; I have ridiculous working hours and I'm single, so I have no help of the childcare issues I would inevitably encounter.

I also didn't consider the fact I technically have a 'tainted' record from when I obtained a DUI back from my college days. I have my beloved father to thank, for the reason I wasn't cast straight out from Harvard following the offense, an extremely sizable donation for the university seemed to help sway their decision. It was the only time I'd asked him for help since we, ever so gracefully, parted ways.

It never affected me from that point, my employers overlooked the minor offense and were more focused on my incredible alumni and the experience I had from volunteering at numerous law firms around the country, as well as my fair share of pro Bono cases I'd lead as my contribution to the lesser community (Allie's idea).

Yet, now it is a huge brick wall standing in my way. It wouldn't be so bad if I had my previous few years of AA meetings to stand on, but I stopped attending them a long time ago.

Probably part of the reason I relapsed.

Being 10 years clean, I thought it wouldn't be able to pull me back into its choke hold, I thought I had the upper hand. But that's the thing about addiction, it's always there lurking in the shadows, waiting to pounce when you hit your most vulnerable stages.

The phone call with Harrison did not go pleasantly, as you could imagine.

At first, he was surprised I was even calling after our last experience, but I was also curious why he was even in my office in the first place.

Turns out, there is a human beating heart inside of the asshole's chest. Not that he'd cared to make the effort over the years to meet his niece, but he's heard through the grapevine that Allie was in intensive care and apparently wanted to 'see how I was doing'. By that he meant if I'd been drinking. Which at that point, I hadn't.

Surprisingly, Harrison was there for me during my college days. We were thick as thieves.

We would take turns being each other's wing-man, until I met Allie of course. He hadn't realized I had a problem with alcohol until later.

It was Allie who had been there for me, who supported me through going to rehab and the extensive AA meetings, the relapses, the doctor's visits and more rehab.

I was only three months clean before Willow came along, knowing I was going to become a father was the final push I needed to remain sober.

But it became apparent, me and Harrison were leading two completely different lives after that point, one choosing to continuously side with dear dad and one of us clearly not.

I hadn't realized what Harrison and Charlotte had been doing behind my back, the meet ups, and the financial aid from my father. It's not that I'd have resented them for it, at first, but the continuous lies and deception just led me to believe they were exactly the same as him.

I explained to Harrison about the custody order, if there was anything at the beginning that I could do to get it completely struck aside. I am on Willow's birth certificate so I'm granted my automatic rights with that but apparently anyone within the family is able to challenge you for those rights if they believe they would be the better choice.

Harrison went through the terms of the law and the way that things can be bent towards my favor, my luxurious salary plays in my favor and shows that I can support Willow financially as well as pay for her college funds. I set up a trust fund for her when she was born and I've added to it over the years, it being a sizable amount.

Willow of course loves me so that is not any sort of issue, her opinion is also taken into account. She will stand up and say she wants to live with me and they have to consider her wishes, as long as I am presented as a fit parent.

Allie's parents really don't have a clue about what Willow wants, they only see her when we visit them in the summer in their Florida residence. Well, I haven't been for the last three summers as I've been swamped with work, but Allie and Willow have still visited.

They have numerous properties all over the states and have their finances on their side. As far as I'm aware, they're both retired and have a lot of time on their hands, but that doesn't prove they have a relationship with Willow.

I don't know enough about them to form an actual argument in my defense, but that is the purpose of having a lawyer. They fish around and try and find any sort of useful information that can weaken the opposing side. And luckily for me, I have the best family lawyer in Atlanta on my side.

"I know this might be a sensitive topic and still too fresh to know this sort of information, but did you consider that Allie may have a will?" Our third phone call about the case.

The question catches me off guard, it wasn't something I've considered prior, I haven't exactly had much of a rationalized approach to this entire situation.

I furrow my brows, genuine wonder plaguing my mind.

"Well, um, she doesn't have one that I'm aware of. Should I be chasing this up, or do they reach out to me? I don't know, I didn't think so, but I suppose she could have had one." The last of my words are more of a discussion to myself.

"Look, Reed. I know that things were rocky with Allie in the upcoming to her de–"

My guard skyrockets. "How the hell would you have any idea about how my relationship with Allie was?" the bitterness drips off my tongue.

His silence awakens a rage in me, a rage that I've became all too familiar with in the past week.

"Are you going to answer me?" I tut impatiently.

"Reed…" he trails off. The silence is taunting me, haunting me.

I practically growl, waiting for him to continue.

"Allie called us a few weeks before she, you know…" he trails off.

My eyes practically bulge out of their sockets, Allie called… them?

What does he mean by them? Him? Charlotte? My father? All of them together? What the fuck is going on?

"Harrison you better start fucking spewing words before I sue you for withholding information."

He lets out a deep sigh in response to my snarl.

"She… God. Reed, you don't understand how hard this is."

My heart is racing, my blood pressure rising every second that I know he knows something about my late wife that I don't.

I wait.

"She… fuck," the frustration in his tone is evident. My mind is running at a million miles an hour, every thought, every wonder crosses my mind.

"She came to us seeking out full custody of Willow as well as a restraining order against you."

Explosions. Confusion. Tsunamis. Anger. Hurricanes.

My entire concept of my life has been thrown into a wind tunnel and shook around until very few parts of it remain.

It feels like my mind is a minefield, each step I take triggering unexpected, unwarranted feelings.

There is no correlation between what Harrison has just said and the memories I am sprinting through in my mind. Each one, blowing my consciousness to smithereens. I can barely breath, let alone speak.

I say the only thing my mind can comprehend right now.

"What?" I blink. And blink.

Harrison goes on to explain how around five weeks before the accident, Allie had sought him out regarding her grounds on seeking custody. It came as a huge shock to him; he hadn't realized we were in any sort of situation that would regard such a knowledge. He had organized to meet up with her a few days after their first phone call, insisting that this sort of topic should be discussed more thoroughly and in person.

They met for lunch, he took down notes about the case which he said he would scan and forward to me over email.

Apparently, Allie wanted to know her legalities of obtaining full custody of Lo, without a divorce. Then with a divorce. Then with a restraining order.

I was taken aback that I hadn't known that this meeting had taken place, but I was none the wiser whilst I was striving for named partner. I threw my heart and soul into my career and hadn't realized I was dragging my family alongside me.

I always wanted to be better than my father had been, I thought I was doing everything I should be by creating a better future for us, providing for my family so they could have anything they wanted. With the news of the divorce, with this new information it turns out I was incredibly wrong.

I asked for more information about why she thought she could obtain a restraining order on me, without any grounds for such.

I edge my way to the alcohol cabinet, looking for something to stabilize my blood pressure, something to numb the sickening feeling twisting in my gut.

I grab the vodka and screw off the top, taking a swig.

I eradicated the use for a glass a few nights ago, it didn't matter anymore.

"Well... I mean, it is innocent until proven guilty, Reed, and she's no longer around to argue that."

I set down the bottle shakily and grip hold of the phone tightly.

"Don't you dare." I spit at him.

Lawyers are known to be ruthless, but the wounds are disgustingly fresh, and he has no clue about anything that me and Allie have been through.

"Shit, no. That came out wrong, I'm sorry. All I meant is– *fuck*. Reed, I'm your brother, okay? You know I've got your back no matter what. I know I haven't been there for you as much as I should have, but I really mean it. Anything you did, it's now in the past, she can't take you down for it."

My thoughts whirl around in my head, processing the words.

"Down for what? What are you talking about?" I rub my hands across my overgrown stubble tightly, my heart thundering.

The pressure in my ears almost makes the next part inaudible, I'm floundering underwater.

"Nothing really, she just... said some things."

I slowly raise my eyes to the blank wall in front of me, the candlelight flickering, reflecting shadows dancing across the ceiling. My senses heighten immediately, I can smell the lemon zest of the bleach used to clean the kitchen, the cinnamon of the candle burning, the lavender spray across pillows of the sofa I'm currently perched on.

Sweat beads down my back.

My mouth is sandpaper.

The deafening sound of silence.

Everything is closing in on me.

I loosen my tie from my neck, unbuttoning the top three buttons of my shirt.

I close my eyes to try and limit the overload my body is experiencing.

"Like I said, Harrison, what the fuck are you talking about?" I grit through my teeth.

"Honestly, it isn't my place to tell you what's right and wrong. I know you've been through a lot." He sighs.

"I have never fucking laid my hands on her, not once." I hiss, trying to deflect in case he's talking about what I think he's talking about.

"Fuck, Reed, that's not what I said. Anyway, this, is meant to be about Willow now. Whatever Allie has said is irrelevant."

"Of course this is fucking relevant! What if she was spouting this bullshit to other people? *Oh my God.* This is why they want custody isn't it, they think I'd hurt Willow," my voice trails off into nothing.

My fingertips caress my lips as I shake my head over and over, my mind running wild.

I grab the bottle and chug.

This choking feeling needs to stop, I need to add a restraint to my emotions. The alcohol needs to grab every single feeling of mine and drown it, encase it and destroy it. Something needs to give.

"Reed, are you seeing anyone?" His question startles me out of the abyss, the obvious change of topic screams suspicion.

"No, why?"

"I just had an idea, never mind." He finishes.

"What idea? What does that have to do with anything?" Genuine curiosity overwhelms me.

"I mean it's nothing really, it's just… if you had a partner, it really could strengthen your case. And before you ask, no it can't be a fling. I mean someone who could be a role model, someone who is a motherly figure, and of course, a clean record."

A partner. What would that prove?

Almost as if he heard my confusion, he continues.

"Having someone who could add a character statement about you as a person, as a partner would help to diminish any sort of comment about abuse. It would add to your profile and prove that you have the resources to provide a stable upbringing for Willow. Someone who can... attempt to fill the void."

I mean, it makes sense.

It makes complete sense. It is incredibly hard enough as it is for fathers to gain rights to their child, it would be a positive addition to have a stable relationship. They could also help out with the childcare issue, I could also see if there was anything I can to do reduce my hours at work, at a push, but not likely.

But, *who?*

I would need someone who wouldn't be a stranger to Willow, someone who would be able to make Willow feel comfortable, and they would be willing to take her on as their own. I can't risk finding some random girl and putting my entire world into her hands, for her to fumble and drop it, smashing my already fragile future into thousands of pieces.

I put the bottle of vodka back on the shelf and press the phone to my ear.

The fireworks of ideas running through my head right now are showering my mind with every possibility of keeping Willow.

Indie.

The thoughts have filled me with a foreign feeling, a warm feeling. A feeling of... *hope.*

Chapter 14

Indie

As much as I am enjoying the comfort of having an entire bed to sprawl in, the bottomless pit in my heart does not seem to falter. The feeling of impending doom rises in my chest as I encounter yet another, lonely day.

I turn my nose into the flattened pillow, taking a mental note to order some new ones online. My limbs and joints ache from the strenuous week of ballet teaching, now finally having one day off to relax and catch up on my much needed episodes of 'The Kardashians'.

Two cups of black coffee (I haven't bought milk) and scrambled eggs later, I've managed to wake myself up enough to open the curtains in the living area.

I turn to drink in the expanse of the room, little bits of Scott here, little bits of Scott there.

Biting my lip, I challenge myself to clear out the apartment this weekend, it can wait. I carry my leftover cups and plate to the sink in the kitchen and begin scrubbing away, using the time to carefully debate the new routine for the classes tomorrow, stretching my limbs as I remain stationary.

My phone vibrates just as I'm putting away the now dried cups. I skip over to the couch, in a seemingly good mood.

Reed: *Are we still on for today?*

I sink myself deeper into the sofa, wishing it would just swallow me up whole. I already know a few things about Reed from our brief encounters.

1. He's a shitty person. (sleeping with someone on the night of your wife's death)

Okay. He's actually worse than a shitty person.

2. He's manipulative in the worst way.

The kind where he's not even aware of his manipulative behaviors. I mean, he is insanely attractive, so that definitely helps his case. Once you look into his eyes, you are instantly falling in love with the way that the blue blends into an almost ice white in the center. The sharp contrast from the warm coloring of his eyes, to the dark and alluring features of his face.

The way his brows furrow, igniting a small crease in the middle of them. The chiseled bone structure of his face, complemented by his thick and shadowy stubble. Full lips that taunt you and tempt the lips of your own, promising that your every desire will come true if they can just have one small touch, just like Satan's own demons would. He is absolutely devastating.

3. He is INSANELY good in the bedroom department.

Ugh, Indie. Get a hold of your ridiculously over-exaggerated, horny feelings. One man makes you feel idolized and that makes you completely and utterly obsessed with him.

I throw a quick response back to his message confirming I'll be there.

As much as I try and convince myself that I'm doing this for Willow's sake, so I can be there for her, there is an extremely selfish side of me that wants to do this for me, so I can see him again.

Looking through my closet, prepared to tug out a pair of jeans and a simple tee, my mind races over our last encounter. My heart starts to quicken in response, causing a thin layer of sweat to form on my upper lip. I wipe it away with the back of my hand and decide against the jeans.

I pull out a short white flowy dress with lace straps and a strapless bra. I tie my hair back into my usual loose bun and pull out a few loose strands at the front to emphasize the 'messy' look. The least I can do is act like I don't care about him, or what he thinks of me, or what I look like. When in fact, I've spent the longest I've ever spent on my makeup today, chosen a slightly revealing low cut dress, and a pair of wedged heels. But as long as he doesn't know, *right?*

The exterior of Coffee & Creamer sports a collection of tables and chairs, each blessed with an assortment of pastry shaped cushions on the chairs. Some have croissants, some have pretzels, some have baguettes.

I make the favorable decision of choosing the one with the croissants, with a pink throw covering the entire chair. I make myself comfortable knowing I am a little early and scan over the menu. The scent of bitter coffee and sweet pastry invade my nostrils, forming a warm rumble in my stomach.

Looks like those scrambled eggs didn't last very long.

"Is this seat taken?" a deep voice interrupts me.

I peer up into rich brown eyes staring back at me. I draw my brows inwards, confused at the interaction. Tilting my head around his large frame, I glance at the expanse of empty tables that he's walked past to get to mine.

He cocks his head with a smirk, the sunlight pouring upon his honey blonde hair. His attire screams entirely professional, but his face preys upon my face, nipping and biting.

"Harrison." he sticks out a hand, which I shake reluctantly.

I let go and look around at the passers by, praying that someone will help me escape from this awkward situation. Despite my void answer, he takes a seat across from me anyway. He picks up the croissant cushion from the chair and lifts it up in front of him. To my delight, he chuckles and releases a wide grin, showcasing his perfect pearly whites.

"Cute, huh?" he gestures to the pillow, still smiling.

I nod slowly, unsure of how to react.

He props his elbows on the table in front of me and leans forward, his head resting above his closed fists.

"So pretty girl, what brings you to this dainty little coffee shop on a fine Thursday afternoon?" He looks at me inquisitively, entertainment playing in his eyes.

For some wild reason, I actually respond.

"I'm actually waiting for someone thank you, *Harrison*." I emphasize his name, hinting that he's just as obnoxious as his name sounds.

The sun beams down from above, heating up the top of my hair. I reach into my bag and grab a pair of sunglasses, expecting the man to leave.

He relaxes in the chair and adjusts the sparkling cuff links on his suit.

Reed is going to be here any minute, and I haven't even gotten around to order myself an iced coffee yet to chill my rising temperature. I can't tell if it's the weather that's rising my body temperature, the unwarranted company from a stranger, or the fact I'm coming face to face for the first time with Reed since… that night.

"So you sit down with a complete stranger, who is meeting somebody, *by the way*, and you don't even offer to buy the girl a drink? Very poor manners, Mr. Harrison," I tut and rise from my seat.

The smell of spice and sandalwood envelops my senses and almost on instinct, I turn around at the source.

Reed *freaking* Breckenridge.

Despite me staring at him, he looks completely past me and to the stranger in the chair across from me.

"What are you doing here?" Reed practically snarls at the man.

I bat a hand against his chest and gesture to Harrison.

"I didn't bring anyone, this guy just invaded my personal space, didn't bother to buy me a drink either." I smirk at Harrison, whose gaze also looks straight through me at Reed.

"Just checking out the girl that's got you so worked up," he responds snarkily.

Reed strides past me and grabs Harrison by his elbow, ushering him to stand up. Harrison raises his hands in defense and begins to laugh.

To his amusement, Reed does not.

I stand completely baffled at the interactions before me, trying to make sense of anything that is going on.

"Get out of here, Harrison before I kick your ass *again* for getting involved in my personal life." Reed shoves him away, throwing Harrison off balance and having him nearly fall flat on the sidewalk.

A few heads have turned from passers-by to zone in on the altercation, but I can tell it's not serious.

"Fine, fine. Well, it was divine to meet you, Indie. Hopefully next time will be better conceived." He turns away, throwing me a small wave.

I... Wait. *Indie?* I didn't even tell him my name.

Reed turns to me, shaking his head and huffing out a sigh before directing his attention to me.

"Are you okay? What did he want, did he say anything?" His tone desperate and panicked.

"No – I mean yes. I'm fine. I don't know, and no," I stutter, barely making sense.

Reed gestures to the seat that I was originally sat in, and I make my way to sit back down, him coming up behind me. He grips the arms of the chair from behind to tuck me further in.

I inhale deeply at his heavenly scent, filling my lungs with all things Reed. He leans down from behind me, almost in the crook of my neck. The hot fan of his breath causes a river of goosebumps to spread across my body, despite the warm weather. I feel all of the blood inside of me split between north and south, the blush growing evident and I clench my thighs together, trying to avoid my obvious bodily responses.

His finger traces my bare shoulder, the touch so small and delicate producing a shudder. I let out a bashful laugh, turning ever so slightly to glance up at his face. His eyes remain closed whilst a soft smile has overtakes his usually serious face. I lift my hand to hold onto his finger that is causing a wild tsunami of emotions to surface. His eyes flick open and I lose my breath.

It reminds me that I've never actually seen Reed in the daylight, only ever in the dark. His eyes pour into mine, the never-ending blanket of blue, puts oceans collectively to shame.

He retreats and asks me if I would like a coffee, to which I respond with an order of pistachio cream-filled croissants and a vanilla foam iced coffee. He nods and disappears through the entrance of the store.

I take this time to gather my thoughts.

Wait, I'm supposed to be hating him right now.

I do hate him.

Why am I acting like a love-sick teenager that has just been asked out on a date by her crush?

Maybe it's because you are?

Well… not quite a teenager but the rest is debatable. I battle will my internal conscience like picking petals from a daisy.

Do I hate him? Do I not?

He returns with a small tray of our pleasantries and I slip him a quick thank you, taking a long sip from my straw.

The awkwardness that I now feel is the juxtaposition of what I felt five minutes ago. I pick at my croissant, mentally cursing for choosing an unflattering snack, unsure how to tackle it without coming across as a starved beast.

My leg jitters underneath the table, waiting for him to speak. He called me here, surely, *he* should begin the conversation.

Or, maybe I could just ask him a simple question like, how are you? How's your day been? How are you coping? Why didn't you tell me–

"The coffee is nice." I say.

Really, Indie? Really.

"Mm, yeah, it is." He responds, taking a sip of his own.

Folding my arms, irritated at his lack of conversation, I demand to get straight to the point. "So, why'd you ask me here?" I ask, briefly looking at him.

His dark stare meets mine, his long lashes float in the slight breeze. Placing down his coffee, he runs a hand through his thick brown hair.

I wait silently, every second feeling like an hour.

"I wanted to ask for your help," he mumbles, barely audible.

I snort. *My help?*

"And why would *I* help *you*? After convincing me to sleep with you, on the same night that your wife died!" I retort, the anger I felt beginning to bubble up inside of me.

Now that I'm pulling back all of the memories of why I hate him, I've decided. I do hate him.

"I mean, you didn't take much convincing."

My jaw drops open. The audacity.

This man reeks of egotistical love for himself, clearly thinking that any woman would stop dead in their tracks to catch a glimpse of him. He's not entirely wrong, based on the time we've been sitting here but, that's not the point.

"Do you really think I would've spent the night with you if I'd have known the circumstances, Reed? Actually, I don't care what you think. I'm telling you; I absolutely would not have!" I scoff at him, taking a large bite of my croissant.

The enduring feeling of his presence no longer bothers me, he can think I look like a ravenous caveman for all I care. The taste of the sweet but nutty cream center helps to lighten my mood, just slightly.

"Come on, Indie, we both know that there is something between us. Whether you want to admit it to yourself or not, it's here and it's not going away." His tone is daring and tempting.

Stop it.

I burst out into a fit of laughter, hoping to dim this man's confidence. It's unfair how some people in this world suffer with their self-value and esteem, and there's men like him who steal it and don't share it with anyone but themselves.

He doesn't falter.

In fact, he thrives.

His smile grows wider and wider until I could almost count every one of his teeth if I wanted to.

"There they are."

I stop laughing immediately and force a grumpy face, only causing him to erupt into laughter.

I truly feel like I can't win here.

"Okay, but that doesn't explain why you asked me here. I thought this wasn't a date?" I state.

"Does this seem like a date to you?" He smirks.

I've really drew the short straw.

I've made it seem like I think of it as a date, and if I try to deny it it's only answering my own question. *Damn.*

"Stop avoiding my question. What do you want my help with?" I deadpan.

He sighs, sitting forward, his eyes dancing around us, before landing back on my own.

"Okay, so Allie's parents are in town, and they've filed to obtain full custody of Willow, excluding me from that completely."

Eyes widening, my hand rises to my mouth in shock. Willow must be absolutely heartbroken right now; she has just lost her mom and now she may also be losing her dad too. I nod, beckoning for him to continue.

"I have a few issues that could prevent me from gaining full custody of her, and her parents are completely set on winning this. They don't leave me many options; they could use anything from my past against me and I need to go into that court room with the strongest case possible."

I'm still waiting for him to explain how he thinks I could help.

"I was hoping we could come to some sort of agreement." His look is skeptical, watching my face closely.

My mouth dries at the word 'agreement'.

Whilst it sounds very white-collar, nothing about our relationship so far has been anything close.

"Agreement?" I ponder, initiating a response.

"It wasn't my idea, I swear. I'm not like… setting you up or anything. Trust me, being in this situation is far beyond anything I'd want right now, she's all I've got left." His eyes drift away at the end of his sentence, the guilt rising in my throat.

I can't even begin to consider how hard it must be to be in his position. Despite my known love-hate relationship with him, I would hate any child have one less parent, let alone two. My upbringing wasn't the easiest in the slightest, the constant ongoing battle between my mother and I proved challenging. Enough so, I moved out as soon as I could.

Swallowing dryly, I offer him an understanding nod.

"What's your grand idea?" Smiling gently, trying to provide him some sort of reassurance from the difficult subject.

"Basically, you enter into a contractual marriage with me. You receive a large sum of money in return of course, but it does mean we're going to have to date in the meantime. Kind of prove that we're not faking it, even if we kind of are?"

I'm pretty sure my jaw sits on the plate that's holding the leftover flakes from my croissant.

"Are you out of your mind?" I fume. He is absolutely *insane*.

This doesn't even make the slightest bit of sense. What would getting married have to do with keeping custody of Willow?

Shaking my head, I struggle to comprehend the logistics of the situation.

"I can assure you, I am of completely sound mind." The fierceness behind his voice, evident.

Combating the thoughts running at a million miles an hour, I attempt to process each of them one by one.

My mind drifts off, thinking of the way I have always wanted to provide free scholarships to those who can't afford tuition, and get to pursue their dreams in ballet. I have been on both sides of the spectrum, the insanely rich and have everything you could ever ask for, and the side which built me to be the woman I am today. I taught myself the importance of becoming strong and independent, and everything I have in my life is what I have worked my damn ass off for. I would absolutely love if I could relieve some of that pressure from young aspiring ballerinas, the incredible art and grace behind it, the competent brilliance of it.

Smiling, I admire the thought of Thorne Ballet as an official scholarship participant, where the most passionate and driven of people will be allocated free tuition and get to thrive and exceed their expectations.

"Those damn dimples, Indie," he teases, squinting his eyes in a seductive way.

He lifts his fingers to his lips and runs them along his lip line, never removing his gaze from me.

Dropping the smile, I grow annoyed at myself for even acting like this would be an option.

Absolutely not.

"I'm sorry, Reed. I can't help you."

I open my purse and fish a twenty dollar bill out. As I go to place it on the table, his huge hand covers the top of mine. I gasp at the intensity diverging from my hand, up my shoulder and through my veins. My nipples begin to bud at the feeling as I snatch my hand away, dropping the bill and rising from my chair.

"Please, Indie." His desperation radiates through his voice.

His eyes are full of hope, need and desire. It feels like I'm walking through an animal rescue shelter, each animal looking at you, trying to communicate how badly they want to come home with you. It makes it hard for me to turn away, my feet frozen in place.

Lifting my purse higher onto my shoulder, I shake my head regretfully.

"I'm sorry, you're going to have to find someone else. Goodbye, Reed," the last of my words barely above a whisper.

Almost running along the sidewalk, I keep my head low.

I can't bring myself to think about the past hour, the constant push-pull I feel towards him.

Unbelievably, I began to consider his offer, it's completely absurd.

I quicken my pace to get to my car down the street, beginning to dig around in my purse for my keys, glancing inside the bottomless pit that may as well belong to Mary Poppins.

My attention is elsewhere when I hear a loud car horn and I lose the ability to function.

To breathe.

To save myself.

Chapter 15

Reed

Of course, she didn't take my fucking offer.

I mean it's not exactly like I even apologized for the way we met. In fact, I provoked her and made her seem like she was to blame at all which, needless to say, she wasn't.

It was all me.

Pulling out my phone, I text Harrison to make him aware she didn't take the offer.

She didn't even ask how much I was willing to pay her, I know she's not well off financially and with her now being on her own, without the shithead fiancé, I thought she'd jump at the chance.

Reaching down, I pick up the bill that Indie dropped and tuck it away in my pocket, I'll return it to her when I next see her.

I leave my now cold cappuccino and stand up, straightening out my navy blazer and adjusting the cuff links. A car horn in the distance draws my attention for a moment before I continue on my way.

Without being able to return to the office for a while, my only priority right now is spending my time with Willow, or what little time I may have left.

We're already on our way to her favorite diner out of town, listening to Willow's choice of music, the *Encanto* soundtrack.

Turns out, it was the last movie that Allie had taken her to watch at the movies and she is adamant that she must listen to the songs every day for the foreseeable.

I've found it interesting how well Willow has taken the death of her mother, the grief is barely evident. She cried for the first few weeks, struggling to sleep at night and forgetting that she is no longer around. I've tried my best to step in and pick up the pieces that Allie left behind, but her shoes are too big, even for me.

The thought of Allie plays in my subconscious more than I let myself admit. The idea of sitting and feeling every negative emotion that I could comprehend, screams idiocy. I've instead, reconnected with my old roots, good old bourbon.

It's been a confusing process. Becoming an alcoholic in the first place was entirely unintentional, I was unaware and unconcerned. Being sober for almost 10 years and returning to the bad habit is like reuniting with an old friend, the nostalgia, the memories, and the pleasure.

I'm not foolish enough to drink around Willow, with everything going on, limiting it to the times when Bridget comes over to help. It usually begins with me retreating to my home office, excusing that I'm working and until late.

My main issue is once I start, it's like I'm chasing the high, never quite getting there, but enjoying the hunt.

I rarely stop before I've finished nearly an entire bottle, it helps wash away any existing memories I have of her, the blonde of her hair haunting me until the early hours. The smell of her perfume is imprinted on my brain, the silhouette of her body is engraved in my eyesight, her shadow seeming to taunt me, watching me.

The diner is busy, with only a few booths left vacant. I glance around at the restaurant, the cherry red chairs and the contrasting turquoise blue booths are utterly, an eyesore. I swear it's the pop colors that draw children in, I can't understand the obsession because the food is utter junk and flavorless.

Willow juts up and down, pointing at the menu above the counter displaying an array of deathly foods. I slip a smile to her as we're escorted to an empty booth, the plump waitress carrying two menus with her.

"Daddy, please, please, please, can I order anything I want? Mommy never let me order both waffles and pancakes, she always said they were practically the same thing. But, daddy, they're really not. I tried to tell her but she didn't listen, please daddy, please." She rambles.

I squint slightly, her voice raising in pitch towards the end, striking my head in numerous places.

"Of course, honey. Anything you want."

I offer a large grin as her eyes widen and light up. She licks her lips and grabs the menu, muttering about how she wants every single topping they have to offer.

I give the menu a once-over and decide on a simple black coffee with a side of fries. I've not been going to the gym as much as I usually do, the downside of not being in the office building. I've always loved the perk of having access to the gym twenty-four hours of the day, it kept me, mostly, sane.

When a waitress with red hair comes over to take our order, Willow begins listing off pancakes and waffles, with all toppings, one with whipped cream and the other with ice cream.

And syrup.

And an Oreo milkshake, with more whipped cream.

The waitress, or 'Penny' as her name tag reads, looks at me in astonishment, clearly expecting me to refute any of what Willow said. She hasn't began writing it down yet and Willow is staring at me with hope in her crystal blue eyes.

"We'll take two orders of that, and a black coffee." I face Willow as she squeals in delight.

What's a few thousand calories at the expense of that kind of reaction? My heart warms as I begin to ask about school, now that she is happy to return.

"Miss Mendoza asked us to do a project on our idol next week, our hero."

I raise an eyebrow, waiting for her to ask me some questions relating to her project.

Willow sits with her hands under her legs, looking nervous.

"Don't worry, I can answer any questions you have, honey. You don't have to look so nervous!" I offer a curt smile as Penny brings over our order of milkshakes and my black coffee.

Willow looks up at me and shakes her head, pulling her milkshake closer.

"It's not that… I just really want to center my project around Miss Indie. I want to be just as good at ballet as her." She slurps her milkshake.

I still, my mug of coffee almost touching my lips. Eyeing her carefully, I try to gauge how I should respond to her.

"That's great, honey. Really great." I tighten my lips in an attempt to smile, then wash it away with the, now bittersweet, coffee.

"I was hoping you could invite her over next week, so I can ask her all of the questions. Well, I don't have anything prepared yet but I will. I want to know her favorite color, her favorite ballerina and her favorite award she has won!" She beams, the sugar from the milkshake clearly impairing her ability to speak slowly.

"Sure, I'm sure she'd like that." The thought of Indie having to spend more time with me thaws at my soul.

Willow barely finishes a singular plate of waffles, let alone two. She passes out the entire ride home, allowing me to finally turn off the *Encanto* soundtrack. I'm almost certain I will never talk about Bruno again.

I grimace at the need to brush my teeth after the devastating amount of sugar that has passed them, but I must admit, the waffles tasted better with ice cream than whipped cream.

I reverse onto the driveway, switching off the engine and sitting in silence for a few minutes, allowing myself to look over at Willow snoring quietly in the back passenger seat.

The innocence that washes over her porcelain skin tugs at my heart and I find it hard to swallow. My throat constricts and my eyes sting, I don't want to lose her.

I would rather die than have to live a life without her in it, the torture would be unbearable. How anyone can let their child slip through their fingers makes me sick to my stomach. There is absolutely nothing or no one that will stop me from ensuring she stays with me, where she belongs.

Bridal carrying Willow into the house, her arm dangles free and she is barely disturbed from the movement. I rest her down in the center of her bed, tucking her into the plush sheets. After kissing her head, I close the door softly behind me and walk over to the most familiar cupboard in the kitchen.

I've been making my way through the selection, and I've already had to restock it twice, switching to bourbon or vodka only. The gin wasn't really to my taste.

Bridget gets here within the hour so that I can finally begin to de-stress and sink away my hidden sorrows.

Swirling the musky liquid around in the glass, I analyze the way the liquid is entirely powerless in its singular form, yet it still manages to have its hold over me. Something that is so inconsequential but so predominant to me. They the dominatrix, I the willing submissive.

I tsk and drink it anyways, admitting my defeat.

I've learned to pick and choose my battles, and tonight is not a war I will be participating in.

In front of me, my computer displays the file that I've been provided by my private investigator. They had got straight to work on the Dawsons, alongside Harrison. The P.I is inevitably faster due to the lack of legality in their methods whereas, Harry must play it by the book.

There are several documents within each of the four files, individually named after them.

Bill Dawson
Rachel Dawson
Allie Dawson
Britney Dawson

Double-clicking on Bill's file first, I discover very little, most of his being a bunch of boring information about his education, outstanding loans, and his portfolio of homes he owns around the world.

Opening Rachel's next, my eyes zone in immediately on the suspicious bank transfers overseas. Now this, has got my attention. Who knew little miss perfect had been transferring money into offshore accounts, no doubt to evade taxes. This could potentially be leverage.

Pouring another drink, the buzz from the alcohol increases my body temperature. Either that or the excitement from finding something, even if it's minimal.

I lift the glass to my lips and sip slowly, hovering over Allie's file. It seems as if there is no point, especially since the P.I tried to convince me out of soliciting information on her. He obliged to my request but, he wasn't pleased about it.

Skipping over onto Britney's file, I see a significant number of files more than her parents. Frowning my brows, I begin to read through.

It appears that the P.I has hacked into Britney's devices, listing each of her chat conversations, emails, and a folder of images. I ignore the images, sensing there may be some explicit photos that I don't want to see in it.

Filtering through the messages I come across her conversations with Indie. My interest peaks and with another drink in hand, I read.

(Indie): *You don't understand! He like literally is entirely gorgeous. Like beautiful. Like imagine Captain America, but x 1000*

(Britney): *Yeah yeah, you say that about everyone. I don't trust your judgment anymore. Not after you said you would pass on Liam Hemsworth*

(Indie): *That was one time and because he'd just split up with Miley! Team Miley all the way girly*

(Britney): *Anyway, does this mystery man have a name?*

So, she thinks I'm gorgeous, beautiful? *Hm.*

So much for trying to resist me when all she can do is gossip about my insanely good looks.

Indie is the type of girl that plays hard to get when in reality, she wants me in the same way I devoured my pancakes earlier. She is my guilty pleasure, as I am hers. There is no denying the connection between us, the ignition within our touch, the acceleration of my pulse. She is the lightening to my thunder, the drug to my addiction, the flames to my hell.

It has caught me off guard that Indie would be so open about her attraction to me with Britney, it's been barely a month since Allie has passed. Surely, it's too sensitive of a topic to discuss with her, and I can't imagine Britney would be supportive in the slightest.

Brit hates me for more reasons than one, and not just because of Allie. Around 3 years ago, at the last family thanksgiving dinner that I attended, I stumbled upon Britney in the bathroom with her best friend Jasmine Rodriquez, the admission written across both of their faces in a state of panic.

I retreated and thought nothing of it, until I mentioned it at the dinner table. I made a few suggestive jokes about what they were up to, all alone in the bathroom. What I hadn't realized is that there was something going on between them and I basically outed Britney to her entire family, wreaking havoc from her very 'traditional' and religious family.

Regretting it deeply, I was ashamed that I hadn't considered that their friendship was actually more of a relationship. Since that point our, already rocky, relationship was completely severed. I completely violated her privacy and any form of trust she may have had in me. It put Allie in an awkward situation knowing that her husband and her sister were at each other's throats constantly, fixing a divide between me and her family.

The conversation continues and I pour another drink.

(Indie): *He does, but I can't reveal all the juicy gossip over text, that would be boring.*

Ah, nice touch. Keep her on her toes, don't spill too much about me or she'll figure it out and then you'll really have someone to answer to.

(Britney): *Let me guess, he's got an embarrassing name, hasn't he? it's not something like Bartholomew is it? Or Willie? What about Dick?*
(Indie): *Hahaha, definitely not, he's got a lovely name, actually.*

Hm, so she likes my name? That's a good start, and she thinks I'm gorgeous. Enough so, she compared me to Captain America, I'll accept the comparison with delight.

I peer out of the window at the city below, the night silent and preying. I release a breath I didn't realize I was holding and find myself searching through another file I have on my computer, one that I find myself searching through practically every night.

Indie Thorne

See, there are few people in the world that pique my interest as much as Indie has. There is something magnetic about her. Something that has drawn me in since the very first time I laid eyes on her.

Strangely enough, it was long before we met, she just didn't have a name back then. There first time I saw her was at a business management event 4 years ago in Rockdale. I'm assuming that this was before she began her ballet school, and that event clearly paid off for her, and me.

The way she was so determined to make it worthwhile, with her pink notebook on her lap and fluffy pink ballerina pen. She wrote with such fierceness that the ballerina bobbed back and forward on the spring, threatening to jump off with each passing second. The concentration etched on her face as she bit her lip, anxiously trying to absorb the extensive amount of information listed on the PowerPoint in front of her. I could barely remove my eyes from her, fascinated by her passion and also the way it didn't matter if anyone in the room was watching her. I knew she could feel my gaze burning into her, she sat up straighter and peered at the keynote speaker with more intensity. I wanted her to look at me, I wanted her to share a moment with me, grant me the luxury of returning the attention. Of course she didn't, otherwise we'd have fucked 4 years ago.

My pulse drums in my neck as I click through a collection of photos of Indie. I tilt my head, glancing at an image I've never seen before. She's sat in front of a wide mirror, in a nude-colored leotard, bare legged and ballet slippers laced up her calves. My cock thrums at the expanse of her pose.

Her legs are completely spread wide into splits, she appears to be in her studio, alone. The lights are dimmed, the background is clear, offering herself as the main attraction. Her back is to the mirror, the leotard slightly wedged between her plump ass checks, providing a worldly view. I blow out a hot breath and bite my lip, imagining the way that I could destroy her in a position like that. Her hair is loosely waved down her back, only partially revealing part of her face as her head is turned to the same side as the phone is.

She knows how insanely fucking sexy she is. She can act coy, she can act shy, but I know deep down just how much she wants to be ravished. She came alive the night we spent together, she was animalistic, desperate, and starved.

I gave her only a small part of myself that night, I want her to crave me. I need her to want me in every way possible, just as much as I want her.

My cock is strained against my trousers, searching for some way to gain release. I focus my attention back on the picture in front of me and submit to it. I grab my throbbing length and use the bead of pre-cum as a lubricant for my hand, spreading it up and down. I shiver at the sensitivity of it, the instant pleasure causing my head to fall backwards.

My eyes flutter closed as I slowly fist myself, replaying the image of Indie sucking my cock over and over. The veins in my forearms pulsing as I rhythmically pump up and down, I grit my teeth and look back toward the picture on my computer screen. My eyes trace over the long, toned, slightly tan legs, the expanse of them destined to be wrapped around my waist whilst I fuck her senselessly. Her ass teases me and displays exactly that I want what I can't have. What I would give to be able to grab onto those juicy shapely cheeks and slam her down onto my face.

I grab onto my desk with my free hand whilst my other acts as a savior for my darkest desires. Following the curve of her back, now imagining I'm taking her from behind and pounding into the soft bliss of her pussy, my legs shaking from the vigorous restraint I've got.

My balls tighten as I quicken my pace, my breathing growing louder and faster, Indie's moans raw and dirty in my mind. The sweat beads across my forehead and my abdominal muscles tighten, preparing for my pending release. I move past her back and look at her side profile, the fullness of her lips prove to be completely irresistible, imagining them kissing the head of my cock. My hand movement grows lazy as the orgasm explodes through me whilst my body spasms and cascades me into nirvana. The creamy liquid fills into my hand as I cup the end, offering light strokes to bring me down from the clouds above, my muscles burn with bliss.

I clean myself up with a tissue from my desk and retreat to my chair, slumping slightly, as my body recovers from the mind-blowing climax. My ragged breathing begins to even and I glance once more at the picture of Indie, noting that it is my new favorite.

I empty the last of the bottle into my whiskey glass and proceed to finish up on the P.I files, sleep beginning to demand control over my actions.

Clicking on Allie's file finally, my is brain quiet and at peace. I cock my head quizzically, noticing a specific file with a note attached to it from new P.I I hired after finding out about the custody case.

I needed someone with more drive, more abilities. The other P.I fell flat too many times. The note reads:

I'm onto this Reed, there is more going on with this than I initially realized. I'll call you when I have an update.

Chapter 16

Indie

Warm hands.
Comfort.
Air.

Breathe.

Indie breathe.

BREATHE my subconscious screams.

Or... *someone?*

"Indie! Breathe!" Huh?

Opening my eyes, not noticing that they were squeezed tightly enough to make me see an abyss of stars. Or is that from the lack of oxygen because I am still struggling to get my lungs to work.

"It's okay, I've got you, look at me." A comforting voice draws me back to life.

Peering up into warm brown eyes and golden hair, he looks kind of familiar. His face is pulled into a grimace, concern etched in every crease. I suck in a harsh breath, the world around me coming back to life.

"Harrison?" I ask.

"You remember me, pretty girl?" He smiles, standing me upright.

My brain is fuzzy, confused how I thought I'd just died moments before and now I'm here staring haphazardly at the stranger from earlier.

"You've crossed paths with me twice now, both times unwarranted," I say, thinking of his intrusion and the croissant pillows.

"Oh excuse me, next time I'll let the girl wander into a road with busy traffic. Which, by the way, is not a good idea with your head buried in your purse. Ever heard of looking left and right before waltzing in front of a car?" He tilts his head as the sarcasm drips from his sultry lips.

"Maybe, I was wrong about you. I thought you had your wits about you," He lets out a dry laugh.

"I don't know what I was thinking, or if I was thinking at all," I mutter, the past few minutes happened so fast I barely remember getting here.

My concentration was clearly clouded with the ridiculous conversation I had with Reed. I can tell Harrison is trying to lighten the situation with a little humor, but I'm plagued with guilt for refusing to not only help Reed, but Willow.

"Hey, is everything okay, Indie?" He reaches down to my jaw and cups it in his hand, the touch tender and caring.

He waits for a response, scanning over my entire body checking for any actual injuries.

I nod and tuck my loose strands of hair behind my ear, the weight of lifting my wrist feeling extra strenuous.

His hand remains cupping my face and I only just realize that our bodies are still pressed together, the proximity heating my core. The blush rises to my cheeks, and I take a step backwards.

He notices my sudden change of demeanor as he returns the gesture, stepping back.

"What I've been meaning to say, is thank you. For uh, saving my life." I offer a genuine smile, trying to highlight the meaning behind my words.

It's probably a given, considering what I'm thanking him for, but otherwise the extra effort makes me feel better for being so drastically cold.

"Anytime, just if you plan on doing that again anytime soon, be sure to give me a call." He winks, his grin widening as he finishes.

Is he… trying to ask for my number?

God, the embarrassment I feel right now is clear. His cheeks are tainted slightly pink on his light tanned skin, his well-kempt stubble barely masking his traitorous cheeks.

Struggling to throw together a sentence, overwhelmed and flattered all at once, I offer my phone out to him instead, implying that I want his number. It's better to have the upper-hand and text him if I really want to, meaning I can call the shots for now. I don't even know this guy, but do I want to get to know him? Maybe.

He takes the phone from my grasp, tapping in his number and returning it to me.

"Try not to die in the meantime, darling. I'd really love to see you alive and well." He displays an audacious smile and turns swiftly, putting his hands in his suit trouser pockets and walking away.

My chest flutters at the confidence he radiates. It's different to the confidence of someone like Reed. He's forward and direct, but to my benefit rather than his own. He makes me feel like I'm the rose that's encased in the glass chamber, priceless and treasured without forgiveness.

Watching as his figure disappears around a corner, I peer down at the phone I'm holding as if it's my most prized possession.

Harry

Harry. I blush at the nickname, it suits him.

***

I walk up to my apartment building, a sudden feeling of anxiety washing over my senses. I stall and turn around, anticipating an unwarranted presence.

Scott.

My instincts heighten and I'm catapulted into defense mode, the proximity of him causing an eruption of outrage and resentment.

"To what do I owe the pleasure?" I snarl towards him.

His eyes remain calm and don't waver, barely acknowledging the disgust in my tone.

"I've come to take what's rightfully mine," he retorts.

I'm taken aback. I glance up at the apartment and return my gaze to him, fire burning through it.

"I burned everything." I include a forced smile, glad that the conversation will be ending.

As I turn my back towards the building entrance, he grabs my elbow, eliciting a shocked gasp from my lips.

"I'm not talking about belongings or the apartment, Indie." His manner growing more aggressive whilst I tense up.

I try to free my arm from his burning grip, but it only tightens.

"What the fuck do you want from me, Scott? You've already ruined my life, what more could you possibly take," I spit out, the tears beginning to well, memories sifting through me with a whirlwind.

"Half of the studio belongs to me."

I snort, convulsing into a fit of laughter. He is entirely insane if he thinks he has any rightful claim to the studio, I completely funded the entire thing and built it up from the dust.

"I'm serious," he continues.

I roll my eyes and try to shake off his grip again, failing again. I look around to see if there is anyone around to witness this, nada.

"As much as you want to rid me of the only thing I have left, it's the one thing you hold no stake over."

He blinks. His face grows nearer, the darkness in his eyes igniting a slither of fear from deep within. For a moment, I think he is going to kiss me with the nearness. His hot breath fans across me as my eyes grow wider.

"I suggest you check the business deed, darling."

What the fuck?

Surely, he's just trying to scare me and intimidate me into offering him fifty percent of the studio, which will certainly never happen.

"The studio belongs to me, Scott. Drop this pathetic scare tactic and get out of my life, for good." My chest rises and falls, fast.

"So, you're not going to allow me to access my rightful shares?" The deepness of his voice sends shock-waves into my brain.

"They're not your shares! The studio is mine, let me live my life. You didn't want to be with me, why do you need to continue to suck the life out of me?" I growl, the heat rises to my cheeks at the newfound confidence in my confrontation.

"Don't think for one single second I'm going to let you keep it, I'll see you in court, sweet." He sneers.

And with that, he releases my arm and stalks away, my heart hammering through my chest. Standing here, I'm completely fixed to the spot, frustration and irritability pulsing to the point I can feel it in my eyeballs.

Storming through the building entrance to the apartment, I'm determined to put this to rest, I need to be relieved that what he's saying isn't true.

There's no possible way for it to be true, is there?

Throwing my bag onto the counter top, I ferociously type on the computer, trying to locate the documentation for the studio deeds.

I pull up the eighty-page-long contract, unsure of where exactly it is I'm meant to find this kind of information. Scanning the pages, hundreds of terms and conditions blur my vision.

That's when I see it.

Shareholders

*Indie Thorne – **50%***

*Scott Lowrey – **50%***

I let out a strained scream, smashing down on the keyboard with my clenched fists. Everything I've fucking worked for. Absolutely everything I've wanted my entire life, is about to be pulled right from under my feet. By the person I shared my bed with only weeks ago. A strangled sob escapes from my mouth as my body folds in on itself, the feeling of failure and loss of control overriding my sanity.

I withdraw to my bedroom, the bed, still unmade and the pillows, still lifeless. Throwing myself onto the bed, I lay, staring at the ceiling, allowing my body to shake and convulse with tears. My mouth dry and my throat hoarse, my cries now barely audible. The weather has taken a turn for the worst, the irony playing strings across my heart.

I don't remember falling asleep, I'm still in the white sundress and the open curtains forecasting that it is late. My skin feels crusty, my eyes swollen as a reminder of the emotional trauma I've experienced.

Barely able to find the energy to pull me out of my slum, self-preservation being the only reason for doing so, I drag myself over to the bathroom. Turning on the shower faucet I take a stance in front of the mirror, analyzing my disheveled appearance.

The red rings around my eyes match perfectly with my crimson tinted nose, black mascara lines the expanse of my cheeks and down to my neck, as well as spreading into my hair, presumably from laying down. I splash water onto my face from the sink, trying to scrub away the freshly inked skin.

Removing my dress and underwear before stepping into the shower, I let the heat of it pierce holes through my skin as I hiss at the contact. I reach to adjust the temperature, before deciding against it. The feeling seemingly numbs the ongoing chaos in my head, finally allowing me a second to breathe without feeling like the world is impacting into my chest.

The water runs over my skin and I step further into it, individual sharp pellets now absorbing into each other as the heat numbs the surface of my skin. I close my eyes and inhale the steam, running my hands over my hair and down my neck, passing over my shoulder gently and smile at the pleasantry of it, when an image pops into my mind.

His blue eyes, his sultry demeanor and antagonistic nature awakens something deep within me. I continue across my chest tickling downwards until I pass over my left breast, goosebumps spreading from the contact and my nipples slowly begin to harden.

Reaching my other hand between my legs, I slightly widen my stance, the ache whirling my insides. He's in here with me, I can smell the sandalwood spice, feel the current between us that heightens all of my senses, the air hot and heavy.

He pulls my hand away and replaces them with his own as I nod fiercely, biting my lip. His large hands begin to circle my peaked nipples, drawing a slow moan from my throat at the union between his skin and my sensitive spots. His lips crash onto my neck and pushes me backwards onto the wall, the coldness only translating further reactivity from my body.

One of his hands leaves my breast, whilst the other playfully tugs and rubs my nipple. It slowly trails lower, over my navel and cups my cunt eliciting a choke from me. He hums in approval, the slickness of my pussy agreeing with him. He sticks out his tongue and licks the side of my neck as I buck my hips closer to his hand, begging for him to relieve me of my darkest desires.

His index finger slips between my slit and I cry out at the sudden contact, his movements slow and teasing. He circles over my clit so slowly that its almost unbearable as his other hand continues to entertain my breasts, alternating between the two, ensuring ultimate pleasure. My greedy mind is already begging for him to fill me with his huge cock, knowing the orgasm that I am so desperately wanting is already close. My moans grow louder and hotter as he slips one finger inside of me.

"Fuck, you're so fucking tight. You're so appetizing, so addictive," his voice is possessed by the filthiest of demons, sparking an agonizing bliss to pool in my stomach.

I follow after the figure in the dark and I'm chasing him through the woods, unknown of the outcome. Begging for mercy, for him to let me live. I squirm under his touch, my yearning for him to release me from his trap, growing wild and frenzied.

"So fucking sinful," he bites my neck, tipping me over the edge as his fingers curl and bury inside of me.

I drive into his hand and enter into my newfound euphoria, the explosive surge of my climax causing my knees to buckle whilst using my free hand to steady myself.

"Reed, *fuck!*" I cry out.

Writhing as he removes his hand from my now seeping pussy, I slump back against the wall, the shower washing away all my sins.

Peeling my eyes open, I look around the emptiness of the shower, shame filling my cheeks. The embarrassment and guilt seeps into my veins, extracting the arousal from my system instantaneously. I shut off the shower, not caring that I haven't bothered to wash my hair and reach for a towel, hugging it tightly around me.

My legs feel weak and unsteady, my head feels light and dizzy. I grip onto the sink counter and wipe away some of the steamed mirror, enough to see my face. I blink at the pink-cheeked, dilated, insatiable woman in front of me. I notice the fullness of my lips, swollen and suggestive.

"What the hell were you thinking?" I ask myself, despite already knowing *exactly* what I was thinking.

A knock on the door disturbs my self-critique and I exit the bathroom. I dry myself quickly, slipping on my robe and tying it whilst I walk to the entrance of my apartment. I check through the peephole, ensuring that it's not some kind of serial killer, or Scott.

I immediately unlock the door and squeal. Lola pulls me into a tight embrace, just as Gracie joins in. I'm practically jumping up and down at the unexpected company, excitement bubbling.

"We haven't seen you in so long, so we thought we'd grab some snacks and have an old-fashioned girl's night!" Gracie says.

"Oh my God, yes! Come in, come in." I move out of the doorway and let them pass before locking the door again.

"Sorry if we interrupted anything, we should have called," Lola cringes.

I bat my hand at her.

"No, nothing of importance. You know you can come over anytime!" I beam, grabbing some cans of diet coke from the refrigerator. My stomach grumbles, reminding me I haven't eaten anything since my croissant earlier.

"I'll just go grab some pajamas, make yourselves at home girls!" I shout to them from the kitchen, their own pajama attire indicating of the vibes.

I pick out some navy-blue plaid shorts and a white tank, slipping them on quickly and returning to the living room.

"So we grabbed three movies, all chick-flicks. We'll let you decide seeing as though we can't come to an agreement." The end of her sentence aimed directly at Gracie, who rolls her eyes.

"Sure." I giggle, grabbing the cases.

Hm. We have *Mean Girls,* a known classic, but I have watched it probably hundreds of times now. *Bride Wars,* another amazing movie that I've definitely watched far too many times and *Me Before You.* I hold up the *Me Before You* case.

"Now this, I haven't seen," I confess.

The girls look at me in disgust, Gracie grabbing it out of my hands.

"Then this is what we're watching, I can't believe you've never seen this!"

"Sam Claflin is *dreamy.*" Lola winks at me.

"Aren't you supposed to be getting married in three weeks?" I say accusingly to Lola.

"Just because I'm getting married doesn't mean I lose my eyesight," she replies, laughing alongside me.

Gracie stakes claim of a bag of salted caramel *M&M's,* whilst I opt for the *Reese's buttercups,* Lola, the *Hershey's kisses.*

The movie begins to play, and I head to the basket in the corner of the room, grabbing two fluffy blankets and throw them at the girls, dimming the lights. We all snuggle up together on the sofa, giggling like we did when we were young.

I stare at the girls beside me in adoration, the fulfillment I get from spending time with these two is incomparable to anything else. The sisterly bond between us is unbreakable, the life we have already endured threw everything it could at us and we held each other's hearts in the center of it all. The fragile composition of the human heart is no match for sisters, the indestructible alliance between us bind us together for life. We guide each other through the dark, even when there is no light to be found.

"What?" Gracie stares back.

"Nothing." I smile, turning my attention back to the movie.

***

I'm bawling. Sobs bounce from one wall to another as we practically cry in harmony.

"But it's not fair! She loved him so much!" I cry, my sisters nodding in agreement and wiping at the inevitable tears.

I reach to the coffee table for the box of tissues as we pass it along us, sniffles and heartache connecting us all together.

"I wouldn't have let him do it, I couldn't!" Lola chokes, clearly imagining Greg in *Sam Claflin*'s shoes.

I pull my knees up to my chest and wrap my arms around them, trying to rearrange my emotions, when the girls both turn to me after sharing a look.

My eyebrow raises. "What?" I question.

They look at each other once more before it appears that Lola is going to be the one to take control of the conversation.

"We just… hm. How can I say this nicely… We noticed you looked like absolute shit earlier and we didn't want to say anything and ruin the night," she cringes at the selective words.

Ouch.

I stay silent for a moment, unsure how to handle this. I could evade the truth and say I'm just tired, still heartbroken over Scott (I'm not), or I could be honest and actually ask them for advice. Even just the thought of Scott makes the peanut buttercups rise in my stomach, threatening to escape.

"I'm fine." Well, wasn't one of your options but pop off. I internally roll my eyes.

"We can see that you're not fine Ind, is something going on?" Lola presses.

I inhale deeply, looking for a way to avoid the questions. I don't normally feel this uncomfortable telling my sisters anything, they usually already know everything about me. The foreign feeling rocks me, sending ice cold signals down my spine. I shake it off and peer back at the two pairs of green eyes looking back at me.

"Girls, you're going to need a drink for this…" I sigh, pointing to the alcohol trolley across the dining room.

Gracie is the first to get up, disappearing into the dark hallway. Lola ponders, unsure of what to do or say, the discomfort obvious.

"Lola?" She startles whilst I instantly grow concerned.

I shift closer to her and wrap an arm around her, pulling her in tight. I breathe in the soft scent of strawberry shampoo in her blonde hair, enjoying the familiar feeling.

"I'm pregnant," she whispers into my ear.

I draw away from her to gauge her facial reaction, trying to work out whether she is playing a prank on me or not.

Her eyes water with tears.

"Oh my god! Lola!" I practically scream and dive on top of her, my celebrations becoming muffled as I face plant into the couch pillows. She laughs and tells me to shush.

"Like, how far along? Who knows? Oh my gosh, the wedding!" I ramble on, the excitement of becoming an aunt overpowering everything else in my brain.

"Ha-ha, well so far I think I'm around five weeks, nobody but Greg knows, it's very early days but I thought you might have needed a bit of good news."

She grabs my hand and squeezes it slightly, the ice in my spine, slowly melting away. My eyes brim with tears of happiness for once, I couldn't have wished this joy on anyone more deserving of it than

Lola. She is definitely the most thoughtful of the trio, the most mature and understanding. I swear we were both born in the wrong order; she should have been the big sister with her incredible attributes.

Gracie walks back into the room with a bottle of red wine and two wine glasses. I wince hoping we didn't spoil the news for Gracie, me and Lola stare at her full of confusion.

"What? You don't think I'd know when my own sister was pregnant?" She smirks, we gasp.

"But, how? This isn't some crazy intuition sister thing, is it?" Lola asks.

"Look, sis. I'm observant. Do you really think there would be any other reason when you've just inhaled a share bag of *Hershey's kisses* two weeks away from your own wedding?" She tuts and places the wine down on the table in front of us.

"Plus, I've noticed you've gained a few pounds." She tests.

And, that's all it takes before Lola launches pillows at where Gracie stands. I join in on cue as we all laugh relentlessly, careful to avoid the bottle of wine.

I've been interrogated, poked, and prodded for answers for the past hour.

My sisters have been going insane that they've been kept out of the loop of this part of my life. I explained it was the shame and guilt of it all weighing me down, which they understood, in regards to Allie.

They want me to file a restraining order against Scott after I told them about our slight altercation earlier, highlighting that a man should never lay a hand on a woman, regardless of the circumstances. I nod in agreement.

"Now, onto the mysterious Mr. Reed who is offering you a lifeline in exchange for a temporary marriage," Lola begins.

"How much is he offering you?" Gracie asks, suspicion in her tone.

"I didn't get that far, I shut him down pretty quickly." I confess.

"Well, I think that's the first thing we need to find out, don't we?" Lola agrees.

Why am I even considering this, wondering what he meant by a 'large sum of money'. Are we walking like thousands? Tens of thousands? Hundreds of thousands?

"Give me your phone." Gracie demands, surprise crosses my face.

"Why would you need my phone?" I retort, my anxiety beginning to rise.

"Relax, sis. I'm not going to post your nudes online. I literally just want to throw a casual text, see if he responds, simple." She holds out her hand, beckoning for me to slip her my phone.

What if he doesn't respond, isn't that going to make me look desperate? I turned his offer down with the highest confidence and if I start sniffing around again, he's going to know that I'm even considering it.

Oh, to hell with it.

Submitting to her, I hand over the phone, she quickly gets to work.

I look at Lola and she yawns, guilt rising for keeping her up this late. She told us about her rough sleep lately, the morning sickness keeping her up at all hours and how ginger biscuits one-hundred-percent *do not* work. My phone notification pings and we all turn our heads in sync as Gracie unlocks my phone again.

"Well shit, sis. I think you're going to want to reconsider his offer."

We all lean over the phone and my eyes bug out of my head. The zeroes blur my vision as I stumble upon what to say, my mouth becoming paralyzed and uncertain how to speak.

"One freaking million dollars!" Lola claps and leaps up from the sofa, shaking her ass and head banging.

I sit, still leaned over the phone and frozen in place. That is one heck of a lot of money. When he originally asked me, I assumed it would be a nice amount, maybe a few thousand.

Not *one million*. I feel sick. He really wasn't lying when he said he was desperate.

"And what are the terms again?" Lola finally gives up her atrocious dancing and comes back down to earth.

"As far as I'm aware… fake dating. Get married. Prove the courts that we're real and retain custody of his daughter Willow."

"Willow as in, ballet Willow?" Gracie asks and I nod eagerly, my heart pulling at the fact I haven't seen her in weeks, releasing a sigh.

The silence washes over the room as my sisters try and grasp the situation I'm in, every possible scenario playing out in my head.

"What about Scott? You could buy him out of his share of the business, giving you full control," Lola murmurs, as she carefully scans my face.

That is certainly a positive. I haven't had much time to process that he owns 50% of the business, let alone come up with a solution to fix my problem.

"And the scholarship program you always wanted to have? I mean, damn, you could move your studio further into the city instead of having it out on the outskirts." Gracie wears a grin, desperately trying to convince me.

"Why do I feel like you both want me to take the deal?" Suspicion lines my words.

"It's not everyday some hot millionaire offers you a million dollars in exchange for fake marrying him." Gracie says.

"Is he at least hot?" Lola asks.

My mind flashes with pictures of him, the hold he has over my sanity.

I bite my lip and nod, feeling flushed.

"Take the damn deal, Indie." Gracie speaks sternly.

I look between my two sisters and sit up straighter, filling myself with the confidence I didn't know I had.

"I'm going to take it?" My voice doesn't match my nodding head.

I repeat. "I'm doing it." The sternness finally coinciding with the intention of my words.

The girls whoop and clap their hands as they tackle me to the floor, laying kisses all over my cheeks. I giggle and try my best to shove them off and calm them down.

"Damn, my sister is a self-established millionaire." Gracie beams, finally relieving me of her weight.

I try to contain my laughter as my phone vibrates again, each of us eyeing each other, wondering who is going to be the one to read it. I lean forward and retrieve it from the table.

"It's from Reed." I state.

"Open it, open it!" Lola squeals, her giddy tone hurting my ears.

I key in my pass code, the message lighting up the screen. I stop dead as my jaw drops open, losing the ability to speak as I put the phone back on the table with a shaky hand. The girls scramble to peer over at the phone.

"TWO FREAKING MILLION!" They both say in unison.

He's just upped his offer, trying to sway my already decided decision.

Gracie grabs the phone and texts him back whilst I sit in silence, the disbelief written across my face.

There must be a catch, it can't be this simple.

Fake marriage doesn't seem worth two million dollars.

Why would he pay that sort of money instead of going out into the real world and finding some sort of desperate woman, eager for a husband?

Why did he choose me, and why is he willing to pay me so much money for it?

Chapter 17

Reed

I pace the living room, nerves wrecking my entire body.

She hasn't responded to my texts, only that she will be here around 5pm for Willow's project.

"Daddy, you keep getting in the way of the TV," she grumbles, shooing her hands at me.

"Sorry, honey."

Walking back into to the kitchen, I take a seat on the stool. My gaze turns to the alcohol cupboard, eyeing up the selection.

Stop.

I'm unable to keep myself sat still for longer than thirty seconds.

A quiet knock on the door has me practically running over to it.

I unlock it just as the wind is knocked out of me at her stunning appearance.

"Hey." Her voice is like melted butter.

I stare at her face, the freckles on her nose, the pink tinted lipstick across her luscious mouth. A mouth I've wanted around the head of my cock since the moment I first laid eyes on her.

"Hey." I choke out, my throat feeling like a chainsaw has been shoved down it.

Following the curve of her tan neck, her halter neck red dress interrupts the revelation of skin. I can make out the outline of her nipples through the thin material, *no bra?*

Hm.

Her dress flows down and cuts off around mid-thigh, showing enough of her silky legs to cause my pulse to race and heat to spread straight to my groin. Those long, flexible, sexy legs.

She stares right back at me, returning the heated gaze, her eyelashes fluttering with every blink.

"INDIE!" Willow barrels right past me and knocks into Indie as she struggles to keep them both upright from the force.

They both wrap their arms around each other, and I watch as they interact, the glimmer in her eyes and the passion behind Willow's. She really does idolize Indie in every way, and I'm thankful she has someone like her to look up to.

"Let's get started!" Indie cheers, Willow grabs her hand and pulls her inside of the house whilst I step out of the way.

Being stampeded by a frantic nine-year-old, is not on my list of tasks to complete today. I close the door, walking back into the living space.

Willow has pulled one of the dining room chairs into the lounge, placing it in the center of the room, in front of one of L-shaped couches. She prompts Indie to sit in the chair, hurrying off to her bedroom to grab her notebook full of burning questions.

Indie sits down, smoothing out her dress and keeping her focus on the rug beneath her. Her hair is down, flowing around the base of her shoulders, partially tucked behind her ear.

"We need to talk later." Her voice is quiet and deeper than her usual tone.

I fold my arms over my chest and lean back against the door frame.

"Is that so?" My tone is cocky and unforgiving.

She looks up at me, her emerald eyes piercing mine in some sort of mental warfare. Her lips purse as she tries to remain emotionless, it's not working.

She's going to accept my offer, isn't she?

I lick around my lips, eager for another taste of her.

"Got it!" Willow shouts, running and jumping onto the sofa, drawing both of our attention on her.

Indie smiles at her and sits up straight, cracking her knuckles.

"Bring it on detective." She winks at Willow.

She giggles and readjusts the notebook, popping the lid from her pen.

"Okay, Miss Thorne. Let's get started with some easy questions, what is your full name?"

"Indie Margot Thorne."

She suits it.

"When is your birthday?"

"September 17, 1995."

"So that makes you… twenty-seven?"

"Twenty-eight." She smiles.

Their introductory questions carry on whilst I slink away to my office.

I still haven't opened a file that my new P.I warned me about. The thought of opening it has been eating away at me. I can't understand what must be so bad, enough for someone in his profession to warn me. He's seen all kinds of things and dealt with some of the worst criminals in the world, but he warns me about something to do with my wife and Willow?

My mouse hovers over the file, the title of it just being a bunch of encrypted numbers. I grab the bottle of bourbon from my drawer and refill the glass next to my computer that has become a part of the furniture. It stays here, permanently.

If whatever is inside of this file carries a warning, I'm going to need something to take the edge of.

I inhale a deep breath through my nose and thin my lips, double-clicking.

A medical document addressed to Allie appears on the screen, with a lot of text. *What the hell is this?*

I scroll down, seeing this dates back to 2014.

So, it's her previous medical history?

I scan through the text, trying to pinpoint whatever the warning was about. I don't see anything but numbers and figures at this point.

Oh, there's my name.

I read through the simple text and it has a few codes along with–

'SPECIMEN SAMPLE: HAIR'

The fuck?

I then scroll down to the final page and choke on my drink.

DNA Test Report

Blinking repeatedly, I don't dare to move my eyes anywhere else across the page.

I can't fucking do this.

Crossing off the document, I shut it out of my mind, not wanting to see any sort of result.

I know Willow is mine, she looks too much like me to not be. But, the fact this test was done in the first place insinuates that Allie was cheating on me when we first met.

My stomach churns and nausea builds up in my throat, saliva filling my mouth. Even if she's not with us anymore, it doesn't make it hurt any less.

After a few more glasses of bourbon, I check in on Willow and Indie, instantly feeling more at ease after a few doses of my favorite medicine.

"How old were you when you decided to become a full-time ballerina?" Willow asks.

Hm, this sounds like she's asking more for herself, than the project.

I keep my presence hidden behind the door frame, Indie now sitting cross legged on the sofa next to Willow. They both face each other, Willow's back to me.

Indie wears a radiant smile, her demeanor showing exactly how unguarded she is right now. She is completely comfortable and relaxed, chatting away with my daughter. I can barely hear their conversation over my complete infatuation with the way she interacts with my daughter.

This right here?

This is why I need her.

She looks up at me, startled and I bring myself into clearer view. Her dress leaves little to the imagination with the position she's sat in, not aware that it gives me a clear view to her nude lacy underwear. I wonder if she's chosen a thong, just for me.

"Daddy, we're hungry." Willow huffs, setting her notebook on the coffee table.

Indie's eyes look at me apologetically as she begins to get up to leave.

"Where are you going?" My voice comes out harsher than intended.

"I really should be going, I have classes early and it's getting late." Her lips tighten as she glances around for her purse.

"Have you eaten already?" I question.

"No, but it's fine, I can pick something up on my way home." She begins to strut past me and I instinctively reach out and grab her by the waist, pulling her body flush against mine.

Her head darts to the direction of Willow, who is engaged with a YouTube video she's chosen. She turns her attention back to me, her breathing ragged and heavy.

I lean down to her face and tuck a piece of hair behind her ear. Bringing myself closer to her ear, I whisper, "Stay."

She can't resist my touch.

The feeling of her body pressed against mine heightens my longing for her. It reminds me of every reason I've been fixated on her with the smell of her perfume offering a temptation that I don't even want to refuse. She hasn't answered my question, she just stares at me with her mouth parted– the mouth I so badly want to taste right now.

Bringing my face closer to hers, I hear her breath hitch. I nudge my nose against hers to try and prompt an answer. Her eyes flutter closed, and I can feel the heat of her breath radiating onto my own. She's trying to talk herself out of staying, but we both already know her answer.

"Stay." I repeat and trail my lips along her jaw, squeezing her hips slightly.

She begins to nod, her nostrils flaring. Offering a sly grin, I pull away from her.

"Pizza or noodles?" I shout towards Willow.

"*Pizza!*" she drags out, laying further back onto the couch and propping her legs up.

I turn back to face Indie, and she looks at me with a defeated face, knowing I've coerced her into staying.

"Oh, one more question Indie," Willow shouts.

"Mm-hmm." Indie doesn't trust her own voice right now, I'm betting that it would betray every single emotion she is feeling inside.

She is most certainly starved, a hunger that only I can fulfill. A desperation so primal, she's letting it overtake her instincts as I torment her, bait her into setting foot right inside of my territory. Little does she know that I plan to devour her in every way possible.

"Pineapple on pizza or not?" The million-dollar question.

Or in this case, *two-million dollars.*

"Absolutely it does." She speaks with confidence.

Me and Willow look at each other, our eyes growing wide.

Thank, God.

Indie looks between us as me and Lo send signals between our gaze, preparing to crack.

"Woo-hoo!" Willow stands up and begins jumping up and down on the sofa doing her 'happy dance'.

Indie lets out a sigh of relief, chuckling.

"Hawaiian pizza it is then," I confirm, leaving the room to order.

***

Willow is crashed out between me and Indie, the *Beauty and the Beast* end credits roll, the room darkening in the process. We consumed the entire pizza between us, ate hot cookies and drank a ridiculous amount of soda.

I stand up, stretching my limbs before peering down at Willow who is snuggled against Indie. Indie glances up at me wearing that adorable smile that makes her dimples pop.

Damn, she is *stunning.*

I carefully scoop Willow up into my arms, setting Indie free, and whisk her away to her bedroom. She is already in her daisy covered pajamas, her hair plastered across her sweaty forehead. I lay her down into the bed and peel back the fresh pink bedspread, her choice of course, and place it back over her, tucking her in tight.

Leaning over, I brush the hair out of her face, a slight snore escaping from her. I wrap my arms around her and place a tender kiss on her cheek, cherishing every single second. Her eyelashes are long and wispy, her skin as smooth as silk, her nose is lightly dotted with tiny freckles.

I realize I'm smiling deeper than I have in months, my heart almost hurts with the amount of love I feel looking at my little girl. I kiss her one last time on her forehead and walk out of the room, closing the door quietly.

Grabbing my cell out of my pocket, I send Bridget a text, telling her there's no need for her to come over tonight. I have a small feeling that tonight isn't going to be spent the usual way, wallowing in self-pity and bourbon.

Indie is standing next to the kitchen sink. Is she washing my dishes? She hasn't noticed that I'm here.

I softly make my way over to her as she hums a song to herself, bobbing her head slightly. Gently moving her hair away from her neck, I expose the section of velvety skin as her body jolts, the same time as my finger makes contact with her.

"Jesus, Reed, you scared me." She blurts, her hand leaving the water to go to her chest.

"Shh," I whisper.

I part my lips, placing them to the side of her neck with such trepidation I can't be quite sure if they made contact. She's stopped washing the dishes, her hands going limp in the sink, her entire body tensed.

"I've missed the smell of your skin," I sigh.

I inhale deeply as she rolls her neck to the side, allowing me to get closer.

"I've missed the feeling of your touch," I say, planting a tender kiss on her shoulder.

Her chest rises and falls quickly.

"I've missed the sight of your angelic body," I continue, planting more kisses further up her neck, feeling a pulse beating hard beneath my lips.

"I've missed the sound of your provocative moans," I tease, and she gulps as I nibble at her earlobe, switching to kissing.

"And most of all, I've missed the taste of your luscious pussy."

I spin her around and her hands fall to my chest as she looks up at me through her lashes. Her eyes are glazed over, and lips parted as her breaths fan over my face.

I place my finger underneath her chin, lifting her jaw as her eyes dart between each of mine, not knowing which one to focus on as I near her.

Licking my lips, I draw her attention to them. She is barely making a sound, but I can clearly feel her nipples against my chest, revealing the truth of her desires. My lips near hers and she begins to close her eyes before popping them wide open again.

"Wait," she pants.

I pull back, almost offended. I lift an eyebrow, suspicion written across my face.

"I didn't just come here for Willow tonight," she begins.

"I came here to take you up on your offer." Her voice is timid.

I pause, processing her words. I blink a few times, trying to comprehend it.

"You're... you're going to help me?" My words are full of hope and desperation, praying that I didn't hear her wrong.

She nods, biting her lip.

A second passes between us before I dart forward, crashing my lips against hers. Her arms wrap around my neck as I part her lips with my tongue, fighting for entry. I run my fingers up her back and through her hair as our tongues dance together, teasing, and playful but filled with passion.

I can't believe she's agreed to help me.

I pull away from her, breathless; her panting breath, matching the rhythm of mine.

"Wait, are you sure?" I ask her in pure disbelief.

"Yes, Reed. I'm sure." She confirms.

That's all I needed.

I pull her back to me and wrap my arms around her, hugging her ridiculously tight. She returns the embrace and I feel like balance has finally been restored. Willow will stay with me, with *us*.

I grasp her face in between my hands, squishing her cheeks slightly causing her lips to pucker. I peck her once before remembering.

"Give me a second."

I rush off into the office, pulling open the bottom drawer. There sits a lonely velvet black box, encasing a four-carat diamond solitaire ring. I grasp hold of it, the box feeling dainty in my large hands.

Entering the kitchen, I notice Indie hasn't moved from where I left her, looking gorgeous as always.

Clearing my throat to prepare, I get down on one knee. Her hands fly to her mouth, eyes wide in awe.

I open the box, the diamond reflecting hundreds of dancing lights across the ceiling.

"Indie Margot Thorne, born on the September 17, 1995." I wink at her as she chuckles.

"I know we've had a bit of a whirlwind romance, and it feels like we've only known each other for weeks," I grin at her, her laughter delighting me.

"But ever since you told me you liked pineapple on pizza, I knew you were the one." She throws her head back, struggling to keep her amusement contained.

"Love is a waiting game, but you proved that time is inconsequential when you stole my heart." Her laughter ceases as she looks down at me, adoration in her eyes.

"Indie, will you marry me?" I finish, eagerness threaded throughout me.

"Of course I will, Mr. Breckenridge!" She squeals in delight, flinging her arms around my neck and throwing me off balance.

We tumble to the floor together, her straddling my hips. I peer up at her, her teeth glisten with her cheesy grin, the dimples never ceasing.

"Give me that hand worth two million dollars." I bait her.

She rolls her eyes and presents her hand. I retrieve the ring and slide it up the fourth finger on her left hand. She lifts her arm, admiring the ring in the light.

"God, Reed. How much is this thing worth?" She studies it.

"Hm, around four-hundred-thousand dollars." I shrug.

She hits my chest playfully. "You're kidding."

I shake my head. "Nope," popping the P.

"Hold up, I can't accept this."

"And, why not?"

"This thing is worth more than my apartment!" She tries to remove the ring to return, and I clasp my hand over hers.

"Speaking of, we need to start house hunting. I want a fresh start." I purse my lips, considering the list of Realtor agents I have stored in my contacts database.

Indie stands up, leaving me laid flat on the floor. She paces a little and I prop myself up on my elbows, leaning back.

"Of course, we need to go over the contract together, but we need Harrison for that. He's already drawn one up and we need witnesses." I inform her, hoping to ease her panic.

"Harrison?"

"Yeah, the guy who harassed you at the coffee shop. He's a lawyer and also unfortunately my brother," I confirm.

"He's your brother!"

"Yeah…" I trail off, confused why she's so astonished.

She stares at the ring on her finger, then at me, then at the ring again.

Great, she's already changing her mind. Maybe I should call Harrison now and get him over here before she can back out. I mean, it's her free will to but I can't lose this chance of winning the custody battle.

"Is everything okay?" I ask softly, hoping not to press her too much.

She nods her head and takes a seat on the island stool, staring at the wall.

I stand up quickly, dusting myself off when she turns to me.

"I'm doing this for Willow," she states.

"Me too." I agree.

I step closer towards her as she scans me up and down.

"I'm doing this…for Willow…" She reiterates.

I stand in front of her, her dress is bunched up and barely covering her ass.

"Me too," I whisper, placing my arms either side of her on the island, trapping her inside of them.

"I'm doing this for…" I grab her waist and greedily take her lips in mine.

I part her legs with my knee and step between them, her hands fly to my belt. *Eager.*

Cupping her left breast in my hand, I feel the pointed nub in the palm of my hand, the friction coercing a moan out of her, against my lips.

She yanks the belt away; it drops to the floor with a clang. I shush her against her lips, smiling slightly. Her tongue is desperate and sends shock-waves to my cock, growing harder by the second. She palms me through my pants, and I let out an animalistic groan, the consuming feeling mind-blowing in itself.

Fuck, my hand has nothing on hers.

We fight each other's clothes off, the urgency between us is agonizing and punishing. We can't get to one another quick enough as our breaths accelerate; the anguish becomes unbearable. I don't even get chance to slip on a condom, but I'm pretty sure she's on birth control anyway. *Not that she seems to care in this moment either.*

I wrestle her dress off her, and bring my cock between her pussy lips, the wetness lining the head and my eyes roll the back of my head at the sensation. She sucks on my tongue, waiting for me to act.

"You're so fucking wet for me, Indie." I growl.

She hums in response as I rub the head of my cock up and down her sopping cunt. She grips onto my shoulders and shuffles further off the stool, leaning back on the island behind her. I grip her hips and stare down at her flushed face, her hair in complete disarray.

She looks *mesmerizing*.

I want to see her like this over and over, I want to bury myself inside of her and never come up for air.

She is my oxygen; she is my only savior.

I push into her tightness, the resistance gripping onto my cock and never wanting to let go. I let out a shaky breath as she drops her head back, her tits somehow becoming more exposed.

I can barely contain myself; I feel like I'm going to come without even moving. How am I meant to satisfy my hunger if her cunt has this sort of effect on me?

I lean down and sweep my tongue over her peaked nipple, she shudders in response.

"Yes." She breathes.

I do it again trying to gauge the same reaction. I start to slowly pump in and out of her, her moans long and hoarse. I bite my lip and increase my pace, ramming into her over and over.

She cries out, bucking her hips as I drive inside of her to the hilt, feeling her body tense every time. I grip her ass cheeks and kick the stool out of the way, holding her body up. She falters on her elbows and readjusts herself, only they remain on the island as I burrow myself inside of her. I indulge in the luscious feeling of her wrapped around me. I'm determined to make her come first; I am a gentleman after all.

I keep a firm grip on her and decide to widen my stance, my heart pounding from my chest at the view of her completely and utterly delirious with pleasure. I pound her harder as she takes me perfectly. Her body shakes uncontrollably as I feel her pulse around me, the sensation driving me crazy.

She lifts her head, opening those stunning green eyes, her pupils dilate as she's shamelessly drunk from the lust.

"Oh, Indie. Don't give me that face, baby– Oh, *fuck.*" I moan.

I try to stop the building orgasm, failing terribly. Her tits are bouncing along with my thrusts, and she is staring at me with the filthiest look in her eyes, her mouth is pouted as she breathes heavily through her nostrils.

"Fuck me, just like that." Her seductive voice, completely possessed.

My eyes roll as I reach up with one hand, pinching her nipple. She moans, rolling her head as her pussy tightens.

Shit. I'm too close.

I use that same hand and press my thumb onto her clit, the action causing her to cry out.

She's close too.

I slam into her as she moans my name, toying with her with my other hand.

"Fuck, uh, I'm gonna…"

Her body reaches forward, her arms lacing around my neck as she shakes and I feel my cock drown in her juices.

That's the only cue I need.

I release my hold and succumb to my own climax, roaring out in ecstasy, every muscle in my body tensing as I spill into her, throbbing in every way possible.

I hold her like that for a few moments, both of us barely able to return to a normal breathing pattern. She hugs onto me like a koala bar, our potion of cum dripping out of her onto the floor.

I slowly set her down on the sofa, not trusting her to be able to stand on those shaky legs yet. I slide alongside her, grasping her hand in mine and rubbing my finger over the diamond ring, a side smile pulling at my lips. She strokes her hand over my abs, the tickling feeling washing away any sort of rigidness in my body.

"Thank you," I whisper to her. *In more ways than one.*

She pulls my head downwards to peer into her green eyes as leans up to give me a longing kiss, one that ignites the carnal predator within me. As much as that was her way of acknowledging my words, it's only made me starve for more.

I flip her over onto her stomach as she squeals excitedly.

Pressing my body into her from behind, I hiss at the skin contact, my cock already throbbing and ready to feast.

"Do you see the effect you have on me?" I snarl into her ear.

Boy is it going to be a long night.

Chapter 18

Indie

I slump into the sofa in the office corner, stretching the length of my legs across it. Since last night, I haven't really had time to stop and process what I've actually agreed to, but the ring on my finger serves as a constant reminder.

I've texted my sisters telling them the facts of how yesterday was with Reed, excluding the raunchy details.

Willow attended classes today, courtesy of Bridget. She was ecstatic that she was back and it was almost like she'd never left, her skills and competence did not falter once. It was incredible to see, she thrives in an environment like this, and I am so proud I get to be the one to watch it.

It's strange to consider that for a period, I'm going to become her stepmother. I love every inch of her, but it's completely different having to raise her. Even if it is for a short time, I'm going to make sure that I am the best motherly figure I can be.

I don't want to act as some sort of replacement for Allie, I will ensure that she is still very much remembered and included in our lives for the perfect woman that she was. The guilt in my throat begins to rise again, remembering only a month ago, I sat here with her and held her against me, absorbing her cries. Now, she is gone, and I am here, wearing a ring on my finger for her husband.

I fiddle with the ring, twisting it around and looking at it from different angles. Contractual or not, this circumstance is completely insane. I knew I didn't want to get into anything serious with anybody after Scott, and I've jumped headfirst into a fake marriage to help someone out.

Why is it always me who tries to save everybody?

Technically this has nothing to do with me.

If I wasn't so close with Willow, would I have taken up this deal?

Absolutely not.

I can't deny that the money was a huge temptation, it was probably one of the leading reasons, especially with Scott's new stakes.

Rubbing my hands over my face, I notice a slight sweat lining my skin.

I head over to my locker and pull out some fresh clothing, prepared to clean myself up. My phone has two missed calls from Reed and a text message letting me know to meet at his house later as Harrison will be there.

When Reed told me that Harrison was indeed his brother, it threw a curve-ball. Harrison is sweet, charming and adorable. Reed on the other hand, he is arrogant, reserved and so damn tempting.

Thinking about it, they do have some similar features but the main difference is the darkness that comes with Reed, the forbidding atmosphere that makes him so captivating that you want to dive blindly into his abyss of sin and destruction.

He makes me want to act reckless, he provokes an animalistic need that I didn't even know I had, the pull between us is so forceful that I can't resist.

Harrison is different. We've barely met but the instant effect he had on me turned me into a deer in headlights. I'm attracted to him immensely, he is exactly the type of guy that I would date. He is wholesome and tempts me in a good way, like a candied apple. A forsaken guilty pleasure but serves a purpose greater than the initial outburst of sweetness.

In less than an hour, I must face them both, in the same room. I can only see one way how this is going to end.

Can you ever have night and day at the same time?

With a sigh, I retreat to the bathroom to take a shower and mentally prepare for it.

I knock twice, my hair is still damp and loose, the air giving it a wavy appearance. I hear footsteps and Reed opens the door, his smile is dazzling under the lights, as does his blue eyes.

"Hey." He props himself against the door frame, folding his arms over his chest.

Blushing, I look to my feet, the memories of last night clouding my brain at the sight of him. I feel exposed and timid, I can't believe we had sex *four* times last night. By the time I peer back up at him, he's biting his lip and giving me a lazy side grin.

So, it's on his mind too?

"Well hello there, my pretty girl." A voice nears.

My gaze switches to Harrison, he looks like a different person outside of his suit attire. He's wearing a black t-shirt and a pair of gym shorts, his hair is spiked in different places, but he looks fresh.

Reed rolls his eyes and steps inside, beckoning for me to come in. I drop my duffel bag in the corridor and grip the wall whilst I take my shoes off, my feet are particularly sore from today's session, I hope Willow's aren't too bad.

"Where's Willow?" I ask, walking into the kitchen.

"She's out with Bridget, they'll be back later."

Harrison sits on a bar stool on one side of the island, whilst Reed stands awkwardly next to the side of the island where he fucked me senseless last night.

I can feel the heat burning in my cheeks once again. I can't explain the person that I become with Reed, I've never acted so promiscuous before.

Feeling Harrison's eyes on me, I don't dare to look at him fully, knowing what he's here for.

"Well, I'm just glad to see you've managed to survive another day." Harrison smirks, drawing laughter from my throat.

Reed shoots a pointed, confused look at Harrison.

"Harrison… kind of saved my life." I thin my lips into a tight line as I gesture to Harrison.

"Please, call me Harry." I swallow and nod, he suits Harry more.

Reed flicks his gaze between me and Harry and offers a small thanks to him.

"Let's get down to business." Reed changes the subject, not wanting to hear anything personal between me and his brother.

We follow him into the lounge as Harry retrieves a thick document from his backpack, bringing it over to the coffee table. Reed flicks on the lamp for better lighting and we crowd around, Harry opposite and Reed next to me on the couch.

Harry looks at me nervously, trying to gauge my emotions about all of this. I offer him a reassuring nod and he lets out a hearty breath.

"Okay, I must go over some things first before we can get down to the essential points of this contract." Harry points out.

"So, you both understand the logistics of a contract. Once signed, it's legally binding and if either of you were to break your side of the contract, the other party has the resources to take legal action against you for the purpose of breaking the contract." I take in his words, the professionalism of it suddenly making this decision more daunting and weightier.

"Yes." we respond.

Harry keeps looking at me, his eyes soft and reassuring. He begins to list the terms of the contract, the monetary exchange, the purpose of this agreement. The only clause for us to end this contract early, is if it is in the best interests of Willow. If for any reason, she wanted us to split apart then the contract would become void immediately. She is the primary reason for this fake marriage, this is to benefit her in every way possible and try to maintain an ordinary life for her. However, she is not to be made aware that the marriage is fake.

Children have a way of relaying information, and we can't trust that she wouldn't slip up, which could cost us the case. We get to the parts where it discusses that our relationship does not require any physical contact, aside from public outings. This can include hand holding, hugging, and kissing (when necessary). This is to ensure that the world can view us like a normal affectionate couple.

We must go on dates twice a week publicly, we need to learn as much about each other as possible in case we are put under any sort of pressure from the courts who may deem our relationship unreliable or false. We must live together for the duration of the contractual marriage and our finances will be covered solely by Reed himself, meaning that the money I acquire will not be used for any sort of living expenses whilst we are 'married'.

I must remain on birth control for the duration, ensuring I keep up to date with any medical appointments that could affect my health. An element of the contract draws my attention.

"I have to change my name?" I grimace.

"Well, it is just to make it so that you are all united. *The Breckenridges.* It will help the opinion of the court if they can visualize you as being part of the family." Harry states.

I swallow anxiously. I don't feel like I've realized the depth of this agreement, the lifestyle changes I'm going to have to make, the commitments.

Tapping my foot on the floor, I chew the inside of my cheek.

Come on, Indie.

Think of the future, think of the people you can help, think of Willow.

You can do this.

I hold my hand out for the pen, the diamond ring on my finger grasping my attention again. I feel like my head is underwater, the sounds in the room sound distant and slow, none of this feels real.

"Indie?" Harry says, concern etched in his sunken brows.

"I'm fine, honestly." I attempt to reassure him.

Reed has barely spoken, keeping to himself which I kind of respect him for. At least he can understand how big of a decision this is for me, without any added pressure.

Gripping the pen firmly, I look at the papers, flipped onto the page that requires my signature, Reed's already signed and complete alongside. I swallow, what feels like a razor blade, and blink slowly, my vision drawing in on the dotted line.

I blow out a breath and lean forward, my hand shaking as I press the ball point to the page. Within a short second, my signature sits there peering up at me in its choke hold. The pen drops to the table with a clatter, breaking the silence.

Harry and Reed both stand up whist I sit here, reserved, and quiet. Harry kneels in front of me, his hand resting on my knee, offering a warming touch.

I look into his honey brown eyes, the soft lighting of the room casts shadows across his jaw. I focus on the indented dimple on his cheek as it flexes with the tensing of his jaw. *That's pretty fucking hot.*

"You've got my number, darling. I'm here if you need anything, anything at all." His large hand squeezes my thigh gently, but not sexually. Everything about him seems genuine, the way he speaks to me is thoughtful and cautious of my internal mindset, always wanting to comfort me in some way.

Reed coughs, earning a scowl from his brother.

"Thank you, Harry." He smiles at the sound of his nickname, knowing that I've taken onboard his comment from earlier.

"That's everything wrapped up on my end, do either of you have any questions?" He stands back up, grabbing onto the thick file of pages. I shake my head as Reed responds *No*, firm, and strong.

"Reed." He tips his head to bid him farewell, as does Reed in response.

"Goodbye, beautiful." He flashes me a wink.

He is baiting Reed *so* badly.

I wave him out and Reed turns his gaze onto me, a wicked look in his eyes.

"So, we're all alone now dimples." He drones out, his voice thick with lust.

I giggle as he crushes me under his weight, all the anxiety from the signing, seeming to dry up.

Chapter 19

Reed

After signing the contract, I've felt a huge weight being lifted from my shoulders. The mornings seem easier to manage, the evenings feel a little less lonely. I think most of all, I've enjoyed feeling like a family again, like I've been given a second shot at this. At life.

Seeing Indie sleeping peacefully beside me, in the bed I once shared with Allie, feels like the exact juxtaposition that it is.

This bed used to be the epitome of too many arguments between us, like who was getting up first, who deserves it most, and which side belongs to whom. I caved eventually, retreating to the spare bedroom as I was so completely sick of it all. I don't think I realized at that specific moment in time, that me giving up this bed, was actually me giving up on *us*. Our marriage.

It feels like from that point, we grew inexplicably different.

It's like the bed was the final thing that kept us together, as mundane as it may be. The only time we resided together, was to sleep at night, in this bed.

People usually have a specific turning point in their marriage, a situation that they can look back on and notice that it was at that moment, that things changed.

There was no dramatic event, it happened gradually.

Sometimes, I wish there had been a moment like that. At least then, we would have been able to attempt to fix things, to even know what to fix. But, I'm as clueless as an outsider with no real indication of our problems, just that we didn't want to be together anymore.

I sit with my back against the wooden headboard, my legs sprawled out in front of me and Indie curled up at my side. Her dark hair fans out beneath her as I peer down at her, appreciating the beauty of her being completely relaxed.

Reaching out my hand, I trace small circles on her shoulder. She doesn't flinch.

Is it too early to admit that I'm falling for her?

Or, that I *already have*.

A slight snore breaks from her mouth and I struggle to mask my laugh as I find her even more adorable.

Willow is sleeping soundly in the room adjacent to us, she didn't ask any questions when she came home to find Indie here. She was thrilled, to be honest.

I'm nervous to tell her that I'm marrying her ballet teacher, especially so soon after her mother's death. I'd be lying if I said it doesn't pain me, to see her go through something this traumatic, so young.

I'm hoping that Indie can give her the hope that she has lost as I know how much she idolizes her.

There isn't a doubt in my mind that during this contract, Indie is going to be the rock at the center of us all, keeping us all in balance.

As much as she is beautiful, she is incredibly smart and caring. She has so many attributes that complement her as a human, it'd be impossible to not fall in love with her.

Sliding my body further down the bed, I rest my head upon the same pillow as Indie. Her breaths are slow and calm as she sleeps in one of my t-shirts.

Wrapping my arm around her waist, I pull her into me. She is completely away with the fairies, she doesn't even stir.

Smiling, I nestle into her, feeling a warmth spread around my body as I close my eyes.

***

"Daddy?" Willow says.

I blink my eyes open, focusing on her small body that's still slightly blurry from my deep sleep.

"Lo?" I reply, stretching my arms wide and then rubbing my hands over my face to try and wake myself up more.

"Daddy..." She lowers her voice to a whisper.

"Yeah?" I whisper back, leaning over the side of the bed to get closer to her.

She crouches down and I furrow my brows in confusion.

Her tiny index finger lifts and points behind me as a quiet giggle escapes her lips.

I crane my head to look at the direction she is pointing, and it dawns on me.

Of course.

"Ah, yeah..." I breath, as if I'd been caught red-handed.

Well, I kinda have.

She stands up to her full height and places her hands on her hips, looking down at me.

I carefully sit up, trying not to wake Indie.

It's difficult not to laugh at Willow when she's looking at me like she's a mother, telling off her son.

"Come on, missus," I say, tipping my head towards the bedroom door.

She steps back and I stand up from the bed, my pajama pants hanging loosely from my hips.

She taps her foot impatiently and rolls her eyes at me, quietly stomping away. Following after her, we head downstairs and into the kitchen.

"You've got some explaining to do, daddy." She pouts her lips and crosses her arms, leaning against the kitchen cupboards.

"Lo, I've got something to tell you…" I wince, getting onto my knees before her so that she has the advantage on the height.

She turns her head away from me with an angry look on her face.

"She's *my* Indie, not yours." She grumbles, avoiding eye contact with me.

I have to bite my cheek to stop myself from laughing at her reaction this this. My moody nine-year-old daughter isn't angry because I'm in bed with another woman, she's angry because she wants Indie all to herself.

"Lo–"

"No, daddy. Indie likes me more than you. It isn't fair she gets to have sleepovers in *your* bed. She should be having sleepovers in *my* bed!" She scowls at me, finally facing me.

"I know, but–"

"No buts, daddy! You say I'm not allowed to say but!" She retorts.

My smart girl.

"Okay, Lo. You're right. It isn't fair." I confess, trying my best to appear sincere.

She scrunches her nose and looks at me fiercely, almost making me smile.

"See, this is what I've wanted to talk to you about," I begin, and she looks at me expectantly, "Indie is going to be around, for a while. You're going to be seeing a lot more of her around here."

I tread lightly, not ready to break the news of the marriage yet.

"Wait, really?" Willow gasps, her eyes growing wide.

"Yeah, I kind of really like her too…" I admit, trying to break this down easily enough for a child to understand.

"So… You're going to be a ballerina?" She looks at me puzzled.

I let out a laugh, "No, darling. I like Indie, more like a friend. But, a little bit more than a friend," I explain.

"Like, a boyfriend?" She asks.

"Kind of, but like a girlfriend." I reply.

"Wait! So you've been *KISSING* my teacher!" She shouts, her jaw drops.

"Shh, and yes, sometimes." I cringe, unsure how to approach this now.

Supposedly, it would make things easier if she can come to terms with the physical connection between us.

"I see," She says, glancing around the room with a skeptical look on her face.

"I'll let you kiss Indie, if you take me to the beach, today." Willow demands, the confidence radiates in her voice.

"The beach is pretty far, it's a very long car journey." I explain and she glares at me.

"I know." Her voice doesn't falter.

Well, I suppose she gets her stubbornness from me.

"Deal."

I erupt into laughter as she breaks out into a grin, wrapping her arms around my neck and squeezing me tightly.

"Can Indie come too?" She asks.

"I'm sure she'd be more than happy to," I chuckle.

***

After the fastest execution of a road trip I've ever experienced, we're now twenty minutes away from Hilton Head.

If there is any way that I can make my little girl happy, I am willing to do it.

I shuffled around my workload, Indie cleared her schedule, and now we're taking a spontaneous overnight vacation.

Our bags were packed within the hour and we were on the road.

"Daddy, I need the toilet." Willow says from the backseat.

"Again?" I whine.

We only stopped half an hour ago for a toilet break. I'm blaming the XL Slurpee Indie got her from the gas station.

"We've only got twenty minutes left before we get to the hotel, can you hold it?" I ask, making eye contact with her through the dash mirror.

"Nope. I need to go, now." She looks at me with pleading eyes, seeing her bounce a little in her seat.

"Okay, okay." I roll my eyes and check the road signs for an upcoming gas station.

"That goddamn Slurpee," I laugh and Indie's head whips towards me.

"Hey! If she's gotta go, she's gotta go!" Indie replies, pushing my shoulder playfully.

***

Despite our last-minute plans, I managed to book us an apartment, only a four-minute walk from the beach itself.

Whatever my girls want, my girls get.

Willow is busy scrambling inside of her bag for her swimming bather, Indie is in the bathroom getting changed, all whilst I'm spread across the super-king bed.

I can't deny that the smell of the fresh ocean air is sensational.

It's been far too long since I've enjoyed a vacation, being a little preoccupied with work and… other things.

At least now, I get to spend quality time with the two people in the world who matter to me most.

"Daddy, help– me." Willow says, struggling to pull her *Barbie* costume over her body.

"Hm, maybe this is a little small. It's been a while since you've been to the beach and for sure, you've grown!" I laugh, tugging on the straps of the material to try and get it over her shoulders.

"There we go!" I cheer, clapping my hands together whilst Willow stands stiffly with her arms outstretched.

"This is– a little too tight." She whines, trying to stretch the material with her movements.

"We'll grab you something else, once we get closer to the beach. Okay?" I propose and she nods, walking in a strange way to grab her flip-flops.

The bathroom door opens and Indie walks out, without a care in the world and proceeding to get something out of her bag.

I'm standing, completely lost for words at the breathtaking view in front of me.

She's wearing a simple white bikini, with a transparent white cover-up that contrasts to her tan skin.

"Everything okay?" She turns to me whilst being bent over her bag.

Random pieces of hair slightly cover her face and she looks so effortlessly put together, without the need for any fancy accessories or makeup.

She is the definition of a natural beauty.

"Yeah… everything is perfect." I grin, admiring the dimples that pop out on her cheeks from my comments.

"I want one of those!" Willow beams, pointing at the bikini that Indie is wearing.

"A bikini?" I say with my face twisted.

"Yes! I'm a grown-up, nearly," She cheers, stomping her tiny feet in her floral daisy flip-flops.

"Hm, I'm not too sure about that, Lo." I ponder, running a hand through my stubble.

It's strange to think that my little girl isn't going to be like this forever. One day, she is going to grow up and be every bit the amazing woman that I imagine her to be.

"I'll think about it." I compromise, still uncertain whether I'm ready for her to change from her *Barbie* swimsuits to a more mature style.

***

We arrive at the beach, Willow in a newly bought sea-horse themed bikini. If it wasn't for Indie being here, I wouldn't have agreed to it. She encouraged me to give Willow the opportunity to feel more grown up, and insisted I was going to have to let go of her childhood one day, I may as well start getting used to it.

I can get used to the bikini situation, as long as that's it for the next five years.

God forbid the day she wants to have a girlfriend or a boyfriend.

Me and Indie stride together, hand in hand, with Willow bolting ahead with a unicorn float. Honestly, I've just been coerced into buying a ton of shit for this singular overnight trip.

The sand sinks in between my toes as we step onto the beach, the use of my flip-flops proves to be useless. Releasing Indie's hand, I reach down and pull them off, dusting off unnecessary sand.

"Ah, give me those," Indie says, holding her hands out.

I pass her the flip-flops and she puts them into her large white beach bag, filled with fresh towels for us to place on our pre-booked cabana.

"Here–" I hand Indie the small map with our cabana booking details on, "I'll stop off at the bar, grab us all a few drinks and I'll meet you there, any special requests?" I ask, pointing over to the crowded station. The sun beams down on us, making it hard to see despite wearing sunglasses.

"I'm a sucker for a piña colada," she laughs, displaying her stunning smile.

"You got it, baby." I wink and head off in the opposite direction from her.

I hear her shouting Willow in the distance and turn to see them meeting up, grasping onto each other's hands.

With the largest grin on my face, I continue walking away.

The beach bar blasts tropical themed music, providing the best vacation vibes. Everyone standing around is singing along, dancing and laughing. It really is a positive atmosphere, especially knowing I'm here with my two girls.

"What can I get ya?" A guy, no older than twenty-one, asks.

"Three straight bourbon shots, a bottled water, a piña colada, and a bottle of *Sprite.*" I respond, pulling out my phone to *Apple Pay* the bill.

"Coming straight up," he nods, moving at the speed of lightning.

I always dreamed of having a summer job, like this. I never got the opportunity to have much of my younger days, I had to mature real fast with having Willow so young. But, if I'm honest, I'm still learning how to be a father every day.

No two days are the same as a parent, you just have to take each day as it comes as you are constantly faced with more challenges, no matter how experienced you are.

I've made mistakes in the past, and I will probably make mistakes in the future. As long as I'm living for the moment, then I know everything will work itself out in the end. Sometimes, it may need a *little* intervention.

"That'll be sixty-four dollars, sir," he says, whilst pushing forward the tray of fulfilled drinks.

I scan my phone on the card machine, then proceed to drinking my three shots whilst I'm standing here.

Leaving the empty shot glasses, I slip my bottled water into my shorts pocket and grab the whole pineapple with the straw sticking out, and the *Sprite*.

As I walk over to our cabana, a warm breeze causes my open cheesecloth shirt to blow behind me, exposing my stomach.

My gaze draws in on Indie, sitting within the cabana and rubbing sun cream on the entirety of Willow's exposed skin.

See? There is so many things I'd forget about, I'm so glad she's here.

"Did you manage to pick up any ladies on your *Baywatch* walk over here?" Indie shouts to me, cupping her hands around the side of her mouth to project her voice.

Chuckling, I shake my head. For some reason, I'm actually blushing a little.

I'm used to compliments from random women, but when she says it, I actually swoon.

"One bottle of *Sprite*, for princess number one," I hand Willow the bottle and lean down to kiss her sticky sun creamed cheek.

"Thank you, Daddy!" She boasts, trying to open it straight away.

"And, one piña colada, for princess number two," I lean down, still holding the pineapple in my hands and press my lips to Indie's. This is an action I'll never grow tired of.

She hums against my lips in an attempt of a thank you. Pulling away, I look back at Willow to see she is still struggling with the lid.

"Here, let me help," I insist, taking the bottle from her and opening it with ease.

"Now, you sit here and relax–" I lean down and place Indie's sunglasses back over her eyes and kissing her forehead, "and *you*, are going to get a five second head start for our race to the ocean!" I shout as Willow squeals happily, putting her bottle down and setting off into a sprint in the direction of the water.

"Enjoy, my love," I beam, placing yet another kiss on Indie's luscious lips.

Throwing the bottled water from my pocket and my shirt onto the cabana, I take off after Willow, kicking the sand behind me as I run.

"Willow!" I taunt, seeing her twist her head behind to see the distance between us.

She screams and begins to giggle, her legs buckling slightly causing her to slow down a little.

I gain on her and she tries even harder to push her legs to their limits as she keeps turning back to see how close I am.

Just as I come up behind her, I stretch my arms out and grab her under her arms, lifting her into the air as I continue to run.

"Daddy! Daddy! Put me down!" She shrieks, flailing her legs in front of me as we near the water.

"I don't think so! You're coming in with me!" I gush, bringing her in to me so her back is flat against my chest.

My feet enter the water and my pace slows down, but still fast enough to be splashing through the water and sinking us in until we're up to my hips, deep.

She screams and thrashes against me, her adorable giggles spill out of her uncontrollably.

Letting her go, she stands on her tiptoes and uses her hands to throw a wave of water towards me.

"Oh, is that how it's going to be?" I raise my eyebrow with a huge smile on my face and she opens her eyes wide, trying to dart away from me, but the water resistance proves to be too much.

"Hold your breath!" I shout, before grabbing her and flipping myself so that she is on top of me as we sink under the crystal blue water together.

Bringing us straight back up to the surface, she coughs and splutters, throwing her hair back and out of her face.

"That's it!" She screams and dives forward, gripping onto my back like a koala bear and trying to pull me back under the surface.

"Oh no! She's got me, ahh!" I pretend to fall under the water and I'm internally laughing as we go under the water again as it's backfired on her, taking her down with me.

Bopping us back up, she lets out exasperated breaths and fans her arms out across the water to steady herself.

"You're so annoying!" She whines, rolling her eyes as she spits out some of the sea water.

"But, unbelievably cool," I counteract, tipping my head to the side to let some water out of my ears. I sink into the water so that I'm down to her level and she swims forward towards me.

"Daddy?" She says, and draws in until she's face to face with me.

"Yeah, Lo?" I respond, waiting for her to continue.

"I love you," She grins, the water runs down her face and into her eyes, so she keeps blinking harshly.

"I love you too, my baby girl," I beam, maintaining eye contact with her.

Within a split second, my eyes are burning and my mouth is slammed shut from the wave of water that's just hit my face.

"I knew that'd be your weakness," she grins, then turns to swim away as fast as her little legs can go.

Shaking my head, I dive after her, "oh, now it's on!"

Chapter 20

Indie

2 Weeks Later

Things have progressed pretty quickly between us, but there is no time like the present. That, and the fact we have a deadline.

We have a preliminary hearing at court in two weeks which determines the temporary custody of Willow until the official verdict has been granted.

We're confident that it's in the court's best interests for Willow to remain with us, rather than uprooting her across the country temporarily.

Reed wanted us to break the news to Willow together but I insisted it was something he had to do alone. I already felt like I was intruding on their family before Allie's bed got cold, I didn't want to force Willow into any sort of reaction to the news if she was uncomfortable that I was there.

She's the kind of sweet little girl that considers your feelings. She's very mature for her age and I'm sure, Allie is to thank for that. She's raised a phenomenal daughter.

As it turned out, Willow was actually ecstatic, she claimed that if she ever wanted another woman in her life, she would choose me. This solidified that I'd made the right decision, to help her stay with her dad.

As much as this marriage will be fake, my love for Willow never will be. I loved her long before any of this happened and I will make sure that she never experiences any kind of hurt again. I want to be the best role model that I can be so that she can excel in life and become the brilliant woman she was always destined to be.

Today is the day that we move into our new house. It's not modest in any way, Reed insisted that the budget was anything I wanted it to be. At first, I felt incredibly uncomfortable shopping around for a house for me to live in temporarily, but I thought about the fact that Reed and Willow no longer have that feminine lead role in their lives, the motherly figure who wants to make sure her family have the best.

Reed urged that we choose a house in Buckhead, even when I told him that the house prices are extortionate.

Nevertheless, I stand before a newly renovated 1930's Mediterranean house. It is cream colored with every window and door being charcoal black, matching the gates to the driveway.

The cobble-stoned driveway leads to the sheltered outbuilding that sports a balcony above it.

It's a *humble,* five-bedroom four-bathroom home, with two lounges, an extremely large kitchen, dining room and an office.

Every other home I'd toured before this one didn't seem to fulfill anything, they were all too clinical, too modern and lack of character.

This one took my breath away the second I pulled onto the driveway, the entire building was full of personality and had the true feeling of a 'home', embedded into it.

I sent the home online link to Reed to gather his thoughts on it. He responded with a text message a few hours later telling me his offer had been accepted.

I'm guessing he liked it as much as me?

When I got in contact with the Realtor agent, she told me how Reed had inputted an offer over the asking price.

That night, I made sure he knew how much I appreciated it.

He returned to work recently, and I've warned him to take it easy and not to become so enthralled by it again. So far, he's been home every night around 6.PM and had his weekends off, Willow has thrived.

The removal men are carrying in all of our new furniture, each piece signposted with the correct room for it to go in. Willow is running around in the the yard, the sprinklers flittering on and off. Reed has taken the day off to help out with the moving process, it's odd to see him in joggers and a loose tee, or intended to be loose. It's practically molded to his abs with the sweat, his hair is damp and has began to grow curly, emphasizing the epitome of *DILF*.

"Throw me my cap." Reed calls to me from the removal's truck.

Men are swarming around me with boxes as I stand in the driveway, taking in the reality of my new home.

I reach into the half-closed box and see it's full of different baseball caps, some vintage looking and others new. I grab a cream colored one and throw it to him, which he puts on backwards, tucking his hair out of his face. Wow, I never really took Reed for a cap kind of guy, turns out he has a full collection of *Atlanta Braves* hats.

Willow comes barreling towards me, her dress partially soaked and her hair wet.

"What on earth am I going to do with you, Lo?" I sing and swing her around, careful not to get in the way of any of the removal men.

I have always called Willow by her full name; not aware she even had a nickname. Reed is the only person who calls her by it, but after spending so much time with them both its slowly become a part of my vocabulary too.

We've had a few occasions where Willow has broken down over the loss of her mom, it's usually triggered by things you'd think were insignificant, but to her they're everything.

One time, we were shopping in the supermarket, and we walked down the cereal aisle. She took once glance at the Lucky Charms and burst into tears. Neither me, or Reed, knew why, so we left all our shopping and drove her straight back home. Later that night, she told us how every single weekend they would visit the pond with a box of Lucky Charms. They would sit together and pick out all of the colored marshmallow cereals, snacking on them whilst admiring the swans.

She told us how her mom always referred to her as a 'Swan' as it symbolized her grace and beauty, how she couldn't wait to see Willow grow up and be old enough to perform the '*Swan Lake*' routine. It brought me to tears, the thoughtfulness behind her kind words, the significance it had on Willow. For this very reason, I instructed the interior designer to design Willow's new bedroom as entirely 'swan' themed.

I never want her to forget about the amazing woman that Allie was, I want to keep her memory alive as much as possible and make sure Willow knows that we want her to remain in the present. She hasn't seen her bedroom yet, both me and Reed have been discussing just how much she's going to love it.

"That's the last of it!" A man with a Texan accent calls to Reed.

Reed hops down out of the removal's van and stands with his hands on his hips. Willow has hold of my hand as we stare at her dad, he stares back with a huge grin.

"Hang on a second," Reed says, pulling his phone out of his pocket.

Me and Willow glance at each other and pull a funny face.

"Perfect, my girls."

We look back at Reed and he has his phone held above him.

Oh, he's taking a photo of us in front of our new home.

"Reed get in the picture!" I call out.

"Hey, would you mind taking a photo of us please?" I ask one of the removal men leaving the house.

"Sure."

Reed hands him the phone and jogs over to join us. He wraps his arm around my waist and leans down in the middle of me and Willow, cupping her shoulders with his other arm.

"Say cheese!" I cheer as we all pose in unison.

"Thanks man," Reed leaves our side and takes his phone back.

He pulls out a few bills and hands them to the removal men as a tip for their help today, as well as thanking them individually. I am really admiring the man I see before me; I can see how Allie loved him all of those years.

The men pull out of the driveway and I turn to look at the house again. I take in the smell of the fresh air, the sounds of the birds in the trees. This neighborhood is a hell of a lot quieter than the sketchy place my apartment resided in.

Reed told me he'd handle the sale of my apartment and just to focus on making our new house, a home.

It's been kind of nice to have a man take control for once, it makes up for all the years I've carried Scott through life. Speaking of, he's been awfully quiet, anxiously quiet. He swore that he was taking his share of the business and so far, nada.

"So, who wants to go and see their new bedroom!" I cheer.

Willow jumps up and down in delight, repeating *'me'* a thousand times over.

We turn towards the huge glass double doors that showcase the center of the property, Reed grasps my hand and squeezes it slightly. I peer down at our interlocked hands and crack a smile at the intimacy. It's slowly becoming more normal for us to interact this way, we're growing comfortable with the idea of us being a couple.

Willow walks with us as we ascend the huge staircase.

"Left or right?" She eagerly asks.

"It's a right." I smirk.

We come up to a black wooden door with a golden handle, I stop us before she can enter.

"Lo, if there is anything at all you don't like, anything at all you'd want to change, just say so. This is your bedroom and I want it to be perfect for you." I place my hand on her cheek and rub it slightly with my thumb.

She nods, and I let go, gesturing to the door handle.

The hallway fills with light, and she gasps at the room before her. The room is huge and bright with the number of windows on the opposing wall. The carpet is a plush cream that your feet sink into when you step on it, the walls are covered in a light pink wallpaper that is covered in white swans and gold crowns. The room matches with golden accents, a dressing table that has a swan carved out of the wood at the top of the mirror, a white dresser with white swan handles and a large white chandelier above the bed. The bed is a king size, and the white wood matches the dressing table, the same swan carved out of the wood at the very top. A princess style drape covers the upper portion of the bed, fairy lights are spread around the headboard of it, the bedspread like the wallpaper but opposing colors. There are several decorative pillows, swans, crowns, clouds and a ballet slipper one. *Nice touch.*

It's only then that I notice the other side of the room, lined with floor to ceiling mirrors, a ballet barre covers the expanse of it. The carpet cuts off at a point and the rest is solid wood flooring.

Who...?

"I made a little call to the designer and asked if it was possible, turns out it is." Reed gestures to the ballet barre portion of the room and shrugs as if it was nothing.

What he doesn't understand is how incredibly valuable that is, how he has taken onboard his daughter's wishes and made them come true.

Willow lets out a sob as we rush to her side, the both of us concerned.

"Willow are you okay, honey?" I ask as Reed rubs her back.

She turns around to us, her face streaked with tears. She wraps an arm around each of our necks and brings us in for a huge group hug and we all tighten our hold on each other. My eyes begin to line with tears at the emotion she is pouring out.

"Thank you, so much," she whispers.

She deserves everything, she is the sweetest and most humble nine-year-old I've ever met. I couldn't wish for a better child.

"You've managed to keep mommy alive!" She cries, gesturing to the numerous swans all around the room.

We nod, both of us sniffling and proud.

"We hope you love it." Reed gestures to the room.

"Are you kidding? You are the best daddy in the world!" She tackles him to the floor, showering him with kisses. I think hearing both of them laughing together is the single most harmonious sound I've ever heard.

"I think this calls for a celebration" Reed cheers.

***

We're all seated on the living room floor, surrounded with cardboard boxes. Our half-eaten takeout sits on the rug before us as the fire crackles in the antique fireplace. We have the TV set up on the floor playing an old episode of *The Suite Life of Zack & Cody*.

Willow lays in my lap whilst I stroke her hair. Reed is keeping himself preoccupied as he focuses on some work on his laptop.

It's dark outside now, the huge, curved windows grant our eyes access to the infinity of stars beyond us, the moonlight glowing.

It's odd how at peace I feel, the calm that's came with this house move is like nothing I've ever felt before. This step has felt monumental to all of our lives, a change that none of us wanted to make originally but needed to happen. It is like the beginning of normality for Reed and Willow, so they can truly begin to live as a family, and I am so thankful that I can be a part of it.

Reed closes his laptop and looks over at us and I notice how his eyes glisten under the moonlight. A lazy smile crosses his face as he looks at us in admiration.

"I just need to finish some work in the office, don't bother waiting up for me I'll probably be a while." Reed states.

I nod whilst Willow sits up to look at him clearer.

"Don't stay up too late daddy," her voice is quiet and almost sad.

Guilt spreads over Reed's face and he rubs a hand over his stubble. He lets out a small breath before turning away.

"Night girls." He says coldly.

What the fuck?

"Willow? What did you mean?"

She wraps her arms around my neck and sits across my lap as she snuggles into my chest. I return the embrace and wait patiently.

"Before you were here, daddy used to stay up *all* night."

"Oh, Lo. I'm sure you know sometimes your daddy has a lot of work to do, sometimes adults go to bed later so that they have chance to catch up on things." I offer a reassuring smile.

She shakes her head and pulls away from me.

"Daddy doesn't work in the office; he drinks that rotten stuff that mommy hated."

I furrow my brows.

"I love him so much, but he can get upset or angry when he drinks it. He goes a little crazy and sometimes he can be too loud, which wakes me up." She sighs.

I bite my lip, wondering how much of this she's possibly seen.

The two weeks I've been living with Reed I haven't seen that at all, he comes to bed with me every night usually. It didn't really set alarm bells off in my head that he wants to work in the office, but maybe the fact that he asked me not to wait up for him, should have.

"I'll see to him, don't you be worrying yourself about it. Now, I think little miss needs some beauty sleep, don't you?" I rub my thumb across her cheek, trying to reassure her.

Her mood is totally off, and I can tell she's worried about Reed. She obviously knows him better than I do. I'll make sure before I go to sleep that I check up on him and make sure that he's not doing anything stupid.

Despite this entire thing being fake, I still have Willow at the forefront of my mind and I won't allow him to do anything that would cause her upset, it doesn't matter that she's not my daughter.

I lay out some pajamas for Willow and leave the room for a moment, allowing her to get changed. Leaning over the banister of the staircase, I look down into the hallway, connected to the office. The door remains closed and I can spot a light peeking out from underneath, but I can't hear anything out of the ordinary. I push away and knock on Willow's door.

"Lo, are you ready?" I double check. She responds with a *yes*.

Opening the door, I see her propped on the end of her bed, her frame appearing tiny in comparison the huge bed behind her. I reach into her dressing room drawers, pulling out the new pink hairbrush.

I beckon for her to sit on the dressing table stool, the fluffy pink fur on the stool tickles my bare legs as I stand against it. She sits down in front of me slightly slouched and I begin to remove the hair tie, letting her brunette waves cascade around her shoulders. I brush her hair as gently as I can, untangling all of the knots that have accumulated over the day. I start to Dutch braid her hair, one of the many perks of growing up with sisters is the amount of practice you can get on braiding. I finish up and tie it with a purple bobble to match her pajamas.

"Where did you learn to do that?" Willow asks.

"I grew up alongside two younger sisters, we used to play 'beauty salons' and give each other makeovers. I got pretty good at it, especially Dutch braids." I smile at the memory.

"Oh." She looks down.

"What's up Lo?" I walk around to the front of her and crouch down on my knees, placing my hand on hers.

"Well… just I'm never going to get to experience that. Not now with mom being gone." She fiddles with her fingers and doesn't meet my eyes.

I didn't think too much around the fact that she is an only child, I do feel for her because I've had my sisters for as long as I can remember. There isn't much of an age gap between the three of us so I've never had to go through the phase of 'wanting' a sibling. But this conversation is incredibly awkward, I can't reassure her that she may possibly have one because I have no idea what Reed's intentions are, once our agreement is over.

I don't know if he'll remarry and begin a family with someone else, but I'm sure that's exactly what Willow expects from me. She's probably getting her hopes up that it could be a possibility when me and Reed both know it's a wasted wish.

I sigh and pull her in for a hug and try to comfort her.

"I'm sure you'll have a sibling one day." I console her.

She yawns and pulls back from the hug.

"I'll just have to dream about it whilst I sleep," she says as a wave of tiredness lines her voice.

She dives onto the expanse of the bed. Her body sinks into the plushness of the duvet covers, I feel like I could just about join her at this rate, the bed looks so cozy. I tuck her in, popping a small peck on her forehead, bidding her goodnight.

On my way out, I use the light switch to dim the chandelier to make the room dark enough for her to sleep and close the door quietly.

I stand with my back against the wall, taking in the difference of my routine compared to only a few weeks ago. I feel like I'm starting to come down with 'impostor syndrome', this doesn't feel like my life. It feels like I've shifted out of my life and stepped directly into Allie's shoes. I'm not sure what I expected truthfully, but transforming from an independent, businesswoman to a family-oriented woman overnight has really begun to take its toll on me.

Hearing the office door open below me, I stay put, listening to what he's doing.

His footsteps disappear towards… the kitchen?

I don't quite have the house mapped out enough yet to differentiate. Waiting a little while, his footsteps don't return so I take this as my chance to go downstairs and into his office.

I tiptoe on the white marble staircase, my ballerina feet allowing me to be as graceful as possible.

Peering down the central hallway to the kitchen, I can see that the garden light is on, the back door left open slightly.

He's…outside?

I dart across the hallway and make a quick left, slipping inside of his office. My chest is heaving from the angst of sneaking around, even when there is practically no reason for me to be doing so. The office is lined with light-wood bookcases and shelving, a large wooden desk is central in the room, a computer sits in the middle of it with hundreds of papers spread around. The computer is on and a crystal decanter is placed next to the keyboard, half-filled.

So, he is drinking in here?

It's strange how he hasn't invited me to join him and wants to be sitting here alone with it. I creep around to his leather office chair, the seat still warm.

I shake the mouse to remove the standby screen and the computer comes to life displaying... nothing.

Not a single tab open.

I startle at the sound of the back door slamming shut, followed by footsteps.

Shit.

I crouch down and crawl under the desk, counting my lucky stars for the wooden wall that shields me from the view of the door.

"Indie?" I hear him call.

I wince, hoping he isn't going to go looking for me. His footsteps begin to come closer again, I try to hold my breath and tuck myself tighter into a ball, praying he isn't going to see me hidden under here. I'm not concerned if he finds me, it just looks a little weird, right?

Hearing the office door close, it shuts off any external sounds and seals me inside with him.

He walks around the desk and I swear if he gets close enough, he will hear my heart thumping out of my chest. His legs stroll past the gap where the chair sits, slightly tucked in.

My ears prick at the sound of him popping the top off the decanter, followed by the sounds of him filling up a glass.

My pulse thrums in my ears, making it hard to figure out if my breaths are quiet enough.

He pulls back the chair and I flinch, pulling myself in as far as I can physically go as he sits down, tucking back in slightly. All I have a view of right now is his crotch in his joggers, I mean it's definitely not a bad view to have.

Sitting with his legs parted, bent at the knee, I notice he's not wearing a shirt anymore, I can see just up to his navel.

He groans and takes another drink. I blink a few times trying to clear my vision, it's a lot darker under here than the rest of the room.

"Hey, Faye. It's me." *Faye?* He must be making a call.

"Yeah, yeah. Any update on the autopsy report?" *Autopsy report?*

"Hm. Right. Can you put an urgent request on this please. Yes, yes I know it's personal and I'm overstepping the boundaries but can you just do as you've been asked. Much appreciated." Woah, is that how Reed speaks to all of his employees?

I'm presuming she's an employee, this sounds work related.

"Oh, one more thing. Tell Scott I said hi." He laughs.

Scott?

Faye?

Scott and Faye?

This can't be a coincidence.

How does he know Scott?

Wait, so his slutty mistress *works* for Reed?

None of this adds up, how does–

My nose tickles for a moment before I burst out into a sneeze, unable to stop myself.

Oh fuck.

I cringe, knowing I've given away my position. Now, this definitely looks weird.

His chair scoots back and he peers down, his gaze burning into mine as I smile at him sheepishly, offering a small wave as if this is a casual way to find someone.

"Indie, what the fuck are you doing?" his voice is angry, not the least bit of kindness. I don't know how to respond, do I tell him the truth about what Willow said? I don't have an answer for him at the minute.

"What the fuck are you doing in my office, Indie?"

I flinch at his raised voice and begin to scramble out from underneath the desk, as if it makes any difference.

"I… Well I–"

"Were you spying on me?" He accuses.

"No!" I burst, hoping he doesn't think that.

Even though that's practically what I'm doing. I wasn't meaning to spy on him, I just wanted to check in on him and he wasn't here and well, oh God. I don't know.

"So, what is it you call someone who sneaks into your office and hides under your desk, listening to private phone calls?"

I tighten my lips.

"Well, when you put it like that…" I try to joke it off, but his face is entirely unforgiving, his eyes are narrowed at me.

"Do you think you had any right to do that?" I look around the room nervously, not sure how to answer without pissing him off, even more.

Within a split second he grips me by the neck and pushes me backwards into the bookcase, earning a gasp from me.

"I said, do you think you had any right to do that?" he snarls into my ear.

My eyes grow wide in shock as my body begins to shake with fear and I can barely remember to breathe. His grip tightens around my neck, warranting me to shake my head ferociously, as best as I can considering the circumstances. He stares into my eyes, his usual bright blue eyes have turned a stormy gray, his face is screwed up and his nostrils flaring.

I flick my sight between each of his eyes, my arms limp at my sides as he presses his body against mine.

"I think we need to set some boundaries, Indie. Don't you?" he purrs.

The tone sends shock waves directly to my lower region, I shift my weight causing a pleasurable friction between my thighs. He leans forward and his lips are only inches away from my own. I part my lips in response, looking into his eyes hungrily.

"Rule number one," he whispers.

I shiver, igniting my body with goosebumps. He keeps one hand to my neck and uses the other to slightly lift my tank top.

"You don't enter my office, without knocking." he declares.

I start to nod my head when he tugs at my short's waistband. I gulp. The slickness between my thighs only grows the longer he stares at me like I'm the most desirable item on the menu.

"Rule number two,"

I practically groan at the arousal lining his voice. My breaths are coming out harsher, but not from the pressure he's placing on my neck.

"You shall never enter my office when I'm not here."

His hand draws closer to my aching cunt and I almost lose all sanity in that singular moment.

"Rule number three,"

I can barely keep my eyes open as the insatiable longing for him envelops me.

Touch me, please.

"If those rules are broken, you will be punished."

I moan in response, hoping that these rules were in place before I walked in here. I can feel myself pulsating with the feral need I have for him, the salacious mind of mine already playing out what I want to happen.

His fingers thrust into me without warning as I cry out at the burn and the sensitivity. He holds me in place by my neck as my legs buckle slightly, the grip cutting off my oxygen. His fingers delve into me recklessly as his thumb massages my clit, my climax rushing to the peak.

My moans have become strangled and I can hear the wetness of myself with his rapid movements. My body begins to spasm as the orgasm starts to spill over. My head feels like it's floating in the clouds–

He pulls his fingers out and releases my neck as my eyes snap open wide. I pant and look at him, a devilish grin on his face. My jaw is dropped open, desperate for him to return me to cloud nine.

"Reed," my voice is sensual and deep.

He takes a step towards me, like an animal stalking its prey.

"I'm going to punish you now."

Wait, *what?*

That wasn't punishment enough?

He tsks and begins to turn away from me before he abruptly grabs me by my hair and throws me face down onto his desk. I squeal and tears spring to my eyes at the sting as he yanks my shorts to my ankles. Out of instinct, my arms spread wide to grip the desk and he takes that as his opportunity to knock my legs wider apart. He pushes into me, filling me fully as I whimper at the feeling.

"I want to hear those filthy fucking cries," he growls into my ear.

I am officially making it my mission to *not cry*.

He twists my hair around his hand, so I bring myself up higher to lessen the strain on my scalp. He withdraws from me completely and slams himself back inside as my body arches to try and accommodate the size of him.

"You take me so fucking good." he spits, pounding his hips against my ass hard enough the skin begins to slap.

The moans fall out of me uncontrollably, his grip tightening on my hair to the point I'm almost standing vertically.

His hand reaches around and gropes my tits through my tank and he groans with frustration. Without saying anything, he tears the tank top enough to rip it off me.

Holy shit. I am so fucking turned on right now.

Finally satisfied, he grabs both of my breasts and leans backwards, thrusting upwards into me, driving his cock to the hilt.

"Oh god, Reed." I sob, the pressure building within me so intense it feels like the floor beneath me has disappeared.

Knowing that he is completely infatuated with me and gaining this reaction from him, drives me insane. Just when it builds to the point my legs shake uncontrollably, he switches.

His palm pushes my back and I'm face down on the desk again. He pushes a hand over my face, the hair, sweat and saliva all mixing into one. The other hand squeezes my ass cheek as he rocks into me hard. His hand comes down on my ass cheek hard, causing a stinging sensation that heightens the sensitivity in my pussy. I whimper which causes him to do it again.

I'm completely dazed with pleasure.

"Do you think you'll come into my office uninvited again?" he says breathlessly.

I am almost completely lost in the kingdom of euphoria that I can barely hear him. I squeeze my eyes shut, as well as my legs, to try to control my delirium. A harsh slap sounds on my other ass cheek and I can't help but cry out. If he carries on, I'm going to come all over his new desk.

"Answer the question, Indie."

I try and grasp a glance of him behind me, my vision disturbed with the amount of hair that covers my face. I nod my head, knowing it'll send him feral. He growls and places more weight on my face as he pushes as far into me as nature will allow.

"Ahh." I sound out, my body struggling to cope.

"I want to hear more of that, my dirty little slut."

He pummels into me, barely pulling out and crashing back inside. He then lets go of my face, grabbing both of my arms behind me and yanking me upright.

"You think that this is meant to be enjoyable for you?" His words are laced with venom.

I moan louder, trying to defy his point. He parts my mouth with his fingers and shoves two of them inside of my mouth to the back of my throat. I gag at the roughness and he only presses deeper. My eyes line with tears and the room is filled with the slapping of our skin and the choking noises coming from my throat.

Whatever it is he's doing, it's fucking working.

The forbidden climax is teasing me, it swells low in my abdomen with every individual thrust as Reed throws filthy words at me, telling me how much I don't deserve to be rewarded with an orgasm. It only tempts my body more, knowing that it wants something that it shouldn't. Feels all the more familiar.

I try to mask my impending doom but my body tenses as my vision starts to become clouded with stars and my brain buzzes with ecstasy.

At the last moment I cave, and throw myself forward onto the desk, but barely reach it as Reed snaps me back up by my hair, the stinging feeling intensifying everything. My body tries to collapse in on itself as I implode, a rush of bliss filling me from the inside out. My juices run down my legs as I feel Reed tense behind me, his body folds over mine and his grunts turn into a forceful cry, feeling his warmth fill me.

We're both panting for air, our chests causing our bodies to rise and fall. My legs feel completely weak, my ass and throat feel sore and I'm still trying to come down from my place in the clouds.

Reed pulls out of me and spins me around, his cheeks are flushed, and his chest is lined with sweat, his cock swollen. He shoves his fingers inside of me unexpectedly, taking my breath away. He pulls his fingers out and lifts them between us, they're lined with a sticky white substance. I glance between his fingers and him, a sadistic look across his face.

"Suck on my fingers and taste how good we are together."

I gulp, slowly nodding. I wrap my hand around his thick wrist and bring his hand closer to my mouth and take my time licking and sucking on his lengthy fingers. The sweet but salty liquid lines my mouth and eventually my throat, heating my core at the mixture we've created. He moans in delight until I pull away, his fingers now clean but still lined with my saliva.

We look at each other and I can't help it, but I burst out laughing. He looks at me with confusion, but I can't stop myself.

I'm full-on belly laughing at Reed Breckenridge after the most heated, intense sexual experience I've had yet.

"What?" he chuckles, my laughter seemingly contagious and flashing me his divine smile.

"I just… did not expect *that*," I confess.

He purses his lips and shrugs, as if this was no big deal to him. He may have had sex like that hundreds of times but for me, it was a first.

Definitely one to remember.

I find Reed's t-shirt in the corner of the room and seize the opportunity to steal it. I slip it over my head, untucking my hair from the collar.

"Just perfect." He mutters quietly, biting his clenched fist.

Blushing, I shake my head, trying to deflect his compliment.

"I can't believe you're all mine." He beams.

Something about the way he said that has my stomach doing backflips. Something about it just made the terms of our contract visually blurry, and I don't think either of us care to rectify that.

Chapter 21

Indie

"These strawberries are sensational!" Erica, one of the bridesmaids confesses.

I pick at the blueberries and top up my champagne flute whilst Lola finishes getting her hair styled.

Gracie is sitting beside me, feasting on a plate of pancakes. I swear her metabolism works on overdrive as she eats a horrendous amount of junk and remains under one-hundred-and-thirty pounds, the number I've battled with for a couple of years. I'll stick to the carb-free for now.

Despite my taller frame, I was blessed with hips and tits after stepping down from my competitive career, which I'm sure, are the reason I can't lose those extra pounds.

I've already had my makeup professionally done and we have around an hour until the ceremony. The Bridal Room is a generous size, sporting an array of 'girly' decorations. There are five 'Hollywood' style dressing tables lined up on one side of the room and on the opposite wall sits every kind of hair styling tool.

It's interesting, considering most women hire professionals to come in to do the hard work.

I *wonder if they've ever been used?*

In the center of the room is a long glass table that currently has a breakfast spread across the expanse of it. There are pastries, every fruit imaginable, pancakes and several bottles of champagne.

All of our dresses are locked away in the back room, none of us risking putting them on until the last minute. Knowing my luck, I'd end up with some sort of monstrosity art design of champagne and orange juice on mine. I'm not dancing with the devil today.

I planned on attending today alone, but Lola insisted that I bring Reed along. I swear she is rooting for my love life more than her own. Bridget is taking care of Willow for the weekend whilst we're away for the night, we're two hours away from home and I already had a room booked here, apart from it was meant to be with Scott.

Surely it won't cause any harm, if anything being seen publicly together will help our 'relationship' along.

Surprisingly, I ended up calling Harrison yesterday. He knew who I was as soon as he picked up. My guess is he actually already had my number, he probably swiped my contact details from the contract. I've invited him to come over once we're home, unbeknownst to Reed. Reed still hasn't fully opened up to me about the situation with his family, he usually skims over it and describes his relationship with his family as 'strained'. But there's got to be more to the story than that.

In regards to family drama, my mother is also here. I've kept my distance and barely acknowledged her except to ensure that her flute is only filled up with the alcohol-free champagne. We've placed a small red tape around the rim of each alcohol-free bottle and removed labels so that nobody gains suspicion of Lola's pregnancy, so it works out even better that we can keep our mother sober.

My big sisterly duty is to ensure that today runs as smoothly as possible and Lola has the wedding that she's always dreamed of.

The wedding planner rushes in, a dense folder in her arms and she looks at us still in 'Bridal Party' pajamas.

"Girls! Why are we not dressed?" Her high pitch making me wince.

Why do they always give the impression of hyper chihuahuas?

"We're just about to." I offer a reassuring smile, hoping to relieve her blood pressure a little bit.

I glance over at Lola and she looks absolutely incredible, the stylist is adding a few diamantes to her loose french braid and after that it'll be dressing time.

"So Indie, I've heard you've got a new boy toy," Dear Mother's whiny voice curses my ears.

"Celia, as much as I appreciate you acting like you care, I don't. Please don't ask about my personal life when you are not part of it." I bite out, not wanting to engage in conversation with her longer than needs be.

"Oh, but what happened to dear old Scotty? He was great, I really liked him. What did you do for him to leave you – Wait. I bet I can guess. You spent too much time at that silly little dance school." She snarls at me.

Well, this woman certainly knows how to press my buttons.

In all honesty, I haven't even thought about Scott or his mistress in a long while.

Oh.

I briefly remember the conversation Reed had on the phone in his office, my mind was a little preoccupied from the events that followed.

Faye. Yes, the lovely redhead that uprooted my entire life, is employed by Reed, or so I suspect.

"Like I said, just keep out of it."

Me and Lola exchange looks in the mirror and oddly enough, I know I have to be the bigger person in this situation, despite her supposedly being a 'mature' adult. She acts like a gossiping teenager that is trying to stir up trouble for a little bit of drama.

I turn away and walk up behind Lola, placing a gentle hand on her shoulder.

"You look absolutely stunning sis. Greg, is one lucky man." I beam.

"Oh stop, it's too early for tears!" she sobs, fanning her face to try and dry up the water in her eyes.

She stands in her white silk robe, her skin a shade darker than usual thanks to her spray tan.

We all gather around the buffet table and I take the opportunity to fill up five flutes with champagne, filling up Lola's and my mother's with a red tape bottle, first.

She is still completely unaware which makes things a lot easier.

"Let's have a toast!" I gesture to the glasses and begin to hand them out, using the mental note of whose drink is whose.

"To Lola, who is about to lose her thorns!" I joke, making reference to her soon to be name change. We all clink glasses and cheer, taking a sip.

"Girls you have five minutes to get into your dresses before I kick you out of here without them!" The wedding planner is back.

Rolling my eyes, I go into the closet to retrieve my dress, unzipping it from the overcoat as the stunning gold silk dress hangs on the plush hanger. The color is phenomenal and makes my green eyes pop.

Entering a cubicle, I remove my button up short pajamas. I pop on a seamless nude thong and decide to go bra-less as the spaghetti straps and thin silk look best without any indentation from undergarments.

Slipping the dress on over my head, I shimmy around until it's past my ass, the rest of the material drops to the floor, flowing and free. The dress hugs me tight around my breasts and waist but the bottom half of the dress is loose and breezy. Sliding on my nude strappy heels, I take a look at myself in the mirror, readjusting my curls and positioning the metal gold leaf headband.

The ring Reed has given me makes the dress look like a million dollars, as if I'm about to walk out onto the red carpet. I check my teeth one more time, applying some extra gloss and powder, before regrouping.

Lola stands central in the room, her gorgeous white A-line gown complementing her in every way she'd hoped it would. Of course, I've already seen the dress but to see her in all of her glory brings a tear to my eye.

My little sister has dreamed of this moment for as long as I can remember. As our father isn't here anymore, Greg's father offered to walk her down the aisle. I recall it being a super emotional moment for them all. Well, at least I won't have to worry about that for my city hall wedding.

"I just want to thank you all for being here today, I've dreamed of this moment for my entire life and all of you helped it come true. Keeping it short and sweet, let's get me married!"

We all join in, cheering and clapping as the wedding planner guides us out of the bridal dressing room.

We cross the gravel walkway, towards the entrance of the hall.

I spare one last smile at a nervous looking Lola and stand at the double doors, waiting for my signal to enter. I know Lola sat Reed rather close to the front in our 'family' section, not quite next to me.

I hear the violin begin to play and the adrenaline courses through my veins.

Don't fuck up, I chant in my head.

The wedding planner gives me a thumbs up and I grip onto my small bouquet as if my life depends on it, taking a shaky step forward.

I walk along the back row of people and everyone's heads are turned in my direction. I plaster a smile on my face as I calmly walk down the aisle, Gracie now on my tail.

One step in front of the other.

I hold my head higher to avoid looking at my feet, I'm so anxious I'm going to trip and ruin the entire thing.

I peer at Greg at the alter, his face is lit up with anticipation to see his darling bride. I'm so glad that Lola met someone like Greg who was willing to give her the fairy-tale wedding, regardless of what he wanted.

Surveying the huge crowd, I near the front and that's when my eyes focus in on the blue eyes that are piercing through mine.

The way he's looking at me, makes me feel naked, like he's never seen a woman before, like I'm the only person in the room.

My fake smile transforms into a cheesy grin, and he returns it. I know the exact reason I've gained that smile.

'Dimples' he mouths.

Blushing instantly, I look away before I forget where I am.

I reach the end of the aisle and stand to the side, followed by Gracie, and then Erica.

The big moment is here.

I grab a tissue from the inside of my bouquet, dotting away the tears that have formed.

Yes, I came prepared.

Lola's veil covers over her face and Greg takes one look at her before his eyes begin to flood. They are *so* meant to be.

I hope I can experience a love like those two one day.

As I turn around to look at Reed, I notice his gaze isn't on Lola, it's on *me.*

***

The day has been perfect, watching Lola transition from a Thorne to a Bateson was one of my proudest moments as a sister. She's gotten the life she wants, and she has been blessed with the gift of an unborn child. I'd be lying if I said I wasn't envious, but it couldn't have happened to a better person.

Reed sits beside me on the circular table, he's been obsessed with me in this dress, insisting that I need to wear something similar to the city hall. I told him that I actually want to sign our marriage papers before I'm shoved into a janitor closet so he can have his way with me.

I haven't given much thought to what I'll actually wear to the city hall, I assumed I'd opt for something a lot more casual but you only get married once right? Ha, maybe not so in my case.

The clinking of a glass draws the rooms attention as Greg stands up with his drink, his suit jacket now draped over the back of his chair.

"Good evening, everyone. I'd just like to begin by saying how incredible today has been and it would never have been anything close without my beautiful wife beside me." The crowd awes at his sweet words.

"Thank you, to everyone who came out to celebrate this special day with us, it's been an important factor to our planning to have our family here, both me and Lola are huge on family and we can't wait to begin our lives together as a married couple."

Reed grips my hand and squeezes it as the tingling sensation works its way up my arm, connecting straight to my heart.

"But, I do have something to show you all."

We all look around in confusion. I of course, play along.

The projector screen switches from a slideshow of pictures of Lola and Greg from all walks of life to a sonogram image displaying the tiny baby, with surprisingly distinguishable features. It has a tiny little button nose and puckered lips, its legs are stretched out long.

The room erupts into celebration as Greg turns around and gives Lola the squeeze of her life, kissing her and then her tummy as she stands up proudly. We applaud and Greg receives numerous pats on the back from his groomsmen and the shaking of hands.

"Wow, it's been a long time since I've seen one of those." Reed coughs, his demeanor slightly awkward.

"It's adorable, isn't it?" I stare fondly at the image of my tiny niece or nephew, my eyes glistening as my lip trembles.

My baby sis is going to have a baby of her own.

"It's even better when it's your own." Reed speaks with confidence.

I pull my lips into a tight smile, knowing it will be years before I get to experience it, if ever.

"I bet." My voice is clipped, not wanting to focus on it for any longer.

Our attention is seized by the woman that brought me into this world. She seats herself on the other side of Reed, further away from me. Her blinding yellow outfit makes it impossible to not notice her as the contrast of her vibrant pink lipstick makes me cringe.

"To what, do we owe the pleasure?" I snarl, already knowing her sour intentions.

"Oh, Indie. Is that how we speak to our darling mothers these days?" She counteracts. Reed looks up at me with wide eyes, realizing exactly who she is.

I've told Reed countless stories about my childhood as they all pretty much link to why I'm so dead-set on doing everything myself and not accepting handouts. Well, until I met Reed.

"You must be Reed." My mother fixates on him, looking him up and down with a tantalizing look.

"Yes, indeed. Reed Breckenridge, and you are?"

I practically spit out my drink at his sarcastic response, knowing how much that will make her blood boil. She scowls at me and sits up straighter.

"Celia Thorne, the one and only."

She offers out her hand for him to kiss. I roll my eyes and slurp on my vodka and coke, turning my nose up at the fact she still uses my father's last name, yet she's remarried. Reed takes her hand and is his usual charming and charismatic self, he places a soft kiss on the upper side of her hand, causing her to blush. I roll my eyes *again*.

"Is that an engagement ring?" she squawks.

I really do not want to be having this conversation right now, and with her of all people.

"Indeed, it is." Reed answers for me and brings my hand with the ring on into his, threading our fingers together.

She peers down at our hands, the wheels turning in her brain.

"Oh, I am so terribly sorry to hear about your late wife, Reed. You must be heartbroken. I can assure you from my experience getting married to the first girl who shows you attention isn't going to be a quick fix and I'm speaking from experience!" She chuckles and takes a sip of her wine.

Wine? Who the hell let this woman have wine?

I look around to see where she's managed to snag a bottle from, unless she brought her own collection. She must have figured out that all the drinks she was served were non-alcoholic.

I scoff at her words, she's clearly done her research about him. Reed looks incredibly uncomfortable and shifts in his seat, the unrelenting stare down from my mother burning holes into his pristine suit.

"Yes, Allie was an incredible woman. But," he pauses, tilting his face towards me. My heart melts when he flashes one of his heart stopping smiles. "It just so turns out that your daughter is phenomenal, I couldn't let that pass."

The smile disappears from my mother's face as Reed continues.

"No amount of time will undo what happened to Allie, but your daughter has proved there is no match for time when it comes to our love."

My heart soars at the confession.

"Indie has been the anchor for my life since we met. She is destined for great things, and I couldn't help but want to join her side every step of the way."

He's speaking with so much confidence, I feel the need to shy away.

It's hard to remember that this isn't actually real and it's all for show.

My mother seems taken aback from his words and unsure how to approach him now.

Take *that*, Celia. Your conniving plan failed.

"Interesting. Well, I hope your happy for as long as it lasts." Her words are directly targeted to Reed rather than me; she wouldn't wish me happiness if it was the last thing that would save her.

She leaves the table with her drink in hand whilst the anxiety of her drinking alcohol sucks away any part of the buzz that existed prior to her interruption.

"Thank you for that, I'm sorry you had to be put in a situation like that. It was completely uncalled for that she mentioned Allie." I gulp as guilt rises in my throat.

"I just spoke the truth." He says solidly, twirling the engagement ring around my finger.

The truth? Well, I'll be damned, it turns out Reed can actually say nice things about me, without me coercing him into it.

"You really meant all of that?" I ask in surprise.

"Every last bit of it." he confirms as his eyes trace over mine as I look at him amazed with his sudden revelations.

"Well, thank you. That was very kind of you."

I present a soft smile on my face as his eyes shift to my cheeks, a wider smile forming on his.

"I'm gonna go grab another drink." I stand up with my empty glass to return it to the bar.

Reed nods in correspondence and I exit the room, disappearing through the hallway.

I swing by the bathroom to relieve myself and re-powder my face. I need to get rid of the clear sheen of sweat that lines face from the awkward conversation with my mother.

Whilst readjusting my dress in the full-length mirror, the door to the bathroom opens, almost knocking into me.

"Oh, sorry." I wince and step out of the way.

I turn just as I hear the bathroom door lock and lose any breath I had in my lungs. My eyes stretch wide and I stare into the dark brown abyss of his eyes.

"What the fuck are you doing here?" I spit, trying to override the fight or flight adrenaline rush working its way through my bloodstream.

"Just came to check how my lovely ex-fiancé is, are you missing me?" he pouts, an alarming look in his eyes.

I swallow razor blades and turn away from him, how many unwanted confrontations can a woman face in one night?

"Come on, Indie. I just wanted to tell you how sorry I am." His tone completely insincere.

"Sorry?" I laugh.

It's a bit fucking late for that.

He squints his eyes at me, looking at me from head to toe. I tap my foot nervously, wanting to be out of here and away from him.

"Don't be like that baby, you know couples just go through rough patches sometimes. It doesn't mean we have to break up."

"A rough patch? Are you just as delusional as you are stupid?" I fume at him, stepping backwards from him as he attempts to close our distance.

"I know you must miss me, but I've decided to come back, to come home."

Shaking my head, I let another laugh erupt from me. This man really can't be serious.

"There is no home for you to return to, Scott, and besides that, we are already done and have been for a while."

"I've been keeping notes, Indie. Do you really think we'd be over and you could just go on with your life, like I never existed?" he mocks.

I look up at him with my eyes wide as my heart begins to thump out of my chest from the anxiety.

"You are sadly mistaken if that's what you think. I'm not going anywhere." His voice sends shivers down my spine, but not the good kind that I've been used to recently.

He steps closer to me, so I take a step back, but he continues until my back is pressed against the tiled wall. I look around frantically, the sense of claustrophobia and threat sending alarm bells ringing in my head.

Placing one arm above my head, I cower, trying to turn myself inside out to get away from him. His breath smells like alcohol and his stubble is outgrown, now beginning to take form as a beard.

"Look at me!" He barks, gripping my face in between his fingers.

The grip is tight enough to bite the inside of my cheek, my lips pushing out from the pressure.

"You belong to me, Indie, and you always will."

I try to fight him off and grip his wrists in an attempt for him to set me free, to which he only pushes my head back against the wall. His eyes glance over my hands that are clawing at his wrists and his eyebrows shoot upwards.

"Oh, Indie. I can see you've been a very busy girl."

He uses his spare hand and grabs onto my left hand, pulling it towards him as I struggle under his weight.

"What a pretty little diamond that is, must have cost a pretty penny." He slurs and tries to pry the ring from my finger.

I wrestle him and bring my knee forward into his groin and his hands let go of me immediately, rushing to his crown jewels.

Taking this as my opportunity, I bolt past him towards the bathroom door.

Just as I get a hold of the handle, I'm yanked backwards by my hair, sending me barreling to the ground. I wince at the angle I fall l onto my wrist, the sound of vibrating piques my attention.

Looking at my clutch on the counter top next to the sink, I reach up to retrieve it. Scott is still focused on his manhood, and I see the phone is lit up with Reed's name. Just as I swipe to accept the call, Scott pushes me downwards onto the floor, his entire weight crushing my rib-cage as I let out a scream, whilst the air disappears from my lungs.

"You stupid little bitch!" His monstrous voice growls.

He begins to scramble at my dress and this is when I really start to panic, beginning to slap at his face, fight mode taking over my body. He slaps me hard across my face and I falter at the sharp sting of the pain as he seizes me by the wrists, pinning them above my head with one hand, whilst I kick my legs desperately.

I'm running out of options, my small frame is no match for his bulky one. I hear the sound of a zipper and I let out another scream, hoping someone will hear me.

Someone has got to notice that the ladies toilet has been locked for the past five minutes, please.

Letting go of my wrists, he clamps a hand over my mouth as well as my nose, cutting off any chance of breathing that I originally had.

I scratch and nip at his hand as I become completely hysterical.

Someone help me.

He bunches up my dress with his other hand and I start to become lightheaded from the lack of oxygen, my eyes feel heavy, and my chest burns.

I find myself looking up at Scott through watery eyes.

My stare becomes blank as the reality of the situation kicks in, no one is coming to save me. I'm going to be raped by my ex-fiancé on the best day of my sister's life, I have no options but to lay here and take it.

My body becomes weak and my arms flop to my sides, my brain beginning to fill with silence as he tears away my thong. I eventually close my eyes as my vision starts to waver, I can't tell how long it's been since I was able to fill my lungs, but I know it's long enough to make my brain feel fuzzy, my senses seem to be closing off one by one. I feel like my head is underwater.

It's like having an out-of-body experience, like I'm stood in the corner, watching Scott strip me of any morality I had and seeing my body give up the fight.

He begins to smirk down at me when the bathroom door is kicked open and Scott is ripped from me by his collar.

My body lays completely frozen as I stand in the corner of the room, my lips are deathly blue and my skin is washed of my usual color. I watch on mesmerized as Reed pummels fists in Scott's face, blood splattering across the white tiles as his body becomes limp, he's been knocked unconscious. Reed lets him go and scrambles on his hands and knees towards my body.

My eyes are open, but nobody is home.

He shakes my shoulders as he cries my name in panic, my body completely unresponsive. He lowers his ear to my lips and then proceeds to blow air into my mouth and–

I gasp a large breath and Reed pulls me into his lap as he ushers, 'thank God' over and over.

My body still feels weak as he cradles me, rubbing his large hands over my hair. He whispers *'it's okay'* and *'I'm here, I've got you'* more times than I can remember.

I remain still and can't bring my brain up to speed, I think I'm still completely traumatized and can't find a way out of this state. He tucks me further into his chest, his embrace protecting me from the monster who is passed out in one of the toilet stalls.

My throat hurts with every intake of breath and the best I can do is offer a shaky hand onto Reed's chest, letting him know that I can hear him. I feel a wet drop onto my cheek and it rolls down past my chin, but I'm not crying?

I finally angle my head upwards and see Reed's eyes red and glistening with tears as his lip trembles.

"I'm sorry," he whispers and nuzzles his face into my hair.

Grabbing onto him tightly, a tsunami of emotions, that I was keeping locked inside, begin to break through the dam. I let out a loud cry and my body shakes uncontrollably, the tears pouring out as I begin to process what very nearly happened.

We stay there for a long time, both of us locked securely together, Reed offering me as much reassurance as he can. My sobs begin to die down and I pull away from him, my big sister duties kicking in.

"You can't mention this to anyone." I speak for the first time since, my voice nasally from how much I've cried.

Reed looks at me, confusion written across his face.

"It will ruin everything, today is about Lola and I'm not being the one to ruin it." I explain.

"*You*, didn't do anything." Reed says sternly, glaring at Scott who is still passed out.

I really don't want to be here when he wakes up, I never want to have to look at those murderous eyes ever again.

"I'm going for a walk," I say, the need for some fresh air has me in a choke-hold.

"Are you sure you want to be alone right now?" He asks.

Nodding, I push up from the floor, finally getting a glance at the damage in the mirror.

My face is almost completely makeup-free, except the obvious black smudges all over my cheeks. My face has a pink colored hand print on the left cheek, a purple bruise beginning to surface underneath it. I'll have to go back to the dressing room later to correct the damage.

Sparing one more look at Reed, I murmur, "Thank you, for saving me."

No words can actually describe how thankful I am that he found me when he did.

Chapter 22

Indie

I push through the glass doors and enter a garden, decorated with bonsai trees and rose bushes.

I walk slowly around the pathway, taking in the skill of the shapely bushes, passing through a hedge, stalling at the breath-taking view.

A large lake covers the land before me. A wooden pier leads out to a wooden structure in the center of the lake that's lit up by fairy lights. I edge closer and the pathway ends, turning to grass.

Reaching down, I untie my heels, leaving them by the pathway and pressing my toes into the spongy earth. It's been so long since I've felt nature like this. It feels like it's rooting me back down, keeping my balance.

Strolling along the pier, I take my time to appreciate the freshness of the air and the sounds of wildlife.

Sometimes, you just need to stop the world and get off, to maintain your sanity. Life can be so overbearing that you lose yourself in the process. I trail my finger along the wooden railing, nearing the end of the pier. The wooden structure is completely open with several benches in a strategic order. I'm assuming that the happy couple can choose to have their ceremony here.

I saunter towards the edge of the platform to get a better visual of the moon's reflection in the stillness of the lake. I inhale deeply, my body beginning to relax and melt away from the stresses of my life, from the haunting image of Scott towered over me.

This feels very similar to meditation, but instead of imagining myself in a better place, I'm imagining myself right here, right now, staring at the stunning landscape. I close my eyes and use the only escape my body is familiar with.

I begin to bring my arms higher above my head and stretch upwards, eventually rising up onto my toes, listening to the sounds of the crickets in the distance. Extending my leg upwards and tightening my abs, I finally form the perfect penché. I hold it, feeling steady and completely in control again.

"Indie."

My eyes burst open as my leg falters and I'm losing control.

Oh, God.

I'm falling, my arms flail and desperately try and grasp onto something – but there's nothing there.

I plunge headfirst into the depth of water, the sounds of nature now completely drowned out. My hair and dress float up and around me as I squeeze my eyes closed tighter. My lungs begin to burn with the intake of water from my inelegant fall. I hear the distance sound of splashing and a pair of hands seize me by my forearms and yank me upwards.

The world takes me back, everything rushing into me all at once as my lungs try and inhale a gasp of air, failing terribly with the water still inside of them. I splutter pathetically.

My soaking hair covers my face as the lake water drips into my mouth and eyes. I'm hauled up onto the embankment and someone moves my hair out of my face, revealing themselves to me.

"Jesus, Indie. Are you fucking crazy?" Reed hovers over me, his significantly darker hair leaks droplets onto my face.

His lips glimmer from the wetness and I become entranced as he licks his lips once. He peers down at me with a panicked expression, waiting for me to answer with a bated breath.

I blink twice, my brain slowly catching up with what the fuck has just happened.

"Am I crazy? Are you delusional, Reed? Who sneaks up on someone like that, huh? You could see I was preoccupied and alone. Damn, who does that?" My words jumbling over the next.

"I thought… I don't know," he confesses.

He peers down at me through his soaked lashes and I can't deny he looks delicious right now.

As if the gods above felt like adding to the nightmare, the heaven's opened. Blinking, trying to avoid the large raindrops from entering my eyes, my chest heaves from the lack of oxygen around me and the deathly stare from Reed.

"Indie." He breathes.

He's staring at me so intensely it's beginning to scare me; I continue to hold his stare. He doesn't say anything for a while as we lay with our legs intertwined, his arms holding up his weight above me, shielding me from the downpour.

"Indie," He starts again.

"Watching the sunrise used to be one of my rituals, until something came along, that was even more breathtaking."

"Fuck, I haven't ever met anyone as fascinating as you, my love." He cups my cheek as I gulp visibly.

"I go to sleep every night, thanking the gods I don't believe in for your existence. You have this energy that I can't explain, it's so much more powerful than anything I've ever experienced. You've ignited the shadowed part of me that has been long forgotten. Indie, I'm falling madly and deeply in love with every inch of you." His voice cracks as he wears his heart on his sleeve.

I cup his face, my eyes filled with tears as the rain seems to fade away in the background.

"Oh, Reed." I caress his face, admiring the vulnerability of this moment.

"I think I'm diving head first off a pier for your love," I sigh with a lazy smile.

"Can I.. can I kiss you?" He asks hesitantly.

It takes me a moment to understand the question, considering how many times we've shared a kiss. It's only then I realize, he wants to kiss me, for me. Not because of the contract.

Instead of responding with words, I place my hand on the back of his head and pull him towards me. Our breaths are heated as we remain only an inch apart, my stomach erupts into butterflies as he nears. The hot fan of his breath provides a comfort, like a wave of protection from the bitterness of the world.

His lips collide with mine, an instant release of pressure as my body subsides and my shoulders roll back. We come together as one, the sealing of our lips prove our love for one another. We put down our weapons and wave the white flag, we have united together, the stars above have crossed paths. He kisses me so tenderly and soft that it feels like I'm kissing him for the first time. Our tongues graze alongside each other but instead of fighting, they lick each other playfully, figuring each other out.

This feels entirely fresh, like we've just began, like there is no contract, no boundaries, no expectations. This is purely just me and him in this moment, admitting our defeat and joining forces to conquer the world together.

His hand skims my left side as he runs his fingers up and down my body, like he's never touched me before. He's acting innocent and nervous to discover what lies beneath the thin material barrier between us, the only barrier that shall ever come between us.

He moves his hand over to my stomach; grazing over my navel and trailing to my peaked nipples. The shock waves from the sensation turn me blind as I writhe underneath him, seeing those stars that have finally met. He pulls away from the kiss, my heart aching for more of him, for more of *this*.

"You will never have to worry about another man ever putting his hands on you again, the only person who will ever touch you will be me," he growls, the protectiveness swirling around my head.

Reed is the kind of man that doesn't usually share his emotions, if I've learned anything so far, it's that he's incredibly hard to read. It's one of the main reasons I was so in awe of his confession to me, not only was he being firm and clear about how he felt but he said it so beautifully I wished I had it recorded so I could listen to it repeatedly.

What he doesn't realize is how sweet and loving he is. He discredits himself a lot of the time and acts like its 'normal' to be as passionate and perfect as he is, but he is one of a kind.

"Shall we head inside?" he asks.

I nod and he stands up, offering me his hand. I pull myself up and notice his suit shirt is completely soaked through, his nipples are visible through the practically see-through material.

"Come on, Princess." He leans down and sweeps me up into his arms bridal style, I squeal and kick my legs, wrapping my arms around his neck.

He leans down and leaves another tender kiss on my lips as the rain falls between us.

My body aches from the entirety of the day. The wedding party is close to being over and I'm pretty sure Lola will be too preoccupied to worry about my whereabouts.

He walks us into the building, his feet squelching along the polished flooring and the water dripping from us both. The receptionist gasps.

"Sir, would you like any assistance?" the woman rushes around the desk towards us.

"No thanks, I've got it covered." Reed lets out a heart laugh at the shocked expression on the lady's face.

I can't imagine what she's thinking right now, we must look ridiculous.

Reed pushes open the door of our suite, the room smelling pleasantly of lavender and soap. He sets me upright on my feet as we both take in the expanse of the room.

"This is spectacular!" I gasp, looking at the huge four poster super-king bed, the two-person bath tub in the center of the room.

The bed is covered in rose petals and there is an ice bucket with champagne and two flutes to accompany it. The lighting of the room is pink, making everything else appear pink. A mini fridge sits under the desk and a large TV is above the desk, adjacent to the bed.

"This is really something." Reed agrees.

"I don't even remember booking anything remotely like this!" I tell him, turning to look at him.

He wears a smirk on his face as he leans against the wall with his arms crossed.

"You didn't." He responds, smugly.

"Reed." My voice warns.

"What? it's our first trip away together. I wanted it to be special." He smiles, pushing off the wall and striding towards me.

"And you say you aren't a hopeless romantic," I joke as a laugh rips from his throat. He turns on the tub and adds the complimentary bubble bath.

"You deserve to be relaxed."

He walks closer to me and leans down to kiss my bare shoulder. I stand still whilst he unzips my dress, letting the material fall to my feet. It's only then, I notice I've left my shoes in the garden outside.

"My shoes!" I exclaim.

"Shh, we'll get them tomorrow." He presses his finger to my lips and places more kisses across my collarbones.

My neck rolls from the bliss, the relief it gives me to know it's him whose touching my skin and it only ever will be him.

Slowly, he peels his own clothes off his body, our outfits forming a damp pile in the middle of the room. He takes hold of my hand and guides me towards the bath, helping me step in without falling.

Like the sweet guy he is, he lights some of the tealights around the bath as I stand in the middle, waiting for him to join me. He climbs in behind me, sitting down with his legs spread wide, allowing me to sit down between them as the water continues to fill around us.

The bubbles smell delightful.

I place some of the bubbles in my hand and gently play with them, working them around my hands.

Reed's hands tickle their way up my back until they reach my shoulders. He kneads his fingers into my shoulders and begins to massage the tight tendons, it feels immensely good, maybe too good.

A moan slips through my lips as he works his way around the knots that have formed, the tension in my body seemingly slipping away from his tender hands. I roll my neck slightly and let my damp hair hang in front of me, appreciating the effort he's putting in to make me feel better.

My mind wanders to a place without Reed, thinking about how

differently tonight could have turned out if he wasn't here with me. Scott still would have been there; he still would have tried to have his way with me and I would have been just as completely helpless.

Not only did Reed save me, but he's now sat behind me trying to put the pieces of me back together. I don't think I understood the depth of my feelings for him until tonight, seeing how much he was willing to put himself on the line just for me to feel more comfortable. Seeing him destroy Scott for what he did to me has my thighs pooling, the concept of having someone to be your knight in shining armor is every girl's dream.

I lean backwards on his firm chest as he moves his hands out of the way, bringing them around to my front. His head rests in the crook of my neck and he splashes the water over my breasts, watching the water run from them. The difference between the hot water and the cold air as the water disappears, has my nipples hardening, earning a chuckle from a thrilled Reed.

"It's not you, it's the water!" I tease him.

His lips run up the expanse of my neck, as I shiver from the delicate touch.

"Is that so?" he taunts, referring to the new coating of goosebumps lining my breasts. I tighten my lips, knowing there is no way to avoid my reactions to him.

I lean forward and turn my body around so that I'm face to face with him. He looks at me with a pout from the loss of contact between us.

I crawl to him on my knees, leaning over his muscular body as the water laps beneath my breasts causing them to bob slightly. His gaze shifts between my face and my breasts whilst a satisfied grin spreads across his face.

"I want to thank you, for everything," I whisper, seductively.

He leans further back in the tub and rests his arms along the side of the tub, catching my drift. It's then that I see his cock is already completely solid and sticking upright out of the water.

Well, that makes things easier.

Smiling up at him, I readjust myself to his waistline, my mouth beginning to water. His breath has already become strained, and I haven't even touched him yet.

"You know that you don't need to thank me for a single thing, Indie. You deserve men to drop to their knees to serve you in their thousands," he whispers, the words binding through my heart.

This man.

I take hold of his member firmly, the veins protruding through the silky skin. A groan escapes his lips as I begin to lower my head, the sound alone sending pleasure signals in between my legs. The bottom half of his cock is still below the water level, meaning I only have the upper half to work with. Most would think it would mean half the work, instead I see it as double the effort.

I dart my tongue out of my mouth a swirl it around the head oh his cock, earning a whimper from his lips. I slide my tongue up and down the underside of his cock, teasing my way up to the top but before I reach the head, I pull my tongue back down, taunting him.

"Oh, Indie. Baby" He moans through gritted teeth.

I continue the rhythm and spontaneously wrap my lips around the head of his cock, his body jolting with arousal every time. He becomes completely breathless as I graze my tongue over his skin, so gently that it's barely noticeable. It keeps him on the edge and desperately wanting more.

I decide he's had enough torture for one night and wrap my lips around his length, kissing and tonguing the top, darting my tongue in and out of his sensitive slit. He grips onto my hair, hissing as I play around with him. I bob my head up and down, swirling my tongue around him when I feel him begin to tense up.

I continue sucking and licking, hollowing out my cheeks and driving him insane. His hips buck and the water swishes with his movements, his grip in my hair tightening and then loosening as he unravels before me. He curls his toes as he cries out, filling my mouth with his rich nectar as I gulp it all down in satisfaction.

I withdraw him from my mouth and make eye contact with him. His eyes shine with ecstasy whilst his body relaxes against the tub again. I wipe my mouth with the back of my hand, removing some of the leftover evidence.

"You know exactly how I like it," he sniggers, pulling me onto him.

I let out a hearty breath at the brush of his throbbing cock between my legs. I try to control myself but the fight inside of me is nowhere to be found, I rub my clit slightly over his length, the yearning for him inside of me only grows. He begins to fondle with my dripping wet breasts as he takes one in his mouth. I arch into him and close my eyes, throwing my head back with gratification for his sinful mouth.

I reach down to him and nudge his cock against my entrance, the minimal touch inflaming my cunt. He shifts underneath me as he pants with anticipation. I slowly lower myself onto him, feeling myself stretch as we become one. My moans fall from my lips as I rise up and down on him, looking down at his charming face.

His eyes are hooded as he watches me, the water slips between us and laps at his stomach, lighting up the indent of his v-line. Reaching back, I yank against the metal chain, allowing the tub to drain as we make love.

I hold onto his shoulders for better balance and begin to buck my hips, the movement easier from the weightlessness of my body in the water.

Reed groans and places his hands on my hips, keeping himself buried inside of me as he rocks me back and forward, the grinding hitting my sweet spot. I dig my nails into his broad shoulders, and I am completely consumed with the overwhelming sensation, throwing all of my rational thoughts to the lions.

I raise my arms above my head and grip my own hair as I ride him to our deaths. I quiver and my legs tense as the excruciating torment explodes throughout my body, I cry out his name as he takes over, thrusting upwards into me and pulling me into him. His pace is completely frenzied and unstoppable as I continue to sob his name into the crevice of his neck, my orgasm still working its way through my body and intensified by his frantic thrusts.

"Ah, Indie," he cries out as he spills himself inside of me, both of our orgasms joining together as our bodies shake and flex from the blinding climax. We lay intertwined for a while, our chests heaving and allowing our heart rates to slow.

Reed's arms wrap around me, his embrace offering solace as my heart skips a beat with the overpowering feeling of love and trust.

"I love you," I whisper into his chest.

His breathing stops for a moment as the silence becomes deafening.

I tense and look straight ahead fiercely, anxiety rising in my stomach as every second that passes feels like eternity.

Hearing the last of the water splash, his presence leaves the bathtub, the water level decreasing with his absence.

Pulling my knees up to my chest, I wrap my arms around them, wishing that the tub would just swallow me up, taking me away from the humility.

"I'm sorry, I just… I find it hard to say those words."

I swallow and offer a slight nod, my mind too busy swirling with embarrassment.

I think back to the words he spoke at the lake, the adoration I felt as he spoke to me with complete honesty and candor.

Right now, feels the opposite.

It's like he's back to being closed off and reserved, the sweetness of the man from earlier has been replaced with the robotic emotionless one. I can understand that he isn't the best at expressing his emotions, but to blow blisteringly hot and then numbingly cold is completely different. I don't want to spend my days wondering which side of him I'm going to get, knowing that I'll be hurt in the process.

I truly felt that we'd made progress tonight, that we'd established that there is something more going on between us. I stupidly thought it would mean that he would want to be with me for *me*, and not the contract. But it seems I have forgotten the true purpose here, that this is purely for business.

He's a guy, wanting to be intimate with me does not make him special, but his words do, and I thought he truly meant what he'd said earlier.

Clearly not.

I'm not going to allow myself to become completely infatuated with him again, all it results in is his heartache and disaster. Reed Breckenridge will not penetrate my barriers again, even if it is to spare me the last bit of dignity I've got.

I climb out of the bathtub and drip onto the surrounding tiled floor, my naked body now feeling exposed and inappropriate.

Taking the white towel from the railing, I wrap it around me as Reed exits the bathroom wearing his boxers, pausing as he looks at me.

I struggle to meet his eyes and I withdraw a complimentary white fluffy robe from the closet, exchanging it for my towel. When I turn around, Reed is sat upon the chaise longue at the end of the bed, his head in his hands.

I almost reach out to touch him when I fixate my hand to my side and decide against it.

For some bizarre reason, after everything that has happened to me tonight, this feels the worst of all. The ache in my chest causes a pain that I'm all too familiar with, in circumstances with my parents and Scott.

It's the unwanted, unloved, unworthy agony that has plagued me since I was young. It's one of my biggest insecurities, my need to be appreciated and cherished clouds my judgment. I've fallen victim to it once again.

I peel back the bed covers, the rose petals fleeing from me with desperation, to get away from the cursed girl, the untouchable girl.

Pulling the sheets over my body, I rest my wet hair onto the pillows, that feel too expensive to support my head. I take one final glance at Reed, still perched at the foot of the bed, his body unmoving and silent.

I turn off the lamp, cascading the room into an eternal darkness.

A small tear escape from my eye as I curl myself tightly into a ball, not wanting to let myself go.

Why is it you can't be loved Indie?

The looming feeling of loneliness smothers me as I close my eyes, escaping to a better place.

Chapter 23

Reed

My vision blurs at the laptop screen, the continuous hours of working have finally begun to take its toll. I close off the case details and shut the laptop, the darkness of the world outside finally registering in my brain.

The half-filled bottle of bourbon eyes me suspiciously from the bookcase. I've placed it over there in a pathetic attempt to stop me from drinking it. All it does is take extra time to fill up my glass.

I sigh and stand up for the sixth time. Grabbing the bottle, I bring it over to the desk. There's no point trying to ignore the fact that this 'plan' is never going to work.

I swallow the brown liquid as it ignites a burn in my throat, relieving me from the dangers of my own mind.

Since we returned from Lola's wedding, things have been different. Actually, things have been incompatible.

Indie has decided to stay in the spare room, leaving 'our' room to me. We've barely spoken since, I know why we're not speaking but what I don't understand is why it's affected her this much. I find saying those three words more difficult than the ability to breathe underwater.

I confessed my true feelings to Indie that night by the lake, I admitted that I was falling in love with her, but that is still different to saying the big three. Allie never heard me say it, but she knew me and understood it was just something I was incapable of. It had never really been an issue in my life until now, until it seems so detrimental to her that I say it, but I can't.

The last woman I'd spoken those words to, was my mother.

I've never repeated them to any other woman, they are purely reserved for her.

Willow is my only exception.

She's spent all her spare time away from the house, I'm assuming at her studio, trying to avoid me. She collects Willow from school and takes her out for dinner every night, and to Willow's delight, it's her choice. I heard them both chatting excitedly about an upcoming ballet show.

But, I've not been invited to it, nor have I been told about it.

It feels like we've backpedaled to a place that never even existed, we've never had this level of animosity between us, and I can't think of a way to fix it, especially before tomorrow. We can't make our first appearance in front of the court being cold and disinterested in one another, this needs to be solved and it needs to be today.

I've originally wanted to plan for us all to use the firm's private jet to get us to New York for the showing of *'Jewels'* at the Metropolitan Opera House. With the ongoing custody battle, I'm not allowed to take Willow out of the country as I may be planning a 'great escape' as they put it.

I've made a mental note to book it in preparation for when this case is closed and we can have a week-long celebration, doing everything that we've missed out on.

Instead, I've had to opt for something a little more humble. We're getting married. I've made a lot of phone calls to find us a space today instead of the original date in a few weeks, but I've managed it.I've also taken it upon myself to purchase the girls a beautiful designer dress each, so that they can look incredible as we unite us as a family.

I see the digital clock flash 3am and I take that as my cue to sleep off the alcohol. I make my way through the silent house, making sure not to wake anyone and sleep alone for the *last time*.

* * *

"Daddy, why aren't I going to school today?" Willow plagues me with questions as she eats her cereal, swinging her legs from the stool.

"It's a surprise, that you can't tell Indie about," I whisper to her, making her pinky promise with me before I tell her.

Her tiny pinky finger wraps around mine as she looks like she's about to explode out of her chair from anticipation.

I cup my hand around her ear and lean in.

"We're having the wedding, *today.*" I smirk as she pulls away with her hand to her open mouth.

"You're kidding!" she bites back, her eyes wide as she claps loudly.

I shush her and point to the hallway, unsure where Indie is in the house.

"Indie is really going to be our family." She says in amazement, her cereal spoon dripping milk onto the counter as she forgets she's in the middle of eating.

Nodding eagerly, I tell her about the plans, and how she needs to be in on it with me. She's never been keener to help me out with something, even though I have offered her an unlimited budget shopping trip to the mall next week.

Willow isn't aware of the court date tomorrow, I've told Indie not to say anything as it will cause her unnecessary worrying when she has nothing to be worried about. I've tried my best to keep some level of normality for her and Indie makes it so much better for her, it's like she's got a best friend who is living with her permanently. They are similar in so many ways it's not hard to figure out why they love each other so much.

Footsteps can be heard coming towards the kitchen and I widen my eyes at Willow as she nods and I turn away, busying myself with rearranging the utensils in the pot next to the stove.

Really, Reed?

"Willow, why aren't you dressed for school?" Indie asks, concern in her voice.

"Oh, gosh. Are you sick?" She raises the back of her hand to Willow's forehead as Lo shakes her head.

"No, I'm not sick silly, we're having a girls day of course!" She lies, I'm impressed so far.

Indie looks over to me, trying to gauge my opinion on the matter.

I shrug and grab my keys from the counter top.

"I'm heading off to work now, have a fun day girls." I keep my words short and concise, grabbing my briefcase filled with all of our essential paperwork and identification for the marriage.

I place the briefcase in the trunk of the car, alongside the dresses for the girls and my new suit, a smile stretched across my face as I think about how the rest of the day is going to turn out.

* * *

Indie

Willow has insisted that we need a girl's day, just me and her. I was surprised that Reed agreed to it if I'm honest, he's been extremely strict about her education since I've been involved, but he has a soft spot for her.

So far, we've had manicures and pedicures, we've been pampered at a beauty salon, and we've got matching fishtail braids with daisies. It's actually been a really sweet day as it's been a long while since I've managed to do a bit of self-loving and it's boosted my confidence massively.

My eyes are bronzed, and my lips are nude, the rest of my face smooth and polished with all of the right amounts of makeup, a lot better than I can usually do. Willow wanted us to have a trial run of services before our big show next weekend.

How could I turn her down?

We've eaten a huge tub of Nutella gelato between us, careful not to ruin our faces.

"Pretty please, can we visit the place where you and daddy are going to be married?" She begs, her hand tugging on mine.

She's been ecstatic about the fact she's going to get to be a bridesmaid, she has the date of the wedding marked down on her calendar and she crosses off each day as they finish, telling me each night that it's one day closer to me joining her family forever. I feel incredibly guilty with the circumstances, but for now I allow myself to believe it, for her sake as well as my own.

I sigh, "Fine, but we can't stay for long, we have the showing of *The Secret Life of Pets 2* in an hour."

"Yeah of course, that's fine, can we go now?" Her eagerness makes me smile, as it warms my heart.

"Come on then." I take her hand as we walk in the direction of the city hall.

* * *

We've been inside for a few minutes and Willow asks a member of staff if there's any toilets on the second level that we could use. I look down at her confused by her question, considering we're on the ground floor, the lady directs us, and Willow runs off with me chasing after her in an attempt not to lose her.

She races up the huge staircase and I call after her, her sudden outburst making my head spin. I climb the staircase as she passes down a hallway and disappearing through a doorway. I push open the toilet entrance and she stands in the center of the room, holding two zip up dust bags.

What the–?

"I got you a gift." She smiles, offering one of the bags to me.

I hesitantly take it, totally baffled at where she got them from.

She begins to unzip her own and a lilac frilly dress spills out, the upper part of it encrusted with pearls and butterflies. It is an absolutely stunning dress but, where the hell did she get it from?

"It's perfect!" she cheers, beginning to remove her shorts and t-shirt. I turn away to offer her some privacy as my mind races with the irrationality of the situation.

"Zip me up." She demands, and I turn around, taken aback by the quality of the dress.

"You look beautiful, honey." I smile and zip the dress up at the back.

She prances around in front of the mirror and turns back towards me.

"Come on, put yours on." She ushers.

I unfold the bag and hang it on the toilet stall door, slowly unzipping it.

A breath-taking off the shoulder dress reveals itself to me, the crimson color deep and seductive. The length of it falls to the floor, the material is a rich silk with a slit up the right thigh, it's only then I realize what's going on.

"Oh, Willow," I gasp, my eyes welling.

I'm here to get married. The silk of the material was the dead giveaway.

My memory floods with the conversation Reed had, insisting I was to wear silk to our wedding. The vivid color of the dress has taken me by surprise, it's a far stretch from the traditional white, but I suppose that is to represent innocence and we both know that I'm far from that.

"Do you like it?" she asks politely, trying to figure out my thoughts.

I nod vigorously and drop down onto my knees, so I am eye level with her.

"Willow, are you completely sure about this? As much as I want to be in your life, I want you to want me there. Your daddy would do anything for you, even if that meant not getting married to me." I hold her hands and squeeze them slightly, encouraging her to be honest.

She takes one hand away from mine and reaches up to my fishtail braid, stroking it slightly and then proceeding to do the same to her own.

She gently smiles, "I've never been surer of anything."

I squeeze her into a tight hug, careful not to disturb her hair as well as my own.

"Well, let's do this then!" I cheer, the adrenaline coursing through my veins.

I remove my plain, boring clothes and slip into the dress. I bend down slightly to allow Willow to zip up the rest of the side that I can't manage alone.

"So, everything today was part of your master plan, I'm assuming," I say, gesturing to the pampered features of us both.

She looks around, pretending to be completely casual. She is the sneakiest but sweetest child ever; I can't believe I didn't assume anything was out of the ordinary.

I slide on the black strappy heels and readjust my diamond ring, making sure it is perfectly central and upright. I take one last look in the mirror at myself and admire the way the dress hugs into my curves perfectly, like it was crafted to mold to my body.

My heart thumps with the rush of getting married spontaneously, but also with the rising anxiety. This is not a small step in life, despite this being somewhat fake, the marriage is legally real. I visualize Reed standing at the end of the aisle, his usual endearing presence watching me from afar, my cheeks faltering at the perfect sight of him in his suit. I swallow the lump that has formed in my throat from the anticipation and let out a shaky breath.

"You look beautiful Indie," Lo praises, standing beside me in the mirror.

"I think you mean *we* look beautiful," I chuckle and grasp a firm grip of her hand.

"Come on or we're going to be late." Lo pulls my hand and yanks open the bathroom door.

She pulls me along the corridor, our attire feeling completely overdressed in this seemingly normal part of the city hall. I find myself admiring the drive behind Lo right now, seeing her eager to get me to the correct room so that I can marry her father.

We pass through a set of double doors and the interior shifts to an old-fashioned oak style hallway, filled with vintage photos and antique looking furniture. I admire the history as we continue, desperate to cloud my mind with thoughts of anything but what is about to happen in the next ten minutes, to curb the nerve-wrecking thoughts.

"I think this is it." She stops.

I look at the huge double doors, analyzing the intricate design carved into them. A thousand and one thoughts are rushing in and out of me all at once, his wife, the first time we met, the proposition, the contract, the intimacy, the suspicion, the confession of feelings, the missing 'I love you', today. I begin to feel lightheaded and steady myself against the frame of the door, the sickness beginning to overpower again. I can't tell if it's the rush of adrenaline or the fear of what's to come, I'm about to sign my life away to someone else, someone who has been oscillating between every emotion I can think of.

The familiar feeling rises from the time we met up for coffee, only this time the daisy I'm picking is 'does he love me' and 'does he not'. I'm mentally tugging the petals away from the flower, desperate to know the answer, but the petals are never-ending as if I'll never find the answer.

The only way I can figure it out is to walk through those doors and face it head on.

Before I've even had chance to decide if I'm going to walk through the doors or not, Willow pushes both handles down and swings them open, the weight of them echoing throughout the entire hall.

My eyes fixate on him, standing directly parallel to where I am, and my heart stops, completely frozen with fear and love and lust and vulnerability.

He planned all of this, he wanted to surprise me, he wanted to prove to me in other ways his kindness, his thoughtfulness. His gaze burns holes through my dress, once again making me feel exposed and naked as the fierceness between us overpowers anything rational I was thinking previously. The one thing I'm sure of is I want him, I want him to be my husband, but not temporarily, I want him to be mine for eternity.

My eyes shift to the ones that are peering right back at me, and that's when I notice them. A hand pulls upwards to my mouth, it's Lola, it's Greg, it's Gracie, it's Harrison, a woman seated next to him that I don't recognize, and it's Britney.

Oh my gosh, it's Britney.

My eyes swell and I let out a slight sob as she smiles at me softly, assuring me that she's here for me and that she supports me.

How did he manage to convince her? We haven't spoken in weeks since I broke the news to her, she was beyond furious that I was not only joining forces with her sister's husband, but her enemy. I just want to rush towards her and wrap her in my arms and tell her about everything that's happened since we've been apart, tell her how sorry I am, tell her how much I've wanted to call her. But I knew she needed her space, knew that I was doing this for a good reason that she may struggle to accept now, but will appreciate in the future.

The music draws me out of my state of shock, and I almost burst into tears from his choice. It's 'Landslide' by Fleetwood Mac, one of the first songs we ever listened to together. I can't deal with the emotions pouring through me right now.

I feel like I'm just going to melt into a puddle of adoration right at the beginning of the aisle before I even get a chance to experience what life has to offer me from him.

"That's me," Willow sings as she skips in front of me, her lilac dress swishing around as she begins her descent through the middle walkway.

I close my eyes and enjoy the beautiful strums of the acoustic guitar and the soft tones of Stevie Nicks' voice. I let out a shaky breath and reopen my eyes, courage surfacing, *finally*.

I keep my focus on Reed at the end, conscious that I'm going to look around for possible escape routes.

He stands with his legs slightly apart and his hands held together at his waist, his black suit and bow tie pristine. He's wearing a crimson rose in the pocket of his suit, the perfect color match to my dress. The both of us certainly look the part.

Flashes catch my eye and I take note of the photographer in the corner, snapping images, I look back at Reed and he is grinning at me. It finally draws a smile from my own lips, the pressure of getting married evidently melting away, along with the devil on the shoulder.

Flash.

I come to a pause at the end as Reed takes my hand and kisses it gently, grasping the other one and doing the same. We stand to face each other, our hands still holding, as our eyes glisten between us and my heart flips.

The officiant begins his speech with his usual '*we are gathered here today*' and my mind can't concentrate on his words, only the man standing before me. It feels surreal knowing that only days ago, I was the bridesmaid to Lola's wedding and watched her do this exact same thing, wishing for the exact same.

And here I am.

"The happy couple will now exchange their vows." The officiants voice startles me, knowing I obviously have nothing prepared.

Reed coughs slightly and reaches into the inside of his suit pocket and pulls out some folded paper. I watch on in awe as Willow appears beside me with a pillow and two silver wedding bands between, one considerably larger than the other.

"Indie, I wasn't sure where to begin with these wedding vows, but not because I had nothing to say. It was because I had *too much* to say. There are so many qualities about you that I adore completely and cannot wait to experience for the rest of our lives, we are going to go on so many adventures together through the sunrises, the sunsets, the storms, and the aftermath. Every single second of my life has built up to this point, the most rewarding climb of all and I am ready to conquer it with you. I make a promise to you today and to the people in this room as our witnesses, to cherish you with my love, to be faithful to you, and to ride our battleship head on into war together. As much as I know you want me to hear the words 'I do', my choice is 'I will'. I will love you when life is peaceful and I will love you when life is painful, I will love you for every one of your successes, but love you twice as much for every one of your failures. Today is just the beginning of our story and I already know how it ends, we are going to have our happily ever after, Indie. I am going to devote my life to you and Willow, till death do us part."

My breath is lost and my eyes are betraying my orders to keep the tears contained. I let out a sob and bring my hand to my mouth with a slight laugh, trying to stop the inevitable.

The officiant reaches into his pocket and brings out a handkerchief, which I kindly accept, dotting at my face.

I look back up at Reed, his eyes also lined with tears and the fullness I feel within me is incomparable to anything I've ever felt before.

I take a shaky breath and straighten myself up, regaining his hands in mine.

"I think we all know that I haven't really had chance to prepare anything, and it's certainly not going to top that," I explain, gaining laughs from the room.

"But all I can do, is speak the truth from my heart. I will honor you, respect you, be faithful to you and love you with my entire being. I want to venture into life blindly with you, knowing that we will always have each other to fall back on. I promise to laugh with you, to hold you and to be by your side throughout our endeavors. I will promise to honor you as your wife and to devote my life to you and to Willow. Every day I want to wake up with you both by my side and I want to return to sleep every night with a smile on my face knowing that I chose this life. Willow, I may not be your mother by blood, but I promise to love you and care for you as a mother would. Reed, I promise to be your best friend, your strength and your wife, until death do us part." I finish, nervous if I managed it okay despite the lack of preparation.

The audience applauses whilst I peer back up at Reed, his jaw tensed whilst his eyes line with water. He's trying to stop himself from crying and something about it makes me feel fuzzy inside. Knowing that I've managed to draw such a raw emotion from him, with his indifference with his own feelings makes me feel like I've succeeded with my vows.

"You shall wear these rings as a reminder of the vows that you have just taken." The officiant gestures to Reed.

Reed picks up the smaller ring of the two, sliding it up my ring finger to meet my engagement ring.

I make a mental note to swap around the order they present on my fingers later.

My hand shakes as I pick up his ring, and grasp his hand to try and steady my own. It's only then that I notice the obvious existing indent on his wedding ring finger, a reminder that a wedding ring sat there only weeks before. A wedding ring that was a reminder of his vows, to another woman.

I gulp and slide the ring further up, feeling nervous as if this is some sort of fever dream.

"I have the pleasure of pronouncing you as husband and wife! You may now kiss your bride!" The officiant announces.

Reed reaches forward and cups my face in his hands, as our lips meet the explosions spread across my skin, forming goosebumps at the physical reminder of our love and connection between each other. He wraps one hand around the back of my head and one at my waist as he leans me backwards, causing my leg with the slit in to rise in the air as I grasp onto him by wrapping my arms around his neck.

Everyone cheers and applauds as we pull away, still leaned over one another. He stares into my eyes passionately as I lick my lips, my breath fanning across his lips.

I am completely breathless and hopelessly in love with Reed Breckenridge.

* * *

It's been several hours of celebrations in *The Peachtree Club* and it's just about ending.

I found out who the mystery woman was, it was Reed's sister Charlotte who I've finally had the honor to meet. She is quite literally stunning, her hair is a mousy brown and she has the same striking blue eyes as Reed. Turns out their entire family followed the law pathway after their father, who is clearly absent from the affair.

It's quite ironic that both of us have a parent that we resent and avoid at all costs, and then a parent who died whilst we were young.

Either way, this full wedding has been parent-less.

There is a small table with a few gifts and sealed envelopes on that I can't wait to tear into once we're home. One of my favorite things about weddings is seeing what you receive in gifts, it can be as normal as a 'Mr & Mrs' mug set, or it can be as wild as a 'Mold-a-dick' set. Either way, I'd be happy.

Surprisingly, Britney offered to have Willow stay overnight which we were hesitant about at first considering it's the day before the preliminary hearing, but she insisted that we get to spend the first night together as newlyweds alone.

Reed seized the opportunity and booked a chartered a flight in his firm's jet directly to Cancun. He showed me a few images of our villa, the private pool and the ocean view and I was practically skipping out of the venue. We've bid our goodbyes to everyone, and we've made a quick pit stop at home to pack an overnight bag.

We've been on the flight for almost two hours now, I insisted on bringing the wedding gifts along our very brief honeymoon as I wanted to try and experience what it feels like to be a bride for as long as possible. Reed sits across from me with one of his legs crossed across his knee, his suit still crisp and clean. Whereas, my dress looks like it could do with an iron and it has a small champagne stain on the right leg.

"I'm going to open the presents." I say excitedly as I get up from my seat and sit back down three seats away, among the gifts.

I start with the envelopes and there is many cards addressed to us both, sending their congratulations and best wishes.

I pick up the last envelope and notice it's not addressed to the both of us, just me. I open it and immediately notice it's completely different to the others.

The front of it says,

'With Deepest Sympathy'.

I frown and open the card, a cursive handwriting fills the inside.

'You've just made a huge mistake'

I swallow, the blood rushing from my face.

Blinking at the card and flipping it over, checking out the envelope for some sort of reasoning behind it.

I would assume that the card was meant for someone else, but it was clearly addressed to me, and it used my now married name.

'Indie Margot Breckenridge'

I check again for any sort of signature as to who it is from, *nothing*.

The lump in my throat rises and I can't decide what to do with the card.

Do I show Reed?

This feels threatening in some form, rather than a warning. I shake my head and tuck the card back into its envelope, placing it at the bottom of the pile of the rest of the cards. I want to enjoy my honeymoon.

I stand up and return to my seat, pushing the thoughts of the card out of my memory for the time being.

"Everything okay?" Reed asks me, cocking an eyebrow.

"Of course, why wouldn't it be?" I smile and take a sip of my champagne. I feel like it's all I've drank the past few days.

"Mr. and Mrs. Breckenridge, we are going to begin our descent now." The crew member informs us.

I blush at the use of of 'Mrs. Breckenridge' and Reed chuckles, seeing the reaction across my cheeks. I tap his leg playfully and shake my head laughing as he holds his hands up in defense.

"You're going to have to get used to it, dimples."

"I'm sure I will." I respond, the image of the envelope ingrained at the forefront of my mind.

* * *

Reed

The honeymoon is short-lived but perfect in every way possible.

I think we only slept for a total of four hours. We made love in every room of the villa, twice in the pool and once on the jet on the way back. I can't get enough of her, as my wife. Seeing her wear her ring with pride, ignites an overbearing love that I've never felt before.

It's more than I've ever felt for anyone, than for Allie.

I can feel the words becoming easier in my head, preparing for me to say them out loud, to provide her with the same devotion and respect she has given me. She has accepted me with every one of my flaws, taken on my daughter and given her a much better life than anything I could have offered her, alone. It's the least that I can do.

I grasp her hand on the drive back, setting it on my leg. She looks exhausted, dressed in her cute Levi shorts and thin t-shirt, her nipples popping through slightly from the air-con on full blast. She has a slight redness to her skin tone from the blazing sun in Mexico for twenty-four hours, it really wasn't enough time, but I don't think any amount of time with her will ever be enough.

She looks lost in her thoughts, so I take this as my opportunity.

"I love you," my voice sings, it rolls off my tongue with desperation, the primal need to let her know how much she means to me.

She looks at me with her jaw open and her eyes wide.

"You what?" she gasps, her eyes already beginning to well with tears.

I feel the need to allow her more of my attention and pull off into a road lay-by, the car skidding to a halt. She grips the dash as her body pushes forward from the force of my sudden halt.

"Jeez, are you trying to kill me?" She breathes, placing a hand on her chest.

"With the car or with my words?" I joke.

She unlocks her seat belt and turns to face me, her pouty lips taunting me from afar.

"Both," she confirms, tucking one of her legs under the other.

"Mrs. Indie Breckenridge, I am utterly, passionately, disgustingly, obsessively, hopelessly in love with you. I love you, I love you, I love you!" I pour out, I can't get enough of saying it, I can't get enough of her.

She climbs over the middle console into my lap and grips both sides of my face, staring intently into my eyes.

"Say it again," she whispers.

"I love you," I breathe, my heart pulling and twisting at the stunning emerald eyes peering back at me.

She kisses me hard and passionately and I run my hand deeply through her hair as she rubs herself across the thin material of my shorts. I let out a groan, my cock hardening despite the triple shift it put in over the past day.

She pulls away. "Say it again," she pants, her hands in my hair.

"I love yo–"

Her lips are back on mine, pulling and tugging at my hair playfully and I breathe harshly out of my nostrils, my heart racing with affection.

We both startle at the deep horn from a truck passing by, sucking us back into reality. We glance at each other and burst out laughing, my stomach aching from how hard I laugh.

It feels good, it feels so right I can't explain it.

She brings out the best in me without even having to try. I've never felt more present than I do right now, I want every second to last a year so that I can cherish every moment we get to spend together.

Watching her laughing before me, I admire how her eyes have little crinkles around them, how her dimples deepen the louder she laughs, and how her nostrils flare slightly every time her body shakes.

I want us to be connected, I want us to be complete, whole, as one.

"Indie," I say nervously.

She stops her laughing and looks at me anxiously, my tone seemingly sucking the fun out of the situation.

"What's wrong?" She holds my face and scans me for answers.

"I want us to scrap the contract," I confess, hoping desperately for her to agree with me.

She swallows before responding and looks around at the rest of the car.

"Have I done something wrong?" She asks quietly.

I pull my brows together, my mouth forming into a tight 'O', trying to understand what she's talking about.

Then it hits me.

"Oh, God no. No, Indie. I don't mean that. What I mean is I want this to be real, I don't want a stupid contract between us. I want us to actually be this happily married couple that we are. I don't want anything about this to be fake, I want us to be a proper family." I explain.

Her shoulders sag with relief as she lets out a breath.

"Oh," she says bashfully.

I shake my head with disbelief, "I can't believe that's the conclusion you jumped to."

She shrugs, looking downwards. I curl my finger under her chin, raising her head so her eyes meet mine.

"Indie, I want you to have my babies," I blurt out, the eagerness inside of me not allowing it to come out smoothly.

Biting my lip, I'm hoping I haven't come onto her too strong, too soon.

When she spoke her vows to me, she included Willow and made it her vow to her as well as me. Our marriage was a lot more than the joining of two people, it was the joining of three.

Indie has never once made Willow feel insignificant, she has placed Willow at the forefront of her mind consistently, never once caring that she is not her mother by blood. I didn't want anymore children with Allie, Willow was enough for me. But Indie, she brings out this other side of me, this side that is primarily focused on family and creating a home. Having a taste of what family is like with Indie, it makes me crave more of it, I want the full three-course meal. This feels like the final piece of the puzzle missing.

"Do you really mean that?" She ponders.

I mean it with my entire being, Indie deserves to have children of her own, I want physical representations of our love between us. I want to see more of what our love has to offer and with having only experienced her love for a short space of time, the future is only going to propel it, intensify it.

"I've never meant anything more in my life," I say sternly, wanting her to know how serious I am.

"Stop taking your birth control, now." I beg, holding onto her stomach, imagining her swollen with my child.

"Now? Are you really sure about this?" She asks, but I think it's more for her own reassurance rather than my own.

I nod firmly and pull her into me.

"I want you to give Willow the siblings she's always wanted, I want you to love our children the way you love her, I want more than anything for you to give me that gift." I plead, my throat closing slightly.

She kisses me softly, just a brush of our lips and she leans backwards.

"Well, I haven't taken my birth control for today, yet." She admits and my smile breaks out into a grin wider than the Cheshire cat.

"I love you." I kiss her.

"I love you." I kiss her neck.

"I love you." I kiss her hands.

"Reed, I love you," she responds.

The words erupt a volcano inside of me as a lava slide of pleasure escapes and forces its way around my heart.

I've never felt anything this strongly towards anyone, ever. Indie Breckenridge is in love with me, she's going to have my babies and she's going to give me the best life I could have ever wished for.

Nothing is going to get in the way of our happiness.

Chapter 24

Reed

I messaged Britney to let her know that we had landed and we would be there in an hour to pick up Willow.

We pull up to her apartment building, me, and Indie both bursting with excitement to see her.

We got her a little present from the airport gift shop on our way back, it's a shell encrusted jewelry box with a clear heart in the middle filled with Mexican sand. It's only something small because as soon as the court case is finished, I intend to take us all back there to celebrate properly, as a family.

We use the elevator to get to her level and come upon her apartment door.

We knock.

Indie grabs my hand and squeezes it as we both smile at each other, knowing that we get to tell Willow that she might get siblings after all. We remain standing there for a while and we knock again, my impatience beginning to irritate me.

"I told her what time we'd get here," I say defensively as Indie pops a hand on her hip, looking at me intensely.

"I swear!" I chuckle, pulling my phone out of my pocket to show her the text messages.

I frown at the undelivered message.

"Huh?" I swear I had signal when I sent it.

"Ugh whatever, I'll call her."

Turning away from the door, I begin to dial her number and make our way back towards the elevators.

The phone goes straight to voicemail.

I pull the phone away from my ear and redial.

Voicemail.

I stop walking, confusion pulling at me.

"Can you try her? I don't think my phone is getting a great signal." I ask Indie.

She nods and tries her phone.

"Voicemail," she says.

I look at her quizzically.

"Maybe they're at the movies and she's turned her phone off?" Indie tries to reassure me.

"Yeah, maybe."

My thoughts are turning more sinister, like she's done this to fuck with the court case because of her hatred for me. She knows we only have two hours until the case begins, and she's not incapable of telling the time.

Anger starts to bubble up, the last thing I need is something like this to throw me off before I need to present my best character in front of a judge.

We walk out of the front of the building and pause, thinking what we should do.

"Have you tried Bridget? Maybe she's been dropped off there?" Indie suggests.

What harm could it do?

Bridget picks up quickly.

"Hey Bridget, is Willow with you?" I ask politely, keeping my cool.

"No, why, should she be?" She responds in a panic.

"No, no. I just wondered, have you seen her at all? She stayed with Britney last night and she's not picking up, she knows how important today is." My tone becomes frustrated towards the end.

"Oh gosh, I haven't seen her but I'll let you know if I do, I'll call you later to check up." She ends the call and Indie is watching me intently.

I shake my head.

I try Britney again, *voicemail*.

What the fuck is going on?

I fist my hair and let out a strangled cry of frustration.

"Where could she be?" Indie sighs, looking around the streets as if she'd just see her strolling by.

I'm beginning to grow more and more suspicious. The way that she agreed almost instantaneously to coming to the wedding, despite the animosity between the three of us. The way she offered to have Willow overnight when previously, it was a mission to get her to look after her for a few hours.

The gnawing feeling in my gut intensifies, my thoughts running wild, thinking of how she could fuck up my life entirely if she doesn't get back here in the next hour.

"There she is!" Indie cries out, pointing across the streets. Britney walks hand in hand with Lo, carrying an ice cream in their free hands.

I let out a hearty breath and rub my hands over my face.

"Fucker." I grit, irritated that she's got me so worked up because she decided to be late on today of all days.

"What time do you call this?" I scream from across the street, passers-by looking at me in shock from my furious tone.

They cross over and Britney's face is confused at why I'm so angry.

"I told you we would be back for one, that was thirty minutes ago!" I bellow, almost falling to my knees in relief.

"Sorry, sorry. We stopped by the animal shelter on the way back to look at all of the puppies, I must have lost track of time," She cringes.

I sigh.

"It's fine, as long as you're here now." Indie smiles and takes Willow's bag from her arm.

"Come on, let's get going. It's a big day." I usher the girls and turn back to Britney, staring at me with wide eyes.

"Brit… Thank you. I just wanted you to know that… I'm sorry." I say quietly as the girls get into the car.

"Oh, don't be sorry, I was the one that was late!" She waves me off.

I gently touch her arm.

"No, I mean… I'm sorry for outing you. I didn't realize that it was something serious going on. I should never have said anything. It wasn't my place," I confess, genuine sorrow in my eyes.

She looks at me, really looks at me.

"It's fine, it's in the past" her voice is clipped and she turns away towards her building.

I exhale harshly.

Well, it was worth a shot, I've done all I can for now to try and mend our broken relationship. Probably marrying her best friend after her sister died was complimentary to her resentment towards me.

Understandable, really.

I enter the driver side of the car and Willow is busy admiring the gift we got her from Mexico.

"You couldn't wait for me, huh?" I tease.

"Sorry, she seen the gift bag in the trunk when I popped her bag in there." Indie winces, her eyes floating back to watch Willow stare in admiration of the box.

I pull away from the sidewalk and head towards home so we can all prepare ourselves to look presentable.

***

We walk into the courtroom, all three of us holding hands. I glance around and see Allie's parents on one side of the room. We take a seat on the opposite side of the room, their eyes following us in disgust.

They can stare at us all they like, it doesn't change the fact that Willow is happy, exactly where she is, where she belongs.

She offers a small wave to her grandparents and their faces change dramatically, waving back with huge smiles plastered on their faces. Rolling my eyes, I adjust my suit before taking a seat.

Willow is dressed in a lemon floaty dress; her hair is braided into Dutch plaits and her finger nails are still manicured. Indie decided to opt for a pantsuit to look professional, it's a nude color with wide legs, a white button up and a nude blazer over the top. She also put on a pair of brown colored aviators, now placed on top of her head whilst her hair is swooped into a ponytail. She looks incredible, I could really get on board with seeing her dressed like this more often. It's the opposite of her usual bubbly dresses, something about it makes her look delicious enough to eat.

Later.

We sit patiently waiting and the lawyers and their people begin to file in.

Harrison walks past us and nods his head at me, reassuring me 'he's got this'.

Willow fidgets in her seat as she sits on top of her hands, swinging her legs. The judge enters the room next and we all stand, Indie leaning down to let Willow know she needs to stand.

"You can all be seated now," the judge states, banging his gavel against the wooden platform.

The court begins with an opening statement from the Dawson's attorney, and we have to sit and listen to their pathetic argument of why they want to uproot Willow's life for their own gain. Or her 'best interests' as they put it.

Harrison begins his case strongly, defining the number of reasons why Willow belongs here, with us. He speaks fondly of Indie as a role model and the importance of ballet in her life, how supportive Indie has been during the loss of her mother.

Dawson states that they have a private school lined up with a ballet program, they have the money to support her through college, they have a close relationship with Willow and so on.

I find myself yawning at their excuses, offering what I could but it causes huge emotional distress on Willow in the process. Harrison bounces back once again, defending our honor and arguing how everything Willow needs is right here, with us.

This goes on for a few hours, Indie's head is resting on my shoulder and Willow is lying across our laps, snoring away from when she grew bored two hours in.

Something about the situation were currently in feels ominous, but I can't quite put a finger on it.

Everything is flowing well, everything is pointing in our direction, the victory is almost ours. But I can't eradicate the gnawing feeling in my gut, that something is going to go wrong.

I listen intently, trying to pinpoint anything that could be suspicious or have a double meaning but nope, nothing. Trying to shake the feeling, I relax a little in my seat, grasping Indie's hand in mine and holding Willow's head tightly.

* * *

The case comes to a close and the judge defines the temporary custody order in our favor, meaning we have our victory, temporarily.

"Your honor, we have some new evidence that we would like to present to the court." the Dawson's attorney rises.

The judge slowly cranes his neck with his eyebrow furrowed. We all freeze in our seats, Willow stirring.

"I'm afraid I have concluded today's case already, Mr. Parkinson," he says, a sigh of relief erupting from us.

"Your honor, I'm afraid this can't wait. It's detrimental to the case" he persists, and Harrison looks back at me, confusion written across his face.

I glance from him to the attorney and back again. Indie sits up straight, her chest barely moving as we sit in anticipation.

"Well then, hand it over." He offers out a hand and their attorney rushes forward, handing it to him.

Harrison is still staring at me and I stare back with anger. What the fuck have they discovered that we haven't?

The judge puts on his glasses and begins to read over the sheet of paper. Time lies heavy as we wait for him to announce to the court whatever nonsense they've come up with. His eyebrows shoot to his hairline, and he looks from the paper to the Dawson's attorney.

"Where did you get this?" He asks.

"We retrieved it from her medical file, your honor," the attorney replies.

My heart sinks.

The judge turns on the projector and places the paper onto it, the screen slowly coming to light on the wall.

I recognize it almost immediately and I look down at the floor.

The sounds drown out as I bury myself inside of my own head, not wanting to be here, not wanting to think, not wanting to breathe.

All of this is over.

The black hole has just exploded into my life, sucking everything out with it.

All of this was for nothing.

Every single nightmare that I've ever had has joined together and targeted me all at once, leaving nothing but the scattered remnants of my heart on the floor before me.

Glancing around, my head still submerged under water, everything is happening in slow motion. Harrison is stood up on his feet, fury evident across his face as he argues back and forth. Indie is standing as well, tears smeared across her face and her finger is pointed at the Dawson's as she shouts something. Willow is slumped against me, her tiny hands hugging around my waist as she sobs.

That's when I break.

I pull her into my arms, wrapping her limbs around me as I bury my face into her neck in an attempt to absorb her cries. Her body shakes uncontrollably and I rub my hand over her hair as my sobs pour out of me without any form of power behind them.

I am completely lost; I am helpless and unable to save my daughter.

The tears emit from me with no resistance, I am completely hysterical. I kneel to the floor with her in my arms and she tightens her grip on me.

I can't do this, I can't lose her. My baby, my daughter, my darling, I can't lose her.

A gentle hand touches my shoulder and I notice the familiarity, the warm touch offering little to console me at the moment. I shake my head and bury my head deeper into Willow, both of us gasping for air among the strangled cries. We're both mourning, howling in pain from the unforgiving world. The world that has torn us apart, when it should be us two together, against the world.

"You are and always will be my Daddy," Willow whispers, her voice nasally from being upset.

I squeeze her tighter. "Always my darling, always." I reassure her.

Rocking us gently, I try to conjure up the courage to look around at the room even though I couldn't care less right now. My irrational thoughts are telling me to get up and run out of here with her in my arms and never look back, escape and build us a life somewhere else in the world.

"You will come back to me, you will," I demand, a new emotion overtaking my emotions.

Determination.

Passion.

This is not the end, they will receive their retribution in due course.

I finally manage to look up, Allie's parents are peering over us expectantly and I use all my being to not stand up and kill them with my bare hands for the cards they've just pulled, just to get their own way. They don't care about what Willow wants, all they care about is themselves, what they see fit.

"Listen, darling. You need to stay strong for me, okay?" I talk quietly into Willow's ear, caressing her back.

She nods and sniffles, pulling back to look at me in the eyes. I almost lose it again, seeing the pain on her face and the torture it's causing her.

I place my hands on her cheeks, wiping away some of her tears with my thumb.

"Daddy will always come back for you, always." I smile at her, a shaky chuckle coming out to absorb my sobs.

My eyes betray me and another tear spills out before I wipe it away quickly. I need to show her strength, show her that I'm not worried, that I've got this.

"I love you so much, Daddy," she cries and I melt underneath her.

Her voice breaks and it yanks at my heart, ripping it out of my chest with such a force that I can barely survive without her.

She has my heart in her tiny hands and she always will.

"I love you Willow, I love you so much." I pull my lips into a tight smile and rub away her tears again.

"Whenever you miss me, think of that. Think of my love for you, think of your love for me. That's what will bring us back together." I assure her and she nods, wiping her nose on the back of her hand.

"Come on Willow, sweetie." Rachel says and I literally want to rip her fucking head off.

Dumb fucking bitch.

Willow stands up on shaky legs, turning to her grandmother.

"I hate you." Willow spits at her, crossing her arms over her chest and stomping past her.

Rachel looks at me in disbelief and I glare at her, hoping that she feels unprepared and nervous to take on Willow. I hope it feels so fucking unnatural to her that she brings Willow right back home, to her home.

God, my eyes are filling up again.

I stand up and watch as they make their way to the exit of the court room. Willow turns back to look at me, for what may be the last time in a long time.

"I love you, Willow Breckenridge!" I shout loud and clear.

She smiles, a genuine smile which makes my heart skip a beat.

"I love you, DADDY!" she shouts back, a prideful grin spreads across my face. That word is the only think that's holding my heart together right now. The fragile thread of my heart very nearly shattered tonight, and her faith is the only thing that can keep me strong.

Her body disappears and I slump against the side of the bench, bringing my knees up and dropping my head in between. I don't have it in me right now to reassure anyone else, I don't want anyone to ask my questions, I don't want anybody's sympathy. I need to get out of here.

"Harrison, take Indie home." I bark, getting to my feet and facing them for the first time.

Indie sits with her hands in between her legs, her head down facing the floor and her trousers are soaked from tears. I don't have the patience to take on anyone else's grief right now apart from my own. Harrison looks at me with a skeptical look on his face and looks at Indie.

"Come on, Reed. We're all here for you." He tries to console me and now that the court case is done, I don't need to keep up the brotherly act anymore.

"Take Indie home and get the *fuck* out of my life," I growl, my patience already wearing thin.

"Don't be like that man, I just wanna–" I shove away his nearing hand and look at him with disgust.

"What? You want to what, Harrison? Help? Look how far that's gotten us. Do you see Willow standing here with us right now? I knew I should never have got in contact with you, you were a lost cause from the beginning!" Spit flies out of my mouth as the fury inside of me resides on him.

He flinches, taken aback from the harshness of my words. But I couldn't care less. The sooner he's out of my life, the better.

I'm going to tackle this on my own.

I don't want to listen to any other comments from them, so I turn on my heel and charge out of the court.

I look up at the darkening sky, the stars beginning to shine through. I take in a harsh breath and cross the street. The City Hall stands before me, the reminder of only yesterday haunts me. The pathetic hope we all had, the short-lived joy we all felt, for it to be burned to ashes today.

I climb into my car and drive towards a bar out of town. After my last experience in a bar in the city, I don't want to be interrupted tonight, I need to let go of myself and blow off this vile feeling of loss.

* * *

Billy's Bar.

This will do.

I can't quite remember much of the drive, my mind was busy preoccupied with scenarios of storming Rachel and Bill's house, snatching Willow from them while I hold them at gunpoint. I really am debating taking extreme measures if it's necessary.

There is this ruthless streak that you inhabit once you become a parent, the kind that mean you would take a bullet for your child, but you would also kill for them. Neither of them intimidates me, both I would do without taking a second thought if it meant keeping my daughter safe and protected.

I order an entire bottle of whiskey at the bar and a glass filled with ice. They looked at me like I'd grown two heads but when I slapped down three hundred-dollar bills on the sticky bar and they scurried off to the back to retrieve the goods.

I stopped off at a gas station on the way to get some cigarettes and by the looks of it in here, they don't care for you to smoke them outside. The room is dimly lit, smoke clouding beneath the dusty lamps and there are six wooden tables with mismatched chairs. It's mainly filled with men but there are a few men here with women considerably younger than them. I turn my nose at them, not interested in anything but my own dramas tonight.

I light a cigarette and sip at the glass, the bottle sitting in the center of the table. The music playing is heavy rock, a mixture of *Metallica*, *Iron Maiden* and *Led Zeppelin*. I vibe along to the music, the loudness making it easier to drown out my own thoughts.

My phone buzzes in my pocket. I pull it out and Indie is calling me, I decline it and power down my phone. If there's anyone that's going to make me think rationally, it's her. And I'm not in the mood to think rationally about anything anymore.

The alcohol buzzes my brain, my muscles feel loose, and I can finally enjoy the atmosphere. As much as I want to pummel the fuck out of some good for nothing junkie to release some steam, I'm actually not interested in wasting my anger. I want to stimulate it and direct it right back at the Dawson's.

"Hey man, mind if we sit?" A man with an Australian accent and a torn denim jacket on, asks.

I look behind him at the other two guys, one in a recognizable Armani suit and the other wearing just a button up shirt. I gesture to the empty table and light up another cigarette, pulling it between my lips and inhaling the toxic air.

They scuffle around the table until they're all seated, I eye each of them carefully, trying to figure them out.

"Sorry, I'm Everett," the blonde guy in the denim jacket says and reaches out his hand across the table for me to shake.

I stare at his hand for a while before he retrieves it and cringes slightly. He looks around at the other guys and takes a swig from his beer bottle nervously.

"I'm not really in the mood for introductory small talk." I state, the conversation boring me to the back teeth.

"Ah I get that, we thought you looked like you could use some company," the chirpy blonde continues, he reminds me of Harry in some ways.

"The name's Devon." A deep voice speaks and I notice it's from the guy in the suit, his jet black hair suiting his name.

I nod and take another drink from my glass, flicking my ash into the tray in the middle of the table.

"And you?" I beckon my glass towards the brunette in the button down, he may as well introduce himself seeing as the others beat down my barriers.

"Oh, I'm Blake," he confesses, startled.

Nodding, I take another drink.

"I'm Reed." I speak into my glass, finishing the last of my cigarette.

The dark haired one sits without a drink, a scowl across his shadowy features. Everett sips at his drink, eyeing the other boys as the silence between us grows.

"So, Reed. What brings you to Billy's?" Everett asks.

"Do you normally pry into everyone's lives?" I chew on some ice.

He looks taken aback by my tone as the one in the suit speaks up, "Look, he's just trying to be nice. There's no need to be a dick about it."

I look at him and he oddly looks like he'd be me in another life. Even his tone is awfully similar to mine.

I call over the bar lady and she struts over, swinging her hips in her, too tight, jean shorts.

"Can we have three more glasses, please?" I gesture to the open bottle of whiskey in the on the table.

"Make it two glasses and a diet coke please, Sarah." He offers a wink at her and she giggles, eating it up. I roll my eyes.

"Not a drinker?" I hold up my glass.

"Ex-drinker," he says and reaches into his pocket, retrieving a green ten-month chip and flicking it between his fingers.

I tip my chin respectfully and peer down into my glass, the reminder of my failed sobriety, sits half-full.

Blake taps Devon on the back and takes another swig of his bottle. Oddly, I'm not getting any negative energy from these guys. I mean fine, Everett is a little loud for my liking, but other than that they seem decent.

"So, what's got your knickers in a twist? Or are you always like this?" Blake asks, relaxing back against the chair.

I let out a heavy sigh and knock back the remainder of the glass, the burn allowing me to actually speak about it.

"Lost custody of my daughter today."

Willow's face fills my mind and my stomach wrenches, pulling at me. I quickly pour more whiskey into my glass and drink again as Devon eyes me suspiciously.

"Damn, that's gotta be hard man." Everett says, the thickness of his accent rolling off his tongue.

I shrug, and drink.

"Sorry about your daughter." Blake offers his condolences and I wave him off, not wanting to dwell on the topic for any longer.

I've got an entire lifetime to think about it.

"What about you?" I don't direct my question at anyone in particular.

Everett is the first to speak up, "Ah, see I grew up here but moved away for college. About two years ago, I came back for an internship in the city. It didn't work out and somehow got involved in motocross. I've been competing in the *Supercross* here in Atlanta ever since. But I'm in and out of town a lot," he confesses.

It explains the heavily patched denim jacket, the icons now becoming familiar.

"Impressive." I purse my lips in admiration.

I've watched the annual motocross in Hampton many a times when I was in college. Me, Harrison and our buddies used to visit and turn it into a sick overnight trip.

"Pilot." Devon says, with no extra information.

I cock my head at him and he looks at me intensely, his almost black eyes piercing into my own.

Well, I suppose that's all he's going to say.

"Okay, well mines going to sound boring now. I work in tech" Blake confesses, rolling his eyes.

His words actually manage to draw a laugh from me, catching him by surprise.

"So, you're all friends?"

They look between each other and a quiet laugh is passed between them before Devon speaks up, "Yeah, you could say that."

Sarah comes over with the glasses and the diet coke, leaning down for an extra long time as she slides the cups into the middle of the table. Devon leans back and checks her out from behind and his face looks unimpressed. He sits back up straight and chooses to blank the woman as she tries to gain his attention.

Damn.

"I'm assuming your taste in women is better than his?" Everett points a thumb at Devon beside him and grimaces, noting the fact I kept my eyes to myself during the exchange.

"Married." I say through tight lips and lift my hand up, revealing my wedding ring.

"Oh, let's see her," Blake says and I furrow my brows at his eagerness.

"Not like that, I'm just interested in getting to know you." He offers a polite smile and I unlock my phone.

I select images and see the last photos I had taken on my phone were from the move in day. The picture of all three of us stood in front of the new house, I feel world's away from that day right now.

I bite my lip and flip the phone around to them, placing it central in the table.

"Ooh damn, she's hot."

"You got yourself a looker there, Reed."

But Devon stays silent, staring at the picture but not saying anything. I look at him, waiting for his response.

"Is that your daughter?" Devon deadpans.

I nod my head slowly as he continues to stare at the photo.

"Are you going to do something about it?" He questions me, genuine curiosity behind it as the other two fight over the whiskey bottle.

"You bet, I'd kill for her." I state, my face unmoving as I feel the anger fueling my emotions again.

Drink.

"You seem like a great father."

I thank him.

Drink.

The music in the room grows louder as the drinks continue to flow and the conversation follows.

By the end of the night, I am drunk up to my eyeballs and can barely stand, following suit with Everett and Blake.

"Where do you live?" Everett shouts over the music, spilling his drink on himself in the process.

"Buckhead." I inform him.

He jabs a thumb into Devon's chest, resulting in a deathly glare from him.

"Mr. designated driver here can take us all home!" He sings and begins swaying his arms to the music whilst Blake looks like he's staring off into the rest of the bar.

"Hey, I'm gonna go talk to that chick, she's been eyeing me up all night." Blake points at a dark-haired woman, and he gets up from the table.

Staggering, he salutes me. "Until next time, Reed." his voice slurs.

I laugh loudly and readjust myself in my seat.

"Good luck." I salute him back, merging my words together to the point they're almost indecipherable.

Everett slumps forward on the table and Devon pulls him back by his collar.

"Alright, I think that's enough for one night, buddy." He stands up and hooks Everett's arm around his neck.

"You want a ride?" He looks down at me and I nod, not caring that I'm leaving my car here.

I'll deal with it in the morning.

We pass by Blake on the way out and as he put it, "I'm in boys, you shall go on without me!" as he returned to kissing the scantily clad woman.

Devon throws Everett down on the backseat of his Range Rover and he mutters a few words that sound like *'cheeseburger'* and *'rabbit tree',* whatever the hell that meant.

I climb into the passenger side of the car and pull my phone out to turn it on, but it flashes with a red battery, and I groan, putting it back in my pocket.

Devon climbs in and sets the GPS on to Everett's address in Brookhaven, the city where Indie used to live, only a short ride from Buckhead.

The beginning of the journey is awkward enough to sober me up to the point I remember the fuck ton of turmoil inside of my head.

"How long has it been since you relapsed?" Devon's question catches me completely off guard.

"What?"

"How long have you been since you relapsed?" He repeats.

I take a moment to form an answer, my confusion evident on how he knows.

"Six weeks" I confess shamefully.

"What caused it? Is it the situation with your daughter?" His gaze remains fixed on the road and he drives with one hand on the steering wheel, one wrapped around his jaw.

"My wife died." I confess and he turns to me with wide eyes.

"Shit, I'm sorry, these guys are so insensitive." He gestures to Everett passed out on the back seat, triple buckled in with the seat belts making him look like he's been caught in a web.

"No, it's fine. It's not my current wife," I explain, but probably only causing more confusion.

His lips part as I can see the wheels turning in his brain, trying to figure out the timeline here.

"Oh, so you were like a widower and then got remarried?" His question not coming across as judgmental, more as understanding.

"Yeah, it's pretty complicated if I'm honest." I rub my hands over my face, my eyes feeling heavy and my chest tight from the cigarettes I'd been smoking.

"So, why is it you were drinking at Billy's tonight, and not at home with her?" He asks.

I ponder, not actually knowing the answer.

I don't quite know why I ran, why I didn't confide in her. She's been the biggest support system for me, my biggest supporter if anything. And I kicked her to the curb like she was nothing more than a quarter.

"I'm asking myself the same thing." My voice is low and I'm deep in thought.

She lost her too. I didn't stop for a single second and think about the fact that she's at home, alone, probably distraught and worried about my whereabouts, all whilst processing that fact that Willow isn't in our custody anymore.

* * *

The rest of the journey is quiet.

I pop my window down to get some air to my sweaty skin, the sudden need to get home to her overpowering my senses.

We both carry Everett into his house, Devon tucks him into his bed on his side and sets up a bucket, a bottle of water and two aspirin on his bedside table.

I am still trying to figure him out, he plays this cool, dark, and mysterious guy that doesn't give much away, but then he looks after his friends like they're his own children. I mean it's great and all, but it makes him so much harder to read. Apparently, I'm an open book.

We lock his door and leave the key under the plant pot, the night still young.

We're almost at my place and I feel the need to ask him.

"What made you get sober?" I'm blunt and concise.

He stares at the road and his jaw tics; I can tell I've asked him a sensitive question.

He sighs, "A girl."

Wow, real elaborate.

I nod and stare out of the window, sensing he doesn't want to talk about it.

"She killed herself," his voice is cold as I turn to look at him with wide eyes.

"We weren't anything serious. But, we had known each other since we were kids, so I took it pretty hard."

I listen intently, the thoughts of my own mother coming to surface.

"Like I knew she was depressed, but I didn't think it was that bad, you know?" His voice cracks at the end and he tenses his jaw, clearly pushing down his feelings.

The car goes silent for a short while.

"She called me, on the night of. I didn't pick up; I was out of my face drunk at some party and declined the call because I was already getting lucky with another girl at the party." He winces at the recollection.

"Turns out, she wasn't calling for a booty call. She was calling because she was struggling and needed help."

I gulp, the weight of his words resting on my shoulders.

I can't imagine how that must feel.

"She hung herself that night in her garage, I found out the morning after. Still hungover."

I shake my head in disbelief.

"From that point, I vowed to never that alcohol rule my life again. I went cold turkey and here I am, ten months sober."

My mouth is dry and making it hard to swallow, but I try anyway. I don't even know what to say, so I do the one thing that I hate, the thing I despise.

I offer him my sympathy.

He shrugs it off like it's not a big deal but his eyes are slightly glazed over.

We pull up to the entrance of my driveway and he puts the car in park.

"Look, I know it's not my place, but you reminded me a lot of myself tonight. Lost in your own head too much to realize what you've got right in front of you. Coming from a man who didn't have a chance to put it right, you need to quit the drinking."

I look at him and feel a strange pull in my heart, the sincerity of his words playing over and over.

"When the time comes, I'd happily be your sponsor," he offers.

I let out a dry laugh and look up at him again, his face stone cold serious. I stop my laughing and nod.

"Here." He reaches in front of me opening the glove compartment and retrieving a card.

I take it from him and see it's an AA group located right here in

Buckhead, a few blocks away from my office.

I twiddle the card in my hands as he stares down at me.

"Just think about it." He offers a tight smile, the first I've seen tonight.

"Thanks, and for the ride."

I exit the car and stalk towards the gates of the driveway, noticing they're still unlocked.

Releasing a pent up breath, I push them open, offering a small wave to Devon as he pulls away.

I walk up to the door and fumble with my keys for a moment, finally unlocking it and pushing it open. Locking it behind me, I chuck my keys into the bowl, meeting the dark expanse of the house.

It's eerily silent and the shadows from the exterior lights offer an assortment of shapes across the walls. I remove my shoes and start to ascend the marble staircase.

Our bedroom door remains closed, and I stop, turning around and look directly across into Willow's bedroom. The fairy lights are still on, lighting up the room with a warm glow, like it's waiting for her, waiting for her to come home.

I bow my head and close her door, not wanting to be taunted by the fact she's not here.

Creaking open our bedroom door, the room is in complete blackness.

My eyes take a few seconds to adjust, and I can make out the boundaries of our bed. I take off my cuff links and blazer, setting them on the dressing table, unbuttoning my shirt, enjoying the silence for a while.

Once I've completely stripped to nothing, I walk around to my side of the bed.

I almost go to dive into it but that's when I notice it.

Indie is wrapped around my pillow, her grip tight and her body is not even under the covers. She is still dressed in her pantsuit from today and I swear my heart breaks for the second time today.

I get onto my knees and crouch before her, her breaths slow and steady. Her hair is spread around her, her eyes look puffy, the black rings around them have bled onto my pillow. Her lips are squashed against the pillow, her breaths fanning across my face and I inhale the sweet scent.

Oh, Reed, why have you fucked up again?

Instead of waking her, I go around to her side of the bed and climb in. I pull the covers back enough to tuck her underneath with me. She stirs slightly, but not enough to wake up. Pulling the pillow from her grip, she flinches until I use those arms to wrap around my stomach. I lay her head on my chest and she snuggles into me, pressing her body flush with mine. Staring up at the ceiling, I rub my hands over her shoulder, trying to lull her back into a deep sleep.

Closing my eyes, I feel a newfound certainty.

I'm going to take Devon up on his offer.

Chapter 25

❦

Indie

I burrow my face into the silkiness of his skin, my nose brushing against his nipple. I wrap my arms tighter around him and then I'm thrown back into reality.

Sitting up abruptly, causing him to stir awake, I look straight ahead, not wanting to face him yet.

My eyes feel worn and heavy, I rub the sleep out of my eyes and they're black from the mascara I'd worn yesterday. I have streaks of black across the sides of my hands from when I've rubbed my eyes. My pantsuit is creased and uncomfortable.

Pulling back the sheets, I climb out of the bed, heading to the bathroom.

"Indie?" Reed's voice calls out sleepily.

I ignore him and lock the door, finally caving in and bursting out into tears, as I turn the shower on to drown out the sounds.

Taking a seat on the side of the tub, I place my head in my hands and feel my body shake, the pain and the overwhelming guilt swallowing me up.

I tried to help her, I miss her, I love her so much.

After Harry brought me home yesterday, he offered to stay with me, but I turned him down, wanting to be ready for when Reed came home. I needed a bit of time on my own to process the details, the huge twist of events in the court case.

The second that the judge displayed the evidence, I couldn't breathe. I couldn't process the information quick enough, but Reed's reaction confirmed it.

Reed was *not* Willow's biological father.

Watching them in the aftermath was absolutely tragic it was by far, the most horrifying scene to watch, it will be something I will never ever forget.

The bond between the pair of them proves more than a stupid piece of paper ever will. It was completely uncalled for, for Allie's parents to reveal something like that in such a desensitized way. Something that should have been approached carefully and with dignity, was abused and used as ammunition.

Regardless of whether they want custody of Willow, the absolute worst thing anyone could do is reveal that kind of information in such a public manner. Willow did not get a chance to even process any of it before she was hauled away by the very people who caused it.

I sobbed and sobbed, barely moving myself from the couch in the lounge, until I went to retrieve a glass of water from the kitchen, as my voice had grown hoarse.

In the center of the island was a bouquet of white roses, the tips rimmed with red paint. A card was attached to it with my full name on.

I didn't know who'd brought them or how I hadn't seen them earlier, but I just assumed they were flowers from the wedding.

Tearing into the envelope, the cover of the card said, *'So sorry for your loss'*, and in the same cursive writing as the previous card, it read, *'You don't belong with them'*.

This is the second card I've had from the mysterious sender.

The irony of the card made my stomach turn and I vomited directly into the kitchen sink, having to clean it up straight away before it happened again.

I stashed the card inside of my wedding dress dust bag along with the other one. I compared the handwriting, it was a perfect match, written with the same ink. Someone is toying with me, trying to make me feel uncomfortable in my own home. But I won't let them win.

Peeling off my clothes, I climb into the walk-in shower, the water rolling across my skin, washing away the evidence of our trauma.

After a long shower, I exit the bathroom with the towel wrapped tightly around me and my hair turban-style in a towel. Reed is lying across the made bed.

He made the bed.

He stares at me from afar, his eyes trailing down the expanse of my legs and then back up to my face. I roll my eyes and sit down at the dressing table, releasing my hair from the towel.

"Indie," he begins.

Before he gets a chance to speak, I turn on my hair dryer. The longer I can avoid speaking to him the better. I can see him through the reflection of the mirror, and he flops backwards on the bed with his hands over his face.

Surely he knows this isn't going to be some sort of easy apology, sweep it under the rug and move on kind of apology. We spoke our vows only the day before, promising to hold each other up and help each other during hard times, he fell completely flat on that one.

Besides that, I have no idea where he was, he wouldn't answer my phone calls and didn't return home until God-knows-what time. It's completely unacceptable and if that is the kind of marriage he is offering me, I'm not interested.

I've got a bunch of paperwork to catch up on and classes today, I don't have time for him to fill my head with his pathetic apology, for where he was last night. I continue drying my hair, occasionally casting a glance at Reed on the bed. He lays there completely unmoving.

Shutting off the hair dryer, I proceed to brush my hair and he sits up, coming back to life.

"Indie, can we talk?" He tries again.

My shoulders slump and I swivel around on the stool to face him, setting the brush in my lap. I look at him expectantly.

"Look, I'm so fucking sorry for yesterday. I failed you, I failed Willow, I let you all down and it's not going to happen again. You don't know too much about my past and I'm going to lay my cards on the table, I want to be completely open and honest with you." He runs a hand through his hair and intertwines his hands in front of him.

"Many years ago, I fell into a seriously bad addiction with alcohol, I've got a long history with it and it began when my mother committed suicide. I was thirteen the first time I touched it, and I used it to numb the pain of losing my mother and losing my father at the same time. As you already know, he left us with my aunt after my mom passed, and I just kind of spiraled. It was a rough time, until I met Allie. She helped me get clean, sober and attended AA meetings with me, avoiding alcohol herself at the beginning, so I couldn't fall back into temptation."

The revelations have be in a choke hold, realizing all of the warning signs that I'd clearly missed.

"Well, when Allie died, I didn't have her anymore. And with that, I kind of felt like my sobriety died alongside her too. I didn't have my person anymore, and I'd fallen into a dark place, and strangely enough, you were there on the very first night that I relapsed."

I gasp, remembering the bar, the complete wasted state he was in.

"Since that moment, I've continued to fall victim again and again to this horrible disease. I've used it as my crutch, to get by. When everything came to a head yesterday, the only thing I wanted to do was to run, to numb it all with the only way I knew how. I should have confided in you, I should have been there for you and I wasn't, for that I am so incredibly sorry."

I gently smile, hoping that he knows how much I appreciate his candor.

"I found myself at a bar on the outskirts of town, and I bought an entire bottle of whiskey to drink alone, to convince myself that I wasn't alone. And, as if the universe decided to offer me a second chance, I met a group of guys. Everett, Devon, and Blake. At first, I was bitter and cold, only caring about the bottle in front of me. But, the longer they were there, the more I began to enjoy myself. I remember what it felt like to be alive, to be a normal guy and have friends. I've spent too long enthralled in my career I left out the most important parts of myself. My family and my friends."

It feels like I've emptied my entire body of its water contents, but here I am, proving myself wrong.

"Devon drove me home; he didn't drink at the bar. When I asked him why, he showed me his chip. I felt like I'd taken a step back in time, remembering my old self doing the same to a friend, I saved him from his illness. It really felt like fate had gifted my back the same kindness, he offered to be my sponsor. He gave me a card with the AA group contact details and I called them this morning whilst you were in the shower. I've taken leave from the office and I'm attending my first meeting tomorrow, I want my life back. I want Willow back," he wails.

I rush over to him and he wraps his arms around my waist as he presses his face into my stomach. I cradle his head as he lets it all out, the sound of his pain reducing me to tears.

In another life, he is that little boy who lost his mother.

He is hurt, he is struggling, he needs help.

He sags against me, completely unguarded and tortured by the agony of his past and the torment of the future.

"This time, I'm doing it for me," he sobs into my towel and I lean down, pressing a kiss into his hair as he hugs onto me like I'll disappear if he lets go.

I peel him away from me and crouch down before him, looking into his bleeding eyes.

"We *will* get her back." I comfort him, my voice stern.

He nods and grasps onto my hands, "Thank you," he whispers as he presses a kiss to my forehead.

My eyes flutter closed and my heart fills with his love.

✳ ✳ ✳

The class feels wrong, it feels empty.

Last time she wasn't here, it was different. I knew she was coming back.

But this time, this time I'm not so sure. I've ran through every possible scenario, and I've drawn a blank every time. I don't know much about the laws regarding children, I don't know if it's possible to gain custody over a family member unless there is something seriously wrong.

After the fourth class of the day, I retire to my office, feeling numb inside.

My students knew something was off, my heart wasn't in it and with ballet your heart is at the forefront of your performance. The emotion flows out of your body with every move and if you aren't there, it's impossible to hide.

I pull open my laptop and begin to organize an advertisement for a ballet teacher. With everything going on at the moment, I need to be selective with my time, meaning I need to cut hours at the studio. It's not even that I don't want to, a bit of relief from this business really would set me free and give me time to work on myself, but it's the fact I know Scott is still on my heels. I don't want him to think I'm an easy push to selling up the studio, but I need a break.

I post the job advertisement and list a decent paying salary to go alongside it. I have some spare cash in the overheads that can cover the monthly salary and it means the girls at the studio don't need to suffer from my lack of passion.

Closing my laptop, I pull my gym bag from my locker, a white envelope dropping out. My full name is addressed on the front.

You've got to be kidding me.

I tear it open with fury.

The card is titled '*Sending my condolences*' and from the title alone I want to tear it up before even reading the inside of it. But, my curiosity gets the best of me.

'*How does it feel to become Mrs. Breckenridge II*', the same cursive handwriting.

I grit my teeth and stuff it into my bag.

Whoever is sending these messages is trying to scare me out of being with Reed. I'm not having it anymore. I don't feel threatened in any way, but it's become a regular occurrence and I don't want to be plagued with these for the rest of my life.

Taking out my phone, I dial Harry and we organize to meet up downtown, at an Italian restaurant. I text Reed to let him know I'm staying late at the studio and hike my bag onto my shoulder.

I have images on my phone of the previous two cards and the picture of the flowers on my kitchen island. I can't keep this to myself anymore, I have to tell someone, or I'll start to think I'm going crazy.

Ordering a glass of house red, Harry interrupts and tells them to bring over the finest Cabernet Sauvignon by the bottle, forgetting that I am now technically a wealthy Breckenridge.

The waiter pours the wine into the large glass, I tell him to just fill it to the top instead of pouring me a 'ladylike' amount.

Taking a few gulps of it, I set the glass back down, instantly feeling more relieved.

"Harry, I don't even know where to begin." I exasperate.

"Start with the beginning." He responds, earning an eye roll from me.

I begin to tell him about the first card, showing him the picture and then the second one and the third. I hand him the card and he picks it up, flipping it over and scrutinizing it for any kind of evidence.

"Do you have the envelope?" he asks.

I nod and pull it from my bag, handing it over.

He checks the seal and groans, "Whoever is sending them is smart enough not to be lick-sealing these shut."

"And they're not posted?" He asks.

I shake my head.

"So, whoever is giving you these, is hand delivering them to you, showing up at your common places, the house, and the studio."

He seems like he's talking to himself rather than me. I drink more of the wine and nibble at the warm bread in the center of the table.

"Each message seems like a coincidence, does it not?" he raises a brow.

"What do you mean?"

"Well, they're all impeccably timed. With the circumstances."

I'm not really catching his drift here.

"The first card was a 'Deepest sympathy' card, telling you that you've made a mistake. And it was a wedding gift, a wedding between you and Reed."

I nod, trying to follow along whilst practically inhaling the home-made bread.

"The second card was 'sorry for your loss' and this was found just after Reed lost custody of Willow."

I blink and stop chewing.

"I thought the cards were just a mockery, like anything they could pick up from the store. I didn't think they had any actual meaning." I explain.

"Well, it doesn't seem that way to me, it seems completely targeted and full of purpose," he continues.

We order our food and I drink more wine.

"Let me know if you receive any more?" he asks, to which I nod.

Now to get onto the gnarly stuff.

"I didn't know about Reed's addiction," I confess.

"Oh." is all he says.

"Did you not think I should have been made aware of that? Before I signed the contract?" I challenge him.

He looks up at me through his long lashes and back down at his wine.

"I wasn't under the impression that you weren't aware," he responds.

"Besides, what does it matter now? You've fulfilled your contract, you're free to continue with your life," he shrugs and drinks from his glass, looking at me whilst doing so.

I don't know why I feel so uncomfortable about telling him, but something about the way he's looking at me makes me wish I had nothing to tell.

The server comes over with our food, I opted for a white wine pasta and Harry chose a Hawaiian pizza.

I'm guessing the love for pineapple on pizza runs in the family.

He begins to cut his pizza into slices as I formulate the words in my mouth, but no sound is coming out.

Just say it, Indie. Why are you being so difficult about it?

I press my fingers into my temples and blink a few times before conjuring the bravery to do it.

"I'm staying."

His knife falls to the plate with a clatter, and he scrambles to pick it up, knocking the wine glass from the table as it clashes to the floor, the red liquid spilling out across the plush flooring.

I cringe as other occupants in the restaurant turn to view the commotion. Rising to my feet, grabbing my napkin, Harry does the same. I get to my knees and begin dotting away at it.

"I've got it," he says.

But, I ignore him and continue absorbing the spill, knowing it was partly my fault.

"I said, I've got it!" he shouts, the loudness throwing me backwards onto my bum. I flinch at a sharp pain in my hand and realize I've dived backwards onto a shard from the broken glass.

Great.

I climb to my feet to assess the damage in better lighting and a waiter comes over with a sweeping brush and some extra napkins, ushering Harry away and ordering another server to grab him a new glass.

I analyze the large gash in the center of my hand and wince as I attempt to pull out the shard, my bodily instinct not allowing me to do it myself.

"Oh, Indie. Let me see it," Harry says, swanning around the table to my side.

He drops down onto one knee and takes my hand in his. He licks his lips as he looks at the gash, figuring out the best way to pull it out.

"It's in there, pretty deep."

His voice vibrates through my body, causing my temperature to spike.

He pulls on the glass slightly and I let out a cry, that sounds more like a moan. The fire rises to my cheeks and I try to turn away but with him holding my hand still, I'm restricted.

The proximity of him is delivering signals to all of the traitorous parts of my body, the hairs stand up on the back of my neck as I try and squash the thoughts.

"What are we going to do with you, my love."

I swear my eyes roll to the back of my head. He knows exactly what he is doing, he knows the effect he has on me, and it's working.

He drops my hand and grabs two of the cloth napkins, handing one to me and keeping hold of one.

"Bite down on this, it's going to hurt, but only for a moment," his voice is lined with seduction and I can't help but rub my thighs together, to give myself some sort of relief under his gaze.

I do as he says and place the napkin in my mouth, he winks.

Oh for fuck's sake.

He returns his attention to my hand and looks up at me one more time through his fluttering eyelashes.

"You ready?"

Harry you dirty little minx.

He's messing with me badly and he knows it by the huge smirk plastered across his face. I almost feel like he planted the glass there on purpose.

"Three...Two...One..." He counts down.

I bite down hard on the napkin as he pulls the piece from my hand, the pain slicing through me thinly, but sharp. The blood pools a little, dripping onto his white shirt as he takes the cloth napkin, wrapping it firmly around my hand.

"See, it wasn't too bad was it?"

I roll my eyes at him and snatch my hand back, anxious that if he holds onto it for any longer, I'm going to end up giving myself an orgasm from the amount I keep rubbing my thighs together.

He returns to his seat as the server brings over another bottle of wine with the new glass. The burden washes over us again as he takes a sip from his fresh glass. His jaw pulses as he sets it back down.

"So, you're staying, huh?"

"Yeah." I breathe, unsure why it feels shameful to admit it to him.

He nods and takes a bite of his food, his chewing seems exaggerated. His hand taps on the table rhythmically and I shovel a forkful of pasta into my mouth.

"Do you love him?" he asks in a plain voice.

He stares at me closely for my answer.

I chew my pasta trying to bide my time because I want to spare him the pain of the truth, knowing he's not going to like it. I can't quite explain what is between me and Harry, it's different to anything I've ever experienced before. With Reed, my love with him is so obvious and so overpowering that it's undeniable.

But this, with Harry is something else. It's something that feels freeing, it feels fun and exciting, but it doesn't feel like love, no. It's like an emotion that hasn't been invented yet, there is no way to describe how it is I feel towards him.

Harry is exactly the guy I'd date, he is my type, he is sweet, caring and harmless. But, it isn't enough for me to put myself on the line, Reed is and will always be the one I love.

"I do."

He shakes his head slowly, looking up at the ceiling and then back down at his lap. He looks at me and then to the window and the outside world, and then back to me. He swallows deeply, his Adam's apple bobs from the action.

"Does he love you?"

He can't keep his eyes focused on me anymore.

"He does." I nod, my hands lay limp in my lap with my appetite disappearing completely.

He cups his mouth with his hand and drags it slowly downwards, letting out a long sigh.

I shift in my seat, not sure whether to direct the conversation somewhere else or ask for the bill. He makes my decision for me and asks for the bill, the bottle of wine still basically full and our food practically untouched.

Regardless of his feelings towards me, he insists on paying the bill, remaining gentlemanly even in his down moments. That's Harry.

We walk out of the restaurant and down the sidewalk, the wave of alcohol beginning to sway my head.

I was meant to eat the pasta, I swear.

Harry decides to walk me home instead of us calling a cab, saying he could do with the stroll.

Most of the way home, he is silent.

I've left my bag in my car but still have my essentials on me, like my keys and phone. We cross over the road and we're in my neighborhood.

The houses are all completely private and gated off from the rest of the world, the road deathly silent.

We surpass a house with an open driveway and the next thing I know I'm shoved up against the wall.

I close my eyes in shock and let out a gasp, my breath being stolen from me. I slowly edge my eyes open, and everything begins to register. His hands are on my hips as he presses into me tightly, making it hard for my lungs to expand.

He peers down at me fiercely through his blue eyes, his breathing ragged and fanning across my face.

"You're telling me you don't feel that?" he argues, his hand cupping my face.

I shake my head, trying to keep my mind clear of the poison he's injecting into me. My body is convulsing with the reaction to his body being so close to me, so warm and comforting but desirable and seductive.

"Kiss me then," he challenges.

I lose my ability to speak as I know my voice will betray the very feeling I am trying to suppress. I shake my head again as his nose grazes mine.

"Kiss me." He taunts, licking his lips as his tongue very nearly grazes my lips from our proximity.

My breathing is staggered and I want to push him away but also pull him into me and smash my lips against his to feel what it would be like.

"Kiss me, Indie," he whispers, his forehead pressed against mine as I feel myself beginning to cave from the sound of my name on his lips. My stomach rolls with butterflies and my heart beats excessively.

A bead of sweat drips down my back as I glance from his eyes, to his lips, to his eyes and his lips.

"Hey! Get off my property!" Someone shouts from a window above and we startle apart, scurrying around the corner.

My head suddenly floods with anger from the ambush.

"I can walk the rest of the way on my own," I mutter to him, picking up my walking pace.

He jogs a little to keep up with me.

"Indie, stop for a second." He grabs onto my elbow to get me to stop.

"What!" I snap, turning around to face him.

He stops and looks at me worried.

"You think you can just ambush me like that? Force me into doing something that I don't want to do?" I cry, feeling myself bubble up.

"It's not like that and you know it isn't," he argues back.

"Then what is it like, Harry? I've done absolutely nothing to insinuate that I want anything remotely close to that, I'm married to your brother in case you've forgotten!" I shout, holding my hand up and pointing at the rings.

"You and I both know that don't mean shit."

My head spins.

"You and Reed would never have been married if it wasn't for that stupid fucking contract!" He continues.

"Yes we would." I defy him, wanting to blank out the nonsense he is spilling.

"Indie, you and Reed were together because of Willow, for money, for whatever gain you got out of it. But without Willow, you have nothing."

I wipe away at my tears. "We love each other," my voice comes out barely as a whisper.

He lets out a frustrated groan and rubs his face.

"Why can't you see it?" He shakes his head repeatedly.

"See what?" I question, my nose completely blocked and my voice now nasally.

He pauses and shakes his head again.

"It doesn't matter." He puts his hands in his pockets and lowers his head.

My anger begins to cease and I wrap my arms around myself at the chilly breeze.

"At least let me walk you home." He counteracts, his voice now quiet and compassionate.

"Fine." I say.

We stride alongside each other for the rest of the way, nearing the gate of the house when he stops again.

I turn to him, "What now?"

My head drops sideways as I peer at him through my lashes that are now clumped together from the crying.

"If it's him you're choosing, there are some things you should know," he begins.

"It's about Allie." He pleads.

I shake my head.

"Keep it to yourself, Harry. I don't want to hear it," and I turn away from him, disappearing through the gates and into the house.

Chapter 26

❦

Reed

I stand outside of the building for a long time before I figure out how to move my feet again. The strangling feeling wraps itself around my neck, knowing that the second I step foot inside, that's it. I must confront my demons head on, no backing down, no second chances. The devil doesn't offer his mercy, just pain and suffering.

I grip the handle shakily and press downwards, the heavy door lifting as I hear chatter in the distance. I almost decide against it, get in my car and drive back home. But I'm confronted with the reasoning behind why I'm here in the first place.

"Reed! Didn't think I'd be seeing you so soon." Devon claps a hand on my back and looks at my hand still firmly gripped on the handle.

He notices I haven't yet moved an inch and a level of understanding washes over him.

"I get it, stepping inside of there is admitting your faults, confronting your failures." It's like he drew the thoughts directly from within me.

"But, that's what sponsors are for." He reaches a hand towards me, waiting patiently.

I struggle to swallow but try anyway, slowly relaxing my grip on the door handle. I remove my hand and grip onto his, his hand firm and controlled. My muscles slowly begin to relax, knowing that I'm not alone in this, these people know the exact struggles, the unworthiness we all dwell on in the first few weeks, wondering if we're even deserving of being helped.

I walk next to him, each step feeling like I'm walking on sand, sinking into the floor beneath me, heavy and slow footsteps until we reach the shore.

"Ah, Devon. I see you've brought a friend today." An elderly man stands up to greet us.

"I'm Tom, welcome to our AA group, I promise we're all lovely most of the time," he jokes, and I attempt a smile at him.

We stalk over to the circle in the middle of the hall and take a seat, joining the existing group of eight.

The group commences and I listen to the stories of the others, a woman in her forties who lost her teenage daughter in a car accident who turned to drinking to cope. A man in his early-twenties who has suffered with addiction since he left the foster care system at eighteen. A woman in her thirties who found out her husband was having an affair with her best friend and got her pregnant, despite them going through rounds of IVF.

The stories were endless and if anything, it made me feel safer and more content.

Each person in the room is of different age groups, from different walks of life, different social classes, and yet here we all are. Suffering with the same disease, battling the same demons.

It comforts me in a strange way to hear their struggles and hear the difference in their sobriety lengths, some as short as two weeks, some as long as four years.

Either way, the strongest thing I've felt here is the lack of judgment, no one is here to comment on whether you've 'been through enough' to have turned to alcohol. It's supportive and reassuring that I can do this, I've got this.

It's my turn to speak, and my mouth has gone dry. I reach down and take a sip of my water bottle, feeling the attention of the room burning into me.

I rub my jaw with my hand and begin.

"My name is Reed."

The familiar unison of 'hello Reed', fills the room.

"I've been struggling with alcohol addiction, and I've been sober for almost two days now." I pull my lips tightly as they all applaud.

I glance over at Devon and see him nodding his head to go on.

I explain the story from when I was younger, my first run with sobriety and how I relapsed, detailing everything up to yesterday when I had my revelation to make a change. I make sure to thank Devon within that and all he does is nod, accepting my thanks.

I receive my twenty-four hour chip and place it in my pocket, making sure that it's secure, knowing I'm going to be needing it a lot in the first few weeks.

* * *

The meeting finishes up and I stay seated in my chair, offering goodbyes to those that are leaving. A hand presses on my shoulder and I glance up, looking into Devon's deep brown eyes.

"What'd ya think?" He asks.

"I think it went well, as well as it can." I frown, the gnawing feeling of Willow being hours away plays in my mind.

I have arranged with Rachel to have a face time call with her tomorrow, and I've also already mailed out a phone, an iPad, and a sim, to her so she can contact me whenever she wants, instead of going through the devil herself.

"Anything you wanna talk about?" He takes the seat next to me and I slouch back into the chair.

"It's just a lot." I sigh.

He nods.

"It just feels like shit, you know? Knowing that I have already done all this hard work before, knowing that I've failed again and I'm back to square one. This time feels so much harder than the first, because this time I'm not blind to the struggle of it."

"Every day that you wake up sober, is a day to be thankful for."

I turn to him, listening.

"I understand you, probably more than you realize. I mean, Jesus. It took a girl to kill herself before I realized how much it had consumed me."

I gulp, remembering the story he told me in the car.

"But, there's not a day that goes by that I don't think of her, I like to think of myself as a better person now. A person that would never be put in a situation like that again, one where it is the difference between life and death. There is no time like the present and you've begun your journey, just take each day as it comes. Don't worry about your past and the mistakes you've made, don't worry about what's going to happen tomorrow, or the next day. All you need to do is walk with one foot in front of the other and you'll find the rest of it follows."

I close my eyes absorbing every word of his, the steadiness of just confronting my battles for the day instead of the next ten years feels so much easier.

"Damn, have you been a sponsor before?" I laugh.

"First time for everything," he bounces back.

I am thoroughly impressed.

"Ah, you'll probably need my number." He holds his hand out for my phone, and I pass it to him unlocked.

He keys in his number and returns it to me.

"I've got somewhere to be but call me anytime you need me, well apart from when I'm flying but I'm only working part-time at the moment anyway."

"Thanks, Devon." I shake his hand as we stand up.

"See you next week."

He disappears out of the exit, and I stand still before the doors, inhaling deeply, the weight of the world slowly beginning to lighten and release me from its burden.

Day two of sobriety has been somewhat successful.

1 Week Later

Indie

It's day three of conducting interviews for the studio.

I was surprised at the quick response from the advert, but there was a mixed bag of applicants. Some younger, some older, some under-qualified and some overqualified. But, none of them seemed to be the right fit, I don't know if it's because of my personal connection with this place, or the fact I want the perfect person to fill my boots.

I don't want to place the studio in the hands of someone who could undo all of my hard work, I want someone who I can trust will keep my high standards and brilliant reputation. I feel like I'm slowly losing hope that this is a good idea after all.

"Amazing choice of flooring." A woman calls from the entrance of the studio. I look up and take in her stunning auburn hair as it flows down her tall frame flawlessly.

"Why, thank you." I respond, walking over to her.

"I seen your ad for the job, I hope you've got time to squeeze me in for an interview!" She's confident and composed.

I check the time.

"Yeah, I've got some time." I nod and point over to my office, beckoning for her to follow.

I take a seat behind my desk and grab my notebook filled with notes from prior interviews and take my purple fluffy pen out of the pot.

"Well, I'm Indie Thorne. Sorry, Indie Breckenridge. I'm the founder of the studio." I blush, still getting used to my new name.

"It's lovely to finally meet you, I've watched you for so many years, especially during your qualifying years, you're phenomenal!" She smiles at me and I feel the heat rising to my cheeks again.

It's still bizarre to have people who recognize me in the ballet world, I'm not a celebrity by any means but any person who has followed the ballet hierarchy would know who I was.

"Oh, stop." I wave her off, laughing.

"Should I begin by telling you a little about myself?" She bats her long eyelashes as I almost forget why she's here in the first place.

"Oh yeah, of course, go ahead." I readjust my notebook and grip my pen.

"Okay so my name is Felicity Smart, I'm twenty-six, I've been involved in ballet since I was seven, I attended Dallas School of Ballet instead of going to college and I have competed in the international ballet competitions since I was fourteen, collecting twenty-four placement awards, four of which have been first place. I have toured around the states with the Oregon State Corps de Ballet for the past two years and I'm wanting a change of direction, into the teaching world."

I sit back, my hand hasn't pressed the ink to the paper since I've been listening in amazement.

"I have a bunch of references I could–"

"The job is yours if you want it."

She looks at me with wide eyes, "Are you sure? I mean yes of course I want it, it would be an honor to work with you." Her voice is breathless as she latches and then unlatches her hands.

"When can you start?" I ask.

I'm astounded at her achievements; they coincide similar to my own apart from I stepped out of the game a little earlier to begin my school.

I take photos of her ID, her social security number and get her to provide her contact information, arranging for her to come in tomorrow and we will run through the different grade classes and the usual routine of the day: Pilates, warm-up, dance routines and the upcoming performances we have.

I'm confident she'll thrive, I can see the fire behind her eyes that I used to have, the drive to succeed.

* * *

I can't see Reed's car; I don't think he is home again.

He's been attending his AA meetings and the extra sessions since last week and it's been rough on him. We've bickered and argued like a real married couple, fighting over whose turn it was to mow the lawn, who forgot to cancel the newspaper subscription, who left the ice out of the freezer, which one of us needs to do the grocery shopping. All fairly common issues, but with Reed currently in a state of detox, he's been extra tense.

I grab the mail from the mailbox and bring it inside, hauling a brown paper bag filled with groceries inside. I set them on the counter top and make my way back to the entrance of the house to close the door. I unpack the groceries, popping away the milk and eggs and the rest of the vegetables.

The sound of a door slamming startles me.

"Reed?" I call out.

Silence.

My heart thrums against my chest and my senses heighten.

"Reed, is that you?" I call out again, frozen to the spot.

I look around for any potential weapons to protect myself from a serial killer.

Pulling out a knife from the knife block, I slowly edge my way to the exit of the kitchen when a shadow crosses the hallway.

I jump out and nearly fall flat on my ass in shock.

"Jesus Christ, Indie! What do you plan on doing with that?" Lola leaps back in surprise.

I put my hand on my chest and use my other hand to steady myself against the wall, the knife clattering to the floor. I'm busy trying to steady my breathing whilst Lola looks around.

"Why are you so paranoid? Enough so to grab a knife and stupidly confront me with it!" She folds her arms across her chest, dropping the gift bag she was holding onto the floor.

"You didn't answer when I called out." I breathe, still trying to gather myself.

"Are you okay?" she questions, taking a step towards me as if I'm a fragile bird with a broken wing.

I flinch, unsure what the hell my mind is thinking right now, all I know is that I am so tense right now, my ribs would be at risk from taking a breath in too harshly.

"I'm fine." I say unconvincingly.

She pulls me in for a hug and at first, I feel the instinct to push her off but then the familiar smell of her melts away my angst.

"You're shaking!" She worries.

I ignore her and tighten the embrace, closing my eyes.

I have no idea what's came over me, I can't tell if it's the stuff that happened with Scott or the messages I've been receiving, or both.

She withdraws and stands back, picking up a gift bag and handing it to me. I take it apprehensively.

"I found this on your doorstep, I thought I'd bring it inside." The blue gift bag is tied at the top with a red ribbon sealing it shut.

I check the tag and it's addressed to me in – *Cursive Handwriting.*

The nausea climb in my throat and I drop the bag to the floor, my blood pressure dropping instantly.

"Indie, what the hell?" Lola touches my arm and I feel the room begin to spin, an array of stars cloud my vision and my legs give out as I fall to the floor.

"Indie!" I hear her distant shouts as I succumb to the darkness that surrounds me.

* * *

Reed

I pace the waiting room, the familiar feeling I know all too well.

The impatience, the anxiety, the helplessness.

I was playing golf with Devon and Blake, when Lola called me and told me something weird was going on with Indie and then she just collapsed in our hallway. She'd called 911 and the ambulance had just arrived as she'd called me and they were blue-lighted to the emergency room.

I got here as soon as I could and we heard the doctors were running a number of tests to try and figure out what had happened, why she had just fainted like that.

She's still unconscious and we're not allowed into her room until she's woken up.

"What did she say to you before it happened?" I ask Lola, trying to fix the puzzle pieces together.

"She didn't say much, she was just completely shaken up. She came into the hallway wielding a knife, Reed. I've never seen her so guarded before." I absorb her words.

A knife?

Why the fuck would she be so terrified that she'd grab a knife?

It can't be Scott.

Harrison rushes down the hallway, his hair ruffled and his face full of worry.

"What the hell happened?" He asks, he practically bounces from one foot to the other, unable to keep still.

"Literally, the second she read the tag on the gift bag she just fell, like a dead weight." Lola says.

"What gift bag?" Me and Harry say in unison.

"It was on the doorstep when I arrived, I brought it inside for her, and then this–" She gestures to the hospital.

"What was inside of it?" I ask.

"What did it say?" Harrison asks at the same time.

I look at him, my brows furrowed as he looks at me disconcertingly.

"I don't know. Everything happened so quickly, I don't think she opened the bag, she just read the tag on it." Lola sits back down and rests a hand on her blooming stomach.

"Is there something I should know about?" I turn to Harry.

He looks at me like a deer in headlights and it forms a sickening feeling in my gut.

"What the fuck is going on?" I grit through my teeth.

Harrison cracks his knuckles and takes a seat. I stand above him, staring him down.

"Harry, you better start giving me answers before I cut out your good for nothing tongue!" I can't contain my rage any longer, he knows something that I don't about my own wife.

"Reed, sit down." He speaks calmly and rubs his hands over his knees.

Lola focuses on Harry as I sit next to him, waiting expectantly.

"She's been getting these notes, or cards I should say," he begins.

I clench my fists and unclench them, trying to contain myself.

"She got the first one on the day of your wedding."

"What kind of notes, Harry? What did they say?" I bite, wishing he would just spit it out.

"I've got photos of them." He pulls up his phone and I look through them.

A *'With Deepest Sympathy'* card and inside it says, *'You've just made a huge mistake'.*

A *'So sorry for your loss'* card and *'You don't belong with them'* inside of it.

A *'Sending my Condolences'* card and *'How does it feel to become Mrs. Breckenridge II'* inside of it.

I'm almost tempted to launch his phone at the nearest wall with the fury pulsing through my blood right now. I flick through the images, trying to make sense of it, reading the cursive writing over and over.

"I'm assuming you've already tested the envelopes for any DNA traces?" I say.

"Whoever it is, isn't stupid enough to leave any traces. They're not posted, they're hand delivered, which is the most alarming part."

"Where have they been found?" I question with worry.

"Your wedding, your home and the studio."

I lean my head back and look up at the blinding hospital lights, becoming desensitized to it the longer I stare at it.

"I have a feeling I know exactly who it is." I spit.

We're pulled away from our conversation by the doctor, "She's awake, you can see her now, I'll be through shortly to discuss the test results."

The relief and concern battle each other internally with the news.

I rush to her room and see her through the window, her head is down whilst she picks at her fingernails absentmindedly.

Lola and Harry have decided to stay in the waiting area so we don't overwhelm her.

I gently push open the door and she lifts her head, her shoulders sagging with relief.

"Reed." She cries out as I rush over to her, wrapping her weak body in my arms.

I kiss her head over and over, my heart aching from the sight of her in a hospital gown, the irony laughing at me.

"You gave us a real scare," I whisper to her as she sobs into my shirt.

"I'm just glad you're okay." I continue.

She pulls me in tighter.

The door opens and the doctor enters into the room, I take the seat next to her bed and grasp onto her hand.

"Good afternoon, Indie. I'm Dr. Khan and I've been reviewing your test results to figure out the cause of your unconscious episode." He taps a few times on the tablet he's holding in front of him and instead of standing at the foot of the bed, he pulls a chair to the midpoint of the bed and sits down.

My leg shakes uncontrollably, the nerves vibrating through my system.

"Are you the husband?" He asks me and I nod in response.

Me and Indie flicker our eyes to one another as I squeeze her hand, seeing the distress on her face.

"We ran multiple blood tests and we had noticed that your red blood cell count was significantly low. At first, we thought it could be down to anemia. But, as we ran a second round of tests, the number had dropped again, which didn't seem to be making sense. That was when we entered your room and found the significant amount of blood loss."

My breath hitches as Indie's hand seems to fall limp in mine.

"Were you aware of the pregnancy, Miss Thorne?"

His words echo around my head, a rush of emotions swirling around, fighting for dominance.

Indie shakes her head as her lip trembles.

"I'm terribly sorry to tell you this, but you have suffered with a first-trimester miscarriage."

The words hit me like a Mack truck.

My body tenses and my mouth instantly dries up as it feels like all of the water in my body rushes up to my eyes. Indie lets out a sob and her hands raise to her mouth in shock and upset.

"We believed you to be around six weeks based on the size of the embryo on the ultrasound."

Her wails bounce from each wall of the room as I pull her head to mine.

She grips onto my shirt and cries, her tears demanding to escape. I can't process the news, the loss of two of my children within the space of ten days seems incomprehensible.

"I am very sorry for your loss, I'll leave you to process everything." He leaves the room and I climb onto the bed, pulling Indie into my as she curls up into a fetal position.

My wife.

My love.

I close my eyes and bite my lip to prohibit the sobs from coming out of me, knowing I need to be strong for her right now, be her shoulder to cry on, her support system.

We lay like that for a while, maybe an hour when a small knock is heard from the door. Indie's crying has ceased, but she is still turned into me, gripping onto my shirt with all of her might. We've not spoken about it, the emotions still too raw to address the reality of it.

Lola pops her head inside and I can see Harry towering over her, their faces are solemn as they look over at the both of us.

"Indie?" Lola's soft voice causes her to shift beneath me.

The moment she sees Lola she reaches her arms out towards her, the cries begin again.

Harry looks at me from the doorway, sympathy spread across his features. I look away, staring at the city below through the window, the sun beginning to set in the far distance.

"It's gone." Indie's whimper is muffled inside of Lola's neck.

Rubbing my hand through my stubble, I try to suppress the emotion bubbling up. Lola looks at me and my face remains still, the disaster of my life beginning to warp and numb everything.

"I'll go grab us something cold to drink." I press off the bed and leave the room, Harry following behind me.

"What's gone?" He asks.

I barely make it ten feet from the room before I collapse to the floor myself. I feel him wrap his arms around me as my body shakes uncontrollably and for once, I let him.

I envelop my arms around him and hold onto him, the comfort and familiarity of him guiding me to a place of solidarity.

"The baby." I choke out before I'm overcome once again with it all.

This doesn't feel real, it seems impossible to suffer so much loss in one's lifetime, especially all at once. Images of Allie, Willow and a faceless child intertwine together and cloud my thoughts. It feels like my world is caving in, the ability to breathe is stolen from me as I gasp, trying to satisfy my lungs but it won't work.

"Shit, Reed. You're having a panic attack" Harry pulls away from me and places is hand on either side of my body, trying to get me to look up at him.

"Focus on me, Reed" His voice drifts in and out of my ears like it's on a boomerang.

My vision pulsates and all I can hear is the pounding inside of my own body, the thumping of my heartbeat. The one that still beats, against the one that doesn't. Indie's cries drown out anything else as I can barely make out the man standing before me.

"Look at me." I hear distantly.

I blink furiously to clear my clouded vision, seeing his mouth moving but the sound is so far away.

"Breathe with me." he repeats over and over, finally able to grasp onto my ability to listen.

He inhales through his nose and out through his mouth repeatedly until I can fixate myself on it, following his lead. He nods his head as I begin to concentrate on it, filling my lungs with precious oxygen and exhaling, the tightness in my chest beginning to subside. Everything seems to feel calmer, slower, easier.

We do this for a few minutes until I'm fully in control of my own breathing.

His warm brown eyes are staring into my opposite blue, and it feels like when we were at college, the old times. It's like my brain flashes with every happy memory I've had with him, the nostalgia overwhelming and taking over everything.

I pull him into a tight hug and he almost topples into me from my sudden movements, but he returns the embrace anyway.

"Thank you." I speak into his neck, his body loosening and accepting it.

With everything going on, I need people around me.

It's time to bury the hatchet and reconnect with those who I've pushed away for too long.

Chapter 27

Reed

Indie's required to stay overnight so they can monitor her blood levels. They're potentially going to offer her a blood transfusion since they're unaware of how much blood she has actually lost. That's what caused her to faint, the sudden plummet in her blood pressure and her body dived into defense mode.

Lola decided to stay with her, Gracie's also coming up to see her once she can get away from work.

Locking the door behind me I take in the drink in our home, alone. It feels daunting to be in a house this large, a house designed to be full of family, but it is just me, for now.

I walk around the staircase and down the hallway towards the kitchen to grab a drink, but that's when I see it.

The blue glitter shines under the streetlight, like it's under a spotlight. The full story of the cards and the bag had escaped my mind once we'd spoken to the doctor. Indie's health had taken the forefront of my thinking.

But, I'm sucked right back into it at the sight of it.

Snatching it up, I take it through to the kitchen, grabbing myself a can of soda and sit on one of the stools in front of the island. I take a sip of my soda and then twist the bag around, looking for any sort of telltale evidence.

I read the tag and it is the same cursive handwriting I'd seen on the other cards.

'*Indie Margot Breckenridge*', it reads.

This person is aware of her full name also? It's not exactly common knowledge for them to know her middle name, her public identity is simply 'Indie Thorne'. So, it narrows it down to someone who knows her closely, personally.

I tug on the red ribbon that seals the bag and it topples onto the island. I open the bag and see there's a wrapped gift and a card.

I open the card first.

The card design says '*Thinking of You*' and there is a field of daisies below it.

I open the card and in the distinct cursive writing is '*You play her so well*'.

Play who?

I frown, confused at first, until I open the gift.

Tearing away the rose decorated wrapping paper and it reveals a pink box with some writing on it. It's fairly heavy and I twist it around, confused by it.

'*Coco Mademoiselle*'

It's a perfume bottle?

If this isn't weird enough already, what does a perfume bottle have to do with this? I unbox it, wondering if something else is inside and the box is a cover up.

Pulling out the cuboid bottle with the frosted lid, the pink liquid inside swishes as I inspect it.

It is perfume.

I uncap the lid and that's when it pierces my senses, raising alarm bells in my head.

You play *her* so well.

Her, as in Allie.

This is Allie's perfume, the one she has worn since she was younger. I could recognize that smell anywhere, it is what she smelled like ever since I met her, she never changed it. The reminiscence invades me like wildfire, heating my skin to the point it's painful, a bead of sweat rolling down my neck. The memories, her face, her laugh, her smile, her smell, her skin, her taste. All of it at once, all connected to this distinct fragrance, all of it trapped inside of a glass bottle.

I close my eyes and allow myself to inhale it, the guilt crushing me within its grip.

Placing the bottle on the counter, beginning to struggle. I rub my hands along my jaw as it tics, the disgusting need to numb it all with alcohol, becoming extreme.

My hands shake as I pull my enemy out from the cabinet, the dark and murky liquid calling out my name.

It offers me everything that I can't have, the numbness, the ability to forget, the relief from real life. I grab a crystal class and pour it to the halfway point, popping the lid back on the bottle, setting my phone beside it.

I stare at the bourbon, its fingers caressing my face, offering me salvation from my pain.

Staring at the phone, I chew on the inside of my cheek as the devil and angel on my shoulders fight it out.

It reminds me so much of my mother and father, my mother being the saving grace, the peace, the tranquility. My father being the assailant, the greed, the instigator. But I love my mother. I love her with such an overpowering fondness that my ability to love had died alongside her, it was buried with her.

I've battled my demons time and time again, making the wrong decisions and sacrificing myself in the process. I lost so much, too much.

Loss is a feeling that I'm far too familiar with, and I want it to end. I want to be happy; I want to take my second chance and build it up, create new life whilst elevating the existing ones.

Indie has shown me what love can do, she has shown me the power and the strength that comes from it. Of course, things can be done alone. But the joining of forces, the building of bridges, the fusion of light elements, each result in something beyond their lone origins.

Picking up the phone, I dial Devon's number. He picks up instantly and I let out a sigh of relief, glad that in my time of need he's not mid-flight.

"I need you, Devon." I say into the phone and without any further comment, he ends the phone call.

* * *

Twenty minutes later, the three of them bustle into the house.

"Reed, man. Long time, no see!" Everett claps me on the back, and I begin to feel at ease, knowing I'm not here alone.

Blake strides past with a pizza slice in his hand.

"Where's the TV?" He asks, his mouth full.

"Right through there." I chuckle and point to the lounge.

"Did I interrupt something?" I ask and Everett shakes his head.

"Just the Monaco Grand Prix, nothing major," he jokes, and they disappear into the lounge.

I stand in the hallway as Devon leans against the wall.

"Everything okay?" he asks, his arms folded across his chest. I shake my head and stare at the wall beside him.

"Indie had a miscarriage." I wince at the word, my body shrinking in on itself.

Devon pushes off the wall and walks past me, nodding his head towards the kitchen. We walk past the lounge and the guys are sprawled out on the couch, fiddling with the control for the TV to get the race back on.

Devon stands at the other side of the island as I take a seat on the same stool I had been sat in earlier, the glass still on the counter top, untouched.

He raises an eyebrow and nods his head in admiration.

"You did it, Reed."

"I didn't" I grit.

"You did, you did the right thing." He continues.

I look back at the glass and the whiskey bottle sat next to it.

"I was too close, Devon, too close. I poured the drink, and I leaned over it like a predator, waiting for my prey to look away so I can attack," my voice is slightly raised from my fury at myself, knowing I was seconds away from throwing away my progress.

"But, you didn't attack." He reiterates.

I blow out a breath and put my face in my hands.

"This is too fucking hard this time, too fucking hard." I choke out, the pain gnawing into me.

"You're doing it though." He rests his hands on the island as he presses his weight on them, his muscles flexing through his white tee.

"I don't think I can do it," I whisper.

There's a long pause.

"You won't if you keep telling yourself that. You need to believe you can do it, you need that fire in your stomach to keep you going. Yes, your circumstances aren't ideal. But you need to learn to channel your anger and use it to fuel your drive to get sober."

His words make perfect sense, if I already think I'm going to fail, how will I ever succeed? I almost, very nearly, drank today.

But I didn't.

The finish line seems to come into the picture now, the line that never existed until right this second.

"You're right." I state and lower my head.

"I know," he responds, his arrogance shining through, earning a laugh from me.

"How about a drink?" He says and I look up at him with a scowl.

"A soda, I mean." He lets out a dry laugh and pulls a few cans out of the fridge.

"Nah, c'mon man, that's a clear time penalty, he overtook him him way off track!" I hear Everett shout from the lounge.

I roll my eyes and pull myself from the stool.

"Let's see what all the fuss is about." Devon says and slings his free arm over my shoulders as we stride towards the lounge, relief and hope swarming my mind.

Indie

I've been home from the hospital for a few days, Reed has made it so that I haven't had to lift a finger since I've came home. I've appreciated the foot massages and the selection of chocolate he's bought for me.

I'm wrapped in a fluffy blanket in the lounge with a hot water bottle and a mug of hot chocolate. The fire crackles in the corner of the room, the smell of it comforting me and making me feel like I'm in some sort of cabin in the woods.

I sip the hot chocolatey goodness and flick through the new releases on *Netflix* whilst Reed is at work.

Felicity came over the day I was home, she brought me a hamper of treats, face masks and two romance novels. I ran through the basics of how the studio works, the schedules, the routines and she genuinely looked like she understood, but I can't tell if that was a delusion from the pain medication. Either way, I've been calling to check up on her every day and so far, it seems to be working. I knew she'd be the perfect fit.

I'm still struggling with the news. It's been a difficult time, to grieve something that I didn't know existed, something I had lost before I had the chance to find it. I went through a number of checks with the gynecology team, making sure that I was miscarrying 'correctly' as if there is even a way to do so. So far so good I suppose, I've finished bleeding as I should have, experiencing pain as I should be, crying as I should be.

I feel like the only thing missing is my outlook on the future. I'm not thinking about what if's or trying again for another baby, I feel frozen. Stuck. Like I'm floating in space through light-years, but to me it feels I'm still in the same place.

Reed suggested we try again on my next cycle as long as the doctor gives me the green light.

I think he's really struggling with it. Of course for him, he's lost two children in such a short space of time I think it's slowly breaking him.

But me? I'm not broken, I just think I've stopped. Like I'm a clock that needs oil for my gears to allow me to keep ticking.

Life at the minute seems inconclusive, uninhabitable, intermittent.

I've spent my days watching home design shows and reality TV and eating copious amounts of chocolate.

Reaching into the bag of M&M's, I realize it's now empty. I groan and slam my hand to my forehead, my cravings demanding more. Throwing the blanket from me, I decide it's time for me to venture back out into the real world, climb out of my slum and face reality. I don't know why it surprises me that a bag of M&M's is the motivation for me to do it.

I quickly get changed out of my pajamas and throw on a pair of sweats, along with one of Reed's hoodies, the size of it swamping me but the smell of it comforting me.

Making sure I have the essentials, my phone, keys and credit card, I leave the house for the first time since I returned home.

The outside air smells of moisture, *it's been raining?*

The ground is damp and the leaves on the bonsai trees are dripping. A lot can happen when you've locked yourself inside away from everything. The sky is cloudy, and the sunshine is lost behind them, strangely coherent with my inner self.

I drive to the nearest grocery store, and park in the disabled bay at the front of it, not caring if I get a ticket. I just want to be in and out.

Grasping a basket, I walk around the store until I enter the candy aisle, the selection they have is fairly limited compared to the larger stores.

The ones I want are the peanut butter ones and the fudge brownie ones. I search along the rows and come across a salted caramel bag. It makes me smile with a fondness, remembering the girl's night with my sisters that got me here. I wouldn't have Reed if it wasn't for them, I wouldn't have Willow either. Well, I suppose I still don't.

Tightening my lips, I grab a bag of the salted caramel ones and continue my search.

"Indie, is that you?" A female voice calls from behind me.

"Charlotte, hey." I am not in the mood for any sort of social conversation right now, and I look like I've crawled out of a crack dealer's den.

"Call me Lottie, I insist."

What is with this family and their nicknames?

I nod and stand there awkwardly, trying to figure out something to say.

"Harry told me about what happened, I'm so sorry." Her voice drones on, I bite my lip and look away, I appreciate the sympathy but not in public, in the middle of a grocery store.

"I'm also sorry about Willow, I bet the time-zone difference will be difficult." She says.

I falter and stop.

"Time zone difference?" I question her.

What is she talking about? There is no difference between Atlanta and Florida.

"Yeah, it must be a pain to have to travel to Dubai the next time you see her." *Dubai?*

"Lottie, what are you talking about?" I deadpan, my voice coming out stern as my fists clench.

"Dubai…" She trails off, a confused look on her face.

"I have to go." I drop my basket and run out of the store, straight to my car.

A note sits tucked into my windscreen wipers.

You've got to be fucking kidding me, I was in there for *five minutes*.

I snatch it from the wipers as the rain begins to downpour.

Thankful I decided to bring my phone with me, I dial Reed. He picks up after three rings.

"Hey, baby." He answers.

My heart is pulsing so hard my ears ring, I close my eyes to try and focus on slowing my heavy breathing.

"Woah, baby what's wrong?" He can hear the turmoil through the phone.

"Lottie… Willow… Dubai…" I manage to choke out, my heavy panting making it difficult to speak.

"What about Lottie? What?"

"Lottie said something about Willow– in Dubai." I finish, but my chest is heaving, my heart is hurting and my head is swirling with worry.

I grip the parking ticket firmly in my hand and I begin to look at it clearly, realizing it's not a ticket at all.

"Where are you baby? I'm coming." His voice trails off in the background as I tear into the envelope, ripping the cursive writing directly in two.

This card is different to the others, it isn't the same style. It's…

I choke as my eyes burn.

It's a pink card, with a white circle in the center, a stork carrying a tiny pink parcel and surrounding it is *'Welcome to the world baby girl'*.

My hands tremble as I carefully open the card.

Reed's voice calling out to me but all I can focus on right now is the card in between my hands.

The phone drops from my ear and I become weak, desolate, destroyed.

'Checkmate'

Chapter 28

Reed

Her screams are all I can hear as I bolt out of the office, gripping the phone to my ear tight enough to break it. Something has happened and it's something unintelligible, something unimaginable. I've never heard those sounds erupt from anyone like what I heard in that moment.

The torture.

The fear.

The agony.

I have no idea where she is, but she mentioned something about Lottie. I flip my car into drive and fly out of the office car park, blitzing the streets and swerving traffic. I use my in-car call system to dial Lottie, but she doesn't answer.

What the fuck is going on?

I try her again and she doesn't pick up.

I call Harry.

"Hey, how are–"

"Have you seen Indie?" I bark, not caring to have any sort of introduction right now. The Adrenalin courses my veins and I grip the steering wheel tightly, my windscreen wipers on full power as a storm brews above.

"No, what's happened?" He asks, his voice dripping with anticipation.

"I don't fucking know." I can't contain my sob as I let out an excruciating cry.

I can't explain it but I just know, something awful, something terrible has happened. She mentioned Willow, and she just went silent for a while. And then, it was like her body had been coated in gasoline and she was set alight, her body being consumed by flames as she screamed out at the insufferable pain.

I accelerate harder, the need to get to her completely overtaking my instincts.

"I'm heading over to your place now, I'll be there in five." He ends the phone call and I'm left with the sound of the rain hammering my car as the darkness rolls in.

I shake my head to try and clear my vision, the tears threatening to spill at any moment.

I call Indie again, but this time she picks up.

"Where are you?" I choke, utterly distraught.

"They've taken her." Her voice is quiet, broken.

"Taken who?" I try my best not to come across as being angry at her, but it's difficult to conceal my emotions.

"Willow," she cries, the sound of her name causing her to erupt back into turmoil.

I blink slowly, my lips thin and my breathing heavy. My nostrils flare as I stare through the windscreen, watching the raindrops pound against the glass, seeing the way they erupt on it, the way they bloom and spread across to the next droplet and then they're wiped away with the plastic wiper as if they never existed.

"Baby, tell me where you are." I manage to regain the ability to form words.

I need to see her; I need her to tell me exactly what has happened. She isn't making sense and is talking about things that have already happened.

I'm praying to God that she isn't broken to the point she needs serious help. It seems as if everything dawned on her all at once, I know she isn't at home because of the volume of the rain, it sounded like she was in her car.

"Barnaby's Convenience," she sniffles.

I check the road signs and see the turn off coming up.

"Baby, I'll be there soon, hang on my love, I'm coming for you." I end the phone call and dial Harry, in case he's closer than I am.

"Harry, she's at Barnaby's on ninety-first," I say and flick on my indicator. I check my rear view mirror and there's a car behind me, pretty darn close.

"I'm about a mile away," he says, and I feel a slight release in the tension of my shoulders.

She's going to be okay.

"Tell her I lo–"

The car on the other side of the road blares its high beams at me and I beep my horn at them for them to stop, my vision becoming incapacitated. The car behind me shines their high beams, I'm assuming at the other car and the inside of my car lights up, the ability to see, completely removed.

I panic and press my breaks, knowing the turn off is coming off, just a few more seconds and the car will have passed.

"Reed?" is the last thing I hear before my car begins to lose control.

The wheels spin and I desperately try to regain control, but the downpour eradicates my efforts. I reach for my seat belt, realizing I hadn't put it on and–

Indie

I bounce my leg up and down impatiently, the rain heavy and the winds beginning to pick up.

C'mon Reed, where are you?

A red Audi pulls up next to me and I notice the familiarity of the man getting out. Harry pulls open the driver side door and I wrap my arms around his neck as he wraps his hand around the back of my head.

"Indie, we have to go." He ushers me out of my car.

"What, what's going on?" I ask, a newfound worry fills my mind.

"I think something bad has happened to Reed." My body sets itself on fire and my adrenaline keeps me alive.

"C'mon." I say, climbing into the passenger side of his car as he starts up the engine.

We race out of the car park as the route we begin to drive becomes recognizable, it's headed to Reed's office.

Just as we're about to pull onto the main interstate, the blue and red flashing lights grabs our attention and Harry heads straight for it.

My heart sinks.

My eyes are wide in fear as we near the wreckage, the car I know all too well is upside down, on its roof. The second he stops, I dart out of the car, pushing through the emergency services, calling his name.

My legs burn with the pace I'm running, my chest heaves with every breath but not from running. There is glass everywhere, cops, firefighters, and EMT's with equipment laid out on the floor.

The rain soaks into my hoodie and my sweats, the coldness of it not affecting me in any way from the heat of my core. My hair sticks to my face as I run, my tears conjoining with the pellets of rain. The mixed voices of the emergency services drown out as my focus is fixated on the vehicle.

I slow as I come up to the car, the police tape surrounding it and I see a pool of blood on the ground, next to where the driver side door used to be.

I sink to my knees before it, pressing one hand to the soaked pavement and one hand covers my mouth as I sob uncontrollably. My throat aches and my heart throbs, I have never ever felt pain like this in my life.

I feel as if every nerve ending in my body is being sliced into slowly to preserve the pain, make it last for as long as possible for ultimate torture.

"Ma'am." Someone places a light hand on my shoulder but I can't face them.

I can't process the fact that in the past two weeks I've lost everything. Absolutely everything. There is no words to describe the epitome of this vicious heartache.

Do people really die of a broken heart? Because I feel like I'm about to.

"Ma'am." The person repeats and I turn my head towards them sharply, furious at the fact I'm sat here as a grieving widow and some fucker doesn't have the decency to grant me his patience.

"Are you a family member of the driver?" He asks kindly, but I couldn't care less right now.

"Wife." I grit, my knuckles pressing into the gravel, inflicting some degree of pain to help numb the emotional one.

"The gentleman is in the ambulance being checked over by the crew, if you'd like to see him."

I pause.

"He's… alive?" My voice is timid with disbelief as I shake my head.

"Oh, yes, absolutely. It was a nasty accident, but he was lucky to be wearing his seat belt. The storm really is treacherous at the moment. He has a few superficial cuts and bruises, a pretty nasty gash on his arm but other than that he's fine."

Squeezing my eyes shut, I let out a heavy exhale.

This doesn't feel real, none of this does. It's almost as if someone is making a story of my life and adding as much drama and trauma that they can to get a better shock factor for their reader.

I take his extended hand and stand up, as graceful as *Bambi*.

We walk around to the back of the ambulance and from the moment I see him, it is like every one of my prayers has been answered.

He is alive, he is sitting up, awake, talking, smiling even.

His gaze falls to me and he stands up immediately, pulling the blood pressure cuff with him as I run to him, wrapping my arms around his warmth, not caring if I get any blood or dirt on me.

"I love you, I love you so much." I cry into his chest, fisting the material and then proceeding the check his face for the damage.

"I love you," he croaks and kisses me, holding my cheeks and pulling me into him.

"Are you hurt?" I ask and he shakes his head.

He tells me about everything that happened and the police said they're trying to track down the vehicle on the other side of the road with the lights, as his actions caused an accident, and he didn't stop to help. After he told me he'd only just managed to get his seat belt on before the accident, I gave him a bit of a lecture.

We leave our contact details with the cops as Reed gets the all clear from EMT. We hold onto each other and walk to meet Harry back at his car.

Once we're seated inside, I muster up the ability to tell them about the Lottie and the note.

"This is crazy, why would Lottie know that?" Harry says, staring at Reed.

"Why wouldn't she say anything to either of us?" Reed responds.

"What was she even doing in town? In a small grocery store near your house?"

"None of this makes any sense."

"Have you tried to get in touch with Willow?" Reed turns to me.

I shake my head and explain that I literally just found out.

He dials the phone that he gave her and it doesn't connect, meaning it's either turned off or… what Lottie said may be true.

"Wait, I have that app," Reed says, his nose buried in his phone as he quickly scans through his phone.

I sit in the middle of the backseat. Harry's eyes pour into mine when I glance up at the dash mirror, looking away quickly as the memory of the last time I seen him comes to the forefront my mind.

"Got it." Reed says.

The dot that usually remains in the Florida region, suddenly jumps as the app updates. The map moves around to the other side of the world, her little icon pings in exactly where Lottie said, Dubai.

"The Dawson's know she's not allowed to leave the country during an active custody case." Harry rubs his hand across his jaw, trying to figure out the game they're playing.

I got so distracted with the conversation about Willow, that I've forgotten to show them the card.

"Guys, I got another envelope, whilst I was in the store."

They both swivel around to look at me.

I pull it out of my pocket and unfold it, handing it to them. They both wince at the card of choice but when they open it, they remain still.

"Checkmate." Harrison says slowly.

"As in, they win. Whoever is sending you these notes, think that they've won something."

"It can't just be a coincidence that this has been sent around the time Willow has been practically kidnapped and taken to Dubai." Harry hisses.

"This seems too specific, too direct." Reed says.

"That would explain the perfume, if it was someone closer, someone who knew Allie on a personal level," Harry responds.

"What perfume?" I ask, losing the conversation now.

Reed lets out a groan and his hands rub down his face, he flinches with the movement of one of his arms.

"The gift bag, it contained another envelope and a gift. The card said *'You play her so well'* and then there was a bottle of perfume in the bag. At first there was no relevance, I thought it was a random gift, like the roses. But then I opened it and I recognized it as Allie's perfume." Reed explains and I nod slowly, not realizing that I'd forgotten all about the bag in the midst of everything.

"Everything is strategic, everything is on a timeline, related to events," Harry mutters, mostly to himself as if he's trying to work through everything and fit them together to form the bigger picture.

"We're missing something here, something huge." Reed says, turning to face frontwards again.

"Should we go to the police about Willow?" I ask, trying to conjure up a way to get her back.

"It's no use, they have no jurisdiction halfway across the world," Harry answers, my mind once again forgetting he specializes in family law.

"Let's just go home and we'll come up with something, okay?" Reed begs, and I begin to feel guilty about the fact he got into an accident, on his way to me.

I need to begin to rationalize my thinking.

If I have learned anything from the past two months, it's that we need to be two steps ahead, instead of two steps behind.

We swing by the grocery store to collect my car from the parking lot, seeing as though we're going to need it now Reed's car is totaled.

We called a private doctor to stop by and give him a real check-up to rule out any other injuries, but everything was fine. Perfect, even.

Reed is sprawled across the couch, I made sure to give him some of my pain medication, knowing it's stronger than anything you can buy over the counter. His face is etched in worry lines as he stares blankly into the fire.

"Hey." I say and sit down on the floor in front of the couch, his eyes unmoving.

I rest my chin on his arm and peer up into his eyes, the sheen of his glowing in the iridescence of the flames.

I admire the way the shadows dance around his eyes, lighting up the different angles, the blue color still enticing me as if we'd just met.

"Can you believe that two months ago, we didn't even know either of us existed?" I sigh, wanting to draw his mind away from the negativity.

He lips pull into a lazy smile, but his eyes don't coordinate with them. I pout my lips and frown my brows, to which he finally looks down at me.

"You are so goddamn beautiful. Do you know that?" He says to me, heat rising to my cheeks.

"You try to tell me everyday." I beam at him from the first bit of happiness I've felt in a while.

He reaches up to my face with his grazed knuckles, brushing my hair aside as he gently touches my skin. My eyes flutter closed with the bliss of the sensation, the opposite of how I've been feeling. His hands continue to the back of my head and he pulls me nearer to him, the gap between us closing as our lips graze one another.

I let out a shallow whimper as he darts his tongue out, skimming the outline of my lips with the tip of it. I give in to my temptations and press my lips flush against his, his mouth tasting of peaches. The smell of his usual sandalwood spice begins to ignite the side of me that has been dormant for too long.

"Reed," I groan, his breath is harsh and his nostrils flare as he pulls me onto him.

I straddle him in my night dress and his hands move down my spine before settling on my hips. We fight for dominance within our mouths, the desperation from me struggling to put up a good enough battle.

Part of me just wants to submit and let him have his way with me, but the fire that's coursing through me keeps me going. I grind myself against him and he falters for a moment, his mouth falling slack as I take the opportunity to nibble at his lip. He hisses as I pull away, a dot of blood draws on his bottom lip.

He looks up at me through hazy eyes as he slides one hand between us, unbuttoning his trousers. The sound of the zipper has me in a frenzy, I feel like I can't wait any longer, the rush is growing, and my head is buzzed with anticipation.

"Sit up, baby," he says, and I suck my lip between my teeth, the sound of his deep husky voice sending signals directly to my already throbbing cunt.

I raise up higher as he pulls out his hard cock, the end of it dripping with his pre-cum. My mouth salivates at the sight of his veins, the silky expanse of it tempting me, baiting me. I shuffle my ass backwards and drop between his legs as he looks at me with pleasant surprise.

"Oh, my sweet, sweet poison," he tuts as I look up at him through my lashes.

I take over his grip of his cock, the resistance pulling back as I try and direct it towards me. His legs sit either side of me as my body spreads out in the middle of him, taking up the rest of the couch.

I part my lips and wet them before placing a soft, sopping kiss on the underside of his cock. He hums in approval as his hips buck slightly. I use my spare hand to hold onto his hip, I want him to give me full control. I don't want him to have to use a muscle tonight. I want it to all come from me, for us to forget about everything for a while. To bury our sorrows into each other.

The thoughts take me back, to that first night we met, the pact we made, to forget. But now, all I want to do is remember that night, think about the goodness and the vows we promised one another.

I slide my tongue up and down his length and he presses his head back further into the sofa cushions, his hands cover his face with his elbows pointing at the ceiling. His breath is rough and uneven as I take him in my mouth, slowly sucking up and down, wrapping my tongue around the head.

He begins to buck his hips, begging for more but I dig my nails into his side, insistent on him remaining still. He translates my signal and his hips relax again as I work my way around him, listening to his reactions and adjusting my pace and harshness accordingly.

"Indie," he grits through his teeth as I feel him pulse in my mouth, knowing his climax has him in a choke hold.

I keep my rhythm but swirl my tongue around his tip for longer whilst his breaths grow ragged. His hand reaches down into my hair but he doesn't pull it, he runs his fingers through it gently and his thumb caresses my cheek. I peer up at him and I realize he's looking directly at me. I hold his stare as I pull him out of my mouth and slowly ease him back in.

His eyes flutter as he tries to keep them open, I smirk slightly and repeat. He takes his hand away from my face and balls them into fists at his side as he tries to hold onto his perseverance. He moans as his eyes narrow at me and I suck him harder, offering a fierce scowl in return. He gasps and I feel his cock twitch and my mouth fills with his salty juices, which I swallow rewardingly. I lick him clean as he lays there, staring at me in bewilderment.

I sit up and one of his leg flops from the sofa onto the floor. He reaches forward for my hands and then pulls me on top of him. He places his hand on the back of my neck and kisses me deeply. Within a brief second, he rolls us from the sofa and onto the floor, him absorbing the impact of the fall. I laugh as he grins up at me, kissing along my jawline and down my neck. He sucks and nibbles on my collarbone to the point I'm sure he's left a mark.

He lays me down on the rug in front of the fire and pulls up my nightgown, revealing my bare stomach. He begins to trace circles around my belly, his eyes following the movements of his finger, then leaning down to place soft kisses around it.

The fire is ridiculously hot, a layer of sweat beads along my stomach as the flames light up my body like the fourth of July. Reed pulls off his shirt and I stare at the colorful bruises dotted along his rib-cage, the graze on his shoulder and his bandaged arm.

I sit up to inspect them.

"They look sore," I say to him, and he shrugs, running a hand through his hair. I absorb the sight of him, his toned stomach and his broad shoulders, his muscular arms, all damaged in some way. I sit up and begin to kiss every bruise that I can see. I butter him up with my lips and he sighs as I feel the muscles in his stomach loosen as my lips touch them.

"Lay down, onto your front," I whisper against his neck, and he nods, obeying my command.

I lean over him, cracking my knuckles before beginning to knead his shoulders, offering him some relief. The tension within them tells me the pain that he is trying so hard to mask.

"That– That feels good." His words fall out of his mouth as he lays his head to the side, the glow from the fire purring over his skin.

Continuing to move from his shoulders, further down his back, I make sure to avoid any of the bruised points and not apply too much pressure.

"I love you so fucking much." He mumbles, his eyes closed as his body rises and falls with every breath.

"I love you," I respond, resting my ear against his toned back, listening to the pounding of his own heart as the butterflies from his words caress my own heart.

I smile against him as his breathing slows.

The calm after the storm.

Pure serenity.

Chapter 29

Reed

"The jet is fueled and ready to go Mr. Breckenridge," the agency says.

"Thank you, let the pilots know we'll be there in an hour," I respond.

Once we'd fallen asleep in front of the fire last night, I found myself wishing that I didn't have to wake up this morning, so that I didn't have to face this vile reality.

Knowing Willow is over seven-thousand miles away, the thought that at any point they could discard her phone and she'd be gone forever is so much more daunting than the court case.

My P.I has been on it since I text him on the way home after Indie told me everything.

He said he would try and investigate the cards, but they're practically untraceable.

I have my suspicions:

~~Scott~~

Britney

Rachel

Lottie?

I hesitated before putting my own sister on the list, but her showing up randomly, the card appearing around the same time, seemed too coincidental to ignore.

Britney has been a bit of a lost cause since we broke the news to her about us, and then she showed up at the wedding with little convincing, had Willow overnight, and then poof. *Gone.*

Rachel is the obvious candidate, she despises me and therefore, despises Indie. The information that was relayed in those cards were too specific and simultaneously connected to events that had happened for it to be someone distant.

* * *

"Reed, you're looking well!" Ever shouts me over as I walk through the bar to our usual table.

"You too, Ever. Sun-kissed as always." I joke, hinting to his Aussie skin tone.

I take the seat across from Devon, beside Blake.

"Have you ever thought, on your days off, to wear anything but a suit?" Blake laughs, aiming his words towards Devon.

"You know, I never have, actually. Thanks, Blake." He responds with a scowl, heightening Blake's laughing.

"So, Reed. We've heard through the grapevine that you need a bit of help, with a problem of yours?" Blake begins.

I take hold of the soda that Devon got for me before I arrived, taking a large gulp and then nodding my head.

"You're in luck, man. Devon here has all of the answers to your problems. There isn't anything he can't do, right Ever?" Blake continues, jabbing his thumb in Devon's direction.

"Yeah, he's not wrong. He's somewhat of a mastermind." Ever smirks.

My eyebrows furrow as Devon stares around the bar absentmindedly, not caring that his two best friends are singing his praises.

I can't understand what they're getting at, they haven't even heard my problem yet.

"Is that so?" I look at Devon and his gaze returns to mine, the darkness within his eyes becomes intimidating.

"They give me far too much credit, I'm one of many. It's not all my doing." Devon responds dryly.

"What's not all your doing? I'm a little lost here, guys." My eyes flick between the three of them, waiting for one of them to spill the beans and let me in on this taboo subject.

"Devon here, is a businessman of sorts. Lets just say, even bad guys don't mess with him." Blake grins, staring admirably at Devon.

"I'm still not following." I groan, wishing they would stop being so evasive.

"Just, just trust him. Okay? Tell him your problem and watch him work his magic." Ever leans forward as Devon continues to look at me with a blank expression.

Exhaling, I rub a hand through my stubble and begin to tell them all about Willow and Dubai.

∗ ∗ ∗

It was difficult to organize the route to Dubai from here, the actual end to end journey is around sixteen hours. Our jet can hold about up to six hours worth of fuel, meaning were going to have to refuel at least three times, prolonging our journey.

The pilots had to plan an entirely different route to the usual because people normally fly commercial to somewhere as far as Dubai, but I need to be off the radar.

The Dawson's probably have someone scanning every flight index for our names so that we can't hijack their plans to 'kidnap' my daughter.

"Reed, honey." Her gentle voice laps at my ears, my heart skipping a beat.

"Yeah, baby?" I turn to her and admire the woman standing before me.

She's dressed in a pair of mom jeans and a cropped sweatshirt. Her hair is pulled back into a pony, her travel case at her side.

She walks into the office, her demeanor different to her chirpy one this morning. I rush to her side, anxiety clawing at me.

"What's wrong?" I ask her, dying to know the answer.

"I have something to tell you, and I don't want you to be mad until you hear my full story."

I gulp and nod.

Whatever she is going to say isn't going to compare to anything else we've been through lately.

"When we lost custody of Willow, I was distraught, I didn't know what to do with the news. And that she wasn't biologically yours."

My throat dries with those words, it'll never get easier to hear them.

"I did what I think any other person would do. You know, like get a second opinion." She fiddles with her hands as she looks down at the floor.

"I went behind your back and used hair from Willow's brush and I swabbed your mouth while you slept," she admits.

I don't feel any sort of anger towards her, if anything I feel glad, she could find the confirmation she needed to help process the news.

"I just wanted to see it for myself, you know?" I nod and pull her in for a cuddle, resting my chin on the top of her head.

She melts into me and hugs me tighter.

As she pulls away, she looks up at me and her eyes are watery.

"She's yours, Reed. She's biologically your daughter."

I allow her to continue.

"I got the results this morning, by email. I can show you them if you'd like," my heart races, knowing that she did this for me.

My eyes read through the document, and I come across the all too familiar looking page.

Probability of Paternity: 99.9998%

"This means…"

"They fabricated the report," she finishes for me.

Willow Breckenridge is my daughter, but little does Indie know, I've known for the past few hours also.

After I'd informed Devon of the drastic measures of my in-laws, he assured me that he could help. What I hadn't realized, is that by 'help', he meant that he would uncover information that turned this entire situation on its head.

He gave me a new level of truth that I would never have believed if he didn't have the proof to back it up.

Devon's entire team belong to a force higher than our law enforcement, a hidden vigilante group that have impacted the world in so many ways without any of them realizing it.

It's not that I didn't trust him, it was just what he told me was so unbelievable that it didn't make sense, it changed everything.

With Devon being able to orchestrate the entire plan, it meant that it actually seemed feasible. The plan he has come up with is far beyond anything a 'normal' human would be able to conjure, the detail and the number of 'back-up' plans is insane, making sure that the plan is flawless.

Of course, Indie will have to be clued in and that is something I'm going to have to spend the next sixteen hours of flight time, explaining.

For now, I let her have her victory.

"Thank you, so fucking much." I kiss her deeply and she sighs into the kiss.

"Let's go and get your daughter back." she grins at me and takes my hand, grabbing her travel case in the other.

"Let's go and get *our* daughter back." I confirm, as she looks at me tearfully.

It feels like my world, divided by oceans, rivers, and lakes, has finally been provided with a passageway to our safe haven.

Chapter 30

Reed

"We really must get you a new car," I insist, listening to the rattle of the engine and shift myself in the uncomfortable seat.

"Oh, stop it. You sound exactly like my mother." She waves me off and places both her hands back on the steering wheel.

The airport is busier than normal for a Thursday, but the perk of chartering a jet is the exclusive VIP route. We're done with security in less than ten minutes and we're having a quick bite to eat.

"Are you scared?" Indie asks me, taking a bite of her bagel.

"Scared for what?" I sip my black coffee and bounce my leg up and down, eager to board the plane.

"I don't know... just, what if something bad happens?" She questions.

I'm not exactly sure what she thinks Rachel and Bill are capable of, but it's definitely more than I expected. They've proved me wrong on that point. Never judge a book by its cover, you never know what's written in between the lines.

In this case, it was the fact that they were clever enough to spring something so detrimental to the case last minute that none of us considered the idea that it could be falsified.

I didn't think that they would have the balls to actually take her to Dubai, but knowing what I know now, their actions aren't that of their own.

"I just can't wait to see her sweet face, Reed. I've missed her so much." Indie grasps hold of my hand, threading her fingers in between mine.

What she hasn't realized is, she's changed everything. She turned this entire thing around, she fulfilled me with hope, she held me up when I couldn't stand, she was the person who kept filling me with the passion to fight. She will never be able to understand how much I appreciate her for that, but I will spend my entire life trying.

"You have no idea, Indie." I smile.

"Mr. and Mrs. Breckenridge, Flight A329 is now boarding. The pilot has requested a quick word with you before take off."

"Come on, my darling wife."

I take her hand as she grabs her iced coffee to take with us and we walk over to the gate. We show our electronic boarding passes, listed under random aliases and we don't provide our passports, which the agency is already aware of.

Sometimes, we have to do similar things for our cases, especially when it's with the top companies who want to keep everything under wraps, so it's not unfamiliar to any of us, but Indie.

Devon has ensured everything is set in place, everything is to run smoothly.

We walk onto the jet and Indie takes a seat in one of the leather recliners, setting down her book and bag.

"I'll be just a moment," I tell her and knock on the cockpit door.

The door opens and I'm met with the dark brown eyes, his face pulled into a grin.

"Devon!" I cheer and pull him in for a brother hug.

"Reed, pleasure to be flying you." His tone is professional but surprisingly joyful.

He looks great in his pilot uniform, the navy blue and the gold stripes wrap around the sleeves, contrasting to his dark features.

I turn around and step out of the way so he can get a view of the cabin.

"This is my wife, Indie Breckenridge. Indie, this is Devon, my sponsor." His eyes shift from me to my wife and he smiles a grin that I haven't seen him provide before, flashing his perfect white teeth.

"Devon Stark, your pilot of the evening." He removes his hat and holds it at his stomach, bowing.

I roll my eyes as Indie raises an eyebrow at me and smirking.

"It's wonderful to finally meet the man who steals my husband away for several nights a week," she jokes, earning a genuine laugh from him.

"Alright, alright. That's enough flirting. Shall we ditch the tarmac?" I usher Devon back into the cockpit and he laughs again, waving at me before sealing himself inside of the tiny room.

I take the seat across from Indie, her legs crossed over and her converse shoe bouncing.

"Is there any need for you to eye fuck my friends right in front of me?" I joke.

Her cheeks deepen a shade of pink and she pretends to read her book, considering it's upside down.

"Bit of advice," I whisper, leaning forward.

"It might help if you turn the book the right way up." I lean back in the chair as she closes the book altogether, tossing it to the side.

"Buckle up ladies," Devon's voice comes through the intercom.

Indie chuckles to herself as we fasten our seat belts.

"Ready for the longest journey of your life?" I ask her.

"I thought I already agreed to that on our wedding day?" she taunts as she twists her wedding rings around her finger playfully.

I shake my head, biting my lip to stop myself from laughing.

I won't give her the satisfaction.

***

We land at our second refueling stop, we're in Morocco. We have a forty-five minute break to use the toilet, grab some snacks and a hot drink. The jet wasn't restocked for us as we requested it with short notice.

"How does it feel to be finally traveling the world?" I ask Indie as she skims through a magazine in the airport cafe.

"It feels like every second that I'm with you, it's dreamy." She smiles, closing her eyes.

I lean down and kiss her. Everything is beginning to feel okay, to feel like the world has been put back on its axis.

"I'm just going to run to the bathroom, do you need anything?" She shakes her head.

As I'm walking to the bathroom, I feel the hairs on the back of my neck stand up. I stop walking, turning around to look at people in the vicinity. I eye each of them carefully, none of them glancing in my direction.

Sighing, I continue to the bathroom.

I walk closer to the cafe, the same feeling that I can't seem to shake, rises.

Someone is watching me.

I can feel it.

I stop and look around again, taking extra caution this time, seeing if there's anyone's face from earlier that I recognize.

Nobody.

I return to the table we were sat at, Devon and the other pilot sit with Indie, chatting about destinations they've visited, selecting their favorites. Indie listens in awe, nodding her head as she finishes her green smoothie.

"Time to go." Devon stands up, buttoning his blazer.

We board the plane and sit in the same seats. As we begin to taxi onto the runway, I glance back at the glass windows of the airport, nearest to our terminal. A figure in dark attire stands there, watching our jet. I squint my eyes to try and get a closer look but before I can distinguish anything, the jet turns away and steals my view.

***

"Welcome to Dubai, ladies. The local time is 13:13, the climate is dry and it's thirty-eight degrees Celsius, one-hundred-point-four degrees Fahrenheit." Devon's voice speaks through the intercom.

We're both peering out of the window at the stunning blue skies and the brightness of it compared to Atlanta.

Grabbing our luggage and hauling it down the steps of the jet, the sun beams down on us.

After explaining everything to Indie, she needed a few hours to digest it, eventually falling into a deep sleep. I don't blame her, it's been a rough few weeks and this really is the tip of the iceberg.

Devon and his team are on standby, waiting for our signal.

It seems completely absurd to be doing something as crazy as this, but desperate times call for desperate measures.

The longer Willow is here, the more chance they have to uproot and jet to another country. The tracker on her phone still says she's here, the place where she is staying is only twenty-five miles away from the airport, so it gives us enough time to go over the plan for the last time, before we put it in action.

We climb into the back of the black SUV and the driver places our luggage in the trunk. We join the busy traffic, the coordinates already provided to the driver.

"We need to lay down a few ground rules here," I begin as Indie rubs her eyes, trying to wake herself up more from the sleep on the jet.

"Please don't panic, don't be alarmed." I pull open the middle compartment of the SUV and slide out the black case that's embedded inside of it.

I flip the locks and open it, the 9mm pistol cushioned in the foam with an 18-bullet loaded magazine held in the corner.

"Reed what the fuck?" She gasps, looking around at the passers-by in case anyone can see.

"The windows are fully tinted and reflective. Don't worry," I assure her and remove the gun from the case.

"Oh my God." She looks away.

"We don't know what game they're going to play here, Indie. We need to be prepared from all angles." I pull out the magazine and push it into the gun, making a note that I haven't reloaded it yet.

I set the gun back in the case and close it.

"Do you even know how to use that thing?" She looks at me with her jaw dropped.

"What do you take me for? An amateur?" I tease, but she doesn't look impressed.

"Look, I have no intention to use it, only as a last resort." I debate with her as she shrinks into the corner of the seat.

I know Indie isn't comfortable in the slightest with the plan, it's totally out of our comfort zones but it's nothing I haven't done before.

We both take in the beautiful architecture of Dubai as we pass by the beaches. I'm jealous that we don't get to lay on a sun lounger and soak up the rays as a family. Instead, I'm wielding a gun to try and bring my daughter home.

The huge white mansion takes us by surprise. I didn't think that the house on the map looked this extravagant, but Dubai is a fast moving country. The driver takes us right up to the gates and I lean over the seat.

"Hey, we just need to be dropped off outside, we're not actually meant to be here."

The gates open and he ignores me, driving the car into the driveway, circling around the fountain. Me and Indie glance at each other. The hair on the back of my neck stands up again, the awful feeling rising in my throat.

I glance down at the casing of the gun and edge my hand towards it, trying to flick the lock on it without it being noticeable.

Think, Reed. Think of the other plan options. Devon told you to be prepared, he covered all potential angles.

I have no fucking clue what's going on, but it's not good.

The case lock pings open and the driver slams on his brakes, throwing me and Indie into the chairs in front as I wince from the instant shooting pain to my head.

Indie screams.

I look up and the driver is aiming a gun between the both of us.

"Either of you move and I won't hesitate to put a bullet through your skull," he snarls, his accent clearly American.

Well, fuck.

Devon was right.

I glance at the case of the gun, now on the floor at my feet. I return my gaze to the driver and he keeps the gun turned in on us, but he's making hand gestures with his other hand to someone outside of the car.

Indie begins to shake her head at me as if she can read exactly what I'm thinking.

I twist my feet, angling them so they have access to the final flip lock. I press one foot on top of the box and the toe of the other shoe below the lock. I push my foot upwards and the lock flicks open, but I cover it up with an obnoxious cough.

Before I even get chance to do anything, Indie's door is pulled open and she's hauled out by her hair, kicking and screaming. I lurch forward after her, but the driver grips me by the hair, shoving the barrel of the gun into my temple.

"Don't even think about moving," he spits, his breath smelling of cigars and whiskey.

Fuck. Fuck. Fuck.

What the fuck kind of mafia shit is going on here?

I stare over to the door that Indie was dragged through and begin to make a note of my surroundings. My phone buzzes in my pocket.

Fuck, yes.

I angle my body so that the left-hand side of my body is pushed up against the seat. I keep my gaze straight ahead, occasionally flicking my eyes down to the screen. Within three seconds, I text Devon '*SOS*' and share my location.

Whatever the fuck is going on here, I'm out of my depth.

"Hey man, do you mind turning the air-con up? I'm roasting in here." I ask.

He grunts in response and leans forward to adjust the dials as I lean up and come down on him with my elbow, knocking the gun from his grip.

He fights back instantly as his fist collides with my brow bone. I lay face down on the seat, acting like I've been knocked unconscious.

I hear him exit the car, walking around the other side to retrieve his gun and I seize the opportunity. I flip the case open and grab the gun. I lay on my back and spread my legs apart as I can see him about to open the door to the backseat in front of me.

I hold the gun in between my legs, my breath shaky and a droplet of sweat running past my temple. He opens the door and I pull the trigger.

His body launches backwards from the impact and he drops to the floor.

My ears ring from the sound and the adrenaline in my veins causes my body to erupt into uncontrollable shakes.

I sit up, glancing at his body with the large pool of blood surrounding him.

Holy fuck.

His body is still, unmoving. Dead, maybe.

Scrambling out of the car, I step over the dead-weight and rush towards the doors that I saw Indie disappear through. As much as I'm wanting to see Willow, I'm praying to God that she's not in this house with these crazy fuckers.

I slip through the door with my back pressed against the wall, the gun held up at my chest. My heart pounds against my chest, making it difficult to hear anything over it.

I hear footsteps down the corridor and I slyly move along the wall, popping my head out to get a better look.

A woman stands with her back to me, her brown hair medium length and she's wearing a pair of jean shorts and a bikini top. I hold my breath and take aim, steadying my stance and my hands.

I think it's about time to see if my training paid off.

My finger hovers over the trigger shakily, I wait until she steps more central into my view.

The fuck?

She turns and I lose my nerve instantly, shrinking back around the corner.

I'm seeing things now, right?

I swallow and blink a few times, bringing my head around the corner again. She sips from a soda can and looks upwards, making the birthmark on her neck prominent. I can't fucking believe it.

It's Lottie.

I fucking knew she had something to do with it, she knew far too much for her role in our lives, the cards, fuck. I need to get to Indie; I don't trust any of them.

A sharp piercing scream can be heard from upstairs as I hear Lottie's footsteps dash up the staircase.

That better not be my wife.

Following after her, I keep myself concealed and climb the double staircase. I flinch at the sound of Indie's voice.

"You crazy fucking bitch!" She screams.

My eyes grow wide, and my instinct almost takes over, my legs almost setting out into a sprint towards the sound of it.

You are going to be no help if you're dead, Reed.

I creep closer to the room, sliding along the wall and following the red train of carpet running through the middle of the tiled flooring. I can hear muffled conversation behind the door and I reload the pistol, letting out a hasty breath. I tighten my lips and then kick the door open, my gun pointed directly into the room.

My legs buckle beneath me as I drop the gun, the air knocked out of me.

"Nice of you to finally join us, my darling husband."

Chapter 31

Reed

I pick my gaze up from the floor in front of me as I struggle to breathe. My mind is rearranging itself, flipping everything inside out, looking for reality. I squeeze my eyes shut tightly and reopen them.

Her blonde hair is cut into a bob, her green eyes burning into me with fury as she points a gun at me. Everything is wrong, everything is confusing and muddled and I can't even string a sentence together for fuck's sake.

Nothing is working, I'm still on my knees, my hands haven't moved and I'm not even sure if I'm still breathing.

"Miss me?" she snarls, and I literally feel like I'm about to vomit everywhere.

Oh fuck, yup.

It's happening.

I keel over and empty the contents of my stomach onto the floor in front of me as she cackles in delight. My throat and eyes burn as I flick through everything in the past two months, trying to find something I missed, but I draw a blank.

"Cat got your tongue, Reed?" I heave every time she speaks, especially when it's my name. This can't be real, I don't want this to be real.

I shakily bring my eyes back up to meet *hers*.

Allie's.

I start to shake my head again as she smirks at me.

"Get up, you look pathetic." She moves the gun, signaling for me to stand up.

I reach to my side for the gun.

"Don't even think about it, I'll have your brain matter sprayed across the wall behind you before I could even say BOO!" She bursts out laughing and I hear another high-pitched laugh and that's when my eyes fixate on my sister.

I scowl as she stares back at me with a blank look. I can't even tie anything together, I feel like my brain has been thrown into a washer and it's been turned on for the last ten minutes.

"I'm very glad you came to visit, but I must admit, it will be short-lived." I glance towards Indie and see that they've bound her to a chair by her hands and legs, a pair of handcuffs across her wrists and then it's tied to the chair with a rope.

She has a gash on the side of her head that's dripped blood down to her neck and it drips onto her thin t-shirt. Her eyes meet mine and the terror that emits from them turns my stomach, the desperate plea to be saved when I'm utterly fucking helpless.

"Are you not going to ask how I did it?" She licks her lips, her finger still hovered over the trigger.

I'm still completely frozen, cemented to the floor and my mouth unable to move.

"Fine, fine, I'll tell you." She waves the gun and grabs a chair, sitting on it the opposite way around.

"Once upon a time, a girl met a boy and they fell in love. She loved him so deeply, she gave up her life for him and she signed her life away to become a mother, to become a loyal wife, to give him the perfect life."

"Oh no, sorry. That was Indie's story." She laughs at herself and Indie lets out a sob.

"Shut up you whiny bitch!" Allie points the gun at Indie and her body tenses up, her mouth sealing shut.

"Let's begin again. We met in college, hooked up and I became pregnant with darling Willow. We got married and gave it a shot at being together, but it was never enough. You didn't want me. You didn't love me. But in reality, I didn't love you either. My heart belonged to someone else." She looks up and stares fondly at the other person in the room.

"Lottie?" I shout, the outburst proving that my brain is slowly playing catch-up.

I'm shaking my head in disbelief; I'm so beyond lost here.

"Anyway, I found your little file on your computer of Indie. The pictures, the P.I you hired, your infatuation with her."

Indies head whips around to me, her eyes wide as her lip trembles.

I remain silent.

"So, I got in touch with your P.I, he revealed a hell of a lot of information to me, Reed. For the right price of course."

I attempt to swallow the lump in my throat.

"Turns out, you were getting suspicious. You were getting too close, and I had to protect us, bide my time. I hired your own P.I to keep me updated on what you were up to and boy oh boy was it *exciting!*" She falls into laughter again and Indie looks at me tearfully, begging me to spare her.

"The hit man you hired? I paid him off, a lot more than you were willing to pay, it was pitiful to be honest, finding out how little I was worth to you. But that's when it sparked the initiation of this entire project."

I can't even meet Indies stare anymore, I focus my eyes on Allie, her green eyes dancing with triumph.

"Obviously, I faked my own death. But it took a lot of effort, you know? We orchestrated the accident, caused it, whatever you want to call it. The plan went a bit off track, and I got a lot more injured than I was meant to. But, my lovely Lottie flew me straight over to the best surgeons in the world, right here in Dubai." She smiles over at my sister fondly.

"She paid off the hospital staff and your P.I came in incredibly handy to formulate our new identities, the cadaver for the funeral, the death certificate blah blah, you get the point. Mommy and daddy were so relieved to find out I was alive and thriving halfway across the other side of the world, and they were more than happy to help bring my daughter back to me." She toys with the gun in her hands.

"Britney too. But she fumbled with her duties last minute. Do you remember the night of your honeymoon? Well, my sister was meant to board a flight with Willow and bring her right to me, but she had some sort of 'moral dilemma' and backed out. Then we had to think fast, cue the formulation of the DNA report arriving at the end of the court hearing. I must admit it was a desperate grab, but you were all stupid enough not to challenge it and we seized the victory!" She claps excitedly.

"Aw, the little 'I love you Willow Breckenridge' at the end was touching, quite the show," she mocks and I grimace.

Indie

"But, little miss Indie Thorne in my ass over here, couldn't keep her nose out, could she?" She spits at me, rolling her eyes.

"The contract really was a clever idea, Reed. It worked exactly how you wanted it to, she fell in love with your sad, pathetic self. I suppose you have me to thank for that, you couldn't have come up with that without the custody battle."

My heart is being torn apart, blown up, shattered, destroyed, massacred, stabbed.

"The cards idea was more of Lottie's thing, she wanted to mess with you, get in your head, throw you off course because you began to look into my death. We had the P.I hack into all of your devices and that's when I discovered your obsession with me."

Obsession?

"I was honored by the 'Swan' reference, truly. If I had been dead, that would have been nice. But if there's anything I know about you, Indie, it's how much you love Willow. I could tell that long before, even when you were just her ballet teacher. And that for me, didn't fit my agenda. I think Willow had grown used to you acting as a mother to her and began to forget about me, which I didn't like. So, we turned things up a notch, we pulled the plans forward and instead of waiting until the court trial was over, we ran with it."

I shake my tears away, not wanting to look like a blubbering baby.

I don't want to be weak, I want to take her down.

"I knew neither of you would give up Willow that easily, you'd start to raise suspicions with the state, and the last thing we need is the FBI up our asses. Lottie planted her seed in you and look around, it blossomed right into the colorful *thorn* bush that we wanted."

I gulp, we walked right into their trap, they weren't a step ahead at all. They were fucking conducting the whole show.

We were the puppets on the strings.

"I really couldn't have orchestrated it better, you two are just so damn fierce, aren't you? You arrived here, just as expected. I had my people tracking you, making sure nothing was going amiss, we swapped out your driver with one of my guys, but made sure you still had your requested weapon of choice, we didn't want to drop the ball early. This is so much more fun." Her smile is haunting, it's like her body is here but she is dead inside.

"I am awfully sorry about your miscarriage Indie. It must have been awful. Being so desperate to put the final nail in my coffin, to give Willow the one thing I couldn't, a precious sibling." The mention of the miscarriage makes my heart ache, the instinct to press my hand to my stomach protectively to shield her evil from it.

"We'd been polluting your water tank in your office for a while with anti-neoplastic drugs, a relatively low dosage so it flew under the radar but enough to render your womb uninhabitable. It's amazing the access you have to drugs over here in Dubai." She laughs.

I.

Can't.

Fucking.

Breathe.

I can't breathe.

Icannotbreathe.

My body begins to shake violently as I choke. Their attention turns to Reed as he rushes to get up.

"Sit your fucking ass down." She points the gun at Reed.

I thrash against my restraints, desperate to be released from them.

Claustrophobia flips the switch in my brain and I become uncontrollable. I twist and writhe as I scream. My head pounds and I can feel the blood vessels in my eyes bursting one by one. The chair I'm strapped to tips onto its side, falling to the floor. I continue to fight it, praying that the ropes will loosen enough to set me free.

But my efforts are unaccounted for.

I pant as the tears flow endlessly, the reality of the situation sinking in. We're going to die here, today. I can't just sit here helpless, weak, and pleading for mercy.

"Is she this feisty in the bedroom?" She directs her question at Reed and I close my eyes.

I need to think.

Why isn't he doing anything?

Is he really just going to sit here and allow the psycho bitch to talk us to our deaths?

"Tragic, really. You came all this way, with some cute idea of holding my parents at gun point and skipping out of here with Willow by your side. If there's anything you need to work on in your next life, it's to stop being so fucking naive. Quite frankly, it's boring." She sighs, glancing out of the window.

I see Reed out of the corner of my eye rush towards the gun he dropped.

"Pick that up and she gets a bullet in the forehead." She states blankly, the gun now turned on me.

I try and look at Reed, but he's too far behind me to see.

"Have I not just told you not to be so fucking naive, Reed? God, you disappoint me."

I'm deathly still, staring down the barrel of her gun.

"Now, there is one thing I have to ask of you, Reed. Something that you might be uncomfortable answering. I need to know what I'm going back to. I don't want to have to clean up any of your messes."

Going back?

To Atlanta?

"What did you do with that, God awful, ex of hers?" She asks.

My eyes grow wide.

Scott?

"The silent treatment, huh?" She taunts.

Next thing I know, she climbs on top of me, legs either side of me, restricting my movements. She yanks my head to the side and she forces the gun into my mouth, it clangs against my teeth on the way in.

I sob uncontrollably, the tears streaming as I try and breath around the cold metal inside of my mouth.

Reed is staring at her, completely calm and collected.

I'm sitting here about to urinate all over the place and he's there, *looking smug?*

She cocks the gun and Reed flinches.

"Fine, I'll tell you. Just take the gun out of her fucking mouth, Allie."

My eyes bounce between him and the psychotic bitch on top of me.

"I really like the atmosphere though, it makes it so much more exciting, don't you think?" She smiles down at me as I shake my head as much as I can under her grip.

"Ergh, fine." She grumbles and drops my head back to the cold tile, climbing off of me and returning to her chair.

I intake a sharp breath, the oxygen flowing freely into my mouth now it's not being obstructed by a *fucking gun.*

"His body is in the quarry." He states plainly.

Body.

Quarry.

"Brilliant work Reed, I'm almost impressed. It's incredible isn't it? How you'll kill for her, but you tried to kill me. The power of love, hm?" She grins at him.

I don't know how much more of this I can take.

"Now, let's get down to business. Who wants to kill who?"

The air is knocked out of me.

"Oh, come on, we can treat it like a pitiful version of Romeo & Juliet. The tragic love story of two forbidden sweethearts, that tried everything they could to be together but ultimately, it was their love for one another that killed them. Oh, I could picture it now." Her face twists as she looks up at the ceiling, the wicked grin spreads across her thin face.

"Lottie, can you grab my phone please?"

I furrow my brows, what more crazy shit is she going to spout now?

She fiddles with it for a while and then turns it around, the sound of crying filling the room.

"Lola, Gracie, say hello." She says and the second I glance at the screen, the nausea overwhelms me.

They're gagged and bound in a dark room, a gun pressed to their heads and their face covered in tears.

I squeeze my eyes shut, unable to look at them any longer. I cry so hard that I can't hear anything but my own wails, anything to drown out the sound of theirs.

"Take the fucking gun, Indie."

She drops a second gun to her feet and kicks it over to me. It hits my shoulder, the barrel of it pointing towards my face.

I shake my head.

"Tyron, shoot them." Everything intensifies all at once.

"NO, no, no, no, I'll do it, I'll do it!" I roar, my throat burning, my head hurts.

I don't even think I'll be able to hold a gun with the shakiness of my hands.

"Tyron, keep them there until I give you the all clear." She ends the phone call and their cries disappear, just the sound of my own filling the room.

"Hm, cut her restraints." She orders Lottie.

I raise my eyes to Reed's and he's still completely expressionless, I can't tell if he's in a state of shock that he can't actually process what's going on.

Lottie leans down and cuts the rope, releasing me.

"Bring her arms around the front." She orders.

Lottie unlocks one of my handcuffs and readjusts me so my arms are in front of my instead of behind.

I bore my eyes into Lottie's, trying to gauge how she feels about all of this. Yes, she may be in love with Allie and vice versa, but this is her brother. I don't think she'd give a shit about me, but the guy over there is her own flesh and blood.

"Pick up the gun." She demands, her voice cold.

I swing my legs around on the floor and twist to pick up the gun.

"Lottie, grab your gun and then stand her up." Lottie yanks me up by my arms and I wince in pain.

"Gun to the head, just like I showed you."

I feel the harsh material press against the back of my skull, the fear erupting into more shakes in my legs and arms.

"Perfect. Beautiful. Now, Indie. Your requirement here is to shoot Reed. If you comply, we set you your sisters free and you get to go on with your life as if we never existed. If you decide to spare his life, how can I put this… Ah, four lives will be lost today!" She beams.

I can't even think about anything but the weight of the gun in my hands.

The weight of my decision.

The weight of the world on my shoulders.

"Would you like me to call Tyron, give you a little bit of persuasion?" She asks, cocking her head at me.

"No." I sob.

"Get to your feet, Breckenridge." She spits, Reed listens and rises to his feet.

His hands shake but the rest of him remains still.

I look into his eyes and that's when I see it.

I see his fear, his surrender, his understanding.

I close my eyes and drop my head, unable to look at him for any longer.

This can't be the only way, I can't do this.

My entire body is vibrating in shock, despair, and intimidation.

The hairs on the back of my neck stand up as I look at him again.

"Oh, come on, any last words?" She looks between us.

"I'm sorry," I sob, my body trying to fold in on itself as I fight the urge to collapse, knowing it will only earn me a bullet in the process.

Reed smiles at me and I shake my head, unable to see his sweet, charming smile in a moment like this.

It's killing me.

As much as Allie thinks that I will walk away a 'free woman' once I shoot him, this will kill me also. But that's probably what the sick bastard hopes.

My gun is pointed at him, and I don't even think I can see through the tears in my eyes.

Everything hurts, it's all playing out in my head, and I seriously don't think I could even pull the trigger if I wanted to.

"I love you," Reed says as he gets onto his knees.

The sight alone will haunt my every waking moment.

I cock the pistol and let out another sob.

He nods at me slowly as Allie stands beside me, bouncing with eagerness like a kid waiting for an ice-cream.

Inhaling a shaky breath, closing my eyes tightly, I pray to the gods above that I don't go to hell.

I pull the trigger.

Chapter 32

Indie

I drop to the floor instantly, tucking myself into the fetal position as all hell breaks loose.

Combat.

Chaos.

Carnage.

I cover my ears from the sounds, my heart drilling into my eardrums with the intensity.

A pair soft hands pull my own hands away from my ears and I open one eye slowly, my body relaxing into an exhausted heap.

"It's over," he whispers, the sounds of footsteps shuffling around the room almost overthrow the volume of his voice.

I gaze absentmindedly into his endless ocean of blue, the familiarity caresses my body with a gentle comfort.

I sit myself up and see I'm still shaking uncontrollably, unable to stop my natural reaction of shock.

He pulls me into his arms as he's kneels down, placing his hand on the back of my head whilst he squeezes me.

"It's all over, dimples." He breathes as we sink into each other.

He pulls away from me and kisses me deeply, repeatedly.

"You did so well, I'm so proud of you." Reed holds my face in his hands as he grins at me.

My heart flutters and I turn my head slightly, seeing the two limp bodies of Allie and Lottie.

"Willow?" I panic.

"She's waiting at the terminal for us."

"Lola and Gracie–" I begin, the frantic sounds in my voice.

"They were Devon's men."

And once again, my muscles relax.

I had put all of my faith, my trust, God, my life into Reed's hands, and he saved us.

He saved us all.

I look over to the corner of the room and see Devon fully kitted out in a bullet-proof vest, cargo trousers and combat boots.

When Reed told me their plans, I was apprehensive.

He shared that Devon served in the military as a pilot for the first seven years of his career, and that he wanted to do his part for the world differently. He didn't want to be on the front line, he wanted to be behind the scenes, in the shadows, defending the innocent as opposed to fighting federal warfare. That's when he found others like him, others who wanted to live the 'double agent' lifestyle. Reed paid for Devon's entire team to fly out to Dubai commercially, they were more than prepared.

Reed told me everything on the flight here, about the first time he ever saw me at the business conference, the P.I, the hit he put out on Allie, the suspicions he had regarding her autopsy report and Scott.

We were both caught off guard with Lottie's involvement and their relationship, we didn't see that one coming.

The miscarriage story was debatable, I think she'd heard about it and tried to use it to her advantage to make it seem like she had more influence on our lives than she actually had.

We had our suspicions, the symptoms never stopped so we called a doctor over on the night of Reed's accident. Once he'd checked over Reed's injuries, we told him about what had happened and if everything that I was experiencing was normal. He laid me down on the couch and took my vitals and then he removed the Doppler from his bag. He pushed it into my pelvis and the thumping of a strong heartbeat flooded the room. The doctor suspected that it had been twins, and I had lost one of them which caused the confusion.

It turns out our little baby was hiding on the ultrasound I had in the hospital, waiting to surprise us in their own special way.

"We have a medic with us, he can fly with you on the way back and get you both checked out. That must have been pretty fucking traumatic." Devon says, crouching down on his knees to lower himself to our height.

"Thank you," I breathe, peering up at the man who spared our lives, the man who gave us the opportunity to keep our family.

He places a gloved hand on my shoulder, patting it slightly, "Honestly, anytime," Devon grins.

Finally building up the courage, I look around.

It's interesting, seeing the complete turmoil around me, the disaster and hatred splattered across the room, like a pitiful version of Romeo & Juliet.

The tragic love story of two forbidden sweethearts, that tried everything they could to be together but ultimately, it was their love for one another that killed them.

A wicked grin spreads across my face.

Chapter 33

Reed

In some weird, fucked-up way, there is something satisfying about seeing the demise of my beloved ex-wife and my sister.

In every way possible, I've replayed the moment in my head, wondering if things could have turned out differently, but ultimately it's inevitable.

Allie was never going to win. I was pushed to limits beyond my control and if anyone was to ask me if I'd have done things differently, I wouldn't have.

I sought out my sweet retribution, she got exactly what she deserved, along with my sister.

There's one thing you should never test in a father, unless you really want to see the deepest, darkest side of him. And, that's questioning how far they will go for their child, in order to keep them safe.

It's pitiful that they thought I would do anything less, that I would put anything before my daughter, regardless of what it is.

I'll never change that. I'll never surrender to anything less than ensuring Willow is protected at all costs, regardless of who or what. This will continue until the day I eventually meet my own demise.

I will still confidently back every decision that I've made so that Willow can prosper. And of course, our sweet new angel baby.

Indie grasps my hand, interlocking her fingers with mine as we journey back to the airport, to our future.

My body buzzes with excitement and love at the thought of our baby girl, waiting at the airport for us, knowing she is returning home *where she belongs.* Happy and safe.

Rachel and Bill have been shaken beyond belief. We made sure that they're terrified for their lives if they ever try to interfere with Willow or any of us again. We made sure of that by showing them their untimely fate if they are to cross with us, ever. The still and lifeless bodies of Allie and Lottie.

In regards to my darling sister, I'm annoyed more than anything. Irritated that she got herself involved in between a situation that didn't concern her, and now she's just a consequence of her actions.

The car stops in front of the entrance of the bustling airport, a mixture of vacationers, businessmen, and staff, line the walkway with their baggage in tow.

I take a glance at Indie, seeing her slightly pale and bruised. My heart strings pull, ashamed that she was harmed in the process but falling more and more in love with her, knowing she did this for Willow. We both did.

If there's one thing more certain now, than ever, it's that our love between the three– *four* of us, is unconditional.

No beginning, no end.

"She's waiting," Indie whispers, trying to pull me back from my inner conscience.

Squeezing her hand twice, I let go as we climb out of opposing sides of the car, meeting back up on the footpath.

Regaining our connection, we stride through the airport with pride bursting out of our chests as we near the lounge where our entire world resides.

It's as if our feet can't move quick enough, we're practically running at this point with our heartbeat matching the strides of our legs.

We look at each other and her green eyes sparkle under the lighting as her dark hair floats through the air from the gravity of our movements. The dimples on her face deepen the longer she looks at me.

The one thing I'm most grateful for is that Willow didn't have to deal with any of this. She didn't even get a chance to reunite with her 'resurrected' mother. And, I'm thankful that she doesn't have to suffer or try to understand this trauma. She's able to continue her life believing that her mother died a tragic death, which she did, but in a way that is easier to process.

Entering into the V.I.P lounge, it's as if everything else in the room stops.

The world stands still, watching.

Our world, sits with her head lowered and her legs swinging as she sits on the bench with her hands wrapped tightly around the wooden structure.

Trying to swallow the lump in my throat, I inhale deeply through my nose, feeling as if I've just taken my very first breath.

Time is inconsequential as her beautiful face picks up, her eyes darting around the room before settling on the two of us.

No money, no time, no action, is a match for the smile that breaks out onto her face.

I watch her eyes crinkle with the smile as she jumps to her feet and sets off into a sprint with her arms stretched outwards.

Before even thinking about it, I'm at my knees and waiting to feel her tiny body fold into my own.

It's as if everything is happening in slow motion, everything else is blurred out except the sight of my little girl running towards me with all of the determination in her body.

This, this right here is the reason I have to keep fighting another day.

I want to make sure everything is corrected for her sake.

One of her arms snakes around my neck, and the other around Indie's as we fall backwards from the force of her impact.

The brimming tears in my eyes don't hold back as my heart aches, but not painfully.

The longer she holds me, I can feel the cracks beginning to subside with the weight in my chest easing.

Everything in this moment is so devastatingly perfect.

Epilogue

❧

Five Years Later
Willow

Where are they?

I can't find them *anywhere*.

Pulling out everything underneath my bed, the dust particles dance in the air tickling my nose.

I groan.

"Mom!" I shout, my frustration growing from looking for my ballet slippers for the past twenty minutes.

I swear, I can't leave anything anywhere in this house.

Shooting up from my knees, I twist my door knob and stomp out of my bedroom and walk across the landing.

"Poppy! Have you taken my slippers again? This isn't a joke, I have to leave for practice!" I push her bedroom door open to see her sat central with my ballet slippers placed over her considerably smaller feet and the silk ribbons wrapped loosely around her calves.

Folding my arms, I lean against the door frame, waiting for her to respond.

"Lolo, look! I'm just like you!" She smiles at me warmly, her bottom two teeth missing.

"Pops, look. I'll give you an old pair of mine if you please, *stop* taking these ones. I can't afford to waste time looking for them before my classes. You know how important these shows are," I sigh, walking over and plonking myself beside her.

Beginning to unlace the ribbons, she nods her head, her brown curls swishing as she does so.

"I just wanted to be like you, Lolo." She frowns, her bottom lip jutting out.

Pausing, I wrap my arm over her shoulder and pull her into me, her head sinking into my armpit crease.

"I know, I know. And you will be. When I was your age, I didn't have slippers like these ones. They were different, slightly softer. These hurt your feet a lot, trust me, Pops." I laugh slightly as she nods her head again and her tiny arms wrap around my waist.

"Really? An actual pair of Lolo's pointe shoes?" She asks, her sweet voice warming my heart.

"Of course, that's what big sisters are for!" I squeeze her shoulders as she pulls away from me.

"Pops pinky swear?" She holds out her pinky finger, offering it to me as she does with everyone who promises her something.

"Pops pinky swear." I laugh, linking my pinky with hers.

Finishing unlacing her legs, I take my slippers and throw them over my shoulder.

"See ya later, we can have a movie night in my room tonight, if you're still awake when I get back?" I say to her from the doorway.

She stands up and runs up to me, wrapping her arms around my waist.

"Always, I'll be waiting, Lolo."

Walking away from her door, I grab my gym bag and throw my slippers in there along with my leotard, tights and hair tie.

Throwing it over my shoulder, I dart down the staircase and straight into the kitchen.

"Mom, I need you to find a pair of my old pointe shoes for Pops. She had my new ones, *again*. I Pops promised her, and we all know that may as well be the law." I laugh as Mom sits at the dining table.

My one-year old sister Olive chows down on some cucumber sticks, her gums baring at me.

"Lolly!" Olive babbles, holding a cucumber out to me.

"No thank you, Olive." I pinch her chubby cheeks and she tries to grab onto me with her sticky hands.

Mom turns to me, her dark braided hair falls over her shoulder as she does.

"Oh, yes. I'll get your dad to get them from the garage, I'm sure they won't be too difficult to find."

"Lolo!" I hear the sound of his footsteps barreling across the tiles before I see him.

Just as I turn to him, I shriek as his chocolate covered hands attack my legs.

"Wren!" I shout, raising my hands in the air in frustration.

"Oh, Wren! What have I told you about going into the pantry?" Mom rushes over, scooping him up into her arms.

I scowl at my three-year-old little brother as he giggles, pointing at my, now chocolate covered, leggings.

"Wren! Stop laughing! I'm already late." I cringe, freeing my bag from my shoulders and dropping it to the floor.

"Sorry, Lo. I'll get your dad to drop you off at practice, don't worry. I'll make sure your not late, now go and get changed." Mom waves me off, carrying Wren over to the sink.

"Poppy! Dinner!" She shouts at the same time, lowering Wren's hands to the bubble-filled sink.

Practically sprinting, I rush upstairs, throwing off my dirty leggings and grabbing a fresh pair of purple Lululemon's, pulling them up my legs as fast as possible.

Slamming my door closed, I take the steps two at a time and run down the corridor.

"Dad, come on. We need to go!" I sweep up my bag and walk towards his office.

I don't bother knocking and push it open, seeing he's on the phone.

"…it isn't the best time, I've been swamped with finding an attorney for the Presley v Scott case…"

I roll my eyes and throw myself in the chair in front of his desk, waiting for him to finish up.

He narrows his eyes at me as he turns his back, looking out of the window and continuing his conversation.

Pulling out my phone, I scroll through Instagram for a while. A text notification comes through whilst my phone is unlocked and my heart swoons when I see who it's from.

(Landon): Lo, I thought we could meet on Friday, figure out what we're going to do for this ass science project. BTW, your most recent insta post sucks. Love, L x

I let a small giggle escape my lips at the text from my best friend, earning a scowl from my dad.

Immediately, I respond that I'll be there on Friday, not caring if I already have plans.

"Right, come on, Lo." Dad lets out a sigh.

I huff and put my phone into my pocket, standing up and following after him.

We climb into the car and I kick my feet up on the dash, folding my arms across my chest.

"You're going to have to talk to me some day, Willow."

He backs out of the driveway and I reach forward to turn up the volume of the music, not wanting to engage in small talk.

Of course, he turns it back down.

"Look, you know it's only because I care about you. I just don't want you throwing your career away over some silly crush." He begins.

I scoff, "Crush? He's not my crush! He's my best friend!"

"Yeah, yeah. We've all seen the way you go googly-eyed around him. He's a good kid. But, so are you. We just want what's best for you." He states.

Rubbing my hands over my face, I let out a groan and try to turn away from him as best as I can.

As much as I appreciate his effort, I'm not talking about boys, with my *dad*.

"As long as it doesn't interfere with your grades and classes, we're all happy. Right?" He continues.

"DAD!" I whip my head around to him, my eyes wide.

He lets out a dry chuckle and shakes his head at me, focusing his attention back on the road.

"It's just because we love you." He murmurs, barely loud enough for me to hear.

My body folds in on itself and my shoulders slump, my guard dropping.

"I love you all too, dad." I sigh, dropping my head to the side and looking out of the window at the trees whizzing by.

"Don't forget, we're having thanksgiving dinner early this year, on Friday."

Closing my eyes, I let out a bated breath, unsure how I'm going to escape out of this one.

* * *

Friday

"Yo, Lo!" I hear his voice shout me from across the hallway as I slam my locker shut, my chemistry books heavy in my hold.

Turning, I take in his outfit of choice: an over-sized beige sweater and a pair of loose Levi's with white chucks. I make a mental note to remind him that I want that sweater. His blonde hair is lengthy and curly, tamed slightly with wax.

I've always loved the fluffiness of his hair, the kind that tempts you to grasp hold of it and sink your fingers in it.

"Landon!" I cheer in response as he scoops me up, spinning me around in a circle before planting me back onto my feet.

"How's my favorite girl? Excited for chemistry, I see?" He pulls at the books in my arms, taking in the titles and cringing.

"Stop, you know what my parents have said. If my grades drop, I can't see you." I pout my lip and he loops an arm over my shoulders, pulling me into him as we begin to walk.

"I don't see all of the fuss to be honest, your parents *love* me." He flashes his perfect smile, the dimples in his cheeks pop slightly, my heart flickering at the sight.

"That's not the point, Landon. Besides, *everyone* loves you, it's not saying much." I roll my eyes as he fist pumps the air, is ego following us like a shadow.

"My Lolo, so perfectly naive and sweet, thinking her grades will impact if we can see each other or not. You know that you're addicted to me just as much as I am to you." He pinches my side and I squeal, almost dropping my books.

"Miss. Breckenridge and Mr. Morgan, do we have somewhere

that we need to be?" Principal Stanley stares down at us through his glasses, raising an eyebrow expectantly.

"You are correct, Principal Stanley. We're just heading to chemistry." Landon grins, his devastating smile has me gawking.

"Then, hurry along. Less of this– contact." He gestures to Landon's arm around my shoulders, making me blush.

I awkwardly try to get out of his embrace, but he only tightens his grip, securing me underneath him.

"Anything for you, Principal Stanley." Landon smirks and leans his head against mine as we begin to walk away.

We erupt into a fit of laughter and break apart, unable to hold ourselves upright from how much our stomachs ache.

"His–His face!" I giggle, not able to stop myself.

"That was a picture perfect moment!" Landon replies, holding the wall to stop himself from keeling over too far.

I try to catch my breath, my ribs aching from how long we've been laughing and earning strange looks from other students.

"Come on then, Lo. Let's get you off to precious chemistry."

He takes my books from my arms, hooking them under his and then looping my backpack onto his shoulder.

I watch on in awe as he begins to walk in the direction of chemistry, but my feet don't dare to move as I look at him. His golden hair moves with the breeze from an open window, the curls lifting and floating higher.

He stops and turns to me.

"Are you coming or not?" His face is only partially angled to me, but he wears that same heart-stopping grin that I love so much.

I smile and nod, skipping to catch up with him.

* * *

"No, because he really did come home with a live turkey, thinking he was some sort of macho guy who can slay a turkey for thanksgiving!" Mom laughs, taking a sip of her wine.

"Indie, come on. It wasn't like that, a guy told me the flavor of it is better with it being so fresh. I just thought we could give it a try, you know? Switch things up a bit." Dad counteracts defensively.

"So, I do have some questions." Devon ponders.

"Go ahead, ask away." Dad responds.

I push around the yams and toy with the rest of my food, waiting for the time to burn down so I can get out of here and go to Landon's.

"How does one transport a live turkey? Don't tell me you just put it in the trunk and hoped for the best?" Devon laughs, taking a drink of his water.

"Of course not! I'm not that stupid. I used Wren's car seat, strapped him in real secure so he couldn't go anywhere, safety first and everything." Dad says proudly, then reaching forward to grab some more green beans.

"You're kidding, right?" Ever says, his fork frozen in mid-air with a piece of turkey hanging from it.

"Please tell me you're joking." Mom winces, eyeing dad carefully.

"Look, I didn't have many options, okay? He was flapping his wings and shit and –"

"Language!" Mom shouts, glaring at dad fiercely and then looking over at Wren, smashing into his food with his fork.

The baby monitor rings out with the sounds of Olive's cries, mom groans and rises to her feet.

Poppy nudges me in the side and I peer down at her with an expectant look.

"Lolo, quick. Get me some marshmallows off the yams." She looks between me and our parents, distracted with Olive.

I laugh and quickly grab the scoop, scraping the top layer of marshmallow from the yams and plonking it onto her plate.

She picks up her fork and begins shoveling it into her mouth at a rapid pace, whilst I silently giggle in delight.

Pops is definitely going to be the trouble-maker.

"Dad?" I stand up, walking around to his side of the table.

He stops his conversation with the boys and looks up at me, twisting his body to meet me.

"Lo?" He raises an eyebrow, already knowing what I'm going to ask.

"Please, can I go to Landon's, we have this science project and–"

"Lo, we've talked about this–"

"Let her live, Reed." Devon speaks up as my dad turns to him with narrowed eyes.

Dad lets out a sigh and turns back to me with a serious look on his face.

"Okay." He states.

"Okay?" I ask, a smile bursting out onto my cheeks.

"Okay." He repeats.

I throw my arms forward and wrap it around his neck, planting a sloppy kiss on his cheek.

"Thanks dad, you're the best!" I squeal, practically jumping up and down.

Pulling away, I turn to Devon, "Lifesaver. Thank you!" I giggle and give him a big cuddle as he laughs obnoxiously at my dad.

"Yeah, yeah. Off you go then, before your mom gets back and scolds me for letting you leave." My dad rolls his eyes and shoos me away.

Putting my phone in my pocket, I kiss my siblings goodbye and rush out of the house, forgetting to even bring a coat.

Landon only lives two blocks away anyway, so I won't be in the cold for long.

I knock on his door and jig up and down, wrapping my arms around myself. I'm glad I'd chosen today to wear a hoodie, but it's still not enough to protect me from the bitterness of the air.

The door pulls open to reveal my best friend, his eyes looking tired as if he'd just woken up from a nap.

"Lo, hey. Come in." He steps aside for me to come in and as I do, he wraps his arms around me. The warmth of his touch is comforting anyways, especially when I've been in the cold outside.

"Jeez, you're freezing!" He grasps hold of my hands, bringing them up to his mouth as he rubs his larger ones over mine.

I'm frozen in place, but not from the weather. Pulling my hands closer, he begins to breath onto them at the same time as rubbing them to warm me up, his lips are mere centimeters away.

"Let's head upstairs, I've got something to show you." He tugs me towards the stairs and I follow after him eagerly, excitement lining my body.

We come up to his bedroom and he kicks the door open, his hand still holding mine as I drink in his room, the smell of it reminds me of every comfort I've ever known.

Being best friends for eight years comes with its perks, but also being in love with your best friend for the past three years has its disadvantages.

He lets go, my hand dropping limply at my side from the loss of contact, my body igniting in shivers.

"So, I know you had your thanksgiving today. I wanted to get you a little something." He begins.

A gift? He's never given me a gift for thanksgiving before.

He reaches down to pull out a medium-sized black box, no tell-tale signs of what's inside.

"Oh, Landon. I haven't gotten you anything!" I blush and look away, embarrassed that he'd been thoughtful enough to get me something, and I hadn't.

"Nonsense, here–" He hands me the box, it feels weighty in my hands, piquing my curiosity more. I inspect the box, a world of ideas of what it could be, runs through my mind.

"Well, go on then. Open it." We giggle as I nod and begin to open the box.

I pull it out and before I get chance to ask what it is, he begins to explain.

"I know how much you hate thunderstorms, and you hate to be alone when it happens. So, I thought that by using this, you would know when a storm was brewing, and you could call me. I'd come to you, and we can get through the storm together." He looks down, and then back up at me, trying to gage my response.

"It can predict when there is going to be a storm, something to do with the crystals, I'm not quite sure of the logistics but, I really hope you love it."

I fixate my gaze back on the teardrop-shaped glass dome, fixated to a wooden base. The wooden base holds the engravings *'Willow & Landon'* and underneath

'Weathering every storm, together'

My eyes begin to well with tears, the thoughtfulness, the raw emotion, the butterflies, all swirling around inside of my head.

I push forward, placing the gift on his dresser top and wrap my arms around him, pulling him into a tight embrace. My nose sniffles slightly as my eyes pour, my heart swimming with so much feeling, I don't know what to do with it.

I've never felt something this strongly before.

He pulls away from me and tries to look at my face, his eyes darting between both of mine.

His hand cups my chin and I feel myself tense, my heart skipping a beat. His eyes search mine for something, like he's asking a question that I don't know how to answer. I remain still as his lips part, the smell of his minty breath waves through my nostrils.

Still within his embrace, he pushes some of my hair out of my face as he looks at me with so much adoration, I think I could die.

On instinct, my eyes flutter closed as he nears, the feel of his hot breath across my skin has every part of my body on high alert, prepared but so completely unprepared for the way he's making me feel.

Landon's lips touch mine, so softly and gently it is like being kissed by a cloud. My heart erupts and somersaults, the explosion of fireworks as my head spins from how long I've loved him.

I am so grateful, for everything in my life. My parents, my siblings, my friends and most of all, *him*.

Everything, is perfect.

About the Author

Jordyn Ellery is a UK-based author. She is a dark romance fanatic with a love for plot twists and unconventional lovers. Jordyn has always been passionate about her love for reading and writing and finally decided to wear her heart on her sleeve, and write a book. She resides in a small village in the countryside with her fiancé and two young daughters, reading and writing to her heart's content.

You can connect with me on:

🌐 https://www.jordyn-ellery.uk

🐦 https://twitter.com/JordynEllery